'Remarkable . . . It has the power to
move hearts and change minds'
Guardian

'Incredibly charming, brutal and brilliant'
Observer

'It wreaks emotional havoc . . . To finish it with
a firm resolve to be a better person – well, you
can't ask much more of any book than that'
Independent

'*Wonder* is destined to go the way of Mark Haddon's
The Curious Incident of the Dog in the Night-Time
and then some . . . It is dark, funny, touching and
no Tube carriage will be without a copy this year'
The Times

'When the kids have finished with this,
the adults will want to read it. Everybody should'
Financial Times

'A glorious exploration of the nature of friendship,
tenacity, fear and, most importantly, kindness'
The Huffington Post

'An amazing book . . . I absolutely loved it.
I cried my eyes out'
Tom Fletcher

'*Wonder* ultimately succeeds in being tremendously uplifting and a novel of all-too-rare power, confronting Auggie's difficulties with an unflinching gaze and creating an unforgettable, deeply moving character'
Sunday Express

'What makes R.J. Palacio's debut novel so remarkable, and so lovely, is the uncommon generosity with which she tells Auggie's story...The result is a beautiful, funny and sometimes sob-making story of quiet transformation'
The Wall Street Journal

'What a gem of a story. Moving and heart-warming. This book made me laugh, made me angry, made me cry'
Malorie Blackman

'Thoughtful but never preachy. A great book'
Sophie Kinsella

Every page is honest, brave and delightful'
Laura Dockrill

'Rich and memorable . . . It's Auggie and the rest of the children who are the real heart of *Wonder* and Palacio captures the voices of girls and boys, fifth graders and teenagers, with equal skill'
New York Times

'Do yourself a favor and read this book – your life will be better for it'
Nicholas Sparks

PREFACE

Wonder was first published in 2012. Since then it has become a critically acclaimed multi-million global best-seller, and has been transformed into a major motion picture starring Julia Roberts, Owen Wilson and Jacob Tremblay. It has also sparked its own movement for kindness and empathy, asking children and adults to #ChooseKind all over the world.

This very special edition brings *Wonder* and its companion book, *Auggie & Me*, together for the first time, and is a celebration of a truly extraordinary book and author.

R. J. Palacio was born and raised in New York City. She attended the High School of Art and Design and the Parsons School of Design, where she majored in illustration. She was a graphic designer and an art director for many years before writing her critically acclaimed debut novel, *Wonder*, which has been on the *New York Times* bestseller list since March 2012 and sold over 12 million copies worldwide.

In addition to *Wonder*, R. J. has written *Auggie & Me: Three Wonder Stories*, *365 Days of Wonder* and a picture book, *We're All Wonders*. She lives in Brooklyn, New York, with her husband, two sons and two dogs (Bear and Beau). Learn more about her at www.wonderthebook.com or on Twitter at @RJPalacio.

Books by R. J. Palacio

Wonder
365 Days of Wonder
Auggie & Me: Three Wonder Stories
We're All Wonders

WONDER

THE COMPLETE COLLECTION

R. J. Palacio

PUFFIN

PUFFIN BOOKS

UK | USA | Canada | Ireland | Australia
India | New Zealand | South Africa

Puffin Books is part of the Penguin Random House group of companies
whose addresses can be found at global.penguinrandomhouse.com.

www.penguin.co.uk
www.puffin.co.uk
www.ladybird.co.uk

Penguin
Random House
UK

Wonder first published in Great Britain in hardback by The Bodley Head 2012
Auggie and Me first published in Great Britain in paperback by Corgi Books 2015
('The Julian Chapter' first published by RHCP Digital 2014;
'Pluto' and 'Shingaling' first published by RHCP Digital 2015)

003

Typeset in Goudy
Printed and bound in Great Britain by Clays Ltd, Elcograf S.p.A.

A CIP catalogue record for this book is available from the British Library

ISBN: 978-0-241-36838-1

All correspondence to:
Puffin Books
Penguin Random House Children's
80 Strand, London WC2R 0RL

Doctors have come from distant cities
just to see me
stand over my bed
disbelieving what they're seeing

They say I must be one of the wonders
of god's own creation
and as far as they can see they can offer
no explanation

—NATALIE MERCHANT, "Wonder"

For Russell, Caleb, and Joseph

Part One

August

Fate smiled and destiny

laughed as she came to my cradle . . .

—Natalie Merchant, "Wonder"

Ordinary

I know I'm not an ordinary ten-year-old kid. I mean, sure, I do ordinary things. I eat ice cream. I ride my bike. I play ball. I have an XBox. Stuff like that makes me ordinary. I guess. And I feel ordinary. Inside. But I know ordinary kids don't make other ordinary kids run away screaming in playgrounds. I know ordinary kids don't get stared at wherever they go.

If I found a magic lamp and I could have one wish, I would wish that I had a normal face that no one ever noticed at all. I would wish that I could walk down the street without people seeing me and then doing that look-away thing. Here's what I think: the only reason I'm not ordinary is that no one else sees me that way.

But I'm kind of used to how I look by now. I know how to pretend I don't see the faces people make. We've all gotten pretty good at that sort of thing: me, Mom and Dad, Via. Actually, I take that back: Via's not so good at it. She can get really annoyed when people do something rude. Like, for instance, one time in the playground some older kids made some noises. I don't even know what the noises were exactly because I didn't hear them myself, but Via heard and she just started yelling at the kids. That's the way she is. I'm not that way.

Via doesn't see me as ordinary. She says she does, but if I were ordinary, she wouldn't feel like she needs to protect me as much. And Mom and Dad don't see me as ordinary, either. They see me as extraordinary. I think the only person in the world who realizes how ordinary I am is me.

My name is August, by the way. I won't describe what I look like. Whatever you're thinking, it's probably worse.

Why I Didn't Go to School

Next week I start fifth grade. Since I've never been to a real school before, I am pretty much totally and completely petrified. People think I haven't gone to school because of the way I look, but it's not that. It's because of all the surgeries I've had. Twenty-seven since I was born. The bigger ones happened before I was even four years old, so I don't remember those. But I've had two or three surgeries every year since then (some big, some small), and because I'm little for my age, and I have some other medical mysteries that doctors never really figured out, I used to get sick a lot. That's why my parents decided it was better if I didn't go to school. I'm much stronger now, though. The last surgery I had was eight months ago, and I probably won't have to have any more for another couple of years.

Mom homeschools me. She used to be a children's-book illustrator. She draws really great fairies and mermaids. Her boy stuff isn't so hot, though. She once tried to draw me a Darth Vader, but it ended up looking like some weird mushroom-shaped robot. I haven't seen her draw anything in a long time. I think she's too busy taking care of me and Via.

I can't say I always wanted to go to school because that wouldn't be exactly true. What I wanted was to go to school, but only if I could be like every other kid going to school. Have lots of friends and hang out after school and stuff like that.

I have a few really good friends now. Christopher is my best friend, followed by Zachary and Alex. We've known each other since we were babies. And since they've always known me the way I am, they're used to me. When we were little, we used to have playdates all the time, but then Christopher moved to Bridgeport in Connecticut. That's more than an hour away from where I live in North River Heights, which is at the top tip of Manhattan. And Zachary and Alex started going to school. It's funny: even though Christopher's the one who moved far away, I still see him more than I see Zachary and Alex. They have all these new friends now. If we bump into each other on the street, they're still nice to me, though. They always say hello.

I have other friends, too, but not as good as Christopher and Zack and Alex were. For instance, Zack and Alex always invited me to their birthday parties when we were little, but Joel and Eamonn and Gabe never did. Emma invited me once, but I haven't seen her in a long time. And, of course, I always go to Christopher's birthday. Maybe I'm making too big a deal about birthday parties.

How I Came to Life

I like when Mom tells this story because it makes me laugh so much. It's not funny in the way a joke is funny, but when Mom tells it, Via and I just start cracking up.

So when I was in my mom's stomach, no one had any idea I would come out looking the way I look. Mom had had Via four years before, and that had been such a "walk in the park" (Mom's expression) that there was no reason to run any special tests. About two months before I was born, the doctors realized there was something wrong with my face, but they didn't think it was going to be bad. They told Mom and Dad I had a cleft palate and some other stuff going on. They called it "small anomalies."

There were two nurses in the delivery room the night I was born. One was very nice and sweet. The other one, Mom said, did not seem at all nice or sweet. She had very big arms and (here comes the funny part), she kept farting. Like, she'd bring Mom some ice chips, and then fart. She'd check Mom's blood pressure, and fart. Mom says it was unbelievable because the nurse never even said excuse me! Meanwhile, Mom's regular doctor wasn't on duty that night, so Mom got stuck with this cranky kid doctor she and Dad nicknamed Doogie after some old TV show or something (they didn't actually call him that to his face). But Mom says that even though everyone in the room was kind of grumpy, Dad kept making her laugh all night long.

When I came out of Mom's stomach, she said the whole room got very quiet. Mom didn't even get a chance to look at me because the nice nurse immediately rushed me out of the room. Dad was in such a hurry to follow her that he dropped the video camera, which broke into a million pieces. And then Mom got very upset and tried to get out of bed to see where they were going, but the farting nurse put her very big arms on Mom to keep her down in the bed. They were practically fighting, because Mom was hysterical and the farting nurse was yelling at her to stay calm, and then they both started screaming for the doctor. But guess what? He had fainted! Right on the floor! So when the farting nurse saw that he had fainted, she started pushing him with her foot to get him to wake up, yelling at him the whole time: "What kind of doctor are you? What kind of doctor are you? Get up! Get up!" And then all of a sudden she let out the biggest, loudest, smelliest fart in the history of farts. Mom thinks it was actually the fart that finally woke the doctor up. Anyway, when Mom tells this story, she acts out all the parts—including the farting noises—and it is so, so, so, *so* funny!

Mom says the farting nurse turned out to be a very nice woman. She stayed with Mom the whole time. Didn't leave her side even after Dad came back and the doctors told them how sick I was. Mom remembers exactly what the nurse whispered in her ear when the doctor told her I probably wouldn't live through the night: "Everyone born of God overcometh the world." And the next day, after I had lived through the night, it was that nurse who held Mom's hand when they brought her to meet me for the first time.

Mom says by then they had told her all about me. She had been preparing herself for the seeing of me. But she says that when she looked down into my tiny mushed-up face for the first time, all she could see was how pretty my eyes were.

Mom is beautiful, by the way. And Dad is handsome. Via is pretty. In case you were wondering.

Christopher's House

I was really bummed when Christopher moved away three years ago. We were both around seven then. We used to spend hours playing with our *Star Wars* action figures and dueling with our lightsabers. I miss that.

Last spring we drove over to Christopher's house in Bridgeport. Me and Christopher were looking for snacks in the kitchen, and I heard Mom talking to Lisa, Christopher's mom, about my going to school in the fall. I had never, ever heard her mention school before.

"What are you talking about?" I said.

Mom looked surprised, like she hadn't meant for me to hear that.

"You should tell him what you've been thinking, Isabel," Dad said. He was on the other side of the living room talking to Christopher's dad.

"We should talk about this later," said Mom.

"No, I want to know what you were talking about," I answered.

"Don't you think you're ready for school, Auggie?" Mom said.

"No," I said.

"I don't, either," said Dad.

"Then that's it, case closed," I said, shrugging, and I sat in her lap like I was a baby.

"I just think you need to learn more than I can teach you," Mom said. "I mean, come on, Auggie, you know how bad I am at fractions!"

"What school?" I said. I already felt like crying.

"Beecher Prep. Right by us."

"Wow, that's a great school, Auggie," said Lisa, patting my knee.

"Why not Via's school?" I said.

"That's too big," Mom answered. "I don't think that would be a good fit for you."

"I don't want to," I said. I admit: I made my voice sound a little babyish.

"You don't have to do anything you don't want to do," Dad said, coming over and lifting me out of Mom's lap. He carried me over to sit on his lap on the other side of the sofa. "We won't make you do anything you don't want to do."

"But it would be good for him, Nate," Mom said.

"Not if he doesn't want to," answered Dad, looking at me. "Not if he's not ready."

I saw Mom look at Lisa, who reached over and squeezed her hand.

"You guys will figure it out," she said to Mom. "You always have."

"Let's just talk about it later," said Mom. I could tell she and Dad were going to get in a fight about it. I wanted Dad to win the fight. Though a part of me knew Mom was right. And the truth is, she really was terrible at fractions.

Driving

It was a long drive home. I fell asleep in the backseat like I always do, my head on Via's lap like she was my pillow, a towel wrapped around the seat belt so I wouldn't drool all over her. Via fell asleep, too, and Mom and Dad talked quietly about grown-up things I didn't care about.

I don't know how long I was sleeping, but when I woke up, there was a full moon outside the car window. It was a purple night, and we were driving on a highway full of cars. And then I heard Mom and Dad talking about me.

"We can't keep protecting him," Mom whispered to Dad, who was driving. "We can't just pretend he's going to wake up tomorrow and this isn't going to be his reality, because it *is*, Nate, and we have to help him learn to deal with it. We can't just keep avoiding situations that . . ."

"So sending him off to middle school like a lamb to the slaughter . . . ," Dad answered angrily, but he didn't even finish his sentence because he saw me in the mirror looking up.

"What's a lamb to the slaughter?" I asked sleepily.

"Go back to sleep, Auggie," Dad said softly.

"Everyone will stare at me at school," I said, suddenly crying.

"Honey," Mom said. She turned around in the front seat and put her hand on my hand. "You know if you don't want to do this, you don't have to. But we spoke to the principal there and told him about you and he really wants to meet you."

"What did you tell him about me?"

"How funny you are, and how kind and smart. When I told

him you read *Dragon Rider* when you were six, he was like, 'Wow, I have to meet this kid.'"

"Did you tell him anything else?" I said.

Mom smiled at me. Her smile kind of hugged me.

"I told him about all your surgeries, and how brave you are," she said.

"So he knows what I look like?" I asked.

"Well, we brought pictures from last summer in Montauk," Dad said. "We showed him pictures of the whole family. And that great shot of you holding that flounder on the boat!"

"You were there, too?" I have to admit I felt a little disappointed that he was a part of this.

"We both talked to him, yes," Dad said. "He's a really nice man."

"You would like him," Mom added.

Suddenly it felt like they were on the same side.

"Wait, so when did you meet him?" I said.

"He took us on a tour of the school last year," said Mom.

"Last *year?*" I said. "So you've been thinking about this for a whole year and you didn't tell me?"

"We didn't know if you'd even get in, Auggie," answered Mom. "It's a very hard school to get into. There's a whole admissions process. I didn't see the point in telling you and having you get all worked up about it unnecessarily."

"But you're right, Auggie, we should've told you when we found out last month that you got in," said Dad.

"In hindsight," sighed Mom, "yes, I guess."

"Did that lady who came to the house that time have something to do with this?" I said. "The one that gave me that test?"

"Yes, actually," said Mom, looking guilty. "Yes."

"You told me it was an IQ test," I said.

"I know, well, that was a white lie," she answered. "It was a test you needed to take to get into the school. You did very well on it, by the way."

"So you lied," I said.

"A white lie, but yes. Sorry," she said, trying to smile, but when I didn't smile back, she turned around in her seat and faced forward.

"What's a lamb to the slaughter?" I said.

Mom sighed and gave Daddy a "look."

"I shouldn't have said that," Dad said, looking at me in the rearview mirror. "It's not true. Here's the thing: Mommy and I love you so much we want to protect you any way we can. It's just sometimes we want to do it in different ways."

"I don't want to go to school," I answered, folding my arms.

"It would be good for you, Auggie," said Mom.

"Maybe I'll go next year," I answered, looking out the window.

"This year would be better, Auggie," said Mom. "You know why? Because you'll be going into fifth grade, and that's the first year of middle school—for everyone. You won't be the only new kid."

"I'll be the only kid who looks like me," I said.

"I'm not going to say it won't be a big challenge for you, because you know better than that," she answered. "But it'll be good for you, Auggie. You'll make lots of friends. And you'll learn things you'd never learn with me." She turned in her seat again and looked at me. "When we took the tour, you know what they had in their science lab? A little baby chick that was just hatching out of its egg. It was so cute! Auggie, it actually kind of reminded me of you when you were a little baby . . . with those big brown eyes of yours. . . ."

I usually love when they talk about when I was a baby. Sometimes I want to curl up into a little tiny ball and let them

14

hug me and kiss me all over. I miss being a baby, not knowing stuff. But I wasn't in the mood for that now.

"I don't want to go," I said.

"How about this? Can you at least meet Mr. Tushman before making up your mind?" Mom asked.

"Mr. Tushman?" I said.

"He's the principal," answered Mom.

"Mr. *Tush*man?" I repeated.

"I know, right?" Dad answered, smiling and looking at me in the rearview mirror. "Can you believe that name, Auggie? I mean, who on earth would ever agree to have a name like Mr. Tushman?"

I smiled even though I didn't want to let them see me smile. Dad was the one person in the world who could make me laugh no matter how much I didn't want to laugh. Dad always made everyone laugh.

"Auggie, you know, you should go to that school just so you can hear his name said over the loudspeaker!" Dad said excitedly. "Can you imagine how funny that would be? Hello, hello? Paging Mr. Tushman!" He was using a fake high, old-lady voice. "Hi, Mr. Tushman! I see you're running a little *behind* today! Did your car get *rear-ended* again? What a *bum* rap!"

I started laughing, not even because I thought he was being that funny but because I wasn't in the mood to stay mad anymore.

"It could be worse, though!" Dad continued in his normal voice. "Mommy and I had a professor in college called Miss Butt."

Mom was laughing now, too.

"Is that for real?" I said.

"Roberta Butt," Mom answered, raising her hand as if to swear. "Bobbie Butt."

"She had huge cheeks," said Dad.

"Nate!" said Mom.

"What? She had big cheeks is all I'm saying."

Mom laughed and shook her head at the same time.

"Hey hey, I know!" said Dad excitedly. "Let's fix them up on a blind date! Can you imagine? Miss Butt, meet Mr. Tushman. Mr. Tushman, here's Miss Butt. They could get married and have a bunch of little Tushies."

"Poor Mr. Tushman," answered Mom, shaking her head. "Auggie hasn't even met the man yet, Nate!"

"Who's Mr. Tushman?" Via said groggily. She had just woken up.

"He's the principal of my new school," I answered.

Paging Mr. Tushman

I would have been more nervous about meeting Mr. Tushman if I'd known I was also going to be meeting some kids from the new school. But I didn't know, so if anything, I was kind of giggly. I couldn't stop thinking about all the jokes Daddy had made about Mr. Tushman's name. So when me and Mom arrived at Beecher Prep a few weeks before the start of school, and I saw Mr. Tushman standing there, waiting for us at the entrance, I started giggling right away. He didn't look at all like what I pictured, though. I guess I thought he would have a huge butt, but he didn't. In fact, he was a pretty normal guy. Tall and thin. Old but not really old. He seemed nice. He shook my mom's hand first.

"Hi, Mr. Tushman, it's so nice to see you again," said Mom. "This is my son, August."

Mr. Tushman looked right at me and smiled and nodded. He put his hand out for me to shake.

"Hi, August," he said, totally normally. "It's a pleasure to meet you."

"Hi," I mumbled, dropping my hand into his hand while I looked down at his feet. He was wearing red Adidas.

"So," he said, kneeling down in front of me so I couldn't look at his sneakers but had to look at his face, "your mom and dad have told me a lot about you."

"Like what have they told you?" I asked.

"Sorry?"

"Honey, you have to speak up," said Mom.

"Like what?" I asked, trying not to mumble. I admit I have a bad habit of mumbling.

"Well, that you like to read," said Mr. Tushman, "and that you're a great artist." He had blue eyes with white eyelashes. "And you're into science, right?"

"Uh-huh," I said, nodding.

"We have a couple of great science electives at Beecher," he said. "Maybe you'll take one of them?"

"Uh-huh," I said, though I had no idea what an elective was.

"So, are you ready to take a tour?"

"You mean we're doing that now?" I said.

"Did you think we were going to the movies?" he answered, smiling as he stood up.

"You didn't tell me we were taking a tour," I said to Mom in my accusing voice.

"Auggie . . . ," she started to say.

"It'll be fine, August," said Mr. Tushman, holding his hand out to me. "I promise."

I think he wanted me to take his hand, but I took Mom's instead. He smiled and started walking toward the entrance.

Mommy gave my hand a little squeeze, though I don't know if it was an "I love you" squeeze or an "I'm sorry" squeeze. Probably a little of both.

The only school I'd ever been inside before was Via's, when I went with Mom and Dad to watch Via sing in spring concerts and stuff like that. This school was very different. It was smaller. It smelled like a hospital.

Nice Mrs. Garcia

We followed Mr. Tushman down a few hallways. There weren't a lot of people around. And the few people who were there didn't seem to notice me at all, though that may have been because they didn't see me. I sort of hid behind Mom as I walked. I know that sounds kind of babyish of me, but I wasn't feeling very brave right then.

We ended up in a small room with the words OFFICE OF THE MIDDLE SCHOOL DIRECTOR on the door. Inside, there was a desk with a nice-seeming lady sitting behind it.

"This is Mrs. Garcia," said Mr. Tushman, and the lady smiled at Mom and took off her glasses and got up out of her chair.

My mother shook her hand and said: "Isabel Pullman, nice to meet you."

"And this is August," Mr. Tushman said. Mom kind of stepped to the side a bit, so I would move forward. Then that thing happened that I've seen happen a million times before. When I looked up at her, Mrs. Garcia's eyes dropped for a second. It was so fast no one else would have noticed, since the rest of her face stayed exactly the same. She was smiling a really shiny smile.

"Such a pleasure to meet you, August," she said, holding out her hand for me to shake.

"Hi," I said quietly, giving her my hand, but I didn't want to look at her face, so I kept staring at her glasses, which hung from a chain around her neck.

"Wow, what a firm grip!" said Mrs. Garcia. Her hand was really warm.

"The kid's got a killer handshake," Mr. Tushman agreed, and everyone laughed above my head.

"You can call me Mrs. G," Mrs. Garcia said. I think she was talking to me, but I was looking at all the stuff on her desk now. "That's what everyone calls me. Mrs. G, I forgot my combination. Mrs. G, I need a late pass. Mrs. G, I want to change my elective."

"Mrs. G's actually the one who runs the place," said Mr. Tushman, which again made all the grown-ups laugh.

"I'm here every morning by seven-thirty," Mrs. Garcia continued, still looking at me while I stared at her brown sandals with small purple flowers on the buckles. "So if you ever need anything, August, I'm the one to ask. And you can ask me anything."

"Okay," I mumbled.

"Oh, look at that cute baby," Mom said, pointing to one of the photographs on Mrs. Garcia's bulletin board. "Is he yours?"

"No, my goodness!" said Mrs. Garcia, smiling a big smile now that was totally different from her shiny smile. "You've just made my day. He's my grandson."

"What a cutie!" said Mom, shaking her head. "How old?"

"In that picture he was five months, I think. But he's big now. Almost eight years old!"

"Wow," said Mom, nodding and smiling. "Well, he is absolutely beautiful."

"Thank you!" said Mrs. Garcia, nodding like she was about to say something else about her grandson. But then all of a sudden her smile got a little smaller. "We're all going to take very good care of August," she said to Mom, and I saw her give Mom's hand a little squeeze. I looked at Mom's face, and that's when I realized she was just as nervous as I was. I guess I liked Mrs. Garcia— when she wasn't wearing her shiny smile.

Jack Will, Julian, and Charlotte

We followed Mr. Tushman into a small room across from Mrs. Garcia's desk. He was talking as he closed the door to his office and sat down behind his big desk, though I wasn't really paying much attention to what he was saying. I was looking around at all the things on his desk. Cool stuff, like a globe that floated in the air and a Rubik's-type cube made with little mirrors. I liked his office a lot. I liked that there were all these neat little drawings and paintings by students on the walls, framed like they were important.

Mom sat down in a chair in front of Mr. Tushman's desk, and even though there was another chair right next to hers, I decided to stand beside her.

"Why do you have your own room and Mrs. G doesn't?" I said.

"You mean, why do I have an office?" asked Mr. Tushman.

"You said she runs the place," I said.

"Oh! Well, I was kind of kidding. Mrs. G is my assistant."

"Mr. Tushman is the director of the middle school," Mom explained.

"Do they call you Mr. T?" I asked, which made him smile.

"Do you know who Mr. T is?" he answered. "I pity the fool?" he said in a funny tough voice, like he was imitating someone.

I had no idea what he was talking about.

"Anyway, no," said Mr. Tushman, shaking his head. "No one calls me Mr. T. Though I have a feeling I'm called a lot of other things I don't know about. Let's face it, a name like mine is not so easy to live with, you know what I mean?"

Here I have to admit I totally laughed, because I knew exactly what he meant.

"My mom and dad had a teacher called Miss Butt," I said.

"Auggie!" said Mom, but Mr. Tushman laughed.

"Now, that's bad," said Mr. Tushman, shaking his head. "I guess I shouldn't complain. Hey, so listen, August, here's what I thought we would do today. . . ."

"Is that a pumpkin?" I said, pointing to a framed painting behind Mr. Tushman's desk.

"Auggie, sweetie, don't interrupt," said Mom.

"You like it?" said Mr. Tushman, turning around and looking at the painting. "I do, too. And I thought it was a pumpkin, too, until the student who gave it to me explained that it is actually not a pumpkin. It is . . . are you ready for this . . . a portrait of me! Now, August, I ask you: do I really look that much like a pumpkin?"

"No!" I answered, though I was thinking yes. Something about the way his cheeks puffed out when he smiled made him look like a jack-o'-lantern. Just as I thought that, it occurred to me how funny that was: cheeks, Mr. Tushman. And I started laughing a little. I shook my head and covered my mouth with my hand.

Mr. Tushman smiled like he could read my mind.

I was about to say something else, but then all of a sudden I heard other voices outside the office: kids' voices. I'm not exaggerating when I say this, but my heart literally started beating like I'd just run the longest race in the world. The laughter I had inside just poured out of me.

The thing is, when I was little, I never minded meeting new kids because all the kids I met were really little, too. What's cool about really little kids is that they don't say stuff to try to hurt your feelings, even though sometimes they do say stuff that hurts your feelings. But they don't actually know what they're saying. Big kids, though: they know what they're saying. And that is definitely not fun for me. One of the reasons I grew my hair long last year was that I like how my bangs cover my eyes: it helps me block out the things I don't want to see.

Mrs. Garcia knocked on the door and poked her head inside.

"They're here, Mr. Tushman," she said.

"Who's here?" I said.

"Thanks," said Mr. Tushman to Mrs. Garcia. "August, I thought it would be a good idea for you to meet some students who'll be in your homeroom this year. I figure they could take you around the school a bit, show you the lay of the land, so to speak."

"I don't want to meet anyone," I said to Mom.

Mr. Tushman was suddenly right in front of me, his hands on my shoulders. He leaned down and said very softly in my ear: "It'll be okay, August. These are nice kids, I promise."

"You're going to be okay, Auggie," Mom whispered with all her might.

Before she could say anything else, Mr. Tushman opened the door to his office.

"Come on in, kids," he said, and in walked two boys and a girl. None of them looked over at me or Mom: they stood by the door looking straight at Mr. Tushman like their lives depended on it.

"Thanks so much for coming, guys—especially since school doesn't start until next month!" said Mr. Tushman. "Have you had a good summer?"

All of them nodded but no one said anything.

"Great, great," said Mr. Tushman. "So, guys, I wanted you

to meet August, who's going to be a new student here this year. August, these guys have been students at Beecher Prep since kindergarten, though, of course, they were in the lower-school building, but they know all the ins and outs of the middle-school program. And since you're all in the same homeroom, I thought it would be nice if you got to know each other a little before school started. Okay? So, kids, this is August. August, this is Jack Will."

Jack Will looked at me and put out his hand. When I shook it, he kind of half smiled and said: "Hey," and looked down really fast.

"This is Julian," said Mr. Tushman.

"Hey," said Julian, and did the same exact thing as Jack Will: took my hand, forced a smile, looked down fast.

"And Charlotte," said Mr. Tushman.

Charlotte had the blondest hair I've ever seen. She didn't shake my hand but gave me a quick little wave and smiled. "Hi, August. Nice to meet you," she said.

"Hi," I said, looking down. She was wearing bright green Crocs.

"So," said Mr. Tushman, putting his hands together in a kind of slow clap. "What I thought you guys could do is take August on a little tour of the school. Maybe you could start on the third floor? That's where your homeroom class is going to be: room 301. I think. Mrs. G, is—"

"Room 301!" Mrs. Garcia called out from the other room.

"Room 301." Mr. Tushman nodded. "And then you can show August the science labs and the computer room. Then work your way down to the library and the performance space on the second floor. Take him to the cafeteria, of course."

"Should we take him to the music room?" asked Julian.

"Good idea, yes," said Mr. Tushman. "August, do you play any instruments?"

"No," I said. It wasn't my favorite subject on account of the fact that I don't really have ears. Well, I do, but they don't exactly look like normal ears.

"Well, you may enjoy seeing the music room anyway," said Mr. Tushman. "We have a very nice selection of percussion instruments."

"August, you've been wanting to learn to play the drums," Mom said, trying to get me to look at her. But my eyes were covered by my bangs as I stared at a piece of old gum that was stuck to the bottom of Mr. Tushman's desk.

"Great! Okay, so why don't you guys get going?" said Mr. Tushman. "Just be back here in . . ." He looked at Mom. "Half an hour, okay?"

I think Mom nodded.

"So, is that okay with you, August?" he asked me.

I didn't answer.

"Is that okay, August?" Mom repeated. I looked at her now. I wanted her to see how mad I was at her. But then I saw her face and just nodded. She seemed more scared than I was.

The other kids had started out the door, so I followed them.

"See you soon," said Mom, her voice sounding a little higher than normal. I didn't answer her.

The Grand Tour

Jack Will, Julian, Charlotte, and I went down a big hallway to some wide stairs. No one said a word as we walked up to the third floor.

When we got to the top of the stairs, we went down a little hallway full of lots of doors. Julian opened the door marked 301.

"This is our homeroom," he said, standing in front of the half-opened door. "We have Ms. Petosa. They say she's okay, at least for homeroom. I heard she's really strict if you get her for math, though."

"That's not true," said Charlotte. "My sister had her last year and said she's totally nice."

"Not what I heard," answered Julian, "but whatever." He closed the door and continued walking down the hallway.

"This is the science lab," he said when he got to the next door. And just like he did two seconds ago, he stood in front of the half-opened door and started talking. He didn't look at me once while he talked, which was okay because I wasn't looking at him, either. "You won't know who you have for science until the first day of school, but you want to get Mr. Haller. He used to be in the lower school. He would play this giant tuba in class."

"It was a baritone horn," said Charlotte.

"It was a tuba!" answered Julian, closing the door.

"Dude, let him go inside so he can check it out," Jack Will told him, pushing past Julian and opening the door.

"Go inside if you want," Julian said. It was the first time he looked at me.

26

I shrugged and walked over to the door. Julian moved out of the way quickly, like he was afraid I might accidentally touch him as I passed by him.

"Nothing much to see," Julian said, walking in after me. He started pointing to a bunch of stuff around the room. "That's the incubator. That big black thing is the chalkboard. These are the desks. These are chairs. Those are the Bunsen burners. This is a gross science poster. This is chalk. This is the eraser."

"I'm sure he knows what an eraser is," Charlotte said, sounding a little like Via.

"How would I know what he knows?" Julian answered. "Mr. Tushman said he's never been to a school before."

"You know what an eraser is, right?" Charlotte asked me.

I admit I was feeling so nervous that I didn't know what to say or do except look at the floor.

"Hey, can you talk?" asked Jack Will.

"Yeah." I nodded. I still really hadn't looked at any of them yet, not directly.

"You know what an eraser is, right?" asked Jack Will.

"Of course!" I mumbled.

"I told you there was nothing to see in here," said Julian, shrugging.

"I have a question . . . ," I said, trying to keep my voice steady. "Um. What exactly is homeroom? Is that like a subject?"

"No, that's just your group," explained Charlotte, ignoring Julian's smirk. "It's like where you go when you get to school in the morning and your homeroom teacher takes attendance and stuff like that. In a way, it's your main class even though it's not really a class. I mean, it's a class, but—"

"I think he gets it, Charlotte," said Jack Will.

"Do you get it?" Charlotte asked me.

"Yeah." I nodded at her.

"Okay, let's get out of here," said Jack Will, walking away.

"Wait, Jack, we're supposed to be answering questions," said Charlotte.

Jack Will rolled his eyes a little as he turned around.

"Do you have any more questions?" he asked.

"Um, no," I answered. "Oh, well, actually, yes. Is your name Jack or Jack Will?"

"Jack is my first name. Will is my last name."

"Oh, because Mr. Tushman introduced you as Jack Will, so I thought . . ."

"Ha! You thought his name was Jackwill!" laughed Julian.

"Yeah, some people call me by my first and last name," Jack said, shrugging. "I don't know why. Anyway, can we go now?"

"Let's go to the performance space next," said Charlotte, leading the way out of the science room. "It's very cool. You'll like it, August."

The Performance Space

Charlotte basically didn't stop talking as we headed down to the second floor. She was describing the play they had put on last year, which was *Oliver!* She played Oliver even though she's a girl. As she said this, she pushed open the double doors to a huge auditorium. At the other end of the room was a stage.

Charlotte started skipping toward the stage. Julian ran after her, and then turned around halfway down the aisle.

"Come on!" he said loudly, waving for me to follow him, which I did.

"There were like hundreds of people in the audience that night," said Charlotte, and it took me a second to realize she was still talking about *Oliver!* "I was so, so nervous. I had so many lines, and I had all these songs to sing. It was so, so, so, so hard!" Although she was talking to me, she really didn't look at me much. "On opening night, my parents were all the way in back of the auditorium, like where Jack is right now, but when the lights are off, you can't really see that far back. So I was like, 'Where are my parents? Where are my parents?' And then Mr. Resnick, our theater-arts teacher last year—he said: 'Charlotte, stop being such a diva!' And I was like, 'Okay!' And then I spotted my parents and I was totally fine. I didn't forget a single line."

While she was talking, I noticed Julian staring at me out of the corner of his eye. This is something I see people do a lot with me. They think I don't know they're staring, but I can tell from the way their heads are tilted. I turned around to see where Jack had gone to. He had stayed in the back of the auditorium, like he was bored.

"We put on a play every year," said Charlotte.

"I don't think he's going to want to be in the school play, Charlotte," said Julian sarcastically.

"You can be in the play without actually being 'in' the play," Charlotte answered, looking at me. "You can do the lighting. You can paint the backdrops."

"Oh yeah, whoopee," said Julian, twirling his finger in the air.

"But you don't have to take the theater-arts elective if you don't want to," Charlotte said, shrugging. "There's dance or chorus or band. There's leadership."

"Only dorks take leadership," Julian interrupted.

"Julian, you're being so obnoxious!" said Charlotte, which made Julian laugh.

"I'm taking the science elective," I said.

"Cool!" said Charlotte.

Julian looked directly at me. "The science elective is supposably the hardest elective of all," he said. "No offense, but if you've never, *ever* been in a school before, why do you think you're suddenly going to be smart enough to take the science elective? I mean, have you ever even studied science before? Like real science, not like the kind you do in kits?"

"Yeah." I nodded.

"He was homeschooled, Julian!" said Charlotte.

"So teachers came to his house?" asked Julian, looking puzzled.

"No, his mother taught him!" answered Charlotte.

"Is she a teacher?" Julian said.

"Is your mother a teacher?" Charlotte asked me.

"No," I said.

"So she's not a real teacher!" said Julian, as if that proved his point. "That's what I mean. How can someone who's not a real teacher actually teach science?"

"I'm sure you'll do fine," said Charlotte, looking at me.

"Let's just go to the library now," Jack called out, sounding really bored.

"Why is your hair so long?" Julian said to me. He sounded like he was annoyed.

I didn't know what to say, so I just shrugged.

"Can I ask you a question?" he said.

I shrugged again. Didn't he just ask me a question?

"What's the deal with your face? I mean, were you in a fire or something?"

"Julian, that's so rude!" said Charlotte.

"I'm not being rude," said Julian, "I'm just asking a question. Mr. Tushman said we could ask questions if we wanted to."

"Not rude questions like that," said Charlotte. "Besides, he was born like that. That's what Mr. Tushman said. You just weren't listening."

"I was so listening!" said Julian. "I just thought maybe he was in a fire, too."

"Geez, Julian," said Jack. "Just shut up."

"You shut up!" Julian yelled.

"Come on, August," said Jack. "Let's just go to the library already."

I walked toward Jack and followed him out of the auditorium. He held the double doors open for me, and as I passed by, he looked at me right in the face, kind of daring me to look back at him, which I did. Then I actually smiled. I don't know. Sometimes when I have the feeling like I'm almost crying, it can turn into an almost-laughing feeling. And that must have been the feeling I was having then, because I smiled, almost like I was going to giggle. The thing is, because of the way my face is, people who don't know me very well don't always get that I'm smiling. My mouth doesn't go up at the corners the way other people's mouths do. It just goes straight across my face. But somehow Jack Will got that I had smiled at him. And he smiled back.

"Julian's a jerk," he whispered before Julian and Charlotte reached us. "But, dude, you're gonna have to talk." He said this seriously, like he was trying to help me. I nodded as Julian and Charlotte caught up to us. We were all quiet for a second, all of us just kind of nodding, looking at the floor. Then I looked up at Julian.

"The word's 'supposedly,' by the way," I said.

"What are you talking about?"

"You said 'supposably' before," I said.

"I did not!"

"Yeah you did," Charlotte nodded. "You said the science elective is *supposably* really hard. I heard you."

"I absolutely did not," he insisted.

"Whatever," said Jack. "Let's just go."

"Yeah, let's just go," agreed Charlotte, following Jack down the stairs to the next floor. I started to follow her, but Julian cut right in front of me, which actually made me stumble backward.

"Oops, sorry about that!" said Julian.

But I could tell from the way he looked at me that he wasn't really sorry at all.

The Deal

Mom and Mr. Tushman were talking when we got back to the office. Mrs. Garcia was the first to see us come back, and she started smiling her shiny smile as we walked in.

"So, August, what did you think? Did you like what you saw?" she asked.

"Yeah." I nodded, looking over at Mom.

Jack, Julian, and Charlotte were standing by the door, not sure where to go or if they were still needed. I wondered what else they'd been told about me before they'd met me.

"Did you see the baby chick?" Mom asked me.

As I shook my head, Julian said: "Are you talking about the baby chicks in science? Those get donated to a farm at the end of every school year."

"Oh," said Mom, disappointed.

"But they hatch new ones every year in science," Julian added. "So August will be able to see them again in the spring."

"Oh, good," said Mom, eyeing me. "They were so cute, August."

I wished she wouldn't talk to me like I was a baby in front of other people.

"So, August," said Mr. Tushman, "did these guys show you around enough or do you want to see more? I realize I forgot to ask them to show you the gym."

"We did anyway, Mr. Tushman," said Julian.

"Excellent!" said Mr. Tushman.

"And I told him about the school play and some of the electives," said Charlotte. "Oh no!" she said suddenly. "We forgot to show him the art room!"

"That's okay," said Mr. Tushman.

"But we can show it to him now," Charlotte offered.

"Don't we have to pick Via up soon?" I said to Mom.

That was our signal for my telling Mom if I really wanted to leave.

"Oh, you're right," said Mom, getting up. I could tell she was pretending to check the time on her watch. "I'm sorry, everybody. I lost track of the time. We have to go pick up my daughter at her new school. She's taking an unofficial tour today." This part wasn't a lie: that Via was checking out her new school today. The part that was a lie was that we were picking her up at the school, which we weren't. She was coming home with Dad later.

"Where does she go to school?" asked Mr. Tushman, getting up.

"She's starting Faulkner High School this fall."

"Wow, that's not an easy school to get into. Good for her!"

"Thank you," said Mom, nodding. "It'll be a bit of a schlep, though. The A train down to Eighty-Sixth, then the crosstown bus all the way to the East Side. Takes an hour that way but it's just a fifteen-minute drive."

"It'll be worth it. I know a couple of kids who got into Faulkner and love it," said Mr. Tushman.

"We should really go, Mom," I said, tugging at her pocketbook.

We said goodbye kind of quickly after that. I think Mr. Tushman was a little surprised that we were leaving so suddenly, and then I wondered if he would blame Jack and Charlotte, even though it was really only Julian who made me feel kind of bad.

"Everyone was really nice," I made sure to tell Mr. Tushman before we left.

"I look forward to having you as a student," said Mr. Tushman, patting my back.

"Bye," I said to Jack, Charlotte, and Julian, but I didn't look at them—or look up at all—until I left the building.

34

Home

As soon as we had walked at least half a block from the school, Mom said: "So . . . how'd it go? Did you like it?"

"Not yet, Mom. When we get home," I said.

The moment we got inside the house, I ran to my room and threw myself onto my bed. I could tell Mom didn't know what was up, and I guess I really didn't, either. I felt very sad and a tiny bit happy at the exact same time, kind of like that laughing-crying feeling all over again.

My dog, Daisy, followed me into the room, jumped on the bed, and started licking me all over my face.

"Who's a good girlie?" I said in my Dad voice. "Who's a good girlie?"

"Is everything okay, sweetness?" Mom said. She wanted to sit down beside me but Daisy was hogging the bed. "Excuse me, Daisy." She sat down, nudging Daisy over. "Were those kids not nice to you, Auggie?"

"Oh no," I said, only half lying. "They were okay."

"But were they nice? Mr. Tushman went out of his way to tell me what sweet kids they are."

"Uh-huh." I nodded, but I kept looking at Daisy, kissing her on the nose and rubbing her ear until her back leg did that little flea-scratch shake.

"That boy Julian seemed especially nice," Mom said.

"Oh, no, he was the least nice. I liked Jack, though. He was nice. I thought his name was Jack Will but it's just Jack."

"Wait, maybe I'm getting them confused. Which one was the one with the dark hair that was brushed forward?"

"Julian."

"And he wasn't nice?"

"No, not nice."

"Oh." She thought about this for a second. "Okay, so is he the kind of kid who's one way in front of grown-ups and another way in front of kids?"

"Yeah, I guess."

"Ah, hate those," she answered, nodding.

"He was like, 'So, August, what's the deal with your face?'" I said, looking at Daisy the whole time. "'Were you in a fire or something?'"

Mom didn't say anything. When I looked up at her, I could tell she was completely shocked.

"He didn't say it in a mean way," I said quickly. "He was just asking."

Mom nodded.

"But I really liked Jack," I said. "He was like, 'Shut up, Julian!' And Charlotte was like, 'You're so rude, Julian!'"

Mom nodded again. She pressed her fingers on her forehead like she was pushing against a headache.

"I'm so sorry, Auggie," she said quietly. Her cheeks were bright red.

"No, it's okay, Mom, really."

"You don't have to go to school if you don't want, sweetie."

"I want to," I said.

"Auggie . . ."

"Really, Mom. I want to." And I wasn't lying.

36

First-Day Jitters

Okay, so I admit that the first day of school I was so nervous that the butterflies in my stomach were more like pigeons flying around my insides. Mom and Dad were probably a little nervous, too, but they acted all excited for me, taking pictures of me and Via before we left the house since it was Via's first day of school, too.

Up until a few days before, we still weren't sure I would be going to school at all. After my tour of the school, Mom and Dad had reversed sides on whether I should go or not. Mom was now the one saying I shouldn't go and Dad was saying I should. Dad had told me he was really proud of how I'd handled myself with Julian and that I was turning into quite the strong man. And I heard him tell Mom that he now thought she had been right all along. But Mom, I could tell, wasn't so sure anymore. When Dad told her that he and Via wanted to walk me to school today, too, since it was on the way to the subway station, Mom seemed relieved that we would all be going together. And I guess I was, too.

Even though Beecher Prep is just a few blocks from our house, I've only been on that block a couple of times before. In general, I try to avoid blocks where there are lots of kids roaming around. On our block, everybody knows me and I know everybody. I know every brick and every tree trunk and every crack in the sidewalk. I know Mrs. Grimaldi, the lady who's always sitting by her window, and the old guy who walks up and down the street whistling like a bird. I know the deli on the corner where Mom gets our bagels, and the waitresses at the coffee shop who all call me "honey" and give me lollipops whenever they see me. I love my neighborhood of North River Heights, which is why it was so strange to be walking down these blocks feeling like it was all new to me suddenly. Amesfort Avenue, a street I've been down a million times, looked totally different for some reason. Full of people I never saw before, waiting for buses, pushing strollers.

We crossed Amesfort and turned up Heights Place: Via walked next to me like she usually does, and Mom and Dad were behind us. As soon as we turned the corner, we saw all the kids in front of the school—hundreds of them talking to each other in little groups, laughing, or standing with their parents, who were talking with other parents. I kept my head way down.

"Everyone's just as nervous as you are," said Via in my ear. "Just remember that this is everyone's first day of school. Okay?"

Mr. Tushman was greeting students and parents in front of the school entrance.

I have to admit: so far, nothing bad had happened. I didn't catch anyone staring or even noticing me. Only once did I look up to see some girls looking my way and whispering with their hands cupped over their mouths, but they looked away when they saw me notice them.

We reached the front entrance.

"Okay, so this is it, big boy," said Dad, putting his hands on top of my shoulders.

"Have a great first day. I love you," said Via, giving me a big kiss and a hug.

"You, too," I said.

"I love you, Auggie," said Dad, hugging me.

"Bye."

Then Mom hugged me, but I could tell she was about to cry, which would have totally embarrassed me, so I just gave her a fast hard hug, turned, and disappeared into the school.

Locks

I went straight to room 301 on the third floor. Now I was glad I'd gone on that little tour, because I knew exactly where to go and didn't have to look up once. I noticed that some kids were definitely staring at me now. I did my thing of pretending not to notice.

I went inside the classroom, and the teacher was writing on the chalkboard while all the kids started sitting at different desks. The desks were in a half circle facing the chalkboard, so I chose the desk in the middle toward the back, which I thought would make it harder for anyone to stare at me. I still kept my head way down, just looking up enough from under my bangs to see everyone's feet. As the desks started to fill up, I did notice that no one sat down next to me. A couple of times someone was about to sit next to me, then changed his or her mind at the last minute and sat somewhere else.

"Hey, August." It was Charlotte, giving me her little wave as she sat down at a desk in the front of the class. Why anyone would ever choose to sit way up front in a class, I don't know.

"Hey," I said, nodding hello. Then I noticed Julian was sitting a few seats away from her, talking to some other kids. I know he saw me, but he didn't say hello.

Suddenly someone was sitting down next to me. It was Jack Will. Jack.

"What's up," he said, nodding at me.

"Hey, Jack," I answered, waving my hand, which I immediately wished I hadn't done because it felt kind of uncool.

"Okay, kids, okay, everybody! Settle down," said the teacher, now facing us. She had written her name, Ms. Petosa, on the chalkboard. "Everybody find a seat, please. Come in," she said to a couple of kids who had just walked in the room. "There's a seat there, and right there."

She hadn't noticed me yet.

"Now, the first thing I want everyone to do is stop talking and . . ."

She noticed me.

". . . put your backpacks down and quiet down."

She had only hesitated for a millionth of a second, but I could tell the moment she saw me. Like I said: I'm used to it by now.

"I'm going to take attendance and do the seating chart," she continued, sitting on the edge of her desk. Next to her were three neat rows of accordion folders. "When I call your name, come up and I'll hand you a folder with your name on it. It contains your class schedule and your combination lock, which you should *not* try to open until I tell you to. Your locker number is written on the class schedule. Be forewarned that some lockers are not right outside this class but down the hall, and before anyone even thinks of asking: no, you cannot switch lockers and you can't switch locks. Then if there's time at the end of this period, we're all going to get to know each other a little better, okay? Okay."

She picked up the clipboard on her desk and started reading the names out loud.

"Okay, so, Julian Albans?" she said, looking up.

Julian raised his hand and said "Here" at the same time.

"Hi, Julian," she said, making a note on her seating chart. She picked up the very first folder and held it out toward him. "Come pick it up," she said, kind of no-nonsense. He got up and took it from her. "Ximena Chin?"

40

She handed a folder to each kid as she read off the names. As she went down the list, I noticed that the seat next to me was the only one still empty, even though there were two kids sitting at one desk just a few seats away. When she called the name of one of them, a big kid named Henry Joplin who already looked like a teenager, she said: "Henry, there's an empty desk right over there. Why don't you take that seat, okay?"

She handed him his folder and pointed to the desk next to mine. Although I didn't look at him directly, I could tell Henry did not want to move next to me, just by the way he dragged his backpack on the floor as he came over, like he was moving in slow motion. Then he plopped his backpack up really high on the right side of the desk so it was kind of like a wall between his desk and mine.

"Maya Markowitz?" Ms. Petosa was saying.

"Here," said a girl about four desks down from me.

"Miles Noury?"

"Here," said the kid that had been sitting with Henry Joplin. As he walked back to his desk, I saw him shoot Henry a "poor you" look.

"August Pullman?" said Ms. Petosa.

"Here," I said quietly, raising my hand a bit.

"Hi, August," she said, smiling at me very nicely when I went up to get my folder. I kind of felt everyone's eyes burning into my back for the few seconds I stood in the front of the class, and everybody looked down when I walked back to my desk. I resisted spinning the combination when I sat down, even though everyone else was doing it, because she had specifically told us not to. I was already pretty good at opening locks, anyway, because I've used them on my bike. Henry kept trying to open his lock but couldn't do it. He was getting frustrated and kind of cursing under his breath.

Ms. Petosa called out the next few names. The last name was Jack Will.

After she handed Jack his folder, she said: "Okay, so, everybody write your combinations down somewhere safe that you won't forget, okay? But if you do forget, which happens at least three point two times per semester, Mrs. Garcia has a list of all the combination numbers. Now go ahead, take your locks out of your folders and spend a couple of minutes practicing how to open them, though I know some of you went ahead and did that anyway." She was looking at Henry when she said that. "And in the meanwhile, I'll tell you guys a little something about myself. And then you guys can tell me a little about yourselves and we'll, um, get to know each other. Sound good? Good."

She smiled at everyone, though I felt like she was smiling at me the most. It wasn't a shiny smile, like Mrs. Garcia's smile, but a normal smile, like she meant it. She looked very different from what I thought teachers were going to look like. I guess I thought she'd look like Miss Fowl from *Jimmy Neutron*: an old lady with a big bun on top of her head. But, in fact, she looked exactly like Mon Mothma from *Star Wars Episode IV*: haircut kind of like a boy's, and a big white shirt kind of like a tunic.

She turned around and started writing on the chalkboard.

Henry still couldn't get his lock to open, and he was getting more and more frustrated every time someone else popped one open. He got really annoyed when I was able to open mine on the first try. The funny thing is, if he hadn't put the backpack between us, I most definitely would have offered to help him.

Around the Room

Ms. Petosa told us a little about who she was. It was boring stuff about where she originally came from, and how she always wanted to teach, and she left her job on Wall Street about six years ago to pursue her "dream" and teach kids. She ended by asking if anyone had any questions, and Julian raised his hand.

"Yes . . ." She had to look at the list to remember his name. "Julian."

"That's cool about how you're pursuing your dream," he said.

"Thank you!"

"You're welcome!" He smiled proudly.

"Okay, so why don't you tell us a little about yourself, Julian? Actually, here's what I want everyone to do. Think of two things you want other people to know about you. Actually, wait a minute: how many of you came from the Beecher lower school? About half the kids raised their hands. "Okay, so a few of you already know each other. But the rest of you, I guess, are new to the school, right? Okay, so everyone think of two things you want other people to know about you—and if you know some of the other kids, try to think of things they don't already know about you. Okay? Okay. So let's start with Julian and we'll go around the room."

Julian scrunched up his face and started tapping his forehead like he was thinking really hard.

"Okay, whenever you're ready," Ms. Petosa said.

"Okay, so number one is that—"

"Do me a favor and start with your names, okay?" Ms. Petosa interrupted. "It'll help me remember everyone."

"Oh, okay. So my name is Julian. And the number one thing I'd like to tell everyone about myself is that . . . I just got Battleground Mystic for my Wii and it's totally awesome. And the number two thing is that we got a Ping-Pong table this summer."

"Very nice, I love Ping-Pong," said Ms. Petosa. "Does anyone have any questions for Julian?"

"Is Battleground Mystic multiplayer or one player?" said the kid named Miles.

"Not those kinds of questions, guys," said Ms. Petosa. "Okay, so how about you. . . ." She pointed to Charlotte, probably because her desk was closest to the front.

"Oh, sure." Charlotte didn't hesitate for even a second, like she knew exactly what she wanted to say. "My name is Charlotte. I have two sisters, and we just got a new puppy named Suki in July. We got her from an animal shelter and she's so, so cute!"

"That's great, Charlotte, thank you," said Ms. Petosa. "Okay, then, who's next?"

Lamb to the Slaughter

"Like a lamb to the slaughter": *Something that you say about someone who goes somewhere calmly, not knowing that something unpleasant is going to happen to them.*

I Googled it last night. That's what I was thinking when Ms. Petosa called my name and suddenly it was my turn to talk.

"My name is August," I said, and yeah, I kind of mumbled it.

"What?" said someone.

"Can you speak up, honey?" said Ms. Petosa.

"My name is August," I said louder, forcing myself to look up. "I, um . . . have a sister named Via and a dog named Daisy. And, um . . . that's it."

"Wonderful," said Ms. Petosa. "Anyone have questions for August?"

No one said anything.

"Okay, you're next," said Ms. Petosa to Jack.

"Wait, I have a question for August," said Julian, raising his hand. "Why do you have that tiny braid in the back of your hair? Is that like a Padawan thing?"

"Yeah." I shrug-nodded.

"What's a Padawan thing?" said Ms. Petosa, smiling at me.

"It's from *Star Wars*," answered Julian. "A Padawan is a Jedi apprentice."

"Oh, interesting," answered Ms. Petosa, looking at me. "So, are you into *Star Wars*, August?"

"I guess." I nodded, not looking up because what I really wanted was to just slide under the desk.

"Who's your favorite character?" Julian asked. I started thinking maybe he wasn't so bad.

"Jango Fett."

"What about Darth Sidious?" he said. "Do you like him?"

"Okay, guys, you can talk about *Star Wars* stuff at recess," said Ms. Petosa cheerfully. "But let's keep going. We haven't heard from *you* yet," she said to Jack.

Now it was Jack's turn to talk, but I admit I didn't hear a word he said. Maybe no one got the Darth Sidious thing, and maybe Julian didn't mean anything at all. But in *Star Wars Episode III: Revenge of the Sith*, Darth Sidious's face gets burned by Sith lightning and becomes totally deformed. His skin gets all shriveled up and his whole face just kind of melts.

I peeked at Julian and he was looking at me. Yeah, he knew what he was saying.

Choose Kind

There was a lot of shuffling around when the bell rang and everybody got up to leave. I checked my schedule and it said my next class was English, room 321. I didn't stop to see if anyone else from my homeroom was going my way: I just zoomed out of the class and down the hall and sat down as far from the front as possible. The teacher, a really tall man with a yellow beard, was writing on the chalkboard.

Kids came in laughing and talking in little groups but I didn't look up. Basically, the same thing that happened in homeroom happened again: no one sat next to me except for Jack, who was joking around with some kids who weren't in our homeroom. I could tell Jack was the kind of kid other kids like. He had a lot of friends. He made people laugh.

When the second bell rang, everyone got quiet and the teacher turned around and faced us. He said his name was Mr. Browne, and then he started talking about what we would be doing this semester. At a certain point, somewhere between *A Wrinkle in Time* and *Shen of the Sea*, he noticed me but kept right on talking.

I was mostly doodling in my notebook while he talked, but every once in a while I would sneak a look at the other students. Charlotte was in this class. So were Julian and Henry. Miles wasn't.

Mr. Browne had written on the chalkboard in big block letters:

P-R-E-C-E-P-T!

"Okay, everybody write this down at the very top of the very first page in your English notebook."

As we did what he told us to do, he said: "Okay, so who can tell me what a precept is? Does anyone know?"

No one raised their hands.

Mr. Browne smiled, nodded, and turned around to write on the chalkboard again:

**PRECEPTS = RULES ABOUT REALLY
IMPORTANT THINGS!**

"Like a motto?" someone called out.

"Like a motto!" said Mr. Browne, nodding as he continued writing on the board. "Like a famous quote. Like a line from a fortune cookie. Any saying or ground rule that can motivate you. Basically, a precept is anything that helps guide us when making decisions about really important things."

He wrote all that on the chalkboard and then turned around and faced us.

"So, what are some *really important* things?" he asked us.

A few kids raised their hands, and as he pointed at them, they gave their answers, which he wrote on the chalkboard in really, really sloppy handwriting:

RULES. SCHOOLWORK. HOMEWORK.

"What else?" he said as he wrote, not even turning around. "Just call things out!" He wrote everything everyone called out.

FAMILY. PARENTS. PETS.

One girl called out: "The environment!"

THE ENVIRONMENT,

he wrote on the chalkboard, and added:

OUR WORLD!

"Sharks, because they eat dead things in the ocean!" said one of the boys, a kid named Reid, and Mr. Browne wrote down

SHARKS.

"Bees!" "Seatbelts!" "Recycling!" "Friends!"

"Okay," said Mr. Browne, writing all those things down. He turned around when he finished writing to face us again. "But no one's named the most important thing of all."

We all looked at him, out of ideas.

"God?" said one kid, and I could tell that even though Mr. Browne wrote "God" down, that wasn't the answer he was looking for. Without saying anything else, he wrote down:

WHO WE ARE!

"Who we are," he said, underlining each word as he said it. "Who we are! Us! Right? What kind of people are we? What kind of person are you? Isn't that the most important thing of all? Isn't that the kind of question we should be asking ourselves all the time? "What kind of person am I?

"Did anyone happen to notice the plaque next to the door of this school? Anyone read what it says? Anyone?"

He looked around but no one knew the answer.

"It says: 'Know Thyself,'" he said, smiling and nodding. "And learning who you are is what you're here to do."

"I thought we were here to learn English," Jack cracked, which made everyone laugh.

"Oh yeah, and that, too!" Mr. Browne answered, which I thought was very cool of him. He turned around and wrote in big huge block letters that spread all the way across the chalkboard:

MR. BROWNE'S SEPTEMBER PRECEPT:

WHEN GIVEN THE CHOICE BETWEEN BEING RIGHT OR BEING KIND, CHOOSE KIND.

"Okay, so, everybody," he said, facing us again, "I want you to start a brand-new section in your notebooks and call it Mr. Browne's Precepts."

He kept talking as we did what he was telling us to do.

"Put today's date at the top of the first page. And from now on, at the beginning of every month, I'm going to write a new Mr. Browne precept on the chalkboard and you're going to write it down in your notebook. Then we're going to discuss that precept and what it means. And at the end of the month, you're going to write an essay about it, about what it means to you. So by the end of the year, you'll all have your own list of precepts to take away with you.

"Over the summer, I ask all my students to come up with their very own personal precept, write it on a postcard, and mail it to me from wherever you go on your summer vacation."

"People really do that?" said one girl whose name I didn't know.

"Oh yeah!" he answered, "people really do that. I've had students send me new precepts years after they've graduated from this school, actually. It's pretty amazing."

He paused and stroked his beard.

"But, anyway, next summer seems like a long way off, I know," he joked, which made us laugh. "So, everybody relax a bit while I take attendance, and then when we're finished with that, I'll start telling you about all the fun stuff we're going to be doing this year—in *English*." He pointed to Jack when he said this, which was also funny, so we all laughed at that.

As I wrote down Mr. Browne's September precept, I suddenly realized that I was going to like school. No matter what.

Lunch

Via had warned me about lunch in middle school, so I guess I should have known it would be hard. I just hadn't expected it to be this hard. Basically, all the kids from all the fifth-grade classes poured into the cafeteria at the same time, talking loudly and bumping into one another while they ran to different tables. One of the lunchroom teachers said something about no seat-saving allowed, but I didn't know what she meant and maybe no one else did, either, because just about everybody was saving seats for their friends. I tried to sit down at one table, but the kid in the next chair said, "Oh, sorry, but somebody else is sitting here."

So I moved to an empty table and just waited for everyone to finish stampeding and the lunchroom teacher to tell us what to do next. As she started telling us the cafeteria rules, I looked around to see where Jack Will was sitting, but I didn't see him on my side of the room. Kids were still coming in as the teachers started calling the first few tables to get their trays and stand on line at the counter. Julian, Henry, and Miles were sitting at a table toward the back of the room.

Mom had packed me a cheese sandwich, graham crackers, and a juice box, so I didn't need to stand on line when my table was called. Instead, I just concentrated on opening my backpack, pulling out my lunch bag, and slowly opening the aluminum-foil wrapping of my sandwich.

I could tell I was being stared at without even looking up. I knew that people were nudging each other, watching me out of the corners of their eyes. I thought I was used to those kinds of stares by now, but I guess I wasn't.

There was one table of girls that I knew were whispering about me because they were talking behind their hands. Their eyes and whispers kept bouncing over to me.

I hate the way I eat. I know how weird it looks. I had a surgery to fix my cleft palate when I was a baby, and then a second cleft surgery when I was four, but I still have a hole in the roof of my mouth. And even though I had jaw-alignment surgery a few years ago, I have to chew food in the front of my mouth. I didn't even realize how this looked until I was at a birthday party once, and one of the kids told the mom of the birthday boy he didn't want to sit next to me because I was too messy with all the food crumbs shooting out of my mouth. I know the kid wasn't trying to be mean, but he got in big trouble later, and his mom called my mom that night to apologize. When I got home from the party, I went to the bathroom mirror and started eating a saltine cracker to see what I looked like when I was chewing. The kid was right. I eat like a tortoise, if you've ever seen a tortoise eating. Like some prehistoric swamp thing.

The Summer Table

"Hey, is this seat taken?"

I looked up, and a girl I never saw before was standing across from my table with a lunch tray full of food. She had long wavy brown hair, and wore a brown T-shirt with a purple peace sign on it.

"Uh, no," I said.

She put her lunch tray on the table, plopped her backpack on the floor, and sat down across from me. She started to eat the mac and cheese on her plate.

"Ugh," she said after the swallowing the first bite. "I should have brought a sandwich like you did."

"Yeah," I said, nodding.

"My name is Summer, by the way. What's yours?"

"August."

"Cool," she said.

"Summer!" Another girl came over to the table carrying a tray. "Why are you sitting here? Come back to the table."

"It was too crowded," Summer answered her. "Come sit here. There's more room."

The other girl looked confused for a second. I realized she had been one of the girls I had caught looking at me just a few minutes earlier: hand cupped over her mouth, whispering. I guess Summer had been one of the girls at that table, too.

"Never mind," said the girl, leaving.

Summer looked at me, shrugged-smiled, and took another bite of her mac and cheese.

"Hey, our names kind of match," she said as she chewed.

I guess she could tell I didn't know what she meant.

"Summer? August?" she said, smiling, her eyes open wide, as she waited for me to get it.

"Oh, yeah," I said after a second.

"We can make this the 'summer only' lunch table," she said. "Only kids with summer names can sit here. Let's see, is there anyone here named June or July?"

"There's a Maya," I said.

"Technically, May is spring," Summer answered, "but if she wanted to sit here, we could make an exception." She said it as if she'd actually thought the whole thing through. "There's Julian. That's like the name Julia, which comes from July."

I didn't say anything.

"There's a kid named Reid in my English class," I said.

"Yeah, I know Reid, but how is Reid a summer name?" she asked.

"I don't know." I shrugged. "I just picture, like, a reed of grass being a summer thing."

"Yeah, okay." She nodded, pulling out her notebook. "And Ms. Petosa could sit here, too. That kind of sounds like the word 'petal,' which I think of as a summer thing, too."

"I have her for homeroom," I said.

"I have her for math," she answered, making a face.

She started writing the list of names on the second-to-last page of her notebook.

"So, who else?" she said.

By the end of lunch, we had come up with a whole list of names of kids and teachers who could sit at our table if they wanted. Most of the names weren't actually summer names, but they were names that had some kind of connection to summer. I even found a way of making Jack Will's name work by pointing out that you could turn his name into a sentence about summer, like "Jack will go to the beach," which Summer agreed worked fine.

"But if someone doesn't have a summer name and wants to sit with us," she said very seriously, "we'll still let them if they're nice, okay?"

"Okay." I nodded. "Even if it's a winter name."

"Cool beans," she answered, giving me a thumbs-up.

Summer looked like her name. She had a tan, and her eyes were green like a leaf.

One to Ten

Mom always had this habit of asking me how something felt on a scale of one to ten. It started after I had my jaw surgery, when I couldn't talk because my mouth was wired shut. They had taken a piece of bone from my hip bone to insert into my chin to make it look more normal, so I was hurting in a lot of different places. Mom would point to one of my bandages, and I would hold up my fingers to show her how much it was hurting. One meant a little bit. Ten meant so, so, so much. Then she would tell the doctor when he made his rounds what needed adjusting or things like that. Mom got very good at reading my mind sometimes.

After that, we got into the habit of doing the one-to-ten scale for anything that hurt, like if I just had a plain old sore throat, she'd ask: "One to ten?" And I'd say: "Three," or whatever it was.

When school was over, I went outside to meet Mom, who was waiting for me at the front entrance like all the other parents or babysitters. The first thing she said after hugging me was: "So, how was it? One to ten?"

"Five," I said, shrugging, which I could tell totally surprised her.

"Wow," she said quietly, "that's even better than I hoped for."

"Are we picking Via up?"

"Miranda's mother is picking her up today. Do you want me to carry your backpack, sweetness?" We had started walking through the crowd of kids and parents, most of whom were noticing me, "secretly" pointing me out to each other.

"I'm fine," I said.

"It looks too heavy, Auggie." She started to take it from me.

"Mom!" I said, pulling my backpack away from her. I walked in front of her through the crowd.

"See you tomorrow, August!" It was Summer. She was walking in the opposite direction.

"Bye, Summer," I said, waving at her.

As soon as we crossed the street and were away from the crowd, Mom said: "Who was that, Auggie?"

"Summer."

"Is she in your class?"

"I have lots of classes."

"Is she in *any* of your classes?" Mom said.

"Nope."

Mom waited for me to say something else, but I just didn't feel like talking.

"So it went okay?" said Mom. I could tell she had a million questions she wanted to ask me. "Everyone was nice? Did you like your teachers?"

"Yeah."

"How about those kids you met last week? Were they nice?"

"Fine, fine. Jack hung out with me a lot."

"That's so great, sweetie. What about that boy Julian?"

I thought about that Darth Sidious comment. By now it felt like that had happened a hundred years ago.

"He was okay," I said.

"And the blond girl, what was her name?"

"Charlotte. Mom, I said everyone was nice already."

"Okay," Mom answered.

I honestly don't know why I was kind of mad at Mom, but I was. We crossed Amesfort Avenue, and she didn't say anything else until we turned onto our block.

"So," Mom said. "How did you meet Summer if she wasn't in any of your classes?"

"We sat together at lunch," I said.

I had started kicking a rock between my feet like it was a soccer ball, chasing it back and forth across the sidewalk.

"She seems very nice."

"Yeah, she is."

"She's very pretty," Mom said.

"Yeah, I know," I answered. "We're kind of like Beauty and the Beast."

I didn't wait to see Mom's reaction. I just started running down the sidewalk after the rock, which I had kicked as hard as I could in front of me.

Padawan

That night I cut off the little braid on the back of my head. Dad noticed first.

"Oh good," he said. "I never liked that thing."

Via couldn't believe I had cut it off.

"That took you years to grow!" she said, almost like she was angry. "Why did you cut it off?"

"I don't know," I answered.

"Did someone make fun of it?"

"No."

"Did you tell Christopher you were cutting it off?"

"We're not even friends anymore!"

"That's not true," she said. "I can't believe you would just cut it off like that," she added snottily, and then practically slammed my bedroom door shut as she left the room.

I was snuggling with Daisy on my bed when Dad came to tuck me in later. He scooched Daisy over gently and lay down next to me on the blanket.

"So, Auggie Doggie," he said, "it was really an okay day?" He got that from an old cartoon about a dachshund named Auggie Doggie, by the way. He had bought it for me on eBay when I was about four, and we watched it a lot for a while—especially in the hospital. He would call me Auggie Doggie and I would call him "dear ol' Dad," like the puppy called the dachshund dad on the show.

"Yeah, it was totally okay," I said, nodding.

"You've been so quiet all night long."

"I guess I'm tired."

"It was a long day, huh?"

I nodded.

"But it really was okay?"

I nodded again. He didn't say anything, so after a few seconds, I said: "It was better than okay, actually."

"That's great to hear, Auggie," he said quietly, kissing my forehead. "So it looks like it was a good call Mom made, your going to school."

"Yeah. But I could stop going if I wanted to, right?"

"That was the deal, yes," he answered. "Though I guess it would depend on why you wanted to stop going, too, you know. You'd have to let us know. You'd have to talk to us and tell us how you're feeling, and if anything bad was happening. Okay? You promise you'd tell us?"

"Yeah."

"So can I ask you something? Are you mad at Mom or something? You've been kind of huffy with her all night long. You know, Auggie, I'm as much to blame for sending you to school as she is."

"No, she's more to blame. It was her idea."

Mom knocked on the door just then and peeked her head inside my room.

"Just wanted to say good night," she said. She looked kind of shy for a second.

"Hi, Momma," Dad said, picking up my hand and waving it at her.

"I heard you cut off your braid," Mom said to me, sitting down at the edge of the bed next to Daisy.

"It's not a big deal," I answered quickly.

"I didn't say it was," said Mom.

"Why don't you put Auggie to bed tonight?" Dad said to

Mom, getting up. "I've got some work to do anyway. Good night, my son, my son." That was another part of our Auggie Doggie routine, though I wasn't in the mood to say Good night, dear ol' Dad. "I'm so proud of you," said Dad, and then he got up out of the bed.

Mom and Dad had always taken turns putting me to bed. I know it was a little babyish of me to still need them to do that, but that's just how it was with us.

"Will you check in on Via?" Mom said to Dad as she lay down next to me.

He stopped by the door and turned around. "What's wrong with Via?"

"Nothing," said Mom, shrugging, "at least that she would tell me. But . . . first day of high school and all that."

"Hmm," said Dad, and then he pointed his finger at me and winked. "It's always something with you kids, isn't it?" he said.

"Never a dull moment," said Mom.

"Never a dull moment," Dad repeated. "Good night, guys."

As soon as he closed the door, Mom pulled out the book she'd been reading to me for the last couple of weeks. I was relieved because I really was afraid she'd want to "talk," and I just didn't feel like doing that. But Mom didn't seem to want to talk, either. She just flipped through the pages until she got to where we had left off. We were about halfway through *The Hobbit*.

" '*Stop! stop!' shouted Thorin,*" said Mom, reading aloud, "*but it was too late, the excited dwarves had wasted their last arrows, and now the bows that Beorn had given them were useless.*

"*They were a gloomy party that night, and the gloom gathered still deeper on them in the following days. They had crossed the enchanted stream; but beyond it the path seemed to straggle on just as before, and in the forest they could see no change.*"

I'm not sure why, but all of a sudden I started to cry.

Mom put the book down and wrapped her arms around me. She didn't seem surprised that I was crying. "It's okay," she whispered in my ear. "It'll be okay."

"I'm sorry," I said between sniffles.

"Shh," she said, wiping my tears with the back of her hand. "You have nothing to be sorry about. . . ."

"Why do I have to be so ugly, Mommy?" I whispered.

"No, baby, you're not . . ."

"I know I am."

She kissed me all over my face. She kissed my eyes that came down too far. She kissed my cheeks that looked punched in. She kissed my tortoise mouth.

She said soft words that I know were meant to help me, but words can't change my face.

September

The rest of September was hard. I wasn't used to getting up so early in the morning. I wasn't used to this whole notion of homework. And I got my first "quiz" at the end of the month. I never got "quizzes" when Mom homeschooled me. I also didn't like how I had no free time anymore. Before, I was able to play whenever I wanted to, but now it felt like I always had stuff to do for school.

And being at school was awful in the beginning. Every new class I had was like a new chance for kids to "not stare" at me. They would sneak peeks at me from behind their notebooks or when they thought I wasn't looking. They would take the longest way around me to avoid bumping into me in any way, like I had some germ they could catch, like my face was contagious.

In the hallways, which were always crowded, my face would always surprise some unsuspecting kid who maybe hadn't heard about me. The kid would make the sound you make when you hold your breath before going underwater, a little "uh!" sound. This happened maybe four or five times a day for the first few weeks: on the stairs, in front of the lockers, in the library. Five hundred kids in a school: eventually every one of them was going to see my face at some time. And I knew after the first couple of days that word had gotten around about me, because every once in a while I'd catch a kid elbowing his friend as they passed me, or talking behind their hands as I walked by them. I can only imagine what they were saying about me. Actually, I prefer not to even try to imagine it.

I'm not saying they were doing any of these things in a mean way, by the way: not once did any kid laugh or make noises or do anything like that. They were just being normal dumb kids. I know that. I kind of wanted to tell them that. Like, it's okay, I'm know I'm weird-looking, take a look, I don't bite. Hey, the truth is, if a Wookiee started going to the school all of a sudden, I'd be curious, I'd probably stare a bit! And if I was walking with Jack or Summer, I'd probably whisper to them: Hey, there's the Wookiee. And if the Wookiee caught me saying that, he'd know I wasn't trying to be mean. I was just pointing out the fact that he's a Wookiee.

It took about one week for the kids in my class to get used to my face. These were the kids I'd see every day in all my classes.

It took about two weeks for the rest of the kids in my grade to get used to my face. These were the kids I'd see in the cafeteria, yard time, PE, music, library, computer class.

It took about a month for the rest of the kids in the entire school to get used to it. These were the kids in all the other grades. They were big kids, some of them. Some of them had crazy haircuts. Some of them had earrings in their noses. Some of them had pimples. None of them looked like me.

Jack Will

I hung out with Jack in homeroom, English, history, computer, music, and science, which were all the classes we had together. The teachers assigned seats in every class, and I ended up sitting next to Jack in every single class, so I figured either the teachers were told to put me and Jack together, or it was a totally incredible coincidence.

I walked to classes with Jack, too. I know he noticed kids staring at me, but he pretended not to notice. One time, though, on our way to history, this huge eighth grader who was zooming down the stairs two steps at a time accidentally bumped into us at the bottom of the stairs and knocked me down. As the guy helped me stand up, he got a look at my face, and without even meaning to, he just said: "Whoa!" Then he patted me on the shoulder, like he was dusting me off, and took off after his friends. For some reason, me and Jack started cracking up.

"That guy made the funniest face!" said Jack as we sat down at our desks.

"I know, right?" I said. "He was like, *whoa!*"

"I swear, I think he wet his pants!"

We were laughing so hard that the teacher, Mr. Roche, had to ask us to settle down.

Later, after we finished reading about how ancient Sumerians built sundials, Jack whispered: "Do you ever want to beat those kids up?"

I shrugged. "I guess. I don't know."

"I'd want to. I think you should get a secret squirt gun or

65

something and attach it to your eyes somehow. And every time someone stares at you, you would squirt them in the face."

"With some green slime or something," I answered.

"No, no: with slug juice mixed with dog pee."

"Yeah!" I said, completely agreeing.

"Guys," said Mr. Roche from across the room. "People are still reading."

We nodded and looked down at our books. Then Jack whispered: "Are you always going to look this way, August? I mean, can't you get plastic surgery or something?"

I smiled and pointed to my face. "Hello? This *is* after plastic surgery!"

Jack clapped his hand over his forehead and started laughing hysterically.

"Dude, you should sue your doctor!" he answered between giggles.

This time the two of us were laughing so much we couldn't stop, even after Mr. Roche came over and made us both switch chairs with the kids next to us.

Mr. Browne's October Precept

Mr. Browne's precept for October was:

YOUR DEEDS ARE YOUR MONUMENTS.

He told us that this was written on the tombstone of some Egyptian guy that died thousands of years ago. Since we were just about to start studying ancient Egypt in history, Mr. Browne thought this was a good choice for a precept.

Our homework assignment was to write a paragraph about what we thought the precept meant or how we felt about it.

This is what I wrote:

This precept means that we should be remembered for the things we do. The things we do are the most important things of all. They are more important than what we say or what we look like. The things we do outlast our mortality. The things we do are like monuments that people build to honor heroes after they've died. They're like the pyramids that the Egyptians built to honor the pharaohs. Only instead of being made out of stone, they're made out of the memories people have of you. That's why your deeds are like your monuments. Built with memories instead of with stone.

Apples

My birthday is October 10. I like my birthday: 10/10. It would've been great if I'd been born at exactly 10:10 in the morning or at night, but I wasn't. I was born just after midnight. But I still think my birthday is cool.

I usually have a little party at home, but this year I asked Mom if I could have a big bowling party. Mom was surprised but happy. She asked me who I wanted to ask from my class, and I said everyone in my homeroom plus Summer.

"That's a lot of kids, Auggie," said Mom.

"I have to invite everyone because I don't want anyone to get their feelings hurt if they find out other people are invited and they aren't, okay?"

"Okay," Mom agreed. "You even want to invite the 'what's the deal' kid?"

"Yeah, you can invite Julian," I answered. "Geez, Mom, you should forget about that already."

"I know, you're right."

A couple of weeks later, I asked Mom who was coming to my party, and she said: "Jack Will, Summer. Reid Kingsley. Both Maxes. And a couple of other kids said they were going to try to be there."

"Like who?"

"Charlotte's mom said Charlotte had a dance recital earlier in the day, but she was going to try to come to your party if time allowed. And Tristan's mom said he might come after his soccer game."

68

"So that's *it*?" I said. "That's like . . . five people."

"That's more than five people, Auggie. I think a lot of people just had plans already," Mom answered. We were in the kitchen. She was cutting one of the apples we had just gotten at the farmers' market into teensy-weensy bites so I could eat it.

"What kind of plans?" I asked.

"I don't know, Auggie. We sent out the evites kind of late."

"Like what did they tell you, though? What reasons did they give?"

"Everyone gave different reasons, Auggie." She sounded a bit impatient. "Really, sweetie, it shouldn't matter what their reasons were. People had plans, that's all."

"What did Julian give as his reason?" I asked.

"You know," said Mom, "his mom was the only person who didn't RSVP at all." She looked at me. "I guess the apple doesn't fall far from the tree."

I laughed because I thought she was making a joke, but then I realized she wasn't.

"What does that mean?" I asked.

"Never mind. Now go wash your hands so you can eat."

My birthday party turned out to be much smaller than I thought it would be, but it was still great. Jack, Summer, Reid, Tristan, and both Maxes came from school, and Christopher came, too—all the way from Bridgeport with his parents. And Uncle Ben came. And Aunt Kate and Uncle Po drove in from Boston, though Tata and Poppa were in Florida for the winter. It was fun because all the grown-ups ended up bowling in the lane next to ours, so it really felt like there were a lot of people there to celebrate my birthday.

Halloween

At lunch the next day, Summer asked me what I was going to be for Halloween. Of course, I'd been thinking about it since last Halloween, so I knew right away.

"Boba Fett."

"You know you can wear a costume to school on Halloween, right?"

"No way, really?"

"So long as it's politically correct."

"What, like no guns and stuff?"

"Exactly."

"What about blasters?"

"I think a blaster's like a gun, Auggie."

"Oh man . . . ," I said, shaking my head. Boba Fett has a blaster.

"At least, we don't have to come like a character in a book anymore. In the lower school that's what you had to do. Last year I was the Wicked Witch of the West from *The Wizard of Oz*."

"But that's a movie, not a book."

"Hello?" Summer answered. "It was a book first! One of my favorite books in the world, actually. My dad used to read it to me every night in the first grade."

When Summer talks, especially when she's excited about something, her eyes squint like she's looking right at the sun.

I hardly ever see Summer during the day, since the only class we have together is English. But ever since that first lunch at school, we've sat at the summer table together every day, just the two of us.

"So, what are you going to be?" I asked her.

"I don't know yet. I know what I'd really want to go as, but I think it might be too dorky. You know, Savanna's group isn't even wearing costumes this year. They think we're too old for Halloween."

"What? That's just dumb."

"I know, right?"

"I thought you didn't care what those girls think."

She shrugged and took a long drink of her milk.

"So, what dorky thing do you want to dress up as?" I asked her, smiling.

"Promise not to laugh?" She raised her eyebrows and her shoulders, embarrassed. "A unicorn."

I smiled and looked down at my sandwich.

"Hey, you promised not to laugh!" she laughed.

"Okay, okay," I said. "But you're right: that is too dorky."

"I know!" she said. "But I have it all planned out: I'd make the head out of papier-mâché, and paint the horn gold and make the mane gold, too. . . . It would be so awesome."

"Okay." I shrugged. "Then you should do it. Who cares what other people think, right?"

"Maybe what I'll do is just wear it for the Halloween Parade," she said, snapping her fingers. "And I'll just be, like, a Goth girl for school. Yeah, that's it, that's what I'll do."

"Sounds like a plan." I nodded.

"Thanks, Auggie," she giggled. "You know, that's what I like best about you. I feel like I can tell you anything."

"Yeah?" I answered, nodding. I gave her a thumbs-up sign. "Cool beans."

School Pictures

I don't think anyone will be shocked to learn I don't want to have my school picture taken on October 22. No way. No thank you. I stopped letting anyone take pictures of me a while ago. I guess you could call it a phobia. No, actually, it's not a phobia. It's an "aversion," which is a word I just learned in Mr. Browne's class. I have an aversion to having my picture taken. There, I used it in a sentence.

I thought Mom would try to get me to drop my aversion to having my picture taken for school, but she didn't. Unfortunately, while I managed to avoid having the portrait taken, I couldn't get out of being part of the class picture. Ugh. The photographer looked like he'd just sucked on a lemon when he saw me. I'm sure he thought I ruined the picture. I was one of the ones in the front, sitting down. I didn't smile, not that anyone could tell if I had.

The Cheese Touch

I noticed not too long ago that even though people were getting used to me, no one would actually touch me. I didn't realize this at first because it's not like kids go around touching each other that much in middle school anyway. But last Thursday in dance class, which is, like, my least favorite class, Mrs. Atanabi, the teacher, tried to make Ximena Chin be my dance partner. Now, I've never actually seen someone have a "panic attack" before, but I have heard about it, and I'm pretty sure Ximena had a panic attack at that second. She got really nervous and turned pale and literally broke into a sweat within a minute, and then she came up with some lame excuse about really having to go to the bathroom. Anyway, Mrs. Atanabi let her off the hook, because she ended up not making anyone dance together.

Then yesterday in my science elective, we were doing this cool mystery-powder investigation where we had to classify a substance as an acid or a base. Everyone had to heat their mystery powders on a heating plate and make observations, so we were all huddled around the powders with our notebooks. Now, there are eight kids in the elective, and seven of them were squished together on one side of the plate while one of them—me—had loads of room on the other side. So of course I noticed this, but I was hoping Ms. Rubin wouldn't notice this, because I didn't want her to say something. But of course she did notice this, and of course she said something.

"Guys, there's plenty of room on that side. Tristan, Nino, go over there," she said, so Tristan and Nino scooted over to my side. Tristan and Nino have always been okay-nice to me. I want to go on record as saying that. Not super-nice, like they go out of their way to hang out with me, but okay-nice, like they say hello to me and talk to me like normal. And they didn't even make a face when Ms. Rubin told them to come on my side, which a lot of kids do when they think I'm not looking. Anyway, everything was going fine until Tristan's mystery powder started melting. He moved his foil off the plate just as my powder began to melt, too, which is why I went to move mine off the plate, and then my hand accidentally bumped his hand for a fraction of a second. Tristan jerked his hand away so fast he dropped his foil on the floor while also knocking everyone else's foil off the heating plate.

"Tristan!" yelled Ms. Rubin, but Tristan didn't even care about the spilled powder on the floor or that he ruined the experiment. What he was most concerned about was getting to the lab sink to wash his hands as fast as possible. That's when I knew for sure that there was this thing about touching me at Beecher Prep.

I think it's like the Cheese Touch in *Diary of a Wimpy Kid*. The kids in that story were afraid they'd catch the cooties if they touched the old moldy cheese on the basketball court. At Beecher Prep, I'm the old moldy cheese.

Costumes

For me, Halloween is the best holiday in the world. It even beats Christmas. I get to dress up in a costume. I get to wear a mask. I get to go around like every other kid with a mask and nobody thinks I look weird. Nobody takes a second look. Nobody notices me. Nobody knows me.

I wish every day could be Halloween. We could all wear masks all the time. Then we could walk around and get to know each other before we got to see what we looked like under the masks.

When I was little, I used to wear an astronaut helmet everywhere I went. To the playground. To the supermarket. To pick Via up from school. Even in the middle of summer, though it was so hot my face would sweat. I think I wore it for a couple of years, but I had to stop wearing it when I had my eye surgery. I was about seven, I think. And then we couldn't find the helmet after that. Mom looked everywhere for it. She figured that it had probably ended up in Grans's attic, and she kept meaning to look for it, but by then I had gotten used to not wearing it.

I have pictures of me in all my Halloween costumes. My first Halloween I was a pumpkin. My second I was Tigger. My third I was Peter Pan (my dad dressed up as Captain Hook). My fourth I was Captain Hook (my dad dressed up as Peter Pan). My fifth I was an astronaut. My sixth I was Obi-Wan Kenobi. My seventh I was a clone trooper. My eighth I was Darth Vader. My ninth I was the Bleeding Scream, the one that has fake blood oozing out over the skull mask.

This year I'm going to be Boba Fett: not Boba Fett the kid in *Star Wars Episode II: Attack of the Clones*, but Boba Fett the man from *Star Wars Episode V: The Empire Strikes Back*. Mom searched everywhere for the costume but couldn't find one in my size, so she bought me a Jango Fett costume—since Jango was Boba's dad and wore the same armor—and then painted the armor green. She did some other stuff to it to make it look worn, too. Anyway, it looks totally real. Mom's good at costumes.

In homeroom we all talked about what we were going to be for Halloween. Charlotte was going as Hermione from Harry Potter. Jack was going as a wolfman. I heard that Julian was going as Jango Fett, which was a weird coincidence. I don't think he liked hearing that I was going as Boba Fett.

On the morning of Halloween, Via had this big crying meltdown about something. Via's always been so calm and cool, but this year she's had a couple of these kinds of fits. Dad was late for work and was like, "Via, let's go! Let's go!" Usually Dad is super patient about things, but not when it comes to his being late for work, and his yelling just stressed out Via even more, and she started crying louder, so Mom told Dad to take me to school and that she'd deal with Via. Then Mom kissed me goodbye quickly, before I even put on my costume, and disappeared into Via's room.

"Auggie, let's go now!" said Dad. "I have a meeting I can't be late for!"

"I haven't put my costume on yet!"

"So put it on, already. Five minutes. I'll meet you outside."

I rushed to my room and started to put on the Boba Fett costume, but all of a sudden I didn't feel like wearing it. I'm not sure why—maybe because it had all these belts that needed to be tightened and I needed someone's help to put it on. Or maybe it was because it still smelled a little like paint. All I knew was that it was a lot of work to put the costume on, and Dad was waiting and would get super impatient if I made him late. So, at the last minute, I threw on the Bleeding Scream costume from last year. It was such an easy costume: just a long black robe and a big white mask. I yelled goodbye from the door on my way out, but Mom didn't even hear me.

"I thought you were going as Jango Fett," said Dad when I got outside.

"Boba Fett!"

"Whatever," said Dad. "This is a better costume anyway."

"Yeah, it's cool," I answered.

The Bleeding Scream

Walking through the halls that morning on my way to the lockers was, I have to say, absolutely awesome. Everything was different now. I was different. Where I usually walked with my head down, trying to avoid being seen, today I walked with my head up, looking around. I wanted to be seen. One kid wearing the same exact costume as mine, long white skull face oozing fake red blood, high-fived me as we passed each other on the stairs. I have no idea who he was, and he had no idea who I was, and I wondered for a second if he would have ever done that if he'd known it was me under the mask.

I was starting to think this was going to go down as one of the most awesome days in the history of my life, but then I got to homeroom. The first costume I saw as I walked inside the door was Darth Sidious. It had one of the rubber masks that are so realistic, with a big black hood over the head and a long black robe. I knew right away it was Julian, of course. He must have changed his costume at the last minute because he thought I was coming as Jango Fett. He was talking to two mummies who must have been Miles and Henry, and they were all kind of looking at the door like they were waiting for someone to come through it. I knew it wasn't a Bleeding Scream they were looking for. It was a Boba Fett.

I was going to go and sit at my usual desk, but for some reason, I don't know why, I found myself walking over to a desk near them, and I could hear them talking.

One of the mummies was saying: "It really does look like him."

"Like this part especially . . . ," answered Julian's voice. He put his fingers on the cheeks and eyes of his Darth Sidious mask.

"Actually," said the mummy, "what he really looks like is one of those shrunken heads. Have you ever seen those? He looks exactly like that."

"I think he looks like an orc."

"Oh yeah!"

"If I looked like that," said the Julian voice, kind of laughing, "I swear to God, I'd put a hood over my face every day."

"I've thought about this a lot," said the second mummy, sounding serious, "and I really think . . . if I looked like him, seriously, I think that I'd kill myself."

"You would not," answered Darth Sidious.

"Yeah, for real," insisted the same mummy. "I can't imagine looking in the mirror every day and seeing myself like that. It would be too awful. And getting stared at all the time."

"Then why do you hang out with him so much?" asked Darth Sidious.

"I don't know," answered the mummy. "Tushman asked me to hang out with him at the beginning of the year, and he must have told all the teachers to put us next to each other in all our classes, or something." The mummy shrugged. I knew the shrug, of course. I knew the voice. I knew I wanted to run out of the class right then and there. But I stood where I was and listened to Jack Will finish what he was saying. "I mean, the thing is: he always follows me around. What am I supposed to do?"

"Just ditch him," said Julian.

I don't know what Jack answered because I walked out of the class without anyone knowing I had been there. My face felt like it was on fire while I walked back down the stairs. I was sweating under my costume. And I started crying. I couldn't keep it from happening. The tears were so thick in my eyes I could barely see, but I couldn't wipe them through the mask as I walked. I was looking for a little tiny spot to disappear into. I wanted a hole I could fall inside of: a little black hole that would eat me up.

Names

Rat boy. Freak. Monster. Freddy Krueger. E.T. Gross-out. Lizard face. Mutant. I know the names they call me. I've been in enough playgrounds to know kids can be mean. I know, I know, I know.

I ended up in the second-floor bathroom. No one was there because first period had started and everyone was in class. I locked the door to my stall and took off my mask and just cried for I don't know how long. Then I went to the nurse's office and told her I had a stomach ache, which was true, because I felt like I'd been kicked in the gut. Nurse Molly called Mom and had me lie down on the sofa next to her desk. Fifteen minutes later, Mom was at the door.

"Sweetness," she said, coming over to hug me.

"Hi," I mumbled. I didn't want her to ask anything until afterward.

"You have a stomach ache?" she asked, automatically putting her hand on my forehead to check for my temperature.

"He said he feels like throwing up," said Nurse Molly, looking at me with very nice eyes.

"And I have a headache," I whispered.

"I wonder if it's something you ate," said Mom, looking worried.

"There's a stomach bug going around," said Nurse Molly.

"Oh geez," said Mom, her eyebrows going up as she shook her head. She helped me to my feet. "Should I call a taxi or are you okay walking home?"

"I can walk."

"What a brave kid!" said Nurse Molly, patting me on the back as she walked us toward the door. "If he starts throwing up or runs a temperature, you should call the doctor."

"Absolutely," said Mom, shaking Nurse Molly's hand. "Thank you so much for taking care of him."

"My pleasure," answered Nurse Molly, putting her hand under my chin and tilting my face up. "You take care of yourself, okay?"

I nodded and mumbled "Thank you." Mom and I hug-walked the whole way home. I didn't tell her anything about what had happened, and later when she asked me if I felt well enough to go trick-or-treating after school, I said no. This worried her, since she knew how much I usually loved trick-or-treating.

I heard her say to Dad on the phone: ". . . He doesn't even have the energy to go trick-or-treating. . . . No, no fever at all . . . Well, I will if he doesn't feel better by tomorrow. . . . I know, poor thing . . . Imagine his missing Halloween."

I got out of going to school the next day, too, which was Friday. So I had the whole weekend to think about everything. I was pretty sure I would never go back to school again.

Part Two

Via

Far above the world

Planet Earth is blue

And there's nothing I can do

—David Bowie, "Space Oddity"

A Tour of the Galaxy

August is the Sun. Me and Mom and Dad are planets orbiting the Sun. The rest of our family and friends are asteroids and comets floating around the planets orbiting the Sun. The only celestial body that doesn't orbit August the Sun is Daisy the dog, and that's only because to her little doggy eyes, August's face doesn't look very different from any other human's face. To Daisy, all our faces look alike, as flat and pale as the moon.

I'm used to the way this universe works. I've never minded it because it's all I've ever known. I've always understood that August is special and has special needs. If I was playing too loudly and he was trying to take a nap, I knew I would have to play something else because he needed his rest after some procedure or other had left him weak and in pain. If I wanted Mom and Dad to watch me play soccer, I knew that nine out of ten times they'd miss it because they were busy shuttling August to speech therapy or physical therapy or a new specialist or a surgery.

Mom and Dad would always say I was the most understanding little girl in the world. I don't know about that, just that I understood there was no point in complaining. I've seen August after his surgeries: his little face bandaged up and swollen, his tiny body full of IVs and tubes to keep him alive. After you've seen someone else going through that, it feels kind of crazy to complain over not getting the toy you had asked for, or your mom missing a school play. I knew this even when I was six years old. No one ever told it to me. I just knew it.

So I've gotten used to not complaining, and I've gotten used to not bothering Mom and Dad with little stuff. I've gotten used to figuring things out on my own: how to put toys together, how to organize my life so I don't miss friends' birthday parties, how to stay on top of my schoolwork so I never fall behind in class. I've never asked for help with my homework. Never needed reminding to finish a project or study for a test. If I was having trouble with a subject in school, I'd go home and study it until I figured it out on my own. I taught myself how to convert fractions into decimal points by going online. I've done every school project pretty much by myself. When Mom or Dad ask me how things are going in school, I've always said "good"—even when it hasn't always been so good. My worst day, worst fall, worst headache, worst bruise, worst cramp, worst mean thing anyone could say has always been nothing compared to what August has gone through. This isn't me being noble, by the way: it's just the way I know it is.

And this is the way it's always been for me, for the little universe of us. But this year there seems to be a shift in the cosmos. The galaxy is changing. Planets are falling out of alignment.

Before August

I honestly don't remember my life before August came into it. I look at pictures of me as a baby, and I see Mom and Dad smiling so happily, holding me. I can't believe how much younger they looked back then: Dad was this hipster dude and Mom was this cute Brazilian fashionista. There's one shot of me at my third birthday: Dad's right behind me while Mom's holding the cake with three lit candles, and in back of us are Tata and Poppa, Grans, Uncle Ben, Aunt Kate, and Uncle Po. Everyone's looking at me and I'm looking at the cake. You can see in that picture how I really was the first child, first grandchild, first niece. I don't remember what it felt like, of course, but I can see it plain as can be in the pictures.

I don't remember the day they brought August home from the hospital. I don't remember what I said or did or felt when I saw him for the first time, though everyone has a story about it. Apparently, I just looked at him for a long time without saying anything at all, and then finally I said: "It doesn't look like Lilly!" That was the name of a doll Grans had given me when Mom was pregnant so I could "practice" being a big sister. It was one of those dolls that are incredibly lifelike, and I had carried it everywhere for months, changing its diaper, feeding it. I'm told I even made a baby sling for it. The story goes that after my initial reaction to August, it only took a few minutes (according to Grans) or a few days (according to Mom) before I was all over him: kissing him, cuddling him, baby talking to him. After that I never so much as touched or mentioned Lilly ever again.

Seeing August

I never used to see August the way other people saw him. I knew he didn't look exactly normal, but I really didn't understand why strangers seemed so shocked when they saw him. Horrified. Sickened. Scared. There are so many words I can use to describe the looks on people's faces. And for a long time I didn't get it. I'd just get mad. Mad when they stared. Mad when they looked away. "What the heck are you looking at?" I'd say to people— even grown-ups.

Then, when I was about eleven, I went to stay with Grans in Montauk for four weeks while August was having his big jaw surgery. This was the longest I'd ever been away from home, and I have to say it was so amazing to suddenly be free of all that stuff that made me so mad. No one stared at Grans and me when we went to town to buy groceries. No one pointed at us. No one even noticed us.

Grans was one of those grandmothers who do everything with their grandkids. She'd run into the ocean if I asked her to, even if she had nice clothes on. She would let me play with her makeup and didn't mind if I used it on her face to practice my face-painting skills. She'd take me for ice cream even if we hadn't eaten dinner yet. She'd draw chalk horses on the sidewalk in front of her house. One night, while we were walking back from town, I told her that I wished I could live with her forever. I was so happy there. I think it might have been the best time in my life.

Coming home after four weeks felt very strange at first. I

remember very vividly stepping through the door and seeing August running over to welcome me home, and for this tiny fraction of a moment I saw him not the way I've always seen him, but the way other people see him. It was only a flash, an instant while he was hugging me, so happy that I was home, but it surprised me because I'd never seen him like that before. And I'd never felt what I was feeling before, either: a feeling I hated myself for having the moment I had it. But as he was kissing me with all his heart, all I could see was the drool coming down his chin. And suddenly there I was, like all those people who would stare or look away.

Horrified. Sickened. Scared.

Thankfully, that only lasted for a second: the moment I heard August laugh his raspy little laugh, it was over. Everything was back the way it had been before. But it had opened a door for me. A little peephole. And on the other side of the peephole there were two Augusts: the one I saw blindly, and the one other people saw.

I think the only person in the world I could have told any of this to was Grans, but I didn't. It was too hard to explain over the phone. I thought maybe when she came for Thanksgiving, I'd tell her what I felt. But just two months after I stayed with her in Montauk, my beautiful Grans died. It was so completely out of the blue. Apparently, she had checked herself into the hospital because she'd been feeling nauseous. Mom and I drove out to see her, but it's a three-hour drive from where we live, and by the time we got to the hospital, Grans was gone. A heart attack, they told us. Just like that.

It's so strange how one day you can be on this earth, and the next day not. Where did she go? Will I really ever see her again, or is that a fairy tale?

You see movies and TV shows where people receive horrible

news in hospitals, but for us, with all our many trips to the hospital with August, there had always been good outcomes. What I remember the most from the day Grans died is Mom literally crumpling to the floor in slow, heaving sobs, holding her stomach like someone had just punched her. I've never, ever seen Mom like that. Never heard sounds like that come out of her. Even through all of August's surgeries, Mom always put on a brave face.

On my last day in Montauk, Grans and I had watched the sun set on the beach. We had taken a blanket to sit on, but it had gotten chilly, so we wrapped it around us and cuddled and talked until there wasn't even a sliver of sun left over the ocean. And then Grans told me she had a secret to tell me: she loved me more than anyone else in the world.

"Even August?" I had asked.

She smiled and stroked my hair, like she was thinking about what to say.

"I love Auggie very, very much," she said softly. I can still remember her Portuguese accent, the way she rolled her r's. "But he has many angels looking out for him already, Via. And I want you to know that you have *me* looking out for *you*. Okay, *menina querida*? I want you to know that you are number one for me. You are my . . ." She looked out at the ocean and spread her hands out, like she was trying to smooth out the waves, "You are my everything. You understand me, Via? *Tu es meu tudo.*"

I understood her. And I knew why she said it was a secret. Grandmothers aren't supposed to have favorites. Everyone knows that. But after she died, I held on to that secret and let it cover me like a blanket.

August
Through the Peephole

His eyes are about an inch below where they should be on his face, almost to halfway down his cheeks. They slant downward at an extreme angle, almost like diagonal slits that someone cut into his face, and the left one is noticeably lower than the right one. They bulge outward because his eye cavities are too shallow to accommodate them. The top eyelids are always halfway closed, like he's on the verge of sleeping. The lower eyelids sag so much they almost look like a piece of invisible string is pulling them downward: you can see the red part on the inside, like they're almost inside out. He doesn't have eyebrows or eyelashes. His nose is disproportionately big for his face, and kind of fleshy. His head is pinched in on the sides where the ears should be, like someone used giant pliers and crushed the middle part of his face. He doesn't have cheekbones. There are deep creases running down both sides of his nose to his mouth, which gives him a waxy appearance. Sometimes people assume he's been burned in a fire: his features look like they've been melted, like the drippings on the side of a candle. Several surgeries to correct his lip have left a few scars around his mouth, the most noticeable one being a jagged gash running from the middle of his upper lip to his nose. His upper teeth are small and splay out. He has a severe overbite and an extremely undersized jawbone. He has a very small chin. When he was very little, before a piece of his hip bone was surgically implanted into his lower jaw, he really had no chin at all. His tongue would just hang out of his mouth with nothing underneath to block it. Thankfully, it's better now. He can eat, at least: when he was younger, he had a feeding tube. And he can talk. And he's learned to keep his tongue inside his mouth, though that took him several years to master. He's also learned to control the drool that used to run down his neck. These are considered miracles. When he was a baby, the doctors didn't think he'd live.

He can hear, too. Most kids born with these types of birth defects have problems with their middle ears that prevent them from hearing, but so far August can hear well enough through his tiny cauliflower-shaped ears. The doctors think that eventually he'll need to wear hearing aids, though. August hates the thought of this. He thinks the hearing aids will get noticed too much. I don't tell him that the hearing aids would be the least of his problems, of course, because I'm sure he knows this.

Then again, I'm not really sure what August knows or doesn't know, what he understands and doesn't understand.

Does August see how other people see him, or has he gotten so good at pretending not to see that it doesn't bother him? Or does it bother him? When he looks in the mirror, does he see the Auggie Mom and Dad see, or does he see the Auggie everyone else sees? Or is there another August he sees, someone in his dreams behind the misshapen head and face? Sometimes when I looked at Grans, I could see the pretty girl she used to be underneath the wrinkles. I could see the girl from Ipanema inside the old-lady walk. Does August see himself as he might have looked without that single gene that caused the catastrophe of his face?

I wish I could ask him this stuff. I wish he would tell me how he feels. He used to be easier to read before the surgeries. You knew that when his eyes squinted, he was happy. When his mouth went straight, he was being mischievous. When his cheeks trembled, he was about to cry. He looks better now, no doubt about that, but the signs we used to gauge his moods are all gone. There are new ones, of course. Mom and Dad can read every single one. But I'm having trouble keeping up. And there's a part of me that doesn't want to keep trying: why can't he just say what he's feeling like everyone else? He doesn't have a trache tube in his mouth anymore that keeps him from talking. His jaw's not wired shut. He's ten years old. He can use his words. But we circle around him like he's still the baby he used to be. We change plans, go to plan B, interrupt conversations, go back on promises depending on his moods, his whims, his needs. That was fine when he was little. But he needs to grow up now. We need to let him, help him, make him grow up. Here's what I think: we've all spent so much time trying to make August think he's normal that he actually thinks he is normal. And the problem is, he's not.

High School

What I always loved most about middle school was that it was separate and different from home. I could go there and be Olivia Pullman—not Via, which is my name at home. Via was what they called me in elementary school, too. Back then, everyone knew all about us, of course. Mom used to pick me up after school, and August was always in the stroller. There weren't a lot of people who were equipped to babysit for Auggie, so Mom and Dad brought him to all my class plays and concerts and recitals, all the school functions, the bake sales and the book fairs. My friends knew him. My friends' parents knew him. My teachers knew him. The janitor knew him. ("Hey, how ya doin', Auggie?" he'd always say, and give August a high five.) August was something of a fixture at PS 22.

But in middle school a lot of people didn't know about August. My old friends did, of course, but my new friends didn't. Or if they knew, it wasn't necessarily the first thing they knew about me. Maybe it was the second or third thing they'd hear about me. "Olivia? Yeah, she's nice. Did you hear she has a brother who's deformed?" I always hated that word, but I knew it was how people described Auggie. And I knew those kinds of conversations probably happened all the time out of earshot, every time I left the room at a party, or bumped into groups of friends at the pizza place. And that's okay. I'm always going to be the sister of a kid with a birth defect: that's not the issue. I just don't always want to be defined that way.

The best thing about high school is that hardly anybody

knows me at all. Except Miranda and Ella, of course. And they know not to go around talking about it.

Miranda, Ella, and I have known each other since the first grade. What's so nice is we never have to explain things to one another. When I decided I wanted them to call me Olivia instead of Via, they got it without my having to explain.

They've known August since he was a little baby. When we were little, our favorite thing to do was play dress up with Auggie; load him up with feather boas and big hats and Hannah Montana wigs. He used to love it, of course, and we thought he was adorably cute in his own way. Ella said he reminded her of E.T. She didn't say this to be mean, of course (though maybe it was a little bit mean). The truth is, there's a scene in the movie when Drew Barrymore dresses E.T. in a blond wig: and that was a ringer for Auggie in our Miley Cyrus heyday.

Throughout middle school, Miranda, Ella, and I were pretty much our own little group. Somewhere between super popular and well-liked: not brainy, not jocks, not rich, not druggies, not mean, not goody-goody, not huge, not flat. I don't know if the three of us found each other because we were so alike in so many ways, or that because we found each other, we've become so alike in so many ways. We were so happy when we all got into Faulkner High School. It was such a long shot that all three of us would be accepted, especially when almost no one else from our middle school was. I remember how we screamed into our phones the day we got our acceptance letters.

This is why I haven't understood what's been going on with us lately, now that we're actually in high school. It's nothing like how I thought it would be.

Major Tom

Out of the three of us, Miranda had almost always been the sweetest to August, hugging him and playing with him long after Ella and I had moved on to playing something else. Even as we got older, Miranda always made sure to try to include August in our conversations, ask him how he was doing, talk to him about *Avatar* or *Star Wars* or *Bone* or something she knew he liked. It was Miranda who had given Auggie the astronaut helmet he wore practically every day of the year when he was five or six. She would call him Major Tom and they would sing "Space Oddity" by David Bowie together. It was their little thing. They knew all the words and would blast it on the iPod and sing the song out loud.

Since Miranda's always been really good about calling us as soon as she got home from summer camp, I was a little surprised when I didn't hear from her. I even texted her and she didn't reply. I figured maybe she had ended up staying in the camp longer, now that she was a counselor. Maybe she met a cute guy.

Then I realized from her Facebook wall that she'd actually been back home for a full two weeks, so I sent her an IM and we chatted online a bit, but she didn't give me a reason for not calling, which I thought was bizarre. Miranda had always been a little flaky, so I figured that's all it was. We made plans to meet downtown, but then I had to cancel because we were driving out to visit Tata and Poppa for the weekend.

So I ended up not seeing either Miranda or Ella until the first day of school. And, I have to admit, I was shocked. Miranda looked so different: her hair was cut in this super-cute bob that she'd dyed bright pink, of all things, and she was wearing a striped tube top that (a) seemed way inappropriate for school, and (b) was totally not her usual style. Miranda had always been such a prude about clothes, and here she was all pink-haired and tube-topped. But it wasn't just the way she looked that was different: she was acting differently, too. I can't say she wasn't nice, because she was, but she seemed kind of distant, like I was a casual friend. It was the weirdest thing in the world.

At lunch the three of us sat together like we always used to, but the dynamics had shifted. It was obvious to me that Ella and Miranda had gotten together a few times during the summer without me, though they never actually said that. I pretended not to be at all upset while we talked, though I could feel my face getting hot, my smile being fake. Although Ella wasn't as over-the-top as Miranda, I noticed a change in her usual style, too. It's like they had talked to each other beforehand about redoing their image at the new school, but hadn't bothered to clue me in. I admit: I had always thought I was above this kind of typical teenage pettiness, but I felt a lump in my throat throughout lunch. My voice quivered as I said "See you later" when the bell rang.

After School

"I hear we're driving you home today."

It was Miranda in eighth period. She had just sat down at the desk right behind me. I had forgotten that Mom had called Miranda's mother the night before to ask if she could drive me home from school.

"You don't have to," I answered instinctively, casually. "My mom can pick me up."

"I thought she had to pick Auggie up or something."

"It turns out she can pick me up afterward. She just texted me. Not a problem."

"Oh. Okay."

"Thanks."

It was all a lie on my part, but I couldn't see sitting in a car with the new Miranda. After school I ducked into a restroom to avoid bumping into Miranda's mother outside. Half an hour later I walked out of the school, ran the three blocks to the bus stop, hopped on the M86 to Central Park West, and took the subway home.

"Hey there, sweetie!" Mom said the moment I stepped through the front door. "How was your first day? I was starting to wonder where you guys were."

"We stopped for pizza." Incredible how easily a lie can slip through your lips.

"Is Miranda not with you?" She seemed surprised that Miranda wasn't right behind me.

"She went straight home. We have a lot of homework."

"On your first day?"

"Yes, on our first day!" I yelled, which completely surprised Mom. But before she could say anything, I said: "School was fine. It's really big, though. The kids seem nice." I wanted to give her enough information so she wouldn't feel the need to ask me more. "How was Auggie's first day of school?"

Mom hesitated, her eyebrows still high up on her forehead from when I'd snapped at her a second earlier. "Okay," she said slowly, like she was letting out a breath.

"What do you mean 'okay'?" I said. "Was it good or bad?"

"He said it was good."

"So why do you think it wasn't good?"

"I didn't say it wasn't good! Geez, Via, what's up with you?"

"Just forget I asked anything at all," I answered, and stormed dramatically into Auggie's room and slammed the door. He was on his PlayStation and didn't even look up. I hated how zombified his video games made him.

"So how was school?" I said, scooching Daisy over so I could sit on his bed next to him.

"Fine," he answered, still not looking up from his game.

"Auggie, I'm talking to you!" I pulled the PlayStation out of his hands.

"Hey!" he said angrily.

"How was school?"

"I said fine!" he yelled back, grabbing the PlayStation back from me.

"Were people nice to you?"

"Yes!"

"No one was mean?"

He put the PlayStation down and looked up at me as if I had just asked the dumbest question in the world. "Why would people be mean?" he said. It was the first time in his life that I heard him be sarcastic like that. I didn't think he had it in him.

The Padawan Bites the Dust

I'm not sure at what point that night Auggie had cut off his Padawan braid, or why that made me really mad. I had always found his obsession with everything *Star Wars* kind of geeky, and that braid in the back of his hair, with its little beads, was just awful. But he had always been so proud of it, of how long it took him to grow it, of how he had chosen the beads himself in a crafts store in Soho. He and Christopher, his best friend, used to play with lightsabers and *Star Wars* stuff whenever they got together, and they had both started growing their braids at the same time. When August cut his braid off that night, without an explanation, without telling me beforehand (which was surprising)—or even calling Christopher—I was just so upset I can't even explain why.

I've seen Auggie brushing his hair in the bathroom mirror. He meticulously tries to get every hair in place. He tilts his head to look at himself from different angles, like there's some magic perspective inside the mirror that could change the dimensions of his face.

Mom knocked on my door after dinner. She looked drained, and I realized that between me and Auggie, today had been a tough day for her, too.

"So you want to tell me what's up?" she asked nicely, softly.

"Not now, okay?" I answered. I was reading. I was tired. Maybe later I'd be up to telling her about Miranda, but not now.

"I'll check in before you go to bed," she said, and then she came over and kissed me on the top of my head.

"Can Daisy sleep with me tonight?"

"Sure, I'll bring her in later."

"Don't forget to come back," I said as she left.

"I promise."

But she didn't come back that night. Dad did. He told me Auggie had had a bad first day and Mom was helping him through it. He asked me how my day had gone and I told him fine. He said he didn't believe me for a second, and I told him Miranda and Ella were acting like jerks. (I didn't mention how I took the subway home by myself, though.) He said nothing tests friendships like high school, and then proceeded to poke fun at the fact that I was reading *War and Peace*. Not real fun, of course, since I'd heard him brag to people that he had a "fifteen-year-old who is reading Tolstoy." But he liked to rib me about where I was in the book, in a war part or in a peace part, and if there was anything in there about Napoleon's days as a hip-hop dancer. It was silly stuff, but Dad always managed to make everyone laugh. And sometimes that's all you need to feel better.

"Don't be mad at Mom," he said as he bent down to give me a good-night kiss. "You know how much she worries about Auggie."

"I know," I acknowledged.

"Want the light on or off? It's getting kind of late," he said, pausing by the light switch at the door.

"Can you bring Daisy in first?"

Two seconds later he came back with Daisy dangling in his arms, and he laid her down next to me on the bed.

"Good night, sweetheart," he said, kissing my forehead. He kissed Daisy on her forehead, too. "Good night, girlie. Sweet dreams."

An Apparition at the Door

Once, I got up in the middle of the night because I was thirsty, and I saw Mom standing outside Auggie's room. Her hand was on the doorknob, her forehead leaning on the door, which was ajar. She wasn't going in his room or stepping out: just standing right outside the door, as if she was listening to the sound of his breathing as he slept. The hallway lights were out. The only thing illuminating her was the blue night-light in August's bedroom. She looked ghostlike standing there. Or maybe I should say angelic. I tried to walk back into my room without disturbing her, but she heard me and walked over to me.

"Is Auggie okay?" I asked. I knew that sometimes he would wake up choking on his own saliva if he accidentally turned over on his back.

"Oh, he's fine," she said, wrapping her arms around me. She walked me back into my room, pulled the covers over me, and kissed me good night. She never explained what she was doing outside his door, and I never asked.

I wonder how many nights she's stood outside his door. And I wonder if she's ever stood outside my door like that.

Breakfast

"Can you pick me up from school today?" I said the next morning, smearing some cream cheese on my bagel.

Mom was making August's lunch (American cheese on whole-wheat bread, soft enough for Auggie to eat) while August sat eating oatmeal at the table. Dad was getting ready to go to work. Now that I was in high school, the new school routine was going to be that Dad and I would take the subway together in the morning, which meant his having to leave fifteen minutes earlier than usual, then I'd get off at my stop and he'd keep going. And Mom was going to pick me up after school in the car.

"I was going to call Miranda's mother to see if she could drive you home again," Mom answered.

"No, Mom!" I said quickly. "You pick me up. Or I'll just take the subway."

"You know I don't want you to take the subway by yourself yet," she answered.

"Mom, I'm fifteen! Everybody my age takes the subway by themselves!"

"She can take the subway home," said Dad from the other room, adjusting his tie as he stepped into the kitchen.

"Why can't Miranda's mother just pick her up again?" Mom argued with him.

"She's old enough to take the subway by herself," Dad insisted.

Mom looked at both of us. "Is something going on?" She didn't address her question to either one of us in particular.

"You would know if you had come back to check on me," I said spitefully, "like you *said* you would."

"Oh God, Via," said Mom, remembering now how she had completely ditched me last night. She put down the knife she was using to cut Auggie's grapes in half (still a choking hazard for him because of the size of his palate). "I am so sorry. I fell asleep in Auggie's room. By the time I woke up . . ."

"I know, I know." I nodded indifferently.

Mom came over, put her hands on my cheeks, and lifted my face to look at her.

"I'm really, really sorry," she whispered. I could tell she was.

"It's okay!" I said.

"Via . . ."

"Mom, it's fine." This time I meant it. She looked so genuinely sorry I just wanted to let her off the hook.

She kissed and hugged me, then returned to the grapes.

"So, is something going on with Miranda?" she asked.

"Just that she's acting like a complete jerk," I said.

"Miranda's not a jerk!" Auggie quickly chimed in.

"She can be!" I yelled. "Believe me."

"Okay then, I'll pick you up, no problem," Mom said decisively, sweeping the half-grapes into a snack bag with the side of her knife. "That was the plan all along anyway. I'll pick Auggie up from school in the car and then we'll pick you up. We'll probably get there about a quarter to four."

"No!" I said firmly, before she'd even finished.

"Isabel, she can take the subway!" said Dad impatiently. "She's a big girl now. She's reading *War and Peace*, for crying out loud."

"What does *War and Peace* have to with anything?" answered Mom, clearly annoyed.

"It means you don't have to pick her up in the car like she's a little girl," he said sternly. "Via, are you ready? Get your bag and let's go."

"I'm ready," I said, pulling on my backpack. "Bye, Mom! Bye, Auggie!"

I kissed them both quickly and headed toward the door.

"Do you even have a MetroCard?" Mom said after me.

"Of course she has a MetroCard!" answered Dad, fully exasperated. "Yeesh, Momma! Stop worrying so much! Bye," he said, kissing her on the cheek. "Bye, big boy," he said to August, kissing him on the top of his head. "I'm proud of you. Have a good day."

"Bye, Daddy! You too."

Dad and I jogged down the stoop stairs and headed down the block.

"Call me after school before you get on the subway!" Mom yelled at me from the window. I didn't even turn around but waved my hand at her so she'd know I heard her. Dad did turn around, walking backward for a few steps.

"*War and Peace*, Isabel!" he called out, smiling as he pointed at me. "*War and Peace!*"

Genetics 101

Both sides of Dad's family were Jews from Russia and Poland. Poppa's grandparents fled the pogroms and ended up in NYC at the turn of the century. Tata's parents fled the Nazis and ended up in Argentina in the forties. Poppa and Tata met at a dance on the Lower East Side while she was in town visiting a cousin. They got married, moved to Bayside, and had Dad and Uncle Ben.

Mom's side of the family is from Brazil. Except for her mother, my beautiful Grans, and her dad, Agosto, who died before I was born, the rest of Mom's family—all her glamorous aunts, uncles, and cousins—still live in Alto Leblon, a ritzy suburb south of Rio. Grans and Agosto moved to Boston in the early sixties, and had Mom and Aunt Kate, who's married to Uncle Porter.

Mom and Dad met at Brown University and have been together ever since. Isabel and Nate: like two peas in a pod. They moved to New York right after college, had me a few years later, then moved to a brick townhouse in North River Heights, the hippie-stroller capital of upper *upper* Manhattan, when I was about a year old.

Not one person in the exotic mix of my family gene pool has ever shown any obvious signs of having what August has. I've pored over grainy sepia pictures of long-dead relatives in babushkas; black-and-white snapshots of distant cousins in crisp white linen suits, soldiers in uniform, ladies with beehive hairdos; Polaroids of bell-bottomed teenagers and long-haired hippies, and not once have I been able to detect even the slightest trace of August's face in their faces. Not a one. But after August was born, my parents underwent genetic counseling. They were told that August had what seemed to be a "previously unknown type of mandibulofacial dysostosis caused by an autosomal recessive mutation in the *TCOF1* gene, which is located on chromosome 5, complicated by a hemifacial microsomia characteristic of OAV spectrum." Sometimes these mutations occur during pregnancy. Sometimes they're inherited from one parent carrying the dominant gene. Sometimes they're caused by the interaction of many genes, possibly in combination with environmental factors. This is called multifactorial inheritance. In August's case, the doctors were able to identify one of the "single nucleotide deletion mutations" that made war on his face. The weird thing is, though you'd never know it from looking at them: both my parents carry that mutant gene.

And I carry it, too.

The Punnett Square

If I have children, there's a one-in-two chance that I will pass on the defective gene to them. That doesn't mean they'll look like August, but they'll carry the gene that got double-dosed in August and helped make him the way he is. If I marry someone who has the same defective gene, there's a one-in-two chance that our kids will carry the gene and look totally normal, a one-in-four chance that our kids will not carry the gene at all, and a one-in-four chance that our kids will look like August.

If August has children with someone who doesn't have a trace of the gene, there's a 100 percent probability that their kids will inherit the gene, but a zero percent chance that their kids will have a double dose of it, like August. Which means they'll carry the gene no matter what, but they could look totally normal. If he marries someone who has the gene, their kids will have the same odds as my kids.

This only explains the part of August that's explainable. There's that other part of his genetic makeup that's not inherited but just incredibly bad luck.

Countless doctors have drawn little tic-tac-toe grids for my parents over the years to try to explain the genetic lottery to them. Geneticists use these Punnett squares to determine inheritance, recessive and dominant genes, probabilities and chance. But for all they know, there's more they don't know. They can try to forecast the odds, but they can't guarantee them. They use terms like "germline mosaicism," "chromosome rearrangement," or "delayed mutation" to explain why their science is not an exact science. I actually like how doctors talk. I like the sound of science. I like how words you don't understand explain things you can't understand. There are countless people under words like "germline mosaicism," "chromosome rearrangement," or "delayed mutation." Countless babies who'll never be born, like mine.

Out with the Old

Miranda and Ella blasted off. They attached themselves to a new crowd destined for high school glory. After a week of painful lunches where all they would do was talk about people that didn't interest me, I decided to make a clean break for it. They asked no questions. I told no lies. We just went our separate ways.

I didn't even mind after a while. I stopped going to lunch for about a week, though, to make the transition easier, to avoid the fake Oh, shoot, there's no room for you at the table, Olivia! It was easier just to go to the library and read.

I finished *War and Peace* in October. It was amazing. People think it's such a hard read, but it's really just a soap opera with lots of characters, people falling in love, fighting for love, dying for love. I want to be in love like that someday. I want my husband to love me the way Prince Andrei loved Natasha.

I ended up hanging out with a girl named Eleanor who I'd known from my days at PS 22, though we'd gone to different middle schools. Eleanor had always been a really smart girl—a little bit of a crybaby back then, but nice. I'd never realized how funny she was (not laugh-out-loud Daddy-funny, but full of great quips), and she never knew how lighthearted I could be. Eleanor, I guess, had always been under the impression that I was very serious. And, as it turns out, she'd never liked Miranda and Ella. She thought they were stuck-up.

I gained entry through Eleanor to the smart-kids' table at lunch. It was a larger group than I'd been accustomed to hanging out with, and a more diverse crowd. It included Eleanor's boyfriend, Kevin, who would definitely become class president someday; a few techie guys; girls like Eleanor who were members of the yearbook committee and the debate club; and a quiet guy named Justin who had small round glasses and played the violin, and who I had an instant crush on.

When I'd see Miranda and Ella, who were now hanging out with the super-popular set, we'd say "Hey, what's up," and move on. Occasionally Miranda would ask me how August was doing, and then say "Tell him I say hello." This I never did, not to spite Miranda, but because August was in his own world these days. There were times, at home, that we never crossed paths.

October 31

Grans had died the night before Halloween. Since then, even though it's been four years, this has always been a sad time of year for me. For Mom, too, though she doesn't always say it. Instead, she immerses herself in getting August's costume ready, since we all know Halloween is his favorite time of year.

This year was no different. August really wanted to be a *Star Wars* character called Boba Fett, so Mom looked for a Boba Fett costume in August's size, which, strangely enough, was out of stock everywhere. She went to every online store, found a few on eBay that were going for an outrageous amount, and finally ended up buying a Jango Fett costume that she then converted into a Boba Fett costume by painting it green. I would say, in all, she must have spent two weeks working on the stupid costume. And no, I won't mention the fact that Mom has never made any of my costumes, because it really has no bearing on anything at all.

The morning of Halloween I woke up thinking about Grans, which made me really sad and weepy. Dad kept telling me to hurry up and get dressed, which just stressed me out even more, and suddenly I started crying. I just wanted to stay home.

So Dad took August to school that morning and Mom said I could stay home, and the two of us cried together for a while. One thing I knew for sure: however much I missed Grans, Mom must have missed her more. All those times August was clinging to life after a surgery, all those rush trips to the ER: Grans had always been there for Mom. It felt good to cry with Mom. For both of us. At some point, Mom had the idea of our watching *The Ghost and Mrs. Muir* together, which was one of our all-time favorite black-and-white movies. I agreed that that was a great idea. I think I probably would have used this weeping session as an opportunity to tell Mom everything that was going on at school with Miranda and Ella, but just as we were sitting down in front of the DVD player, the phone rang. It was the nurse from August's school calling to tell Mom that August had a stomach ache and should be picked up. So much for the old movies and the mother-daughter bonding.

Mom picked August up, and the moment he came home, he went straight to the bathroom and threw up. Then he went to his bed and pulled the covers over his head. Mom took his temperature, brought him some hot tea, and assumed the "August's mom" role again. "Via's mom," who had come out for a little while, was put away. I understood, though: August was in bad shape.

Neither one of us asked him why he had worn his Bleeding Scream costume to school instead of the Boba Fett costume Mom had made for him. If it annoyed Mom to see the costume she had worked on for two weeks tossed on the floor, unused, she didn't show it.

Trick or Treat

August said he wasn't feeling well enough to go trick-or-treating later in the afternoon, which was sad for him because I know how much he loved to trick-or-treat—especially after it got dark outside. Even though I was well beyond the trick-or-treating stage myself, I usually threw on some mask or other to accompany him up and down the blocks, watching him knocking on people's doors, giddy with excitement. I knew it was the one night a year when he could truly be like every other kid. No one knew he was different under the mask. To August, that must have felt absolutely amazing.

At seven o'clock that night, I knocked on his door.

"Hey," I said.

"Hey," he said back. He wasn't using his PlayStation or reading a comic book. He was just lying in his bed looking at the ceiling. Daisy, as always, was next to him on the bed, her head draped over his legs. The Bleeding Scream costume was crumpled up on the floor next to the Boba Fett costume.

"How's your stomach?" I said, sitting next to him on the bed.

"I'm still nauseous."

"You sure you're not up for the Halloween Parade?"

"Positive."

This surprised me. Usually August was such a trouper about his medical issues, whether it was skateboarding a few days after a surgery or sipping food through a straw when his mouth was practically bolted shut. This was a kid who's gotten more shots, taken more medicines, put up with more procedures by the age of

113

ten than most people would have to put up with in ten lifetimes, and he was sidelined from a little nausea?

"You want to tell me what's up?" I said, sounding a bit like Mom.

"No."

"Is it school?"

"Yes."

"Teachers? Schoolwork? Friends?"

He didn't answer.

"Did someone say something?" I asked.

"People always say something," he answered bitterly. I could tell he was close to crying.

"Tell me what happened," I said.

And he told me what happened. He had overheard some *very* mean things some boys were saying about him. He didn't care about what the other boys had said, he expected that, but he was hurt that one of the boys was his "best friend" Jack Will. I remembered his mentioning Jack a couple of times over the past few months. I remembered Mom and Dad saying he seemed like a really nice kid, saying they were glad August had already made a friend like that.

"Sometimes kids are stupid," I said softly, holding his hand. "I'm sure he didn't mean it."

"Then why would he say it? He's been pretending to be my friend all along. Tushman probably bribed him with good grades or something. I bet you he was like, hey, Jack, if you make friends with the freak, you don't have to take any tests this year."

"You know that's not true. And don't call yourself a freak."

"Whatever. I wish I'd never gone to school in the first place."

"But I thought you were liking it."

"I hate it!" He was angry all of a sudden, punching his pillow.

"I hate it! I hate it! I hate it!" He was shrieking at the top of his lungs.

I didn't say anything. I didn't know what to say. He was hurt. He was mad.

I let him have a few more minutes of his fury. Daisy started licking the tears off of his face.

"Come on, Auggie," I said, patting his back gently. "Why don't you put on your Jango Fett costume and—"

"It's a Boba Fett costume! Why does everyone mix that up?"

"Boba Fett costume," I said, trying to stay calm. I put my arm around his shoulders. "Let's just go to the parade, okay?"

"If I go to the parade, Mom will think I'm feeling better and make me go to school tomorrow."

"Mom would never make you go to school," I answered. "Come on, Auggie. Let's just go. It'll be fun, I promise. And I'll let you have all my candy."

He didn't argue. He got out of bed and slowly started pulling on his Boba Fett costume. I helped him adjust the straps and tighten the belt, and by the time he put his helmet on, I could tell he was feeling better.

Time to Think

August played up the stomach ache the next day so he wouldn't have to go to school. I admit I felt a little bad for Mom, who was genuinely concerned that he had a stomach bug, but I had promised August I wouldn't tell her about the incident at school.

By Sunday, he was still determined not to go back to school.

"What are you planning on telling Mom and Dad?" I asked him when he told me this.

"They said I could quit whenever I wanted to." He said this while he was still focused on a comic book he was reading.

"But you've never been the kind of kid who quits things," I said truthfully. "That's not like you."

"I'm quitting."

"You're going to have to tell Mom and Dad why," I pointed out, pulling the comic book out of his hands so he'd have to look up at me while we were talking. "Then Mom will call the school and everyone will know about it."

"Will Jack get in trouble?"

"I would think so."

"Good."

I have to admit, August was surprising me more and more. He pulled another comic book off his shelf and started leafing through it.

"Auggie," I said. "Are you really going to let a couple of stupid kids keep you from going back to school? I know you've been enjoying it. Don't give them that power over you. Don't give them the satisfaction."

"They have no idea I even heard them," he explained.

"No, I know, but . . ."

"Via, it's okay. I know what I'm doing. I've made up my mind."

"But this is crazy, Auggie!" I said emphatically, pulling the new comic book away from him, too. "You have to go back to school. Everyone hates school sometimes. I hate school sometimes. I hate my friends sometimes. That's just life, Auggie. You want to be treated normally, right? This is normal! We all have to go to school sometimes despite the fact that we have bad days, okay?"

"Do people go out of their way to avoid touching you, Via?" he answered, which left me momentarily without an answer. "Yeah, right. That's what I thought. So don't compare your bad days at school to mine, okay?"

"Okay, that's fair," I said. "But it's not a contest about whose days suck the most, Auggie. The point is we all have to put up with the bad days. Now, unless you want to be treated like a baby the rest of your life, or like a kid with special needs, you just have to suck it up and go."

He didn't say anything, but I think that last bit was getting to him.

"You don't have to say a word to those kids," I continued. "August, actually, it's so cool that you know what they said, but they don't know you know what they said, you know?"

"What the heck?"

"You know what I mean. You don't have to talk to them ever again, if you don't want. And they'll never know why. See? Or you can pretend to be friends with them, but deep down inside you know you're not."

"Is that how you are with Miranda?" he asked.

"No," I answered quickly, defensively. "I never faked my feelings with Miranda."

"So why are you saying I should?"

"I'm not! I'm just saying you shouldn't let those little jerks get to you, that's all."

"Like Miranda got to you."

"Why do you keep bringing Miranda up?" I yelled impatiently. "I'm trying to talk to you about your friends. Please keep mine out of it."

"You're not even friends with her anymore."

"What does that have to do with what we're talking about?"

The way August was looking at me reminded me of a doll's face. He was just staring at me blankly with his half-closed doll eyes.

"She called the other day," he said finally.

"What?" I was stunned. "And you didn't tell me?"

"She wasn't calling you," he answered, pulling both comic books out of my hands. "She was calling me. Just to say hi. To see how I was doing. She didn't even know I was going to a real school now. I can't believe you hadn't even told her. She said the two of you don't hang out as much anymore, but she wanted me to know she'd always love me like a big sister."

Double-stunned. Stung. Flabbergasted. No words formed in my mouth.

"Why didn't you tell me?" I said, finally.

"I don't know." He shrugged, opening the first comic book again.

"Well, I'm telling Mom and Dad about Jack Will if you stop going to school," I answered. "Tushman will probably call you into school and make Jack and those other kids apologize to you in front of everyone, and everyone will treat you like a kid who should be going to a school for kids with special needs. Is that what you want? Because that's what's going to happen. Otherwise, just go back to school and act like nothing happened. Or if you want to confront Jack about it, fine. But either way, if you—"

"Fine. Fine. Fine," he interrupted.

"What?"

"Fine! I'll go!" he yelled, not loudly. "Just stop talking about it already. Can I please read my book now?"

118

"Fine!" I answered. Turning to leave his room, I thought of something. "Did Miranda say anything else about me?"

He looked up from the comic book and looked right into my eyes.

"She said to tell you she misses you. Quote unquote."

I nodded.

"Thanks," I said casually, too embarrassed to let him see how happy that made me feel.

Part Three

SUMMER

You are beautiful no matter what they say

Words can't bring you down

You are beautiful in every single way

Yes, words can't bring you down

—Christina Aguilera, "Beautiful"

Weird Kids

Some kids have actually come out and asked me why I hang out with "the freak" so much. These are kids that don't even know him well. If they knew him, they wouldn't call him that.

"Because he's a nice kid!" I always answer. "And don't call him that."

"You're a saint, Summer," Ximena Chin said to me the other day. "I couldn't do what you're doing."

"It's not a big deal," I answered her truthfully.

"Did Mr. Tushman ask you to be friends with him?" Charlotte Cody asked.

"No. I'm friends with him because I want to be friends with him," I answered.

Who knew that my sitting with August Pullman at lunch would be such a big deal? People acted like it was the strangest thing in the world. It's weird how weird kids can be.

I sat with him that first day because I felt sorry for him. That's all. Here he was, this strange-looking kid in a brand-new school. No one was talking to him. Everyone was staring at him. All the girls at my table were whispering about him. He wasn't the only new kid at Beecher Prep, but he was the only one everyone was talking about. Julian had nicknamed him the Zombie Kid, and that's what everyone was calling him. "Did you see the Zombie Kid yet?" Stuff like that gets around fast. And August knew it. It's hard enough being the new kid even when you have a normal face. Imagine having his face?

So I just went over and sat with him. Not a biggie. I wish people would stop trying to turn it into something major.

He's just a kid. The weirdest-looking kid I've ever seen, yes. But just a kid.

The Plague

I do admit August's face takes some getting used to. I've been sitting with him for two weeks now, and let's just say he's not the neatest eater in the world. But other than that, he's pretty nice. I should also say that I don't really feel sorry for him anymore. That might have been what made me sit down with him the first time, but it's not why I keep sitting down with him. I keep sitting down with him because he is fun.

One of the things I'm not loving about this year is how a lot of the kids are acting like they're too grown-up to play things anymore. All they want to do is "hang out" and "talk" at recess. And all they talk about now is who likes who and who is cute and isn't cute. August doesn't bother about that stuff. He likes to play Four Square at recess, which I love to play, too.

It was actually because I was playing Four Square with August that I found out about the Plague. Apparently this is a "game" that's been going on since the beginning of the year. Anyone who accidentally touches August has only thirty seconds to wash their hands or find hand sanitizer before they catch the Plague. I'm not sure what happens to you if you actually catch the Plague because nobody's touched August yet—not directly.

How I found out about this is that Maya Markowitz told me that the reason she won't play Four Square with us at recess is that she doesn't want to catch the Plague. I was like, "What's the Plague?" And she told me. I told Maya I thought that was really dumb and she agreed, but she still wouldn't touch a ball that August just touched, not if she could help it.

The Halloween Party

I was really excited because I got an invitation to Savanna's Halloween party.

Savanna is probably the most popular girl in the school. All the boys like her. All the girls want to be friends with her. She was the first girl in the grade to actually have a "boyfriend." It was some kid who goes to MS 281, though she dumped him and started dating Henry Joplin, which makes sense because the two of them totally look like teenagers already.

Anyway, even though I'm not in the "popular" group, I somehow got invited, which is very cool. When I told Savanna I got her invitation and would be going to her party, she was really nice to me, though she made sure to tell me that she didn't invite a lot of people, so I shouldn't go around bragging to anyone that I got invited. Maya didn't get invited, for instance. Savanna also made sure to tell me not to wear a costume. It's good she told me because, of course, I would have worn a costume to a Halloween party—not the unicorn costume I made for the Halloween Parade, but the Goth girl getup that I'd worn to school. But even that was a no-no for Savanna's party. The only negative about my going to Savanna's party was that now I wouldn't be able to go the parade and the unicorn costume would be wasted. That was kind of a bummer, but okay.

Anyway, the first thing that happened when I got to her party was that Savanna greeted me at the door and asked: "Where's your boyfriend, Summer?"

I didn't even know what she was talking about.

"I guess he doesn't have to wear a mask at Halloween, right?" she added. And then I knew she was talking about August.

"He's not my boyfriend," I said.

"I know. I'm just kidding!" She kissed my cheek (all the girls in her group kissed each other's cheeks now whenever they said hello), and threw my jacket on a coatrack in her hallway. Then she took me by the hand down the stairs to her basement, which is where the party was. I didn't see her parents anywhere.

There were about fifteen kids there: all of them were popular kids from either Savanna's group or Julian's group. I guess they've all kind of merged into one big supergroup of popular kids, now that some of them have started dating each other.

I didn't even know there were so many couples. I mean, I knew about Savanna and Henry, but Ximena and Miles? And Ellie and Amos? Ellie's practically as flat as I am.

Anyway, about five minutes after I got there, Henry and Savanna were standing next to me, literally hovering over me.

"So, we want to know why you hang out with the Zombie Kid so much," said Henry.

"He's not a zombie," I laughed, like they were making a joke. I was smiling but I didn't feel like smiling.

"You know, Summer," said Savanna, "you would be a lot more popular if you didn't hang out with him so much. I'm going to be completely honest with you: Julian likes you. He wants to ask you out."

"He does?"

"Do you think he's cute?"

"Um . . . yeah, I guess. Yeah, he's cute."

"So you have to choose who you want to hang out with," Savanna said. She was talking to me like a big sister would talk to a little sister. "Everyone likes you, Summer. Everyone thinks you're really nice and that you're really, really pretty. You could totally be part of our group if you wanted to, and believe me, there are a lot of girls in our grade who would love that."

"I know." I nodded. "Thank you."

"You're welcome," she answered. "You want me to tell Julian to come and talk to you?"

I looked over to where she was pointing and could see Julian looking over at us.

"Um, I actually need to go to the bathroom. Where is that?"

I went to where she pointed, sat down on the side of the bathtub, and called Mom and asked her to pick me up.

"Is everything okay?" said Mom.

"Yeah, I just don't want to stay," I said.

Mom didn't ask any more questions and said she'd be there in ten minutes.

"Don't ring the bell," I told her. "Just call me when you're outside."

I hung out in the bathroom until Mom called, and then I snuck upstairs without anyone seeing me, got my jacket, and went outside.

It was only nine-thirty. The Halloween Parade was in full swing down Amesfort Avenue. Huge crowds everywhere. Everyone was in costume. Skeletons. Pirates. Princesses. Vampires. Superheroes.

But not one unicorn.

November

The next day at school I told Savanna I had eaten some really bad Halloween candy and gotten sick, which is why I went home early from her party, and she believed me. There was actually a stomach bug going around, so it was a good lie.

I also told her that I had a crush on someone else that wasn't Julian so she would leave me alone about that and hopefully spread the word to Julian that I wasn't interested. She, of course, wanted to know who I had a crush on, and I told her it was a secret.

August was absent the day after Halloween, and when he came back, I could tell something was up with him. He was acting so weird at lunch!

He barely said a word, and kept looking down at his food when I talked to him. Like he wouldn't look me in the eye.

Finally, I was like, "Auggie, is everything okay? Are you mad at me or something?"

"No," he said.

"Sorry you weren't feeling well on Halloween. I kept looking for Boba Fett in the hallways."

"Yeah, I was sick."

"Did you have that stomach bug?"

"Yeah, I guess."

He opened a book and started to read, which was kind of rude.

"I'm so excited about the Egyptian Museum project," I said. "Aren't you?"

He shook his head, his mouth full of food. I actually looked away because between the way he was chewing, which almost seemed like he was being gross on purpose, and the way his eyes were just kind of closed down, I was getting a really bad vibe from him.

"What project did you get?" I asked.

He shrugged, pulled out a little scrap of paper from his jeans pocket, and flicked it across the table to me.

Everyone in the grade got assigned an Egyptian artifact to work on for Egyptian Museum Day, which was in December. The teachers wrote all the assignments down on tiny scraps of paper, which they put into a fishbowl, and then all us kids in the grade took turns picking the papers out of the fishbowl in assembly.

So I unfolded Auggie's little slip of paper.

"Oh, cool!" I said, maybe a little overexcited because I was trying to get him psyched up. "You got the Step Pyramid of Sakkara!"

"I know!" he said.

"I got Anubis, the god of the afterlife."

"The one with the dog head?"

"It's actually a jackal head," I corrected him. "Hey, you want to start working on our projects together after school? You could come over to my house."

He put his sandwich down and leaned back in his chair. I can't even describe the look he was giving me.

"You know, Summer," he said. "You don't have to do this."

"What are you talking about?"

"You don't have to be friends with me. I know Mr. Tushman talked to you."

"I have no idea what you're talking about."

"You don't have to pretend, is all I'm saying. I know Mr.

Tushman talked to some kids before school started and told them they had to be friends with me."

"He did not talk to me, August."

"Yeah, he did."

"No, he did not."

"Yeah, he did."

"No he didn't!! I swear on my life!" I put my hands up in the air so he could see I wasn't crossing my fingers. He immediately looked down at my feet, so I shook off my UGGs so he could see my toes weren't crossed.

"You're wearing tights," he said accusingly.

"You can see my toes are flat!" I yelled.

"Okay, you don't have to scream."

"I don't like being accused of things, okay?"

"Okay. I'm sorry."

"You should be."

"He really didn't talk to you?"

"Auggie!"

"Okay, okay, I'm really sorry."

I would have stayed mad at him longer, but then he told me about something bad that had happened to him on Halloween and I couldn't stay mad at him anymore. Basically, he heard Jack bad-mouthing him and saying really horrible things behind his back. It kind of explained his attitude, and now I knew why he'd been out "sick."

"Promise you won't tell anyone," he said.

"I won't." I nodded. "Promise you won't ever be mean like that to me again?"

"Promise," he said, and we pinky swore.

Warning: This Kid Is Rated R

I had warned Mom about August's face. I had described what he looked like. I did this because I know she's not always so good at faking her feelings, and August was coming over for the first time today. I even sent her a text at work to remind her about it. But I could tell from the expression on her face when she came home after work that I hadn't prepared her enough. She was shocked when she came through the door and saw his face for the first time.

"Hi, Mom, this is Auggie. Can he stay for dinner?" I asked quickly.

It took a second for my question to even register.

"Hi, Auggie," she said. "Um, of course, sweetheart. If it's okay with Auggie's mother."

While Auggie called his mother on his cell phone, I whispered to Mom: "Stop making that weirded-out face!" She had that look like when she's watching the news and some horrific event has happened. She nodded quickly, like she hadn't realized she was making a face, and was really nice and normal to Auggie afterward.

After a while, Auggie and I got tired of working on our projects and went to hang out in the living room. Auggie was looking at the pictures on the mantel, and he saw a picture of me and Daddy.

"Is that your dad?" he said.

"Yeah."

"I didn't know you were . . . what's the word?"

"Biracial."

"Right! That's the word."

"Yeah."

He looked at the picture again.

"Are your parents divorced? I've never seen him at drop-off or anything."

"Oh, no," I said. "He was a platoon sergeant. He died a few years ago."

"Whoa! I didn't know that."

"Yeah." I nodded, handing him a picture of my dad in his uniform.

"Wow, look at all those medals."

"Yeah. He was pretty awesome."

"Wow, Summer. I'm sorry."

"Yeah, it sucks. I really miss him a lot."

"Yeah, wow." He nodded, handing me back the picture.

"Have you ever known anyone who died?" I asked.

"Just my grandmother, and I don't really even remember her."

"That's too bad."

Auggie nodded.

"You ever wonder what happens to people when they die?" I asked.

He shrugged. "Not really. I mean, I guess they go to heaven? That's where my Grans went."

"I think about it a lot," I said. "I think when people die, their souls go to heaven but just for a little while. Like that's where they see their old friends and stuff, and kind of catch up on old times. But then I actually think the souls start thinking about their lives on earth, like if they were good or bad or whatever. And then they get born again as brand-new babies in the world."

"Why would they want to do that?"

"Because then they get another chance to get it right," I answered. "Their souls get a chance to have a do-over."

He thought about what I was saying and then nodded. "Kind of like when you get a makeup test," he said.

"Right."

"But they don't come back looking the same," he said. "I mean, they look completely different when they come back, right?"

"Oh yeah," I answered. "Your soul stays the same but everything else is different."

"I like that," he said, nodding a lot. "I really like that, Summer. That means in my next life I won't be stuck with this face."

He pointed to his face when he said that and batted his eyes, which made me laugh.

"I guess not." I shrugged.

"Hey, I might even be handsome!" he said, smiling. "That would be so awesome, wouldn't it? I could come back and be this good-looking dude and be super buff and super tall."

I laughed again. He was such a good sport about himself. That's one of the things I like the most about Auggie.

"Hey, Auggie, can I ask you a question?"

"Yeah," he said, like he knew exactly what I wanted to ask.

I hesitated. I've been wanting to ask him this for a while but I've always lost the guts to ask.

"What?" he said. "You want to know what's wrong with my face?"

"Yeah, I guess. If it's okay for me to ask."

He shrugged. I was so relieved that he didn't seem mad or sad.

"Yeah, it's no big deal," he said casually. "The main thing I have is this thing called man-di-bu-lo-facial dys-os-tosis—which took me forever to learn how to pronounce, by the way. But I also have this other syndrome thing that I can't even pronounce. And these things kind of just morphed together into one big superthing, which is so rare they don't even have a name for it. I mean, I don't want to brag or anything, but I'm actually considered something of a medical wonder, you know."

He smiled.

"That was a joke," he said. "You can laugh."

I smiled and shook my head.

"You're funny, Auggie." I said.

"Yes, I am," he said proudly. "I am cool beans."

The Egyptian Tomb

Over the next month, August and I hung out a lot after school, either at his house or my house. August's parents even invited Mom and me over for dinner a couple of times. I overheard them talking about fixing Mom up on a blind date with August's uncle Ben.

On the day of the Egyptian Museum exhibit, we were all really excited and kind of giddy. It had snowed the day before— not as much as it had snowed over the Thanksgiving break, but still, snow is snow.

The gym was turned into a giant museum, with everyone's Egyptian artifact displayed on a table with a little caption card explaining what the thing was. Most of the artifacts were really great, but I have to say I really think mine and August's were the best. My sculpture of Anubis looked pretty real, and I had even used real gold paint on it. And August had made his step pyramid out of sugar cubes. It was two feet high and two feet long, and he had spray painted the cubes with this kind of fake-sand paint or something. It looked so awesome.

We all dressed up in Egyptian costumes. Some of the kids were Indiana Jones–type archaeologists. Some of them dressed up like pharaohs. August and I dressed up like mummies. Our faces were covered except for two little holes for the eyes and one little hole for the mouth.

When the parents showed up, they all lined up in the hallway in front of the gym. Then we were told we could go get our parents, and each kid got to take his or her parent on a flashlight tour through the dark gym. August and I took our moms around together. We stopped at each exhibit, explaining what it was, talking in whispers, answering questions. Since it was dark, we used our flashlights to illuminate the artifacts while we were talking. Sometimes, for dramatic effect, we would hold the flashlights under our chins while we were explaining something in detail. It was so much fun, hearing all these whispers in the dark, seeing all the lights zigzagging around the dark room.

At one point, I went over to get a drink at the water fountain. I had to take the mummy wrap off my face.

"Hey, Summer," said Jack, who came over to talk to me. He was dressed like the man from *The Mummy*. "Cool costume."

"Thanks."

"Is the other mummy August?"

"Yeah."

"Um . . . hey, do you know why August is mad at me?"

"Uh-huh." I nodded.

"Can you tell me?"

"No."

He nodded. He seemed bummed.

"I told him I wouldn't tell you," I explained.

"It's so weird," he said. "I have no idea why he's mad at me all of a sudden. None. Can't you at least give me a hint?"

I looked over at where August was across the room, talking to our moms. I wasn't about to break my solid oath that I wouldn't tell anyone about what he overheard at Halloween, but I felt bad for Jack.

"Bleeding Scream," I whispered in his ear, and then walked away.

Part Four

JACK

Now here is my secret. It is very simple.

It is only with one's heart that one can see clearly.

What is essential is invisible to the eye.

—Antoine de Saint-Exupéry, *The Little Prince*

The Call

So in August my parents got this call from Mr. Tushman, the middle-school director. And my Mom said: "Maybe he calls all the new students to welcome them," and my dad said: "That's a lot of kids he'd be calling." So my mom called him back, and I could hear her talking to Mr. Tushman on the phone. This is exactly what she said:

"Oh, hi, Mr. Tushman. This is Amanda Will, returning your call? *Pause.* Oh, thank you! That's so nice of you to say. He is looking forward to it. *Pause.* Yes. *Pause.* Yeah. *Pause.* Oh. Sure. *Long pause.* Ohhh. Uh-huh. *Pause.* Well, that's so nice of you to say. *Pause.* Sure. Ohh. Wow. Ohhhh. *Super long pause.* I see, of course. I'm sure he will. Let me write it down . . . got it. I'll call you after I've had a chance to talk to him, okay? *Pause.* No, thank you for thinking of him. Bye bye!"

And when she hung up, I was like, "what's up, what did he say?"

And Mom said: "Well, it's actually very flattering but kind of sad, too. See, there's this boy who's starting middle school this year, and he's never been in a real school environment before because he was homeschooled, so Mr. Tushman talked to some of the lower-school teachers to find out who they thought were some of the really, really great kids coming into fifth grade, and the teachers must have told him you were an especially nice kid—which I already knew, of course—and so Mr. Tushman is wondering if he could count on you to sort of shepherd this new boy around a bit?"

"Like let him hang out with me?" I said.

"Exactly," said Mom. "He called it being a 'welcome buddy.'"

"But why me?"

"I told you. Your teachers told Mr. Tushman that you were the kind of kid who's known for being a good egg. I mean, I'm so proud that they think so highly of you. . . ."

"Why is it sad?"

"What do you mean?"

"You said it's flattering but kind of sad, too."

"Oh." Mom nodded. "Well, apparently this boy has some sort of . . . um, I guess there's something wrong with his face . . . or something like that. Not sure. Maybe he was in an accident. Mr. Tushman said he'd explain a bit more when you come to the school next week."

"School doesn't start till September!"

"He wants you to meet this kid before school starts."

"Do I have to?"

Mom looked a bit surprised.

"Well, no, of course not," she said, "but it would be the nice thing to do, Jack."

"If I don't have to do it," I said, "I don't want to do it."

"Can you at least think about it?"

"I'm thinking about it and I don't want to do it."

"Well, I'm not going to force you," she said, "but at least think about it some more, okay? I'm not calling Mr. Tushman back until tomorrow, so just sit with it a bit. I mean, Jack, I really don't think it's that much to ask that you spend a little extra time with some new kid. . . ."

"It's not just that he's a new kid, Mom," I answered. "He's deformed."

"That's a terrible thing to say, Jack."

"He is, Mom."

"You don't even know who it is!"

"Yeah, I do," I said, because I knew the second she started talking about him that it was that kid named August.

Carvel

I remember seeing him for the first time in front of the Carvel on Amesfort Avenue when I was about five or six. Me and Veronica, my babysitter, were sitting on the bench outside the store with Jamie, my baby brother, who was sitting in his stroller facing us. I guess I was busy eating my ice cream cone, because I didn't even notice the people who sat down next to us.

Then at one point I turned my head to suck the ice cream out of the bottom of my cone, and that's when I saw him: August. He was sitting right next to me. I know it wasn't cool, but I kind of went "Uhh!" when I saw him because I honestly got scared. I thought he was wearing a zombie mask or something. It was the kind of "uhh" you say when you're watching a scary movie and the bad guy like jumps out of the bushes. Anyway, I know it wasn't nice of me to do that, and though the kid didn't hear me, I know his sister did.

"Jack! We have to go!" said Veronica. She had gotten up and was turning the stroller around because Jamie, who had obviously just noticed the kid, too, was about to say something embarrassing. So I jumped up kind of suddenly, like a bee had landed on me, and followed Veronica as she zoomed away. I could hear the kid's mom saying softly behind us: "Okay, guys, I think it's time to go," and I turned around to look at them one more time. The kid was licking his ice cream cone, the mom was picking up his scooter, and the sister was glaring at me like she was going to kill me. I looked away quickly.

"Veronica, what was wrong with that kid?" I whispered.

"Hush, boy!" she said, her voice angry. I love Veronica, but when she got mad, she got *mad*. Meanwhile, Jamie was practically spilling out of his stroller trying to get another look as Veronica pushed him away.

"But, Vonica . . . ," said Jamie.

"You boys were very naughty! Very naughty!" said Veronica as soon as we were farther down the block. "Staring like that!"

"I didn't mean to!" I said.

"Vonica," said Jamie.

"Us leaving like that," Veronica was muttering. "Oh Lord, that poor lady. I tell you, boys. Every day we should thank the Lord for our blessings, you hear me?"

"Vonica!"

"What is it, Jamie?"

"Is it Halloween?"

"No, Jamie."

"Then why was that boy wearing a mask?"

Veronica didn't answer. Sometimes, when she was mad about something, she would do that.

"He wasn't wearing a mask," I explained to Jamie.

"Hush, Jack!" said Veronica.

"Why are you so mad, Veronica?" I couldn't help asking.

I thought this would make her angrier, but actually she shook her head.

"It was bad how we did that," she said. "Just getting up like that, like we'd just seen the devil. I was scared for what Jamie was going to say, you know? I didn't want him to say anything that would hurt that little boy's feelings. But it was very bad, us leaving like that. The momma knew what was going on."

"But we didn't mean it," I answered.

"Jack, sometimes you don't have to mean to hurt someone to hurt someone. You understand?"

That was the first time I ever saw August in the neighborhood, at least that I remember. But I've seen him around ever since then: a couple of times in the playground, a few times in the park. He used to wear an astronaut helmet sometimes. But I always knew it was him underneath the helmet. All the kids in the neighborhood knew it was him. Everyone has seen August at some point or another. We all know his name, though he doesn't know ours.

And whenever I've seen him, I try to remember what Veronica said. But it's hard. It's hard not to sneak a second look. It's hard to act normal when you see him.

Why I Changed My Mind

"Who else did Mr. Tushman call?" I asked Mom later that night. "Did he tell you?"

"He mentioned Julian and Charlotte."

"Julian!" I said. "Ugh. Why Julian?"

"You used to be friends with Julian!"

"Mom, that was like in kindergarten. Julian's the biggest phony there is. And he's trying so hard to be popular all the time."

"Well," said Mom, "at least Julian agreed to help this kid out. Got to give him credit for that."

I didn't say anything because she was right.

"What about Charlotte?" I asked. "Is she doing it, too?"

"Yes," Mom said.

"Of course she is. Charlotte's such a Goody Two-Shoes," I answered.

"Boy, Jack," said Mom, "you seem to have a problem with everybody these days."

"It's just . . . ," I started. "Mom, you have no idea what this kid looks like."

"I can imagine."

"No! You can't! You've never seen him. I have."

"It might not even be who you're thinking it is."

"Trust me, it is. And I'm telling you, it's really, *really* bad. He's deformed, Mom. His eyes are like down here." I pointed to my cheeks. "And he has no ears. And his mouth is like . . ."

Jamie had walked into the kitchen to get a juice box from the fridge.

"Ask Jamie," I said. "Right, Jamie? Remember that kid we saw in the park after school last year? The kid named August? The one with the face?"

"Oh, that kid?" said Jamie, his eyes opening wide. "He gave me a nightmare!! Remember, Mommy? That nightmare about the zombies from last year?"

"I thought that was from watching a scary movie!" answered Mom.

"No!" said Jamie, "it was from seeing that kid! When I saw him, I was like, 'Ahhh!' and I ran away. . . ."

"Wait a minute," said Mom, getting serious. "Did you do that in front of him?"

"I couldn't help it!" said Jamie, kind of whining.

"Of course you could help it!" Mom scolded. "Guys, I have to tell you, I'm really disappointed by what I'm hearing here." And she looked like how she sounded. "I mean, honestly, he's just a little boy—just like you! Can you imagine how he felt to see you running away from him, Jamie, screaming?"

"It wasn't a scream," argued Jamie. "It was like an 'Ahhh!'" He put his hands on his cheeks and started running around the kitchen.

"Come on, Jamie!" said Mom angrily. "I honestly thought both my boys were more sympathetic than that."

"What's sympathetic?" said Jamie, who was only going into the second grade.

"You know exactly what I mean by sympathetic, Jamie," said Mom.

"It's just he's so ugly, Mommy," said Jamie.

"Hey!" Mom yelled, "I don't like that word! Jamie, just get your juice box. I want to talk to Jack alone for a second."

"Look, Jack," said Mom as soon as he left, and I knew she was about to give me a whole speech.

"Okay, I'll do it," I said, which completely shocked her.

"You will?"

"Yes!"

"So I can call Mr. Tushman?"

"Yes! Mom, yes, I said yes!"

Mom smiled. "I knew you'd rise to the occasion, kiddo. Good for you. I'm proud of you, Jackie." She messed up my hair.

So here's why I changed my mind. It wasn't so I wouldn't have to hear Mom give me a whole lecture. And it wasn't to protect this August kid from Julian, who I knew would be a jerk about the whole thing. It was because when I heard Jamie talking about how he had run away from August going 'Ahhh,' I suddenly felt really bad. The thing is, there are always going to be kids like Julian who are jerks. But if a little kid like Jamie, who's usually a nice enough kid, can be that mean, then a kid like August doesn't stand a chance in middle school.

Four Things

First of all, you do get used to his face. The first couple of times I was like, whoa, I'm never going to get used to this. And then, after about a week, I was like, huh, it's not so bad.

Second of all, he's actually a really cool dude. I mean, he's pretty funny. Like, the teacher will say something and August will whisper something funny to me that no one else hears and totally make me crack up. He's also just, overall, a nice kid. Like, he's easy to hang out with and talk to and stuff.

Third of all, he's really smart. I thought he'd be behind everyone because he hadn't gone to school before. But in most things he's way ahead of me. I mean, maybe not as smart as Charlotte or Ximena, but he's up there. And unlike Charlotte or Ximena, he lets me cheat off of him if I really need to (though I've only needed to a couple of times). He also let me copy his homework once, though we both got in trouble for it after class.

"The two of you got the exact same answers wrong on yesterday's homework," Ms. Rubin said, looking at both of us like she was waiting for an explanation. I didn't know what to say, because the explanation would have been: Oh, that's because I copied August's homework.

But August lied to protect me. He was like, "Oh, that's because we did our homework together last night," which wasn't true at all.

"Well, doing homework together is a good thing," Ms. Rubin answered, "but you're supposed to still do it separately, okay? You could work side by side if you want, but you can't actually do your homework together, okay? Got it?"

After we left the classroom, I said: "Dude, thanks for doing that." And he was like, "No problem."

That was cool.

Fourthly, now that I know him, I would say I actually do want to be friends with August. At first, I admit it, I was only friendly to him because Mr. Tushman asked me to be especially nice and all that. But now I would choose to hang out with him. He laughs at all my jokes. And I kind of feel like I can tell August anything. Like he's a good friend. Like, if all the guys in the fifth grade were lined up against a wall and I got to choose anyone I wanted to hang out with, I would choose August.

Ex-Friends

Bleeding Scream? What the heck? Summer Dawson has always been a bit out there, but this was too much. All I did was ask her why August was acting like he was mad at me or something. I figured she would know. And all she said was "Bleeding Scream"? I don't even know what that means.

It's so weird because one day, me and August were friends. And the next day, whoosh, he was hardly talking to me. And I haven't the slightest idea why. When I said to him, "Hey, August, you mad at me or something?" he shrugged and walked away. So I would take that as a definite yes. And since I know for a fact that I didn't do anything to him to be mad about, I figured Summer could tell me what's up. But all I got from her was "Bleeding Scream"? Yeah, big help. Thanks, Summer.

You know, I've got plenty of other friends in school. So if August wants to officially be my ex-friend, then fine, that is okay by me, see if I care. I've started ignoring him like he's ignoring me in school now. This is actually kind of hard since we sit next to each other in practically every class.

Other kids have noticed and have started asking if me and August have had a fight. Nobody asks August what's going on. Hardly anyone ever talks to him, anyway. I mean, the only person he hangs out with, other than me, is Summer. Sometimes he hangs out with Reid Kingsley a little bit, and the two Maxes got him playing Dungeons & Dragons a couple of times at recess. Charlotte, for all her Goody Two-Shoeing, doesn't ever do more than nod hello when she's passing him in the hallway. And I

146

don't know if everyone's still playing the Plague behind his back, because no one ever really told me about it directly, but my point is that it's not like he has a whole lot of other friends he could be hanging out with instead of me. If he wants to dis me, he's the one who loses—not me.

So this is how things are between us now. We only talk to each other about school stuff if we absolutely have to. Like, I'll say, "What did Rubin say the homework was?" and he'll answer. Or he'll be like, "Can I use your pencil sharpener?" and I'll get my sharpener out of my pencil case for him. But as soon as the bell rings, we go our separate ways.

Why this is good is because I get to hang out with a lot more kids now. Before, when I was hanging out with August all the time, kids weren't hanging out with me because they'd have to hang out with him. Or they would keep things from me, like the whole thing about the Plague. I think I was the only one who wasn't in on it, except for Summer and maybe the D&D crowd. And the truth is, though nobody's that obvious about it: nobody wants to hang out with him. Everyone's way too hung up on being in the popular group, and he's just as far from the popular group as you can get. But now I can hang out with anyone I want. If I wanted to be in the popular group, I could totally be in the popular group.

Why this is bad is because, well, (a) I don't actually enjoy hanging out with the popular group that much. And (b) I actually liked hanging out with August.

So this is kind of messed up. And it's all August's fault.

Snow

The first snow of winter hit right before Thanksgiving break. School was closed, so we got an extra day of vacation. I was glad about that because I was so bummed about this whole August thing and I just wanted some time to chill without having to see him every day. Also, waking up to a snow day is just about my favorite thing in the world. I love that feeling when you first open your eyes in the morning and you don't even know why everything seems different than usual. Then it hits you: Everything is quiet. No cars honking. No buses going down the street. Then you run over to the window, and outside everything is covered in white: the sidewalks, the trees, the cars on the street, your windowpanes. And when that happens on a school day and you find out your school is closed, well, I don't care how old I get: I'm always going to think that that's the best feeling in the world. And I'm never going to be one of those grown-ups that use an umbrella when it's snowing—ever.

Dad's school was closed, too, so he took me and Jamie sledding down Skeleton Hill in the park. They say a little kid broke his neck while sledding down that hill a few years ago, but I don't know if this is actually true or just one of those legends. On the way home, I spotted this banged-up wooden sled kind of propped up against the Old Indian Rock monument. Dad said to leave it, it was just garbage, but something told me it would make the greatest sled ever. So Dad let me drag it home, and I spent the rest of the day fixing it up. I super-glued the broken slats together and wrapped some heavy-duty white duct tape around them for extra strength. Then I spray painted the whole thing white with the paint I had gotten for the Alabaster Sphinx I was making for the Egyptian Museum project. When it was all dry, I painted LIGHTNING in gold letters on the middle piece of wood, and I made a little lightning-bolt symbol above the letters. It looked pretty professional, I have to say. Dad was like, "Wow, Jackie! You were right about the sled!"

The next day, we went back to Skeleton Hill with *Lightning*. It was the fastest thing I've ever ridden—so, so, so much faster than the plastic sleds we'd been using. And because it had gotten warmer outside, the snow had become crunchier and wetter: good packing snow. Me and Jamie took turns on *Lightning* all afternoon. We were in the park until our fingers were frozen and our lips had turned a little blue. Dad practically had to drag us home.

By the end of the weekend, the snow had started turning gray and yellow, and then a rainstorm turned most of the snow to slush. When we got back to school on Monday, there was no snow left.

It was rainy and yucky the first day back from vacation. A slushy day. That's how I was feeling inside, too.

I nodded "hey" to August the first time I saw him. We were in front of the lockers. He nodded "hey" back.

I wanted to tell him about *Lightning*, but I didn't.

Fortune Favors the Bold

Mr. Browne's December precept was: Fortune favors the bold. We were all supposed to write a paragraph about some time in our lives when we did something very brave and how, because of it, something good happened to us.

I thought about this a lot, to be truthful. I have to say that I think the bravest thing I ever did was become friends with August. But I couldn't write about that, of course. I was afraid we'd have to read these out loud, or Mr. Browne would put them up on the bulletin board like he does sometimes. So, instead, I wrote this lame thing about how I used to be afraid of the ocean when I was little. It was dumb but I couldn't think of anything else.

I wonder what August wrote about. He probably had a lot of things to choose from.

Private School

My parents are not rich. I say this because people sometimes think that everyone who goes to private school is rich, but that isn't true with us. Dad's a teacher and Mom's a social worker, which means they don't have those kinds of jobs where people make gazillions of dollars. We used to have a car, but we sold it when Jamie started kindergarten at Beecher Prep. We don't live in a big townhouse or in one of those doorman buildings along the park. We live on the top floor of a five-story walk-up we rent from an old lady named Doña Petra all the way on the "other" side of Broadway. That's "code" for the section of North River Heights where people don't want to park their cars. Me and Jamie share a room. I overhear my parents talk about things like "Can we do without an air conditioner one more year?" or "Maybe I can work two jobs this summer."

So today at recess I was hanging out with Julian and Henry and Miles. Julian, who everyone knows is rich, was like, "I hate that I have to go back to Paris this Christmas. It's *so* boring!"

"Dude, but it's, like, *Paris*," I said like an idiot.

"Believe me, it's *so* boring," he said. "My grandmother lives in this house in the middle of nowhere. It's like an hour away from Paris in this tiny, tiny, tiny village. I swear to God, *nothing* happens there! I mean, it's like, oh wow, there's another fly on the wall! Look, there's a new dog sleeping on the sidewalk. Yippee."

I laughed. Sometimes Julian could be very funny.

"Though my parents are talking about throwing a big party this year instead of going to Paris. I hope so. What are you doing over break?" said Julian.

"Just hanging out," I said.

"You're so lucky," he said.

"I hope it snows again," I answered. "I got this new sled that is so amazing." I was about to tell them about *Lightning* but Miles started talking first.

"I got a new sled, too!" he said. "My dad got it from Hammacher Schlemmer. It's so state of the art."

"How could a sled be state of the art?" said Julian.

"It was like eight hundred dollars or something."

"Whoa!"

"We should all go sledding and have a race down Skeleton Hill," I said.

"That hill is so lame," answered Julian.

"Are you kidding?" I said. "Some kid broke his neck there. That's why it's called Skeleton Hill."

Julian narrowed his eyes and looked at me like I was the biggest moron in the world. "It's called Skeleton Hill because it was an ancient Indian burial ground, duh," he said. "Anyway, it should be called Garbage Hill now, it's so freakin' junky. Last time I was there it was so gross, like with soda cans and broken bottles and stuff." He shook his head.

"I left my old sled there," said Miles. "It was the crappiest piece of junk—and someone took it, too!"

"Maybe a hobo wanted to go sledding!" laughed Julian.

"Where did you leave it?" I said.

"By the big rock at the bottom of the hill. And I went back the next day and it was gone. I couldn't believe somebody actually took it!"

"Here's what we can do," said Julian. "Next time it snows, my dad could drive us all up to this golf course in Westchester that makes Skeleton Hill look like nothing. Hey, Jack, where are you going?"

I had started to walk away.

"I've got to get a book out of my locker," I lied.

I just wanted to get away from them fast. I didn't want anyone to know that I was the "hobo" who had taken the sled.

In Science

I'm not the greatest student in the world. I know some kids actually like school, but I honestly can't say I do. I like some parts of school, like PE and computer class. And lunch and recess. But all in all, I'd be fine without school. And the thing I hate the most about school is all the homework we get. It's not enough that we have to sit through class after class and try to stay awake while they fill our heads with all this stuff we will probably never need to know, like how to figure out the surface area of a cube or what the difference is between kinetic and potential energy. I'm like, who cares? I've never, ever heard my parents say the word "kinetic" in my entire life!

I hate science the most out of all my classes. We get so much work it's not even funny! And the teacher, Ms. Rubin, is so strict about everything—even the way we write our headings on the top of our papers! I once got two points off a homework assignment because I didn't put the date on top. Crazy stuff.

When me and August were still friends, I was doing okay in science because August sat next to me and always let me copy his notes. August has the neatest handwriting of anybody I've ever seen who's a boy. Even his script is neat: up and down perfectly, with really small round loopy letters. But now that we're ex-friends, it's bad because I can't ask him to let me copy his notes anymore.

So I was kind of scrambling today, trying to take notes about what Ms. Rubin was saying (my handwriting is awful), when all of a sudden she started talking about the fifth-grade science-fair project, how we all had to choose a science project to work on.

While she was saying this, I was thinking, We just finished

the freakin' Egypt project, now we have to start a whole new thing? And then in my head I was going, Oh noooooo! like that kid in *Home Alone* with his mouth hanging open and his hands on his face. That was the face I was making on the inside. And then I thought of those pictures of melting ghost faces I've seen somewhere, where the mouths are open wide and they're screaming. And then all of a sudden this picture flew into my head, this memory, and I knew what Summer had meant by "bleeding scream." It's so weird how it all just came to me in this flash. Someone in homeroom had dressed up in a Bleeding Scream costume on Halloween. I remember seeing him a few desks away from me. And then I remember not seeing him again.

Oh man. It was August!

All of this hit me in science class while the teacher was talking.

Oh man.

I'd been talking to Julian about August. Oh man. Now I understood! I was so mean. I don't even know why. I'm not even sure what I said, but it was bad. It was only a minute or two. It's just that I knew Julian and everybody thought I was so weird for hanging out with August all the time, and I felt stupid. And I don't know why I said that stuff. I just was going along. I was stupid. I am stupid. Oh God. He was supposed to come as Boba Fett! I would never have said that stuff in front of Boba Fett. But that was him, that Bleeding Scream sitting at the desk looking over at us. The long white mask with the fake squirting blood. The mouth open wide. Like the ghoul was crying. That was him.

I felt like I was going to puke.

Partners

I didn't hear a word of what Ms. Rubin was saying after that. Blah blah blah. Science-fair project. Blah blah blah. Partners. Blah blah. It was like the way grown-ups talk in Charlie Brown movies. Like someone talking underwater. *Mwah-mwah-mwahhh, mwah mwahh.*

Then all of a sudden Ms. Rubin started pointing to kids around the class. "Reid and Tristan, Maya and Max, Charlotte and Ximena, August and Jack." She pointed to us when she said this. "Miles and Amos, Julian and Henry, Savanna and . . ." I didn't hear the rest.

"Huh?" I said.

The bell rang.

"So don't forget to get together with your partners to choose a project from the list, guys!" said Ms. Rubin as everyone started taking off. I looked up at August, but he had already put his backpack on and was practically out the door.

I must have had a stupid look on my face because Julian came over and said: "Looks like you and your best bud are partners." He was smirking when he said this. I hated him so much right then.

"Hello, earth to Jack Will?" he said when I didn't answer him.

"Shut up, Julian." I was putting my loose-leaf binder away in my backpack and just wanted him away from me.

"You must be so bummed you got stuck with him," he said. "You should tell Ms. Rubin you want to switch partners. I bet she'd let you."

"No she wouldn't," I said.

"Ask her."

"No, I don't want to."

"Ms. Rubin?" Julian said, turning around and raising his hand at the same time.

Ms. Rubin was erasing the chalkboard at the front of the room. She turned when she heard her name.

"No, Julian!" I whisper-screamed.

"What is it, boys?" she said impatiently.

"Could we switch partners if we wanted to?" said Julian, looking very innocent. "Me and Jack had this science-fair project idea we wanted to work on together. . . ."

"Well, I guess we could arrange that . . . ," she started to say.

"No, it's okay, Ms. Rubin," I said quickly, heading out the door. "Bye!"

Julian ran after me.

"Why'd you do that?" he said, catching up to me at the stairs. "We could have been partners. You don't have to be friends with that freak if you don't want to be, you know. . . ."

And that's when I punched him. Right in the mouth.

Detention

Some things you just can't explain. You don't even try. You don't know where to start. All your sentences would jumble up like a giant knot if you opened your mouth. Any words you used would come out wrong.

"Jack, this is very, very serious," Mr. Tushman was saying. I was in his office, sitting on a chair across from his desk and looking at this picture of a pumpkin on the wall behind him. "Kids get expelled for this kind of thing, Jack! I know you're a good kid and I don't want that to happen, but you have to explain yourself."

"This is so not like you, Jack," said Mom. She had come from work as soon as they had called her. I could tell she was going back and forth between being really mad and really surprised.

"I thought you and Julian were friends," said Mr. Tushman.

"We're not friends," I said. My arms were crossed in front of me.

"But to punch someone in the mouth, Jack?" said Mom, raising her voice. "I mean, what were you thinking?" She looked at Mr. Tushman. "Honestly, he's never hit anyone before. He's just not like that."

"Julian's mouth was bleeding, Jack," said Mr. Tushman. "You knocked out a tooth, did you know that?"

"It was just a baby tooth," I said.

"Jack!" said Mom, shaking her head.

"That's what Nurse Molly said!"

"You're missing the point!" Mom yelled.

"I just want to know why," said Mr. Tushman, raising his shoulders.

"It'll just make everything worse," I sighed.

"Just tell me, Jack."

I shrugged but I didn't say anything. I just couldn't. If I told him that Julian had called August a freak, then he'd go talk to Julian about it, then Julian would tell him how I had bad-mouthed August, too, and everybody would find out about it.

"Jack!" said Mom.

I started to cry. "I'm sorry . . ."

Mr. Tushman raised his eyebrows and nodded, but he didn't say anything. Instead, he kind of blew into his hands, like you do when your hands are cold. "Jack," he said, "I don't really know what to say here. I mean, you punched a kid. We have rules about that kind of thing, you know? Automatic expulsion. And you're not even trying to explain yourself."

I was crying a lot by now, and the second Mom put her arms around me, I started to bawl.

"Let's, um . . . ," said Mr. Tushman, taking his glasses off to clean them, "let's do this, Jack. We're out for winter break as of next week anyway. How about you stay home for the rest of this week, and then after winter break you'll come back and everything will be fresh and brand new. Clean slate, so to speak."

"Am I being suspended?" I sniffled.

"Well," he said, shrugging, "technically yes, but it's only for a couple of days. And I'll tell you what. While you're at home, you take the time to think about what's happened. And if you want to write me a letter explaining what happened, and a letter to Julian apologizing, then we won't even put any of this in your permanent record, okay? You go home and talk about it with your mom and dad, and maybe in the morning you'll figure it all out a bit more."

"That sounds like a good plan, Mr. Tushman," said Mom, nodding. "Thank you."

"Everything is going to be okay," said Mr. Tushman, walking over to the door, which was closed. "I know you're a nice kid, Jack. And I know that sometimes even nice kids do dumb things, right?" He opened the door.

"Thank you for being so understanding," said Mom, shaking his hand at the door.

"No problem." He leaned over and told her something quietly that I couldn't hear.

"I know, thank you," said Mom, nodding.

"So, kiddo," he said to me, putting his hands on my shoulders. "Think about what you've done, okay? And have a great holiday. Happy Chanukah! Merry Christmas! Happy Kwanzaa!"

I wiped my nose with my sleeve and started walking out the door.

"Say thank you to Mr. Tushman," said Mom, tapping my shoulder.

I stopped and turned around, but I couldn't look at him. "Thank you, Mr. Tushman," I said.

"Bye, Jack," he answered.

Then I walked out the door.

Season's Greetings

Weirdly enough, when we got back home and Mom brought in the mail, there were holiday cards from both Julian's family and August's family. Julian's holiday card was a picture of Julian wearing a tie, looking like he was about to go to the opera or something. August's holiday card was of a cute old dog wearing reindeer antlers, a red nose, and red booties. There was a cartoon bubble above the dog's head that read: "Ho-Ho-Ho!" On the inside of the card it read:

> To the Will family,
> Peace on Earth.
> Love, Nate, Isabel, Olivia, August (and Daisy)

"Cute card, huh?" I said to Mom, who had hardly said a word to me all the way home. I think she honestly just didn't know what to say. "That must be their dog," I said.

"Do you want to tell me what's going on inside your head, Jack?" she answered me seriously.

"I bet you they put a picture of their dog on the card every year," I said.

She took the card from my hands and looked at the picture carefully. Then she raised her eyebrows and her shoulders and gave me back the card. "We're very lucky, Jack. There's so much we take for granted. . . ."

"I know," I said. I knew what she was talking about without her having to say it. "I heard that Julian's mom actually

Photoshopped August's face out of the class picture when she got it. She gave a copy to a couple of the other moms."

"That's just awful," said Mom. "People are just . . . they're not always so great."

"I know."

"Is that why you hit Julian?"

"No."

And then I told her why I punched Julian. And I told her that August was my ex-friend now. And I told her about Halloween.

Letters, Emails, Facebook, Texts

December 18

Dear Mr. Tushman,

I am very, very sorry for punching Julian. It was very, very wrong for me to do that. I am writing a letter to him to tell him that, too. If it's okay, I would really rather not tell you why I did what I did because it doesn't really make it right anyway. Also, I would rather not make Julian get in trouble for having said something he should not have said.

Very sincerely,
Jack Will

December 18

Dear Julian,

I am very, very, very sorry for hitting you. It was wrong of me. I hope you are okay. I hope your grown-up tooth grows in fast. Mine always do.

Sincerely,
Jack Will

December 26

Dear Jack,

Thank you so much for your letter. One thing I've learned after being a middle-school director for twenty years: there are almost always more than two sides to every story. Although I don't know the details, I have an inkling about what may have sparked the confrontation with Julian.

While nothing justifies striking another student—ever—I also know good friends are sometimes worth defending. This has been a tough year for a lot of students, as the first year of middle school usually is.

Keep up the good work, and keep being the fine boy we all know you are.

All the best,
Lawrence Tushman
Middle-School Director

To: ltushman@beecherschool.edu
Cc: johnwill@phillipsacademy.edu; amandawill@copperbeech.org
Fr: melissa.albans@rmail.com
Subject: Jack Will

Dear Mr. Tushman,

I spoke with Amanda and John Will yesterday, and they expressed their regret at Jack's having punched our son, Julian, in the mouth. I am writing to let you know that my husband and I support your decision to allow Jack to return to Beecher Prep after a two-day suspension. Although I think hitting a child would be valid grounds for expulsion in other schools, I agree such extreme measures aren't warranted here. We have known the Will family since our boys were in kindergarten, and are confident that every measure will be taken to ensure this doesn't happen again.

To that end, I wonder if Jack's unexpectedly violent behavior might have been a result of too much pressure being placed on his young shoulders? I am speaking specifically of the new child with special needs who both Jack and Julian were asked to "befriend." In retrospect, and having now seen the child in question at various school functions and in the class pictures, I think it may have been too much to ask of our children to be able to process all that. Certainly, when Julian mentioned he was having a hard time befriending the boy, we told him he was "off the hook" in that regard. We think the transition to middle school is hard enough without having to place greater burdens or hardships on these young, impressionable minds. I should also mention that, as a member of the school board, I was a little disturbed that more consideration was not given during this child's application process to the fact that Beecher Prep is not an inclusion school. There are many parents—myself included—who question the decision to let this child into our school at all. At the very least, I am somewhat troubled that this child was not held to the same stringent application standards (i.e. interview) that the rest of the incoming middle-school students were.

Best,
Melissa Perper Albans

To: melissa.albans@rmail.com
Fr: ltushman@beecherschool.edu
Cc: johnwill@phillipsacademy.edu; amandawill@copperbeech.org
Subject: Jack Will

Dear Mrs. Albans,

Thanks for your email outlining your concerns. Were I not convinced that Jack Will is extremely sorry for his actions, and were I not confident that he would not repeat those actions, rest assured that I would not be allowing him back to Beecher Prep.

164

As for your other concerns regarding our new student August, please note that he does not have special needs. He is neither disabled, handicapped, nor developmentally delayed in any way, so there was no reason to assume anyone would take issue with his admittance to Beecher Prep—whether it is an inclusion school or not. In terms of the application process, the admissions director and I both felt it within our right to hold the interview off-site at August's home for reasons that are obvious. We felt that this slight break in protocol was warranted but in no way prejudicial—in one way or another—to the application review. August is an extremely good student, and has secured the friendship of some truly exceptional young people, including Jack Will.

At the beginning of the school year, when I enlisted certain children to be a "welcoming committee" to August, I did so as a way of easing his transition into a school environment. I did not think asking these children to be especially kind to a new student would place any extra "burdens or hardships" on them. In fact, I thought it would teach them a thing or two about empathy, and friendship, and loyalty.

As it turns out, Jack Will didn't need to learn any of these virtues—he already had them in abundance.

Thank you again for being in touch.

Sincerely,
Lawrence Tushman

To: melissa.albans@rmail.com
Fr: johnwill@phillipsacademy.edu
Cc: ltushman@beecherschool.edu; amandawill@copperbeech.org
Subject: Jack

Hi Melissa,

Thank you for being so understanding about this incident with Jack. He is, as you know, extremely sorry for his actions. I hope you do accept our offer to pay Julian's dental bills.

We are very touched by your concern regarding Jack's friendship
with August. Please know we have asked Jack if he felt any undue
pressure about any of this, and the answer was a resolute "no."
He enjoys August's company and feels like he has made a good
friend.

                              Hope you have a
                              Happy New Year!
                              John and Amanda Will

Hi August,

Jacklope Will wants to be friends with you on Facebook.

                              Jackalope Will
                              32 mutual friends
                              Thanks,
                              The Facebook Team

To: auggiedoggiepullman@email.com
Subject: Sorry ! ! ! ! ! !
Message:

Hey august. Its me Jack Will. I noticed im not on ur friends list
anymore. Hope u friend me agen cuz im really sorry. I jus wanted 2
say that. Sorry. I know why ur mad at me now Im sorry I didn't mean
the stuff I said. I was so stupid. I hope u can 4give me

                              Hope we can b friends agen.
                              Jack

166

1 New Text Message
From: AUGUST
Dec 31 4:47PM

got ur message u know why im mad at u now?? did Summer tell u?

1 New Text Message
From: JACKWILL
Dec 31 4:49PM

She told me bleeding scream as hint but didn't get it at first then I
remember seeing bleeding scream in homeroom on Hallween. didn't
know it was you thought u were coming as Boba Fett.

1 New Text Message
From: AUGUST
Dec 31 4:51PM

I changed my mind at the last minute. Did u really punch Julian?

1 New Text Message
From: JACKWILL
Dec 31 4:54PM

Yeah i punchd him knocked out a tooth in the back. A baby tooth.

1 New Text Message
From: AUGUST
Dec 31 4:55PM

whyd u punch him????????

1 New Text Message
From: JACKWILL
Dec 31 4:56PM

I dunno

1 New Text Message
From: AUGUST
Dec 31 4:58PM

liar. I bet he said something about me right?

1 New Text Message
From: JACKWILL
Dec 31 5:02PM

he's a jerk. but I was a jerk too. really really really sorry for wat I
said dude, Ok? can we b frenz agen?

1 New Text Message
From: AUGUST
Dec 31 5:03PM

ok

1 New Text Message
From: JACKWILL
Dec 31 5:04PM

awsum!!!!

1 New Text Message
From: AUGUST
Dec 31 5:06PM

but tell me the truth, ok?

wud u really wan to kill urself if u wer me???

1 New Text Message
From: JACKWILL
Dec 31 5:08PM

no!!!!!

I swear on my life
but dude-

I would want 2 kill myself if I were Julian ;)

1 New Text Message
From: AUGUST
Dec 31 5:10PM

lol

yes dude we'r frenz agen.

Back from Winter Break

Despite what Tushman said, there was no "clean slate" when I went back to school in January. In fact, things were totally weird from the second I got to my locker in the morning. I'm next to Amos, who's always been a pretty straight-up kid, and I was like, "Yo, what up?" and he basically just nodded a half hello and closed his locker door and left. I was like, okay, that was bizarre. And then I said: "Hey, what up?" to Henry, who didn't even bother half-smiling but just looked away.

Okay, so something's up. Dissed by two people in less than five minutes. Not that anyone's counting. I thought I'd try one more time, with Tristan, and boom, same thing. He actually looked nervous, like he was afraid of talking to me.

I've got a form of the Plague now, is what I thought. This is Julian's payback.

And that's pretty much how it went all morning. Nobody talked to me. Not true: the girls were totally normal with me. And August talked to me, of course. And, actually, I have to say both Maxes said hello, which made me feel kind of bad for never, ever hanging out with them in the five years I've been in their class.

I hoped lunch would be better, but it wasn't. I sat down at my usual table with Luca and Isaiah. I guess I thought since they weren't in the super-popular group but were kind of middle-of-the-road jock kids that I'd be safe with them. But they barely nodded when I said hello. Then, when our table was called, they got their lunches and never came back. I saw them find a table way over at the other end of the cafeteria. They weren't at Julian's table, but they were near him, like on the fringe of popularity. So anyway, I'd been ditched. I knew table switching was something that happened in the fifth grade, but I never thought it would happen to me.

It felt really awful being at the table by myself. I felt like everyone was watching me. It also made me feel like I had no friends. I decided to skip lunch and go read in the library.

The War

It was Charlotte who had the inside scoop on why everyone was dissing me. I found a note inside my locker at the end of the day.

Meet me in room 301 right after school. Come by yourself! Charlotte.

She was already inside the room when I walked in. "Sup," I said.

"Hey," she said. She went over to the door, looked left and right, and then closed the door and locked it from the inside. Then she turned to face me and started biting her nail as she talked. "Look, I feel bad about what's going on and I just wanted to tell you what I know. Promise you won't tell anyone I talked to you?"

"Promise."

"So Julian had this huge holiday party over winter break," she said. "I mean, *huge.* My sister's friend had had her sweet sixteen at the same place last year. There were like two hundred people there, so I mean it's a *huge* place."

"Yeah, and?"

"Yeah, and . . . well, pretty much everybody in the whole grade was there."

"Not everybody," I joked.

"Right, not everybody. Duh. But like even parents were there, you know. Like my parents were there. You know Julian's mom is the vice president of the school board, right? So she knows a *lot* of people. Anyway, so basically what happened at the party was that Julian went around telling everyone that you punched him because you had emotional problems. . . ."

"What?!"

"And that you would have gotten expelled, but his parents begged the school not to expel you . . ."

"What?!"

"And that none of it would have happened in the first place if Tushman hadn't forced you to be friends with Auggie. He said his mom thinks that you, quote unquote, snapped under the pressure. . . ."

I couldn't believe what I was hearing. "No one bought into that, right?" I said.

She shrugged. "That's not even the point. The point is he's really popular. And, you know, my mom heard that his mom is actually pushing the school to review Auggie's application to Beecher."

"Can she do that?"

"It's about Beecher not being an inclusion school. That's a type of school that mixes normal kids with kids with special needs."

"That's just stupid. Auggie doesn't have special needs."

"Yeah, but she's saying that if the school is changing the way they usually do things in some ways . . ."

"But they're not changing anything!"

"Yeah, they did. Didn't you notice they changed the theme of the New Year Art Show? In past years fifth graders painted self-portraits, but this year they made us do those ridiculous self-portraits as animals, remember?"

"So big freakin' deal."

"I know! I'm not saying I agree, I'm just saying that's what she's saying."

"I know, I know. This is just so messed up. . . ."

"I know. Anyway, Julian said that he thinks being friends with Auggie is bringing you down, and that for your own good you need to stop hanging out with him so much. And if you start losing all your old friends, it'll be like a big wake-up call. So basically, for your own good, he's going to stop being your friend completely."

"News flash: I stopped being his friend completely first!"

"Yeah, but he's convinced all the boys to stop being your friend—for your own good. That's why nobody's talking to you."

"You're talking to me."

"Yeah, well, this is more of a boy thing," she explained. "The girls are staying neutral. Except Savanna's group, because they're going out with Julian's group. But to everybody else this is really a boy war."

I nodded. She tilted her head to one side and pouted like she felt sorry for me.

"Is it okay that I told you all this?" she said.

"Yeah! Of course! I don't care who talks to me or not," I lied. "This is all just so dumb."

She nodded.

"Hey, does Auggie know any of this?"

"Of course not. At least, not from me."

"And Summer?"

"I don't think so. Look, I better go. Just so you know, my mom thinks Julian's mom is a total idiot. She said she thinks people like her are more concerned about what their kids' class pictures look like than doing the right thing. You heard about the Photoshopping, right?"

"Yeah, that was just sick."

"Totally," she answered, nodding. "Anyway, I better go. I just wanted you to know what was up and stuff."

"Thanks, Charlotte."

"I'll let you know if I hear anything else," she said. Before she went out, she looked left and right outside the door to make sure no one saw her leaving. I guess even though she was neutral, she didn't want to be seen with me.

Switching Tables

The next day at lunch, stupid me, I sat down at a table with Tristan, Nino, and Pablo. I thought maybe they were safe because they weren't really considered popular, but they weren't out there playing D&D at recess, either. They were sort of in-betweeners. And, at first, I thought I scored because they were basically too nice to not acknowledge my presence when I walked over to the table. They all said "Hey," though I could tell they looked at each other. But then the same thing happened that happened yesterday: our lunch table was called, they got their food, and then headed toward a new table on the other side of the cafeteria.

Unfortunately, Mrs. G, who was the lunch teacher that day, saw what happened and chased after them.

"That's not allowed, boys!" she scolded them loudly. "This is not that kind of school. You get right back to your table."

Oh great, like that was going to help. Before they could be forced to sit back down at the table, I got up with my tray and walked away really fast. I could hear Mrs. G call my name, but I pretended not to hear and just kept walking to the other side of the cafeteria, behind the lunch counter.

"Sit with us, Jack."

It was Summer. She and August were sitting at their table, and they were both waving me over.

Why I Didn't Sit with August the First Day of School

Okay, I'm a total hypocrite. I know. That very first day of school I remember seeing August in the cafeteria. Everybody was looking at him. Talking about him. Back then, no one was used to his face or even knew that he was coming to Beecher, so it was a total shocker for a lot of people to see him there on the first day of school. Most kids were even afraid to get near him.

So when I saw him going into the cafeteria ahead of me, I knew he'd have no one to sit with, but I just couldn't bring myself to sit with him. I had been hanging out with him all morning long because we had so many classes together, and I guess I was just kind of wanting a little normal time to chill with other kids. So when I saw him move to a table on the other side of the lunch counter, I purposely found a table as far away from there as I could find. I sat down with Isaiah and Luca even though I'd never met them before, and we talked about baseball the whole time, and I played basketball with them at recess. They became my lunch table from then on.

I heard Summer had sat down with August, which surprised me because I knew for a fact she wasn't one of the kids that Tushman had talked to about being friends with Auggie. So I knew she was doing it *just* to be nice, and that was pretty brave, I thought.

So now here I was sitting with Summer and August, and they were being totally nice to me as always. I filled them in about everything Charlotte had told me, except for the whole big part about my having "snapped" under the pressure of being Auggie's friend, or the part about Julian's mom saying that Auggie had special needs, or the part about the school board. I guess all I really told them about was how Julian had had a holiday party and managed to turn the whole grade against me.

"It just feels so weird," I said, "to not have people talking to you, pretending you don't even exist."

Auggie started smiling.

"Ya think?" he said sarcastically. "Welcome to my world!"

Sides

"So here are the official sides," said Summer at lunch the next day. She pulled out a folded piece of loose-leaf paper and opened it. It had three columns of names.

Jack's side	Julian's side	Neutrals
Jack	Miles	Malik
August	Henry	Remo
Reid	Amos	Jose
Max G	Simon	Leif
Max W	Tristan	Ram
	Pablo	Ivan
	Nino	Russell
	Isaiah	
	Luca	
	Jake	
	Toland	
	Roman	
	Ben	
	Emmanuel	
	Zeke	
	Tomaso	

"Where did you get this?" said Auggie, looking over my shoulder as I read the list.

"Charlotte made it," Summer answered quickly. "She gave it to me last period. She said she thought you should know who was on your side, Jack."

"Yeah, not many people, that's for sure," I said.

"Reid is," she said. "And the two Maxes."

"Great. The nerds are on my side."

"Don't be mean," said Summer. "I think Charlotte likes you, by the way."

"Yeah, I know."

"Are you going to ask her out?"

"Are you kidding? I can't, now that everybody's acting like I have the Plague."

The second I said it, I realized I shouldn't have said it. There was this awkward moment of silence. I looked at Auggie.

"It's okay," he said. "I knew about that."

"Sorry, dude," I said.

"I didn't know they called it the Plague, though," he said. "I figured it was more like the Cheese Touch or something."

"Oh, yeah, like in *Diary of a Wimpy Kid*." I nodded.

"The Plague actually sounds cooler," he joked. "Like someone could catch the 'black death of ugliness.'" As he said this, he made air quotes.

"I think it's awful," said Summer, but Auggie shrugged while taking a big sip from his juice box.

"Anyway, I'm not asking Charlotte out," I said.

"My mom thinks we're all too young to be dating anyway," she answered.

"What if Reid asked you out?" I said. "Would you go?"

I could tell she was surprised. "No!" she said.

"I'm just asking," I laughed.

She shook her head and smiled. "Why? What do you know?"

"Nothing! I'm just asking!" I said.

"I actually agree with my mom," she said. "I do think we're too young to be dating. I mean, I just don't see what the rush is."

"Yeah, I agree," said August. "Which is kind of a shame, you know, what with all those babes who keep throwing themselves at me and stuff?"

He said this in such a funny way that the milk I was drinking came out my nose when I laughed, which made us all totally crack up.

August's House

It was already the middle of January, and we still hadn't even chosen what science-fair project we were going to work on. I guess I kept putting it off because I just didn't want to do it. Finally, August was like, "Dude, we have to do this." So we went to his house after school.

I was really nervous because I didn't know if August had ever told his parents about what we now called the Halloween Incident. Turns out the dad wasn't even home and the mom was out running errands. I'm pretty sure from the two seconds I'd spent talking to her that Auggie had never mentioned a thing about it. She was super cool and friendly toward me.

When I first walked into Auggie's room, I was like, "Whoa, Auggie, you have got a serious *Star Wars* addiction."

He had ledges full of *Star Wars* miniatures, and a huge *The Empire Strikes Back* poster on his wall.

"I know, right?" he laughed.

He sat down on a rolling chair next to his desk and I plopped down on a beanbag chair in the corner. That's when his dog waddled into the room right up to me.

"He was on your holiday card!" I said, letting the dog sniff my hand.

"She," he corrected me. "Daisy. You can pet her. She doesn't bite."

When I started petting her, she basically just rolled over onto her back.

"She wants you to rub her tummy," said August.

"Okay, this is the cutest dog I've ever seen," I said, rubbing her stomach.

"I know, right? She's the best dog in the world. Aren't you, girlie?"

As soon as she heard Auggie's voice say that, the dog started wagging her tail and went over to him.

"Who's my little girlie? Who's my little girlie?" Auggie was saying as she licked him all over the face.

"I wish I had a dog," I said. "My parents think our apartment's too small." I started looking around at the stuff in his room while he turned on the computer. "Hey, you've got an Xbox 360? Can we play?"

"Dude, we're here to work on the science-fair project."

"Do you have *Halo*?"

"Of course I have *Halo*."

"Please can we play?"

He had logged on to the Beecher website and was now scrolling down Ms. Rubin's teacher page through the list of science-fair projects. "Can you see from there?" he said.

I sighed and went to sit on a little stool that was right next to him.

"Cool iMac," I said.

"What kind of computer do you have?"

"Dude, I don't even have my own room, much less my own computer. My parents have this ancient Dell that's practically dead."

"Okay, how about this one?" he said, turning the screen in my direction so I would look. I made a quick scan of the screen and my eyes literally started blurring.

"Making a sun clock," he said. "That sounds kind of cool."

I leaned back. "Can't we just make a volcano?"

"Everyone makes volcanoes."

"Duh, because it's easy," I said, petting Daisy again.

"What about: How to make crystal spikes out of Epsom salt?"

"Sounds boring," I answered. "So why'd you call her Daisy?"

He didn't look up from the screen. "My sister named her. I wanted to call her Darth. Actually, technically speaking, her full name is Darth Daisy, but we never really called her that."

"Darth Daisy! That's funny! Hi, Darth Daisy!" I said to the dog, who rolled onto her back again for me to rub her tummy.

"Okay, this one is the one," said August, pointing to a picture on the screen of a bunch of potatoes with wires poking out of them. "How to build an organic battery made of potatoes. Now, that's cool. It says here you could power a lamp with it. We could call it the Spud Lamp or something. What do you think?"

"Dude, that sounds way too hard. You know I suck at science."

"Shut up, you do not."

"Yeah I do! I got a fifty-four on my last test. I suck at science!"

"No you don't! And that was only because we were still fighting and I wasn't helping you. I can help you now. This is a good project, Jack. We've got to do it."

"Fine, whatever." I shrugged.

Just then there was a knock on the door. A teenage girl with long dark wavy hair poked her head inside the door. She wasn't expecting to see me.

"Oh, hey," she said to both of us.

"Hey, Via," said August, looking back at the computer screen. "Via, this is Jack. Jack, that's Via."

"Hey," I said, nodding hello.

"Hey," she said, looking at me carefully. I knew the second Auggie said my name that he had told her about the stuff I had said about him. I could tell from the way she looked at me. In fact, the way she looked at me made me think she remembered me from that day at Carvel on Amesfort Avenue all those years ago.

184

"Auggie, I have a friend I want you to meet, okay?" she said. "He's coming over in a few minutes."

"Is he your new *boyfriend*?" August teased.

Via kicked the bottom of his chair. "Just be nice," she said, and left the room.

"Dude, your sister's hot," I said.

"I know."

"She hates me, right? You told her about the Halloween Incident?"

"Yeah."

"Yeah, she hates me or yeah, you told her about Halloween?"

"Both."

The Boyfriend

Two minutes later the sister came back with this guy named Justin. Seemed like a cool enough dude. Longish hair. Little round glasses. He was carrying a big long shiny silver case that ended in a sharp point on one end.

"Justin, this is my little brother, August," said Via. "And that's Jack."

"Hey, guys," said Justin, shaking our hands. He seemed a little nervous. I guess maybe it was because he was meeting August for the first time. Sometimes I forget what a shock it is the first time you meet him. "Cool room."

"Are you Via's boyfriend?" Auggie asked mischievously, and his sister pulled his cap down over his face.

"What's in your case?" I said. "A machine gun?"

"Ha!" answered the boyfriend. "That's funny. No, it's a, uh . . . fiddle."

"Justin's a fiddler," said Via. "He's in a zydeco band."

"What the heck is a zydeco band?" said Auggie, looking at me.

"It's a type of music," said Justin. "Like Creole music."

"What's Creole?" I said.

"You should tell people that's a machine gun," said Auggie. "Nobody would ever mess with you."

"Ha, I guess you're right," Justin said, nodding and tucking his hair behind his ears. "Creole's the kind of music they play in Louisiana," he said to me.

"Are you from Louisiana?" I asked.

"No, um," he answered, pushing up his glasses. "I'm from Brooklyn."

I don't know why this made me want to laugh.

"Come on, Justin," said Via, pulling him by the hand. "Let's go hang out in my room."

"Okay, see you guys later. Bye," he said.

"Bye!"

"Bye!"

As soon as they left the room, Auggie looked at me, smiling.

"I'm from Brooklyn," I said, and we both started laughing hysterically.

Part Five

Justin

Sometimes I think my head is so big

because it is so full of dreams.

— John Merrick in Bernard Pomerance's

The Elephant Man

Olivia's Brother

the first time i meet Olivia's little brother, i have to admit i'm totally taken by surprise.

i shouldn't be, of course. olivia's told me about his "syndrome." has even described what he looks like. but she's also talked about all his surgeries over the years, so i guess i assumed he'd be more normal-looking by now. like when a kid is born with a cleft lip and has plastic surgery to fix it sometimes you can't even tell except for the little scar above the lip. i guess i thought her brother would have some scars here and there. but not this. i definitely wasn't expecting to see this little kid in a baseball cap who's sitting in front of me right now.

actually there are two kids sitting in front me: one is a totally normal-looking kid with curly blond hair named jack; the other is auggie.

i like to think i'm able to hide my surprise. i hope i do. surprise is one of those emotions that can be hard to fake, though, whether you're trying to look surprised when you're not or trying to not look surprised when you are.

i shake his hand. i shake the other kid's hand. don't want to focus on his face. cool room, I say.

are you via's boyfriend? he says. i think he's smiling.

olivia pushes down his baseball cap.

is that a machine gun? the blond kid asks, like i haven't heard that one before. and we talk about zydeco for a bit. and then via's taking my hand and leading me out of the room. as soon as we close the door behind us, we hear them laughing.

i'm from brooklyn! one of them sings.

olivia rolls her eyes as she smiles. let's go hang out in my room, she says.

we've been dating for two months now. i knew from the moment i saw her, the minute she sat down at our table in the cafeteria, that i liked her. i couldn't keep my eyes off of her. really beautiful. with olive skin and the bluest eyes i've ever seen in my life. at first she acted like she only wanted to be friends. i think she kind of gives off that vibe without even meaning to. stay back. don't even bother. she doesn't flirt like some other girls do. she looks you right in the eye when she talks to you, like she's daring you. so i just kept looking her right in the eye, too, like i was daring her right back. and then i asked her out and she said yes, which rocked.

she's an awesome girl and i love hanging out with her.

she didn't tell me about august until our third date. i think she used the phrase "a craniofacial abnormality" to describe his face. or maybe it was "craniofacial anomaly." i know the one word she didn't use was "deformed," though, because that word would have registered with me.

so, what did you think? she asks me nervously the second we're inside her room. are you shocked?

no, i lie.

she smiles and looks away. you're shocked.

i'm not, i assure her. he's just like what you said he'd be.

she nods and plops down on her bed. kind of cute how she still has a lot of stuffed animals on her bed. she takes one of them, a polar bear, without thinking and puts it in her lap.

i sit down on the rolling chair by her desk. her room is immaculate.

when i was little, she says, there were lots of kids who never came back for a second playdate. i mean, *lots* of kids. i even had

190

friends who wouldn't come to my birthdays because he would be there. they never actually told me this, but it would get back to me. some people just don't know how to deal with auggie, you know?

i nod.

it's not even like they know they're being mean, she adds. they were just scared. i mean, let's face it, his face is a little scary, right?

i guess, i answer.

but you're okay with it? she asks me sweetly. you're not too freaked out? or scared?

i'm not freaked out or scared. i smile.

she nods and looks down at the polar bear on her lap. i can't tell whether she believes me or not, but then she gives the polar bear a kiss on the nose and tosses it to me with a little smile. i think that means she believes me. or at least that she wants to.

Valentine's Day

i give olivia a heart necklace for valentine's day, and she gives me a messenger bag she's made out of old floppy disks. very cool how she makes things like that. earrings out of pieces of circuit boards. dresses out of t-shirts. bags out of old jeans. she's so creative. i tell her she should be an artist someday, but she wants to be a scientist. a geneticist, of all things. she wants to find cures for people like her brother, i guess.

we make plans for me to finally meet her parents. a mexican restaurant on amesfort avenue near her house on saturday night.

all day long i'm nervous about it. and when i get nervous my tics come out. i mean, my tics are always there, but they're not like they used to be when i was little: nothing but a few hard blinks now, the occasional head pull. but when i'm stressed they get worse—and i'm definitely stressing about meeting her folks.

they're waiting inside when i get to the restaurant. the dad gets up and shakes my hand, and the mom gives me a hug. i give auggie a hello fist-punch and kiss olivia on the cheek before i sit down.

it's so nice to meet you, justin! we've heard so much about you!

her parents couldn't be nicer. put me at ease right away. the waiter brings over the menus and i notice his expression the moment he lays eyes on august. but i pretend not to notice. i guess we're all pretending not to notice things tonight. the waiter. my tics. the way august crushes the tortilla chips on the table and spoons the crumbs into his mouth. i look at olivia and she smiles at me. she knows. she sees the waiter's face. she sees my tics. olivia is a girl who sees everything.

we spend the entire dinner talking and laughing. olivia's parents ask me about my music, how i got into the fiddle and stuff like that. and i tell them about how i used to play classical violin but I got into appalachian folk music and then zydeco. and they're listening to every word like they're really interested. they tell me to let them know the next time my band's playing a gig so they can come listen.

i'm not used to all the attention, to be truthful. my parents don't have a clue about what I want to do with my life. they never ask. we never talk like this. i don't think they even know i traded my baroque violin for an eight-string hardanger fiddle two years ago.

after dinner we go back to olivia's for some ice cream. their dog greets us at the door. an old dog. super sweet. she'd thrown up all over the hallway, though. olivia's mom rushes to get paper towels while the dad picks the dog up like she's a baby.

what's up, ol' girlie? he says, and the dog's in heaven, tongue hanging out, tail wagging, legs in the air at awkward angles.

dad, tell justin how you got daisy, says olivia.

yeah! says auggie.

the dad smiles and sits down in a chair with the dog still cradled in his arms. it's obvious he's told this story lots of times and they all love to hear it.

so i'm coming home from the subway one day, he says, and a homeless guy i've never seen in this neighborhood before is pushing this floppy mutt in a stroller, and he comes up to me and says, hey, mister, wanna buy my dog? and without even thinking about it, i say sure, how much you want? and he says ten bucks, so i give him the twenty dollars i have in my wallet and he hands me the dog. justin, i'm telling you, you've never smelled anything so bad in your life! she stank so much i can't even tell you! so i took her right from there to the vet down the street and then i brought her home.

didn't even call me first, by the way! the mom interjects as she cleans the floor, to see if i'm okay with his bringing home some homeless guy's dog.

the dog actually looks over at the mom when she says this, like she understands everything everyone is saying about her. she's a happy dog, like she knows she lucked out that day finding this family.

i kind of know how she feels. i like olivia's family. they laugh a lot.

my family's not like this at all. my mom and dad got divorced when i was four and they pretty much hate each other. i grew up spending half of every week in my dad's apartment in chelsea and the other half in my mom's place in brooklyn heights. i have a half brother who's five years older than me and barely knows i exist. for as long as i can remember, i've felt like my parents could hardly wait for me to be old enough to take care of myself. "you can go to the store by yourself." "here's the key to the apartment." it's funny how there's a word like overprotective to describe some parents, but no word that means the opposite. what word do you use to describe parents who don't protect enough? underprotective? neglectful? self-involved? lame? all of the above.

olivia's family tell each other "i love you" all the time.

i can't remember the last time anyone in my family said that to me.

by the time i go home, my tics have all stopped.

194

OUR TOWN

we're doing the play *our town* for the spring show this year. olivia dares me to try out for the lead role, the stage manager, and somehow i get it. total fluke. never got any lead roles in anything before. i tell olivia she brings me good luck. unfortunately, she doesn't get the female lead, emily gibbs. the pink-haired girl named miranda gets it. olivia gets a bit part and is also the emily understudy. i'm actually more disappointed than olivia is. she almost seems relieved. i don't love people staring at me, she says, which is sort of strange coming from such a pretty girl. a part of me thinks maybe she blew her audition on purpose.

the spring show is at the end of april. it's mid-march now, so that's less than six weeks to memorize my part. plus rehearsal time. plus practicing with my band. plus finals. plus spending time with olivia. it's going to be a rough six weeks, that's for sure. mr. davenport, the drama teacher, is already manic about the whole thing. will drive us crazy by the time it's over, no doubt. i heard through the grapevine that he'd been planning on doing *the elephant man* but changed it to *our town* at the last minute, and that change took a week off of our rehearsal schedule.

not looking forward to the craziness of the next month and a half.

Ladybug

olivia and i are sitting on her front stoop. she's helping me with my lines. it's a warm march evening, almost like summer. the sky is still bright cyan but the sun is low and the sidewalks are streaked with long shadows.

i'm reciting: yes, the sun's come up over a thousand times. summers and winters have cracked the mountains a little bit more and the rains have brought down some of the dirt. some babies that weren't even born before have begun talking regular sentences already; and a number of people who thought they were right young and spry have noticed that they can't bound up a flight of stairs like they used to, without their heart fluttering a little. . . .

i shake my head. can't remember the rest.

all that can happen in a thousand days, olivia prompts me, reading from the script.

right, right, right, i say, shaking my head. i sigh. i'm wiped, olivia. how the heck am i going to remember all these lines?

you will, she answers confidently. she reaches out and cups her hands over a ladybug that appears out of nowhere. see? a good luck sign, she says, slowly lifting her top hand to reveal the ladybug walking on the palm of her other hand.

good luck or just the hot weather, i joke.

of course good luck, she answers, watching the ladybug crawl up her wrist. there should be a thing about making a wish on a ladybug. auggie and I used to do that with fireflies when we were little. she cups her hand over the ladybug again. come on, make a wish. close your eyes.

i dutifully close my eyes. a long second passes, then I open them.

did you make a wish? she asks.

yep.

she smiles, uncups her hands, and the ladybug, as if on cue, spreads its wings and flits away.

don't you want to know what I wished for? i ask, kissing her.

no, she answers shyly, looking up at the sky, which, at this very moment, is the exact color of her eyes.

i made a wish, too, she says mysteriously, but she has so many things she could wish for I have no idea what she's thinking.

The Bus Stop

olivia's mom, auggie, jack, and daisy come down the stoop just as i'm saying goodbye to olivia. slightly awkward since we are in the middle of a nice long kiss.

hey, guys, says the mom, pretending not to see anything, but the two boys are giggling.

hi, mrs. pullman.

please call me isabel, justin, she says again. it's like the third time she's told me this, so i really need to start calling her that.

i'm heading home, i say, as if to explain.

oh, are you heading to the subway? she says, following the dog with a newspaper. can you walk jack to the bus stop?

no problem.

that okay with you, jack? the mom asks him, and he shrugs. justin, can you stay with him till the bus comes?

of course!

we all say our goodbyes. olivia winks at me.

you don't have to stay with me, says jack as we're walking up the block. i take the bus by myself all the time. auggie's mom is way too overprotective.

he's got a low gravelly voice, like a little tough guy. he kind of looks like one of those little-rascal kids in old black-and-white movies, like he should be wearing a newsboy cap and knickers.

we get to the bus stop and the schedule says the bus will be there in eight minutes. i'll wait with you, i tell him.

up to you. he shrugs. can i borrow a dollar? i want some gum.

i fish a dollar out of my pocket and watch him cross the

street to the grocery store on the corner. he seems too small to be walking around by himself, somehow. then i think how i was that young when i was taking the subway by myself. way too young. i'm going to be an overprotective dad someday, i know it. my kids are going to know i care.

i'm waiting there a minute or two when i notice three kids walking up the block from the other direction. they walk right past the grocery store, but one of them looks inside and nudges the other two, and they all back up and look inside. i can tell they're up to no good, all elbowing each other, laughing. one of them is jack's height but the other two look much bigger, more like teens. they hide behind the fruit stand in front of the store, and when jack walks out, they trail behind him, making loud throw-up noises. jack casually turns around at the corner to see who they are and they run away, high-fiving each other and laughing. little jerks.

jack crosses the street like nothing happened and stands next to me at the bus stop, blowing a bubble.

friends of yours? i finally say.

ha, he says. he's trying to smile but i can see he's upset.

just some jerks from my school, he says. a kid named julian and his two gorillas, henry and miles.

do they bother you like that a lot?

no, they've never done that before. they'd never do that in school or they'd get kicked out. julian lives two blocks from here, so I guess it was just bad luck running into him.

oh, okay. i nod.

it's not a big deal, he assures me.

we both automatically look down amesfort avenue to see if the bus is coming.

we're sort of in a war, he says after a minute, as if that explains everything. then he pulls out this crumpled piece of loose-leaf paper from his jean pocket and gives it to me. i unfold it, and it's a list of names in three columns. he's turned the whole grade against me, says jack.

not the whole grade, i point out, looking down at the list.

he leaves me notes in my locker that say stuff like *everybody hates you*.

you should tell your teacher about that.

jack looks at me like i'm an idiot and shakes his head.

anyway, you have all these neutrals, i say, pointing to the list. if you get them on your side, things will even up a bit.

yeah, well, that's really going to happen, he says sarcastically.

why not?

he shoots me another look like i am absolutely the stupidest guy he's ever talked to in the world.

what? i say.

he shakes his head like i'm hopeless. let's just say, he says, i'm friends with someone who isn't exactly the most popular kid in the school.

then it hits me, what's he's not coming out and saying: august. this is all about his being friends with august. and he doesn't want to tell me because i'm the sister's boyfriend. yeah, of course, makes sense.

we see the bus coming down amesfort avenue.

well, just hang in there, i tell him, handing back the paper. middle school is about as bad as it gets, and then it gets better. everything'll work out.

he shrugs and shoves the list back into his pocket.

we wave bye when he gets on the bus, and i watch it pull away.

when i get to the subway station two blocks away, i see the same three kids hanging out in front of the bagel place next door. they're still laughing and yuck-yucking each other like they're some kind of gangbangers, little rich boys in expensive skinny jeans acting tough.

don't know what possesses me, but i take my glasses off, put them in my pocket, and tuck my fiddle case under my arm so the pointy side is facing up. i walk over to them, my face scrunched up, mean-looking. they look at me, laughs dying on their lips when they see me, ice cream cones at odd angles.

yo, listen up. don't mess with jack, i say really slowly, gritting my teeth, my voice all clint eastwood tough-guy. mess with him again and you will be very, *very* sorry. and then i tap my fiddle case for effect.

got it?

they nod in unison, ice cream dripping onto their hands.

good. i nod mysteriously, then sprint down the subway two steps at a time.

Rehearsal

the play is taking up most of my time as we get closer to opening night. lots of lines to remember. long monologues where it's just me talking. olivia had this great idea, though, and it's helping. i have my fiddle with me onstage and play it a bit while i'm talking. It's not written that way, but mr. davenport thinks it adds an extra-folksy element to have the stage manager plucking on a fiddle. and for me it's so great because whenever i need a second to remember my next line, i just start playing a little "soldier's joy" on my fiddle and it buys me some time.

i've gotten to know the kids in the show a lot better, especially the pink-haired girl who plays emily. turns out she's not nearly as stuck-up as i thought she was, given the crowd she hangs out with. her boyfriend's this built jock who's a big deal on the varsity sports circuit at school. it's a whole world that i have nothing to do with, so i'm kind of surprised that this miranda girl turns out to be kind of nice.

one day we're sitting on the floor backstage waiting for the tech guys to fix the main spotlight.

so how long have you and olivia been dating? she asks out of the blue.

about four months now, i say.

have you met her brother? she says casually.

it's so unexpected that i can't hide my surprise.

you know olivia's brother? i ask.

via didn't tell you? we used to be good friends. i've known auggie since he was a baby.

oh, yeah, i think i knew that, i answer. i don't want to let on that olivia had not told me any of this. i don't want to let on how surprised i am that she called her via. nobody but olivia's family calls her via, and here this pink-haired girl, who i thought was a stranger, is calling her via.

miranda laughs and shakes her head but she doesn't say anything. there's an awkward silence and then she starts fishing through her bag and pulls out her wallet. she rifles through a couple of pictures and then hands one to me. it's of a little boy in a park on a sunny day. he's wearing shorts and a t-shirt—and an astronaut helmet that covers his entire head.

it was like a hundred degrees that day, she says, smiling at the picture. but he wouldn't take that helmet off for anything. he wore it for like two years straight, in the winter, in the summer, at the beach. it was crazy.

yeah, i've seen pictures in olivia's house.

i'm the one who gave him that helmet, she says. she sounds a little proud of that. she takes the picture and carefully inserts it back into her wallet.

cool, i answer.

so you're okay with it? she says, looking at me.

i look at her blankly. okay with what?

she raises her eyebrows like she doesn't believe me. you know what i'm talking about, she says, and takes a long drink from her water bottle. let's face it, she continues, the universe was not kind to auggie pullman.

Bird

why didn't you tell me that you and miranda navas used to be friends? i say to olivia the next day. i'm really annoyed at her for not telling me this.

it's not a big deal, she answers defensively, looking at me like i'm weird.

it is a big deal, i say. i looked like an idiot. how could you not tell me? you've always acted like you don't even know her.

i don't know her, she answers quickly. i don't know who that pink-haired cheerleader is. the girl i knew was a total dork who collected american girl dolls.

oh come on, olivia.

you come on!

you could have mentioned it to me at some point, i say quietly, pretending not to notice the big fat tear that's suddenly rolling down her cheek.

she shrugs, fighting back bigger tears.

it's okay, i'm not mad, i say, thinking the tears are about me.

i honestly don't care if you're mad, she says spitefully.

oh, that's real nice, i fire back.

she doesn't say anything. the tears are about to come.

olivia, what's the matter? i say.

she shakes her head like she doesn't want to talk about it, but all of a sudden the tears start rolling a mile a minute.

i'm sorry, it's not you, justin. i'm not crying because of you, she finally says through her tears.

then why are you crying?

because i'm an awful person.

what are you talking about?

she's not looking at me, wiping her tears with the palm of her hand.

i haven't told my parents about the show, she says quickly.

i shake my head because i don't quite get what she's telling me. that's okay, i say. it's not too late, there are still tickets available—

i don't want them to come to the show, justin, she interrupts impatiently. don't you see what i'm saying? i don't want them to come! if they come, they'll bring auggie with them, and i just don't feel like . . .

here she's hit by another round of crying that doesn't let her finish talking. i put my arm around her.

i'm an awful person! she says through her tears.

you're not an awful person, i say softly.

yes i am! she sobs. it's just been so nice being in a new school where nobody knows about him, you know? nobody's whispering about it behind my back. it's just been so nice, justin. but if he comes to the play, then everyone will talk about it, everyone will know. . . . i don't know why i'm feeling like this. . . . i swear i've never been embarrassed by him before.

i know, i know, i say, soothing her. you're entitled, olivia. you've dealt with a lot your whole life.

olivia reminds me of a bird sometimes, how her feathers get all ruffled when she's mad. and when she's fragile like this, she's a little lost bird looking for its nest.

so i give her my wing to hide under.

The Universe

i can't sleep tonight. my head is full of thoughts that won't turn off. lines from my monologues. elements of the periodic table that i'm supposed to be memorizing. theorems i'm supposed to be understanding. olivia. auggie.

miranda's words keep coming back: the universe was not kind to auggie pullman.

i'm thinking about that a lot and everything it means. she's right about that. the universe was not kind to auggie pullman. what did that little kid ever do to deserve his sentence? what did the parents do? or olivia? she once mentioned that some doctor told her parents that the odds of someone getting the same combination of syndromes that came together to make auggie's face were like one in four million. so doesn't that make the universe a giant lottery, then? you purchase a ticket when you're born. and it's all just random whether you get a good ticket or a bad ticket. it's all just luck.

my head swirls on this, but then softer thoughts soothe, like a flatted third on a major chord. no, no, it's not all random. if it really was all random, the universe would abandon us completely. and the universe doesn't. it takes care of its most fragile creations in ways we can't see. like with parents who adore you blindly. and a big sister who feels guilty for being human over you. and a little gravelly-voiced kid whose friends have left him over you. and even a pink-haired girl who carries your picture in her wallet. maybe it is a lottery, but the universe makes it all even out in the end. the universe takes care of all its birds.

Part Six

AUGUST

What a piece of work is a man! how noble in reason! how

infinite in faculty! in form and moving how express and

admirable! in action how like an angel! in apprehension

how like a god! the beauty of the world! . . .

—Shakespeare, *Hamlet*

North Pole

The Spud Lamp was a big hit at the science fair. Jack and I got an A for it. It was the first A Jack got in any class all year long, so he was psyched.

All the science-fair projects were set up on tables in the gym. It was the same setup as the Egyptian Museum back in December, except this time there were volcanoes and molecule dioramas on the tables instead of pyramids and pharaohs. And instead of the kids taking our parents around to look at everybody else's artifact, we had to stand by our tables while all the parents wandered around the room and came over to us one by one.

Here's the math on that one: Sixty kids in the grade equals sixty sets of parents—and doesn't even include grandparents. So that's a minimum of one hundred and twenty pairs of eyes that find their way over to me. Eyes that aren't as used to me as their kids' eyes are by now. It's like how compass needles always point north, no matter which way you're facing. All those eyes are compasses, and I'm like the North Pole to them.

That's why I still don't like school events that include parents. I don't hate them as much as I did at the beginning of the school year. Like the Thanksgiving Sharing Festival: that was the worst one, I think. That was the first time I had to face the parents all at once. The Egyptian Museum came after that, but that one was okay because I got to dress up as a mummy and nobody noticed me. Then came the winter concert, which I totally hated because I had to sing in the chorus. Not only can I not sing at all, but it felt like I was on display. The New Year

Art Show wasn't quite as bad, but it was still annoying. They put up our artwork in the hallways all over the school and had the parents come and check it out. It was like starting school all over again, having unsuspecting adults pass me on the stairway.

Anyway, it's not that I care that people react to me. Like I've said a gazillion times: I'm used to that by now. I don't let it bother me. It's like when you go outside and it's drizzling a little. You don't put on boots for a drizzle. You don't even open your umbrella. You walk through it and barely notice your hair getting wet.

But when it's a huge gym full of parents, the drizzle becomes like this total hurricane. Everyone's eyes hit you like a wall of water.

Mom and Dad hang around my table a lot, along with Jack's parents. It's kind of funny how parents actually end up forming the same little groups their kids form. Like my parents and Jack's and Summer's mom all like and get along with each other. And I see Julian's parents hang out with Henry's parents and Miles's parents. And even the two Maxes' parents hang out together. It's so funny.

I told Mom and Dad about it later when we were walking home, and they thought it was a funny observation.

I guess it's true that like seeks like, said Mom.

The Auggie Doll

For a while, the "war" was all we talked about. February was when it was really at its worst. That's when practically nobody was talking to us, and Julian had started leaving notes in our lockers. The notes to Jack were stupid, like: *You stink, big cheese!* and *Nobody likes you anymore!*

I got notes like: *Freak!* And another that said: *Get out of our school, orc!*

Summer thought we should report the notes to Ms. Rubin, who was the middle-school dean, or even Mr. Tushman, but we thought that would be like snitching. Anyway, it's not like we didn't leave notes, too, though ours weren't really mean. They were kind of funny and sarcastic.

One was: *You're so pretty, Julian! I love you. Will you marry me? Love, Beulah*

Another was: *Love your hair! xox Beulah*

Another was: *You're a babe. Tickle my feet. xo Beulah*

Beulah was a made-up person that me and Jack came up with. She had really gross habits, like eating the green stuff in between her toes and sucking on her knuckles. And we figured someone like that would have a real crush on Julian, who looked and acted like someone in a KidzBop commercial.

There were also a couple of times in February when Julian, Miles, and Henry played tricks on Jack. They didn't play tricks on me, I think, because they knew that if they got caught "bullying" me, it would be big-time trouble for them. Jack, they figured, was an easier target. So one time they stole his gym shorts and played Monkey in the Middle with them in the locker room. Another time Miles, who sat next to Jack in homeroom, swiped Jack's worksheet off his desk, crumpled it in a ball, and tossed it to Julian across the room. This wouldn't have happened if Ms. Petosa had been there, of course, but there was a substitute teacher that day, and subs never really know what's going on. Jack was good about this stuff. He never let them see he was upset, though I think sometimes he was.

The other kids in the grade knew about the war. Except for Savanna's group, the girls were neutral at first. But by March they were getting sick of it. And so were some of the boys. Like another time when Julian was dumping some pencil-sharpener shavings into Jack's backpack, Amos, who was usually tight with them, grabbed the backpack out of Julian's hands and returned it to Jack. It was starting to feel like the majority of boys weren't buying into Julian anymore.

Then a few weeks ago, Julian started spreading this ridiculous rumor that Jack had hired some "hit man" to "get" him and Miles and Henry. This lie was so pathetic that people were actually laughing about him behind his back. At that point, any boys who had still been on his side now jumped ship and were clearly neutral. So by the end of March, only Miles and Henry were on Julian's side—and I think even they were getting tired of the war by then.

I'm pretty sure everyone's stopped playing the Plague game behind my back, too. No one really cringes if I bump into them anymore, and people borrow my pencils without acting like the pencil has cooties.

People even joke around with me now sometimes. Like the other day I saw Maya writing a note to Ellie on a piece of Uglydoll stationery, and I don't know why, but I just kind of randomly said: "Did you know the guy who created the Uglydolls based them on me?"

Maya looked at me with her eyes wide open like she totally believed me. Then, when she realized I was only kidding, she thought it was the funniest thing in the world.

"You are so funny, August!" she said, and then she told Ellie and some of the other girls what I had just said, and they all thought it was funny, too. Like at first they were shocked, but then when they saw I was laughing about it, they knew it was okay to laugh about it, too. And the next day I found a little Uglydoll key chain sitting on my chair with a nice little note from Maya that said: *For the nicest Auggie Doll in the world! xo Maya.*

Six months ago stuff like that would never have happened, but now it happens more and more.

Also, people have been really nice about the hearing aids I started wearing.

Lobot

Ever since I was little, the doctors told my parents that someday I'd need hearing aids. I don't know why this always freaked me out a bit: maybe because anything to do with my ears bothers me a lot.

My hearing was getting worse, but I hadn't told anyone about it. The ocean sound that was always in my head had been getting louder. It was drowning out people's voices, like I was underwater. I couldn't hear teachers if I sat in the back of the class. But I knew if I told Mom or Dad about it, I'd end up with hearing aids—and I was hoping I could make it through the fifth grade without having that happen.

But then in my annual checkup in October I flunked the audiology test and the doctor was like, "Dude, it's time." And he sent me to a special ear doctor who took impressions of my ears.

Out of all my features, my ears are the ones I hate the most. They're like tiny closed fists on the sides of my face. They're too low on my head, too. They look like squashed pieces of pizza dough sticking out of the top of my neck or something. Okay, maybe I'm exaggerating a little. But I really hate them.

When the ear doctor first pulled the hearing aids out for me and Mom to look at, I groaned.

"I am not wearing that thing," I announced, folding my arms in front of me.

"I know they probably look kind of big," said the ear doctor, "but we had to attach them to the headband because we had no other way of making them so they'd stay in your ears."

See, normal hearing aids usually have a part that wraps around the outer ear to hold the inner bud in place. But in my case, since I don't have outer ears, they had to put the earbuds on this heavy-duty headband that was supposed to wrap around the back of my head.

"I can't wear that, Mom," I whined.

"You'll hardly notice them," said Mom, trying to be cheerful. "They look like headphones."

"Headphones? Look at them, Mom!" I said angrily. "I'll look like Lobot!"

"Which one is Lobot?" said Mom calmly.

"Lobot?" The ear doctor smiled as he looked at the headphones and made some adjustments. *The Empire Strikes Back?* The bald guy with the cool bionic radio-transmitter thing that wraps around the back of his skull?"

"I'm drawing a blank," said Mom.

"You know *Star Wars* stuff?" I asked the ear doctor.

"Know *Star Wars* stuff?" he answered, slipping the thing over my head. "I practically invented *Star Wars* stuff!" He leaned back in his chair to see how the headband fit and then took it off again.

"Now, Auggie, I want to explain what all this is," he said, pointing to the different parts of one of the hearing aids. "This curved piece of plastic over here connects to the tubing on the ear mold. That's why we took those impressions back in December, so that this part that goes inside your ear fits nice and snug. This part here is called the tone hook, okay? And this thing is the special part we've attached to this cradle here."

"The Lobot part," I said miserably.

"Hey, Lobot is cool," said the ear doctor. "It's not like we're saying you're going to look like Jar Jar, you know? That would be bad." He slid the earphones on my head again carefully. "There you go, August. So how's that?"

"Totally uncomfortable!" I said.

"You'll get used to them very quickly," he said.

I looked in the mirror. My eyes started tearing up. All I saw were these tubes jutting out from either side of my head—like antennas.

"Do I really have to wear this, Mom?" I said, trying not to cry. "I hate them. They don't make any difference!"

"Give it a second, buddy," said the doctor. "I haven't even turned them on yet. Wait until you hear the difference: you'll want to wear them."

"No I won't!"

And then he turned them on.

Hearing Brightly

How can I describe what I heard when the doctor turned on my hearing aids? Or what I didn't hear? It's too hard to think of words. The ocean just wasn't living inside my head anymore. It was gone. I could hear sounds like shiny lights in my brain. It was like when you're in a room where one of the lightbulbs on the ceiling isn't working, but you don't realize how dark it is until someone changes the lightbulb and then you're like, whoa, it's so bright in here! I don't know if there's a word that means the same as "bright" in terms of hearing, but I wish I knew one, because my ears were hearing brightly now.

"How does it sound, Auggie?" said the ear doctor. "Can you hear me okay, buddy?"

I looked at him and smiled but I didn't answer.

"Sweetie, do you hear anything different?" said Mom.

"You don't have to shout, Mom." I nodded happily.

"Are you hearing better?" asked the ear doctor.

"I don't hear that noise anymore," I answered. "It's so quiet in my ears."

"The white noise is gone," he said, nodding. He looked at me and winked. "I told you you'd like what you heard, August." He made more adjustments on the left hearing aid.

"Does it sound very different, love?" Mom asked.

"Yeah." I nodded. "It sounds . . . lighter."

"That's because you have bionic hearing now, buddy," said the ear doctor, adjusting the right side. "Now touch here." He put my hand behind the hearing aid. "Do you feel that? That's the volume. You have to find the volume that works for you. We're going to do that next. Well, what do you think?" He picked up a small mirror and had me look in the big mirror at how the hearing aids looked in the back. My hair covered most of the headband. The only part that peeked out was the tubing.

"Are you okay with your new bionic Lobot hearing aids?" the ear doctor asked, looking in the mirror at me.

"Yeah," I said. "Thank you."

"Thank you so much, Dr. James," said Mom.

The first day I showed up at school with the hearing aids, I thought kids would make a big deal about it. But no one did. Summer was glad I could hear better, and Jack said it made me look like an FBI agent or something. But that was it. Mr. Browne asked me about it in English class, but it wasn't like, what the heck is that thing on your head?! It was more like, "If you ever need me to repeat something, Auggie, make sure you tell me, okay?"

Now that I look back, I don't know why I was so stressed about it all this time. Funny how sometimes you worry a lot about something and it turns out to be nothing.

Via's Secret

A couple of days after spring break ended, Mom found out that Via hadn't told her about a school play that was happening at her high school the next week. And Mom was mad. Mom doesn't really get mad that much (though Dad would disagree with that), but she was really mad at Via for that. She and Via got into a huge fight. I could hear them yelling at each other in Via's room. My bionic Lobot ears could hear Mom saying: "But what is with you lately, Via? You're moody and taciturn and secretive. . . ."

"What is so wrong with my not telling you about a stupid play?" Via practically screamed. "I don't even have a speaking part in it!"

"Your boyfriend does! Don't you want us to see him in it?"

"No! Actually, I don't!"

"Stop screaming!"

"You screamed first! Just leave me alone, okay? You've been really good about leaving me alone my whole life, so why you choose high school to suddenly be interested I have no idea. . . ."

Then I don't know what Mom answered because it all got very quiet, and even my bionic Lobot ears couldn't pick up a signal.

My Cave

By dinner they seemed to have made up. Dad was working late. Daisy was sleeping. She'd thrown up a lot earlier in the day, and Mom made an appointment to take her to the vet the next morning.

The three of us were sitting down and no one was talking.

Finally, I said: "So, are we going to see Justin in a play?"

Via didn't answer but looked down at her plate.

"You know, Auggie," said Mom quietly. "I hadn't realized what play it was, and it really isn't something that would be interesting to kids your age."

"So I'm not invited?" I said, looking at Via.

"I didn't say that," said Mom. "It's just I don't think it's something you'd enjoy."

"You'd get totally bored," said Via, like she was accusing me of something.

"Are you and Dad going?" I asked.

"Dad'll go," said Mom. "I'll stay home with you."

"What?" Via yelled at Mom. "Oh great, so you're going to punish me for being honest by not going?"

"You didn't want us to go in the first place, remember?" answered Mom.

"But now that you know about it, of course I want you to go!" said Via.

"Well, I've got to weigh *everyone's* feelings here, Via," said Mom.

"What are you two talking about?" I shouted.

"Nothing!" they both snapped at the same time.

"Just something about Via's school that has nothing to do with you," said Mom.

"You're lying," I said.

"Excuse me?" said Mom, kind of shocked. Even Via looked surprised.

"I said you're lying!" I shouted. "You're lying!" I screamed at Via, getting up. "You're both liars! You're both lying to my face like I'm an idiot!"

"Sit down, Auggie!" said Mom, grabbing my arm.

I pulled my arm away and pointed at Via.

"You think I don't know what's going on?" I yelled. "You just don't want your brand-new fancy high school friends to know your brother's a freak!"

"Auggie!" Mom yelled. "That's not true!"

"Stop lying to me, Mom!" I shrieked. "Stop treating me like a baby! I'm not retarded! I know what's going on!"

I ran down the hallway to my room and slammed the door behind me so hard that I actually heard little pieces of the wall crumble inside the door frame. Then I plopped onto my bed and pulled the covers up on top of me. I threw my pillows over my disgusting face and then piled all my stuffed animals on top of the pillows, like I was inside a little cave. If I could walk around with a pillow over my face all the time, I would.

I don't even know how I got so mad. I wasn't really mad at the beginning of dinner. I wasn't even sad. But then all of a sudden it all kind of just exploded out of me. I knew Via didn't want me to go to her stupid play. And I knew why.

I figured Mom would follow me into my room right away, but she didn't. I wanted her to find me inside my cave of stuffed animals, so I waited a little more, but even after ten minutes she still didn't come in after me. I was pretty surprised. She always checks on me when I'm in my room, upset about stuff.

220

I pictured Mom and Via talking about me in the kitchen. I figured Via was feeling really, really, really bad. I pictured Mom totally laying on the guilt. And Dad would be mad at her when he came home, too.

I made a little hole through the pile of pillows and stuffed animals and peeked at the clock on my wall. Half an hour had passed and Mom still hadn't come into my room. I tried to listen for the sounds in the other rooms. Were they still having dinner? What was going on?

Finally, the door opened. It was Via. She didn't even bother coming over to my bed, and she didn't come in softly like I thought she would. She came in quickly.

Goodbye

"Auggie," said Via. "Come quick. Mom needs to talk to you."

"I'm not apologizing!"

"This isn't about you!" she yelled. "Not everything in the world is about you, Auggie! Now hurry up. Daisy's sick. Mom's taking her to the emergency vet. Come say goodbye."

I pushed the pillows off my face and looked up at her. That's when I saw she was crying. "What do you mean 'goodbye'?"

"Come on!" she said, holding out her hand.

I took her hand and followed her down the hall to the kitchen. Daisy was lying down sideways on the floor with her legs straight out in front of her. She was panting a lot, like she'd been running in the park. Mom was kneeling beside her, stroking the top of her head.

"What happened?" I asked.

"She just started whimpering all of a sudden," said Via, kneeling down next to Mom.

I looked down at Mom, who was crying, too.

"I'm taking her to the animal hospital downtown," she said. "The taxi's coming to pick me up."

"The vet'll make her better, right?" I said.

Mom looked at me. "I hope so, honey," she said quietly. "But I honestly don't know."

"Of course he will!" I said.

"Daisy's been sick a lot lately, Auggie. And she's old . . ."

"But they can fix her," I said, looking at Via to agree with me, but Via wouldn't look up at me.

Mom's lips were trembling. "I think it might be time we say goodbye to Daisy, Auggie. I'm sorry."

"No!" I said.

"We don't want her to suffer, Auggie," she said.

The phone rang. Via picked it up, said, "Okay, thanks," and then hung up.

"The taxi's outside," she said, wiping her tears with the backs of her hands.

"Okay, Auggie, open the door for me, sweetie?" said Mom, picking Daisy up very gently like she was a huge droopy baby.

"Please, no, Mommy?" I cried, putting myself in front of the door.

"Honey, please," said Mom. "She's very heavy."

"What about Daddy?" I cried.

"He's meeting me at the hospital," Mom said. "He doesn't want Daisy to suffer, Auggie."

Via moved me away from the door and held it open it for Mom.

"My cell phone's on if you need anything," Mom said to Via. "Can you cover her with the blanket?"

Via nodded, but she was crying hysterically now.

"Say goodbye to Daisy, kids," Mom said, tears streaming down her face.

"I love you, Daisy," Via said, kissing Daisy on the nose. "I love you so much."

"Bye, little girlie . . . ," I whispered into Daisy's ear. "I love you. . . ."

Mom carried Daisy down the stoop. The taxi driver had opened the back door and we watched her get in. Just before she closed the door, Mom looked up at us standing by the entrance to the building and she gave us a little wave. I don't think I've ever seen her look sadder.

"I love you, Mommy!" said Via.

"I love you, Mommy!" I said. "I'm sorry, Mommy!"

Mom blew a kiss to us and closed the door. We watched the car leave and then Via closed the door. She looked at me a second, and then she hugged me very, very tight while we both cried a million tears.

Daisy's Toys

Justin came over about half an hour later. He gave me a big hug and said: "Sorry, Auggie." We all sat down in the living room, not saying anything. For some reason, Via and I had taken all of Daisy's toys from around the house and had put them in a little pile on the coffee table. Now we just stared at the pile.

"She really is the greatest dog in the world," said Via.

"I know," said Justin, rubbing Via's back.

"She just started whimpering, like all of a sudden?" I said.

Via nodded. "Like two seconds after you left the table," she said. "Mom was going to go after you, but Daisy just started, like, whimpering."

"Like how?" I said.

"Just whimpering, I don't know," said Via.

"Like howling?" I asked.

"Auggie, like whimpering!" she answered impatiently. "She just started moaning, like something was really hurting her. And she was panting like crazy. Then she just kind of plopped down, and Mom went over and tried to pick her up, and whatever, she was obviously hurting. She bit Mom."

"What?" I said.

"When Mom tried to touch her stomach, Daisy bit her hand," Via explained.

"Daisy never bites anybody!" I answered.

"She wasn't herself," said Justin. "She was obviously in pain."

"Daddy was right," said Via. "We shouldn't have let her get this bad."

"What do you mean?" I said. "He knew she was sick?"

"Auggie, Mom's taken her to the vet like three times in the last two months. She's been throwing up left and right. Haven't you noticed?"

"But I didn't know she was sick!"

Via didn't say anything, but she put her arm around my shoulders and pulled me closer to her. I started to cry again.

"I'm sorry, Auggie," she said softly. "I'm really sorry about everything, okay? You forgive me? You know how much I love you, right?"

I nodded. Somehow that fight didn't matter much now.

"Was Mommy bleeding?" I asked.

"It was just a nip," said Via. "Right there." She pointed to the bottom of her thumb to show me exactly where Daisy had bitten Mom.

"Did it hurt her?"

"Mommy's okay, Auggie. She's fine."

Mom and Dad came home two hours later. We knew the second they opened the door and Daisy wasn't with them that Daisy was gone. We all sat down in the living room around the pile of Daisy's toys. Dad told us what happened at the animal hospital, how the vet took Daisy for some X-rays and blood tests, then came back and told them she had a huge mass in her stomach. She was having trouble breathing. Mom and Dad didn't want her to suffer, so Daddy picked her up in his arms like he always liked to do, with her legs straight up in the air, and he and Mom kissed her goodbye over and over again and whispered to her while the vet put a needle into her leg. And then after about a minute she died in Daddy's arms. It was so peaceful, Daddy said. She wasn't in any pain at all. Like she was just going to sleep. A couple of times while he talked, Dad's voice got trembly and he cleared his throat.

226

I've never seen Dad cry before, but I saw him cry tonight. I had gone into Mom and Dad's bedroom looking for Mom to put me to bed, but saw Dad sitting on the edge of the bed, taking off his socks. His back was to the door, so he didn't know I was there. At first I thought he was laughing because his shoulders were shaking, but then he put his palms on his eyes and I realized he was crying. It was the quietest crying I've ever heard. Like a whisper. I was going to go over to him, but then I thought maybe he was whisper-crying because he didn't want me or anyone else to hear him. So I walked out and went to Via's room, and I saw Mom lying next to Via on the bed, and Mom was whispering to Via, who was crying.

So I went to my bed and put on my pajamas without anyone telling me to and put the night-light on and turned the light off and crawled into the little mountain of stuffed animals I had left on my bed earlier. It felt like that all had happened a million years ago. I took my hearing aids off and put them on the night table and pulled the covers up to my ears and imagined Daisy snuggling with me, her big wet tongue licking my face all over like it was her favorite face in the world. And that's how I fell asleep.

Heaven

I woke up later on and it was still dark. I got out of bed and walked into Mom and Dad's bedroom.

"Mommy?" I whispered. It was completely dark, so I couldn't see her open her eyes. "Mommy?"

"You okay, honey?" she said groggily.

"Can I sleep with you?"

Mom scooted over toward Daddy's side of the bed, and I snuggled up next to her. She kissed my hair.

"Is your hand okay?" I said. "Via told me Daisy bit you."

"It was only a nip," she whispered in my ear.

"Mommy . . ." I started crying. "I'm sorry about what I said."

"Shhh . . . There's nothing to be sorry about," she said, so quietly I could barely hear her. She was rubbing the side of her face against my face.

"Is Via ashamed of me?" I said.

"No, honey, no. You know she's not. She's just adjusting to a new school. It's not easy."

"I know."

"I know you know."

"I'm sorry I called you a liar."

"Go to sleep, sweet boy. . . . I love you so much."

"I love you so much, too, Mommy."

"Good night, honey," she said very softly.

"Mommy, is Daisy with Grans now?"

"I think so."

"Are they in heaven?"

"Yes."

"Do people look the same when they get to heaven?"

"I don't know. I don't think so."

"Then how do people recognize each other?"

"I don't know, sweetie." She sounded tired. "They just feel it. You don't need your eyes to love, right? You just feel it inside you. That's how it is in heaven. It's just love, and no one forgets who they love."

She kissed me again.

"Now go to sleep, honey. It's late. And I'm so tired."

But I couldn't go to sleep, even after I knew she had fallen asleep. I could hear Daddy sleeping, too, and I imagined I could hear Via sleeping down the hallway in her room. And I wondered if Daisy was sleeping in heaven right then. And if she was sleeping, was she dreaming about me? And I wondered how it would feel to be in heaven someday and not have my face matter anymore. Just like it never, ever mattered to Daisy.

Understudy

Via brought home three tickets to her school play a few days after Daisy died. We never mentioned the fight we had over dinner again. On the night of the play, right before she and Justin were leaving to get to their school early, she gave me a big hug and told me she loved me and she was proud to be my sister.

This was my first time in Via's new school. It was much bigger than her old school, and a thousand times bigger than my school. More hallways. More room for people. The only really bad thing about my bionic Lobot hearing aids was the fact that I couldn't wear a baseball cap anymore. In situations like these, baseball caps come in really handy. Sometimes I wish I could still get away with wearing that old astronaut helmet I used to wear when I was little. Believe it or not, people would think seeing a kid in an astronaut helmet was a lot less weird than seeing my face. Anyway, I kept my head down as I walked right behind Mom through the long bright hallways.

We followed the crowd to the auditorium, where students handed out programs at the front entrance. We found seats in the fifth row, close to the middle. As soon as we sat down, Mom started looking inside her pocketbook.

"I can't believe I forgot my glasses!" she said.

Dad shook his head. Mom was always forgetting her glasses, or her keys, or something or other. She is flaky that way.

"You want to move closer?" said Dad.

Mom squinted at the stage. "No, I can see okay."

"Speak now or forever hold your peace," said Dad.

"I'm fine," answered Mom.

"Look, there's Justin," I said to Dad, pointing out Justin's picture in the program.

"That's a nice picture of him," he answered, nodding.

"How come there's no picture of Via?" I said.

"She's an understudy," said Mom. "But, look: here's her name."

"Why do they call her an understudy?" I asked.

"Wow, look at Miranda's picture," said Mom to Dad. "I don't think I would have recognized her."

"Why do they call it understudy?" I repeated.

"It's what they call someone who replaces an actor if he can't perform for some reason," answered Mom.

"Did you hear Martin's getting remarried?" Dad said to Mom.

"Are you kidding me?!" Mom answered, like she was surprised.

"Who's Martin?" I asked.

"Miranda's father," Mom answered, and then to Dad: "Who told you?"

"I ran into Miranda's mother in the subway. She's not happy about it. He has a new baby on the way and everything."

"Wow," said Mom, shaking her head.

"What are you guys talking about?" I said.

"Nothing," answered Dad.

"But why do they call it understudy?" I said.

"I don't know, Auggie Doggie," Dad answered. "Maybe because the actors kind of study under the main actors or something? I really don't know."

I was going to say something else but then the lights went down. The audience got very quiet very quickly.

"Daddy, can you please not call me Auggie Doggie anymore?" I whispered in Dad's ear.

Dad smiled and nodded and gave me a thumbs-up.

The play started. The curtain opened. The stage was completely empty except for Justin, who was sitting on an old rickety chair tuning his fiddle. He was wearing an old-fashioned type of suit and a straw hat.

"This play is called 'Our Town,'" he said to the audience. "It was written by Thornton Wilder; produced and directed by Philip Davenport. . . . The name of the town is Grover's Corners, New Hampshire—just across the Massachusetts line: latitude 42 degrees 40 minutes; longitude 70 degrees 37 minutes. The First Act shows a day in our town. The day is May 7, 1901. The time is just before dawn."

I knew right then and there that I was going to like the play. It wasn't like other school plays I've been to, like *The Wizard of Oz* or *Cloudy with a Chance of Meatballs*. No, this was grown-up seeming, and I felt smart sitting there watching it.

A little later in the play, a character named Mrs. Webb calls out for her daughter, Emily. I knew from the program that that was the part Miranda was playing, so I leaned forward to get a better look at her.

"That's Miranda," Mom whispered to me, squinting at the stage when Emily walked out. "She looks so different. . . ."

"It's not Miranda," I whispered. "It's Via."

"Oh my God!" said Mom, lurching forward in her seat.

"Shh!" said Dad.

"It's Via," Mom whispered to him.

"I know," whispered Dad, smiling. "Shhh!"

The Ending

The play was so amazing. I don't want to give away the ending, but it's the kind of ending that makes people in the audience teary. Mom totally lost it when Via-as-Emily said:

"Good-by, Good-by world! Good-by, Grover's Corners . . . Mama and Papa. Good-by to clocks ticking and Mama's sunflowers. And food and coffee. And new-ironed dresses and hot baths . . . and sleeping and waking up. Oh, earth, you're too wonderful for anybody to realize you!"

Via was actually crying while she was saying this. Like real tears: I could see them rolling down her cheeks. It was totally awesome.

After the curtain closed, everyone in the audience started clapping. Then the actors came out one by one. Via and Justin were the last ones out, and when they appeared, the whole audience rose to their feet.

"Bravo!" I heard Dad yelling through his hands.

"Why is everyone getting up?" I said.

"It's a standing ovation," said Mom, getting up.

So I got up and clapped and clapped. I clapped until my hands hurt. For a second, I imagined how cool it would be to be Via and Justin right then, having all these people standing up and cheering for them. I think there should be a rule that everyone in the world should get a standing ovation at least once in their lives.

Finally, after I don't know how many minutes, the line of actors onstage stepped back and the curtain closed in front of them. The clapping stopped and the lights went up and the audience started getting up to leave.

Me and Mom and Dad made our way to the backstage. Crowds of people were congratulating the performers, surrounding them, patting them on the back. We saw Via and Justin at the center of the crowd, smiling at everyone, laughing and talking.

"Via!" shouted Dad, waving as he made his way through the crowd. When he got close enough, he hugged her and lifted her off the floor a little. "You were amazing, sweetheart!"

"Oh my God, Via!" Mom was screaming with excitement. "Oh my God, oh my God!" She was hugging Via so hard I thought Via would suffocate, but Via was laughing.

"You were brilliant!" said Dad.

"Brilliant!" Mom said, kind of nodding and shaking her head at the same time.

"And you, Justin," said Dad, shaking Justin's hand and giving him a hug at the same time. "You were fantastic!"

"Fantastic!" Mom repeated. She was, honestly, so emotional she could barely talk.

"What a shock to see you up there, Via!" said Dad.

"Mom didn't even recognize you at first!" I said.

"I didn't recognize you!" said Mom, her hand over her mouth.

"Miranda got sick right before the show started," said Via, all of out of breath. "There wasn't even time to make an announcement." I have to say she looked kind of strange, because she was wearing all this makeup and I'd never seen her like this before.

"And you just stepped in there right at the last minute?" said Dad. "Wow."

"She was amazing, wasn't she?" said Justin, his arm around Via.

"There wasn't a dry eye in the house," said Dad.

"Is Miranda okay?" I said, but no one heard me.

At that moment, a man who I think was their teacher came over to Justin and Via, clapping his hands.

"Bravo, bravo! Olivia and Justin!" He kissed Via on both cheeks.

"I flubbed a couple of lines," said Via, shaking her head.

"But you got through it," said the man, smiling ear to ear.

"Mr. Davenport, these are my parents," said Via.

"You must be so proud of your girl!" he said, shaking their hands with both his hands.

"We are!"

"And this is my little brother, August," said Via.

He looked like he was about to say something but suddenly froze when he looked at me.

"Mr. D," said Justin, pulling him by the arm, "come meet my mom."

Via was about to say something to me, but then someone else came over and started talking to her, and before I knew it, I was kind of alone in the crowd. I mean, I knew where Mom and Dad were, but there were so many people all around us, and people kept bumping into me, spinning me around a bit, giving me that one-two look, which made me feel kind of bad. I don't know if it was because I was feeling hot or something, but I kind of started getting dizzy. People's faces were blurring in my head. And their voices were so loud it was almost hurting my ears. I tried to turn the volume down on my Lobot ears, but I got confused and turned them louder at first, which kind of shocked me. And then I looked up and I didn't see Mom or Dad or Via anywhere.

"Via?" I yelled out. I started pushing through the crowd to find Mom. "Mommy!" I really couldn't see anything but people's stomachs and ties all around me. "Mommy!"

Suddenly someone picked me up from behind.

"Look who's here!" said a familiar voice, hugging me tight. I thought it was Via at first, but when I turned around, I was completely surprised. "Hey, Major Tom!" she said.

"Miranda!" I answered, and I gave her the tightest hug I could give.

Part Seven

MiRANDA

I forgot that I might see

So many beautiful things

I forgot that I might need

To find out what life could bring

—Andain, "Beautiful Things"

Camp Lies

My parents got divorced the summer before ninth grade. My father was with someone else right away. In fact, though my mother never said so, I think this was the reason they got divorced.

After the divorce, I hardly ever saw my father. And my mother acted stranger than ever. It's not that she was unstable or anything: just distant. Remote. My mother is the kind of person who has a happy face for the rest of the world but not a lot left over for me. She's never talked to me much—not about her feelings, her life. I don't know much about what she was like when she was my age. Don't know much about the things she liked or didn't like. The few times she mentioned her own parents, who I've never met, it was mostly about how she wanted to get as far away from them as she could once she'd grown up. She never told me why. I asked a few times, but she would pretend she hadn't heard me.

I didn't want to go to camp that summer. I had wanted to stay with her, to help her through the divorce. But she insisted I go away. I figured she wanted the alone time, so I gave it to her.

Camp was awful. I hated it. I thought it would be better being a junior counselor, but it wasn't. No one I knew from the previous year had come back, so I didn't know anyone—not a single person. I'm not even sure why, but I started playing this little make-believe game with the girls in the camp. They'd ask me stuff about myself, and I'd make things up: my parents are in

Europe, I told them. I live in a huge townhouse on the nicest street in North River Heights. I have a dog named Daisy.

Then one day I blurted out that I had a little brother who was deformed. I have absolutely no idea why I said this: it just seemed like an interesting thing to say. And, of course, the reaction I got from the little girls in the bungalow was dramatic. Really? So sorry! That must be tough! Et cetera. Et cetera. I regretted saying this the moment it escaped from my lips, of course: I felt like such a fake. If Via ever found out, I thought, she'd think I was such a weirdo. And I felt like a weirdo. But, I have to admit, there was a part of me that felt a little entitled to this lie. I've known Auggie since I was six years old. I've watched him grow up. I've played with him. I've watched all six episodes of *Star Wars* for his sake, so I could talk to him about the aliens and bounty hunters and all that. I'm the one that gave him the astronaut helmet he wouldn't take off for two years. I mean, I've kind of earned the right to think of him as my brother.

And the strangest thing is that these lies I told, these fictions, did wonders for my popularity. The other junior counselors heard it from the campers, and they were all over it. Never in my life have I ever been considered one of the "popular" girls in anything, but that summer in camp, for whatever reason, I was the girl everybody wanted to hang out with. Even the girls in bungalow 32 were totally into me. These were the girls at the top of the food chain. They said they liked my hair (though they changed it). They said they liked the way I did my makeup (though they changed that, too). They showed me how to turn my T-shirts into halter tops. We smoked. We snuck out late at night and took the path through the woods to the boys' camp. We hung out with boys.

When I got home from camp, I called Ella right away to make plans with her. I don't know why I didn't call Via. I guess I just didn't feel like talking about stuff with her. She would have asked me about my parents, about camp. Ella never really asked me about things. She was an easier friend to have in that way. She wasn't serious like Via. She was fun. She thought it was cool when I dyed my hair pink. She wanted to hear all about those trips through the woods late at night.

School

I hardly saw Via at school this year, and when I did it was awkward. It felt like she was judging me. I knew she didn't like my new look. I knew she didn't like my group of friends. I didn't much like hers. We never actually argued: we just drifted away. Ella and I badmouthed her to each other: She's such a prude, she's so this, she's so that. We knew we were being mean, but it was easier to ice her out if we pretended she had done something to us. The truth is she hadn't changed at all: we had. We'd become these other people, and she was still the person she'd always been. That annoyed me so much and I didn't know why.

Once in a while I'd look to see where she was sitting in the lunchroom, or check the elective lists to see what she'd signed up for. But except for a few nods in the hallway and an occasional "hello," we never really spoke to each other.

I noticed Justin about halfway through the school year. I hadn't noticed him at all before then, other than that he was this skinny cutish dude with thick glasses and longish hair who carried a violin everywhere. Then one day I saw him in front of the school with his arm around Via. "So Via has a boyfriend!" I said to Ella, kind of mocking. I don't know why it surprised me that she'd have a boyfriend. Out of the three of us, she was totally the prettiest: blue, blue eyes and long wavy dark hair. But she'd just never acted like she was at all interested in boys. She acted like she was too smart for that kind of stuff.

I had a boyfriend, too: a guy named Zack. When I told him I was choosing the theater elective, he shook his head and said: "Careful you don't turn into a drama geek." Not the most sympathetic dude in the world, but very cute. Very high up on the totem pole. A varsity jock.

I wasn't planning on taking theater at first. Then I saw Via's name on the sign-up sheet and just wrote my name down on the list. I don't even know why. We managed to avoid one another throughout most of the semester, like we didn't even know each other. Then one day I got to theater class a little early, and Davenport asked me to run off additional copies of the play he was planning on having us do for the spring production: *The Elephant Man*. I'd heard about it but I didn't really know what it was about, so I started skimming through the pages while I was waiting for the xerox machine. It was about a man who lived more than a hundred years ago named John Merrick who was terribly deformed.

"We can't do this play, Mr. D," I told him when I got back to class, and I told him why: my little brother has a birth defect and has a deformed face and this play would hit too close to home. He seemed annoyed and a little unsympathetic, but I kind of said that my parents would have a real issue with the school doing this play. So anyway, he ended up switching to *Our Town*.

I think I went for the role of Emily Gibbs because I knew Via was going to go for it, too. It never occurred to me that I'd beat her for the role.

What I Miss Most

One of the things I miss the most about Via's friendship is her family. I loved her mom and dad. They were always so welcoming and nice to me. I knew they loved their kids more than anything. I always felt safe around them: safer than anywhere else in the world. How pathetic that I felt safer in someone else's house than in my own, right? And, of course, I loved Auggie. I was never afraid of him: even when I was little. I had friends that couldn't believe I'd ever go over to Via's house. "His face creeps me out," they'd say. "You're stupid," I'd tell them. Auggie's face isn't so bad once you get used to it.

I called Via's house once just to say hello to Auggie. Maybe part of me was hoping Via would answer, I don't know.

"Hey, Major Tom!" I said, using my nickname for him.

"Miranda!" He sounded so happy to hear my voice it actually kind of took me by surprise. "I'm going to a regular school now!" he told me excitedly.

"Really? Wow!" I said, totally shocked. I guess I never thought he'd go to a regular school. His parents have always been so protective of him. I guess I thought he'd always be that little kid in the astronaut helmet I gave him. Talking to him, I could tell he had no idea that Via and I weren't close anymore. "It's different in high school," I explained to him. "You end up hanging out with loads of different people."

"I have some friends in my new school," he told me. "A kid named Jack and a girl named Summer."

"That's awesome, Auggie," I said. "Well, I was just calling to tell you I miss you and hope you're having a good year. Feel free to call me whenever you want, okay, Auggie? You know I love you always."

"I love you, too, Miranda!"

"Say hi to Via for me. Tell her I miss her."

"I will. Bye!"

"Bye!"

Extraordinary,
but No One There to See

Neither my mother nor my father could come see the play on opening night: my mother because she had this thing at work, and my dad because his new wife was going to have her baby any second now, and he had to be on call.

Zack couldn't come to opening night, either: he had a volleyball game against Collegiate he couldn't miss. In fact, he had wanted me to miss the opening night so I could come cheer him on. My "friends" all went to the game, of course, because all their boyfriends were playing. Even Ella didn't come. Given a choice, she chose the crowd.

So on opening night no one that was remotely close to me was even there. And the thing is, I realized in my third or fourth rehearsal that I was good at this acting thing. I felt the part. I understood the words I spoke. I could read the lines as if they were coming from my brain and my heart. And on opening night, I can honestly say I knew I was going to be more than good: I was going to be great. I was going to be extraordinary, but there would be no one there to see.

We were all backstage, nervously running through our lines in our heads. I peeked through the curtain at the people taking their seats in the auditorium. That's when I saw Auggie walking down the aisle with Isabel and Nate. They took three seats in the fifth row, near the middle. Auggie was wearing a bow tie, looking around excitedly. He had grown up a bit since I'd last seen him, almost a year ago. His hair was shorter, and he was wearing some kind of hearing aid now. His face hadn't changed a bit.

Davenport was running through some last-minute changes with the set decorator. I saw Justin pacing off stage left, mumbling his lines nervously.

"Mr. Davenport," I said, surprising myself as I spoke. "I'm sorry, but I can't go on tonight."

Davenport turned around slowly.

"What?" he said.

"I'm sorry."

"Are you kidding?"

"I'm just . . . ," I muttered, looking down, "I don't feel well. I'm sorry. I feel like I'm going to throw up." This was a lie.

"It's just last-minute jitters. . . ."

"No! I can't do it! I'm telling you."

Davenport looked furious. "Miranda, this is outrageous."

"I'm sorry!"

Davenport took a deep breath, like he was trying to restrain himself. To be truthful, I thought he looked like he was going to explode. His forehead turned bright pink. "Miranda, this is absolutely unacceptable! Now go take a few deep breaths and—"

"I'm *not* going on!" I said loudly, and the tears came to my eyes fairly easily.

"Fine!" he screamed, not looking at me. Then he turned to a kid named David, who was a set decorator. "Go find Olivia in the lighting booth! Tell her she's filling in for Miranda tonight!"

"What?" said David, who wasn't too swift.

"Go!" shouted Davenport in his face. "Now!" The other kids had caught on to what was happening and gathered around.

"What's going on?" said Justin.

"Last-minute change of plans," said Davenport. "Miranda doesn't feel well."

"I feel sick," I said, trying to sound sick.

"So why are you still here?" Davenport said to me angrily.

"Stop talking, take off your costume, and give it to Olivia! Okay? Come on, everybody! Let's go! Go! Go!"

I ran backstage to the dressing room as quickly as I could and started peeling off my costume. Two seconds later there was a knock and Via half opened the door.

"*What* is going on?" she said.

"Hurry up, put it on," I answered, handing her the dress.

"You're sick?"

"Yeah! Hurry up!"

Via, looking stunned, took off her T-shirt and jeans and pulled the long dress over her head. I pulled it down for her, and then zipped up the back. Luckily, Emily Webb didn't go on until ten minutes into the play, so the girl handling hair and makeup had time to put Via's hair up in a twist and do a quick makeup job. I'd never seen Via with a lot of makeup on: she looked like a model.

"I'm not even sure I'll remember my lines," Via said, looking at herself in the mirror. "*Your* lines."

"You'll do great," I said.

She looked at me in the mirror. "Why are you doing this, Miranda?"

"Olivia!" It was Davenport, hush-shouting from the door. "You're on in two minutes. It's now or never!"

Via followed him out the door, so I never got the chance to answer her question. I don't know what I would have said, anyway. I wasn't sure what the answer was.

The Performance

I watched the rest of the play from the wings just offstage, next to Davenport. Justin was amazing, and Via, in that heartbreaking last scene, was awesome. There was one line she flubbed a bit, but Justin covered for her, and no one in the audience even noticed. I heard Davenport muttering under his breath: "Good, good, good." He was more nervous than all of the students put together: the actors, the set decorators, the lighting team, the guy handling the curtains. Davenport was a wreck, frankly.

The only time I felt any regret, if you could even call it that, was at the end of the play when everyone went out for their curtain calls. Via and Justin were the last of the actors walking out onstage, and the audience rose to their feet when they took their bows. That, I admit, was a little bittersweet for me. But just a few minutes later I saw Nate and Isabel and Auggie make their way backstage, and they all seemed so happy. Everyone was congratulating the actors, patting them on the back. It was that crazy backstage theater mayhem where sweaty actors stand euphoric while people come worship them for a few seconds. In that crush of people, I noticed Auggie looking kind of lost. I cut through the crowd as fast as I could and came up behind him.

"Hey!" I said. "Major Tom!"

After the Show

I can't say why I was so happy to see August again after so long, or how good it felt when he hugged me.

"I can't believe how big you've gotten," I said to him.

"I thought you were going to be in the play!" he said.

"I wasn't up to it," I said. "But Via was great, don't you think?"

He nodded. Two seconds later Isabel found us.

"Miranda!" she said happily, giving me a kiss on the cheek. And then to August: "Don't ever disappear like that again."

"You're the one who disappeared," Auggie answered back.

"How are you feeling?" Isabel said to me. "Via told us you got sick. . . ."

"Much better," I answered.

"Is your mom here?" said Isabel.

"No, she had work stuff, so it's actually not a big deal for me," I said truthfully. "We have two more shows anyway, though I don't think I'll be as good an Emily as Via was tonight."

Nate came over and we had basically the same exact conversation. Then Isabel said: "Look, we're going to have a late-night dinner to celebrate the show. Are you feeling up to joining us? We'd love to have you!"

"Oh, no . . . ," I started to say.

"Pleeease?" said Auggie.

"I should go home," I said.

"We insist," said Nate.

By now Via and Justin had come over with Justin's mom, and Via put her arm around me.

"You're definitely coming," she said, smiling her old smile at me. They started leading me out of the crowd, and I have to admit, for the first time in a very, very long time, I felt absolutely happy.

Part Eight

AuGuST

You're gonna reach the sky

Fly . . . Beautiful child

—Eurythmics, "Beautiful Child"

The Fifth-Grade Nature Retreat

Every year in the spring, the fifth graders of Beecher Prep go away for three days and two nights to a place called the Broarwood Nature Reserve in Pennsylvania. It's a four-hour bus drive away. The kids sleep in cabins with bunk beds. There are campfires and s'mores and long walks through the woods. The teachers have been prepping us about this all year long, so all the kids in the grade are excited about it—except for me. And it's not even that I'm not excited, because I kind of am—it's just I've never slept away from home before and I'm kind of nervous.

Most kids have had sleepovers by the time they're my age. A lot of kids have gone to sleepaway camps, or stayed with their grandparents or whatever. Not me. Not unless you include hospital stays, but even then Mom or Dad always stayed with me overnight. But I never slept over Tata and Poppa's house, or Aunt Kate and Uncle Po's house. When I was really little, that was mainly because there were too many medical issues, like my trache tube needing to be cleared every hour, or reinserting my feeding tube if it got detached. But when I got bigger, I just never felt like sleeping anywhere else. There was one time when I half slept over Christopher's house. We were about eight, and we were still best friends. Our family had gone for a visit to his house, and me and Christopher were having such a great time playing Legos *Star Wars* that I didn't want to leave when it was time to go. We were like, "Please, please, please can we have a sleepover?" So our parents said yes, and Mom and Dad and Via drove home. And me and Christopher stayed up till midnight playing, until Lisa, his mom, said: "Okay, guys, time to go to bed." Well, that's when I kind of panicked a bit. Lisa tried to help me go to sleep, but I just started crying that I wanted to go home. So at one a.m. Lisa called Mom and Dad, and Dad drove all the way back out to Bridgeport to pick me up. We didn't get home until three a.m. So my one and only sleepover, up until now, was pretty much of a disaster, which is why I'm a little nervous about the nature retreat.

On the other hand, I'm really excited.

Known For

I asked Mom to buy me a new rolling duffel bag because my old one had *Star Wars* stuff on it, and there was no way I was going to take that to the fifth-grade nature retreat. As much as I love *Star Wars*, I don't want that to be what I'm known for. Everyone's known for something in middle school. Like Reid is known for really being into marine life and the oceans and things like that. And Amos is known for being a really good baseball player. And Charlotte is known for having been in a TV commercial when she was six. And Ximena's known for being really smart.

My point is that in middle school you kind of get known for what you're into, and you have to be careful about stuff like that. Like Max G and Max W will never live down their Dungeons & Dragons obsession.

So I was actually trying to ease out of the whole *Star Wars* thing a bit. I mean, it'll always be special to me, like it is with the doctor who put in my hearing aids. It's just not the thing I wanted to be known for in middle school. I'm not sure what I want to be known for, but it's not that.

That's not exactly true: I do know what I'm *really* known for. But there's nothing I can do about that. A *Star Wars* duffel bag I could do something about.

Packing

Mom helped me pack the night before the big trip. We put all the clothes I was taking on my bed, and she folded everything neatly and put it inside the bag while I watched. It was a plain blue rolling duffel, by the way: no logos or artwork.

"What if I can't sleep at night?" I asked.

"Take a book with you. Then if you can't sleep, you can pull out your flashlight, and read for a bit until you get sleepy," she answered.

I nodded. "What if I have a nightmare?"

"Your teachers will be there, sweetie," she said. "And Jack. And your friends."

"I can bring Baboo," I said. That was my favorite stuffed animal when I was little. A small black bear with a soft black nose.

"You don't really sleep with him anymore, do you?" said Mom.

"No, but I keep him in my closet in case I wake up in the middle of the night and can't get back to sleep," I said. "I could hide him in my bag. No one would know."

"Then let's do that." Mom nodded, getting Baboo from inside my closet.

"I wish they allowed cell phones," I said.

"I know, me too!" she said. "Though I know you're going to have a great time, Auggie. You sure you want me to pack Baboo?"

"Yeah, but way down where no one can see him," I said.

She stuck Baboo deep inside the bag and then stuffed the last of my T-shirts on top of him. "So many clothes for just two days!"

"Three days and two nights," I corrected her.

"Yep." She nodded, smiling. "Three days and two nights." She zipped up the duffel bag and picked it up. "Not too heavy. Try it."

I picked up the bag. "Fine." I shrugged.

She sat on the bed. "Hey, what happened to your *Empire Strikes Back* poster?"

"Oh, I took that down ages ago," I answered.

She shook her head. "Huh, I didn't notice that before."

"I'm trying to, you know, change my image a bit," I explained.

"Okay." She smiled, nodding like she understood. "Anyway, honey, you have to promise me you won't forget to put on the bug spray, okay? On the legs, especially when you're hiking through the woods. It's right here in the front compartment."

"Uh-huh."

"And put on your sunscreen," she said. "You do not want to get a sunburn. And don't, I repeat, do *not* forget to take your hearing aids off if you go swimming."

"Would I get electrocuted?"

"No, but you'd be in real hot water with Daddy because those things cost a fortune!" she laughed. "I put the rain poncho in the front compartment, too. Same thing goes if it rains, Auggie, okay? Make sure you cover the hearing aids with the hood."

"Aye, aye, sir," I said, saluting.

She smiled and pulled me over.

"I can't believe how much you've grown up this year, Auggie," she said softly, putting her hands on the sides of my face.

"Do I look taller?"

"Definitely." She nodded.

"I'm still the shortest one in my grade."

"I'm not really even talking about your height," she said.

"Suppose I hate it there?"

"You're going to have a great time, Auggie."

256

I nodded. She got up and gave me a quick kiss on the forehead. "Okay, so I say we get to bed now."

"It's only nine o'clock, Mom!"

"Your bus leaves at six a.m. tomorrow. You don't want to be late. Come on. Chop chop. Your teeth are brushed?"

I nodded and climbed into bed. She started to lie down next to me.

"You don't need to put me to bed tonight, Mom," I said. "I'll read on my own till I get sleepy."

"Really?" She nodded, impressed. She squeezed my hand and gave it a kiss. "Okay then, goodnight, love. Have sweet dreams."

"You too."

She turned on the little reading light beside the bed.

"I'll write you letters," I said as she was leaving. "Even though I'll probably be home before you guys even get them."

"Then we can read them together," she said, and threw me a kiss.

When she left my room, I took my copy of *The Lion, the Witch and the Wardrobe* off the night table and started reading until I fell asleep.

> . . . *though the Witch knew the Deep Magic, there is a magic deeper still which she did not know. Her knowledge goes back only to the dawn of time. But if she could have looked a little further back, into the stillness and the darkness before Time dawned, she would have read there a different incantation.*

Daybreak

The next day I woke up really early. It was still dark inside my room and even darker outside, though I knew it would be morning soon. I turned over on my side but didn't feel at all sleepy. That's when I saw Daisy sitting near my bed. I mean, I knew it wasn't Daisy, but for a second I saw a shadow that looked just like her. I didn't think it was a dream then, but now, looking back, I know it must have been. It didn't make me sad to see her at all: it just filled me up with nice feelings inside. She was gone after a second, and I couldn't see her again in the darkness.

The room slowly started lightening. I reached for my hearing aid headband and put it on, and now the world was really awake. I could hear the garbage trucks clunking down the street and the birds in our backyard. And down the hallway I heard Mom's alarm beeping. Daisy's ghost made me feel super strong inside, knowing wherever I am, she'd be there with me.

I got up out of bed and went to my desk and wrote a little note to Mom. Then I went into the living room, where my packed bag was by the door. I opened it up and fished inside until I found what I was looking for.

I took Baboo back to my room, and I laid him in my bed and taped the little note to Mom on his chest. And then I covered him with my blanket so Mom would find him later. The note read:

Dear Mom, I won't need Baboo, but if you miss me, you can cuddle with him yourself. xo Auggie

Day One

The bus ride went really fast. I sat by the window and Jack was next to me in the aisle seat. Summer and Maya were in front of us. Everyone was in a good mood. Kind of loud, laughing a lot. I noticed right away that Julian wasn't on our bus, even though Henry and Miles were. I figured he must be on the other bus, but then I overheard Miles tell Amos that Julian ditched the grade trip because he thought the whole nature-retreat thing was, quote unquote, dorky. I got totally pumped because dealing with Julian for three days in a row—and two nights—was a major reason that I was nervous about this whole trip. So now without him there, I could really just relax and not worry about anything.

We got to the nature reserve at around noon. The first thing we did was put our stuff down in the cabins. There were three bunk beds to every room, so me and Jack did rock, paper, scissors for the top bunk and I won. Woo-hoo. And the other guys in the room were Reid and Tristan, and Pablo and Nino.

After we had lunch in the main cabin, we all went on a two-hour guided nature hike through the woods. But these were not woods like the kind they have in Central Park: these were real woods. Giant trees that almost totally blocked out the sunlight. Tangles of leaves and fallen tree trunks. Howls and chirps and really loud bird calls. There was a slight fog, too, like a pale blue smoke all around us. So cool. The nature guide pointed everything out to us: the different types of trees we were passing, the insects inside the dead logs on the trail, the signs of deer and bears in the woods, what types of birds were whistling and where to look for them. I realized that my Lobot hearing aids actually made me hear better than most people, because I was usually the first person to hear a new bird call.

It started to rain as we headed back to camp. I pulled on my rain poncho and pulled the hood up so my hearing aids wouldn't get wet, but my jeans and shoes got soaked by the time we reached our cabins. Everyone got soaked. It was fun, though. We had a wet-sock fight in the cabin.

Since it rained for the rest of the day, we spent most of the afternoon goofing off in the rec room. They had a Ping-Pong table and old-style arcade games like *Pac-Man* and *Missile Command* that we played until dinnertime. Luckily, by then it had stopped raining, so we got to have a real campfire cookout. The log benches around the campfire were still a little damp, but we threw our jackets over them and hung out by the fire, toasting s'mores and eating the best roasted hot dogs I have ever, ever tasted. Mom was right about the mosquitoes: there were tons of them. But luckily I had spritzed myself before I left the cabin, and I wasn't eaten alive like some of the other kids were.

I loved hanging out by the campfire after dark. I loved the way bits of fire dust would float up and disappear into the night air. And how the fire lit up people's faces. I loved the sound the fire made, too. And how the woods were so dark that you couldn't see anything around you, and you'd look up and see a billion stars in the sky. The sky doesn't look like that in North River Heights. I've seen it look like that in Montauk, though: like someone sprinkled salt on a shiny black table.

I was so tired when I got back to the cabin that I didn't need to pull out the book to read. I fell asleep almost as fast as my head hit the pillow. And maybe I dreamed about the stars, I don't know.

The Fairgrounds

The next day was just as great as the first day. We went horseback riding in the morning, and in the afternoon we rappelled up some ginormous trees with the help of the nature guides. By the time we got back to the cabins for dinner, we were all really tired again. After dinner they told us we had an hour to rest, and then we were going to take a fifteen-minute bus ride to the fairgrounds for an outdoor movie night.

I hadn't had the chance to write a letter to Mom and Dad and Via yet, so I wrote one telling them all about the stuff we did that day and the day before. I pictured myself reading it to them out loud when I got back, since there was just no way the letter would get home before I did.

When we got to the fairgrounds, the sun was just starting to set. It was about seven-thirty. The shadows were really long on the grass, and the clouds were pink and orange. It looked like someone had taken sidewalk chalk and smudged the colors across the sky with their fingers. It's not that I haven't seen nice sunsets before in the city, because I have—slivers of sunsets between buildings—but I wasn't used to seeing so much sky in every direction. Out here in the fairgrounds, I could understand why ancient people used to think the world was flat and the sky was a dome that closed in on top of it. That's what it looked like from the fairgrounds, in the middle of this huge open field.

Because we were the first school to arrive, we got to run around the field all we wanted until the teachers told us it was time to lay out our sleeping bags on the ground and get good viewing seats. We unzipped our bags and laid them down like picnic blankets on the grass in front of the giant movie screen in the middle of the field. Then we went to the row of food trucks parked at the edge of the field to load up on snacks and sodas and stuff like that. There were concession stands there, too, like at a farmers' market, selling roasted peanuts and cotton candy. And up a little farther was a short row of carnival-type stalls, the kind where you can win a stuffed animal if you throw a baseball into a basket. Jack and I both tried—and failed—to win anything, but we heard Amos won a yellow hippo and gave it to Ximena. That was the big gossip that went around: the jock and the brainiac.

From the food trucks, you could see the cornstalks in back of the movie screen. They covered about a third of the entire field. The rest of the field was completely surrounded by woods. As the sun sank lower in the sky, the tall trees at the entrance to the woods looked dark blue.

By the time the other school buses pulled into the parking lots, we were back in our spots on the sleeping bags, right smack in front of the screen: the best seats in the whole field. Everyone was passing around snacks and having a great time. Me and Jack and Summer and Reid and Maya played Pictionary. We could hear the sounds of the other schools arriving, the loud laughing and talking of kids coming out on the field on both sides of us, but we couldn't really see them. Though the sky was still light, the sun had gone down completely, and everything on the ground had turned deep purple. The clouds were shadows now. We had trouble even seeing the Pictionary cards in front of us.

Just then, without any announcement, all the lights at the ends of the field went on at once. They were like big bright stadium lights. I thought of that scene in *Close Encounters* when the alien ship lands and they're playing that music: *duh-dah-doo-da-dunnn*. Everyone in the field started applauding and cheering like something great had just happened.

Be Kind to Nature

An announcement came over the huge speakers next to the stadium lights:

"Welcome, everyone. Welcome to the twenty-third annual Big Movie Night at the Broarwood Nature Reserve. Welcome, teachers and students from . . . MS 342: the William Heath School. . . ." A big cheer went up on the left side of the field. "Welcome, teachers and students from Glover Academy. . . ." Another cheer went up, this time from the right side of the field. "And welcome, teachers and students from . . . the Beecher Prep School!" Our whole group cheered as loudly as we could. "We're thrilled to have you as our guests here tonight, and thrilled that the weather is cooperating—in fact, can you believe what a beautiful night this is?" Again, everyone whooped and hollered. "So as we prepare the movie, we do ask that you take a few moments to listen to this important announcement. The Broarwood Nature Reserve, as you know, is dedicated to preserving our natural resources and the environment. We ask that you leave no litter behind. Clean up after yourselves. Be kind to nature and it will be kind to you. We ask that you keep that in mind as you walk around the grounds. Do not venture beyond the orange cones at the edges of the fairgrounds. Do not go into the cornfields or the woods. Please keep the free roaming to a minimum. Even if you don't feel like watching the movie, your fellow students may feel otherwise, so please be courteous: no talking, no playing music, no running around. The restrooms are located on the other side of the concession stands. After the movie is over, it will be quite dark, so we ask that all of you stay with your schools as you make your way back to your buses. Teachers, there's usually at least one lost party on Big Movie Nights at Broarwood: don't let it happen to you! Tonight's movie presentation will be . . . *The Sound of Music!*"

I immediately started clapping, even though I'd seen it a few times before, because it was Via's favorite movie of all time. But I was surprised that a whole bunch of kids (not from Beecher) booed and hissed and laughed. Someone from the right side of the field even threw a soda can at the screen, which seemed to surprise Mr. Tushman. I saw him stand up and look in the direction of the can thrower, though I knew he couldn't see anything in the dark.

The movie started playing right away. The stadium lights dimmed. Maria the nun was standing at the top of the mountain twirling around and around. It had gotten chilly all of a sudden, so I put on my yellow Montauk hoodie and adjusted the volume on my hearing aids and leaned against my backpack and started watching.

The hills are alive . . .

The Woods Are Alive

Somewhere around the boring part where the guy named Rolf and the oldest daughter are singing *You are sixteen, going on seventeen*, Jack nudged me.

"Dude, I've got to pee," he said.

We both got up and kind of hopscotched over the kids who were sitting or lying down on the sleeping bags. Summer waved as we passed and I waved back.

There were lots of kids from the other schools walking around by the food trucks, playing the carnival games, or just hanging out.

Of course, there was a huge line for the toilets.

"Forget this, I'll just find a tree," said Jack.

"That's gross, Jack. Let's just wait," I answered.

But he headed off to the row of trees at the edge of the field, which was past the orange cones that we were specifically told not to go past. And of course I followed him. And of course we didn't have our flashlights because we forgot to bring them. It was so dark now we literally couldn't see ten steps ahead of us as we walked toward the woods. Luckily, the movie gave off some light, so when we saw a flashlight coming toward us out of the woods, we knew immediately that it was Henry, Miles, and Amos. I guess they hadn't wanted to wait on line to use the toilets, either.

Miles and Henry were still not talking to Jack, but Amos had let go of the war a while ago. And he nodded hello to us as they passed by.

"Be careful of the bears!" shouted Henry, and he and Miles laughed as they walked away.

Amos shook his head at us like, Don't pay attention to them.

Jack and I walked a little farther until we were just inside the woods. Then Jack hunted around for the perfect tree and finally did his business, though it felt like he was taking forever.

The woods were loud with strange sounds and chirps and croaks, like a wall of noise coming out of the trees. Then we started hearing loud snaps not far from us, almost like cap gun pops, that definitely weren't insect noises. And far away, like in another world, we could hear *Raindrops on roses and whiskers on kittens*.

"Ah, that's much better," said Jack, zipping up.

"Now I have to pee," I said, which I did on the nearest tree. No way I was going farther in like Jack did.

"Do you smell that? Like firecrackers," he said, coming over to me.

"Oh yeah, that's what that is," I answered, zipping up. "Weird."

"Let's go."

Alien

We headed back the way we came, in the direction of the giant screen. That's when we walked straight into a group of kids we didn't know. They'd just come out of the woods, doing stuff I'm sure they didn't want their teachers to know about. I could smell the smoke now, the smell of both firecrackers and cigarettes. They pointed a flashlight at us. There were six of them: four boys and two girls. They looked like they were in the seventh grade.

"What school are you from?" one of the boys called out.

"Beecher Prep!" Jack started to answer, when all of a sudden one of the girls started screaming.

"Oh my God!" she shrieked, holding her hand over her eyes like she was crying. I figured maybe a huge bug had just flown into her face or something.

"No way!" one of the boys cried out, and he started flicking his hand in the air like he'd just touched something hot. And then he covered his mouth. "No freakin' way, man! No freakin' way!"

All of them started half laughing and half covering their eyes now, pushing each other and cursing loudly.

"What is that?" said the kid who was pointing the flashlight at us, and it was only then that I realized that the flashlight was pointed right at my face, and what they were talking about— screaming about—was me.

"Let's get out of here," Jack said to me quietly, and he pulled me by my sweatshirt sleeve and started walking away from them.

"Wait wait wait!" yelled the guy with the flashlight, cutting us off. He pointed the flashlight right in my face again, and now he was only about five feet away. "Oh man! Oh man!!" he said, shaking his head, his mouth wide open. "What happened to your face?"

"Stop it, Eddie," said one of the girls.

"I didn't know we were watching *Lord of the Rings* tonight!" he said. "Look, guys, it's Gollum!"

This made his friends hysterical.

Again we tried to walk away from them, and again the kid named Eddie cut us off. He was at least a head taller than Jack, who was about a head taller than me, so the guy looked huge to me.

"No man, it's *Alien*!" said one of the other kids.

"No, no, no, man. It's an orc!" laughed Eddie, pointing the flashlight in my face again. This time he was right in front of us.

"Leave him alone, okay?" said Jack, pushing the hand holding the flashlight away.

"Make me," answered Eddie, pointing the flashlight in Jack's face now.

"What's your problem, dude?" said Jack.

"Your boyfriend's my problem!"

"Jack, let's just go," I said, pulling him by the arm.

"Oh man, it talks!" screamed Eddie, shining the flashlight in my face again. Then one of the other guys threw a firecracker at our feet.

Jack tried to push past Eddie, but Eddie shoved his hands into Jack's shoulders and pushed him hard, which made Jack fall backward.

"Eddie!" screamed one of the girls.

"Look," I said, stepping in front of Jack and holding my hands up in the air like a traffic cop. "We're a lot smaller than you guys . . ."

"Are you talking to me, Freddie Krueger? I don't think you want to mess with me, you ugly freak," said Eddie. And this was the point where I knew I should run away as fast as I could, but Jack was still on the ground and I wasn't about to leave him.

"Yo, dude," said a new voice behind us. "What's up, man?"

Eddie spun around and pointed his flashlight toward the voice. For a second, I couldn't believe who it was.

"Leave them alone, dude," said Amos, with Miles and Henry right behind him.

"Says who?" said one of the guys with Eddie.

"Just leave them alone, dude," Amos repeated calmly.

"Are you a freak, too?" said Eddie.

"They're all a bunch of freaks!" said one of his friends.

Amos didn't answer them but looked at us. "Come on, guys, let's go. Mr. Tushman's waiting for us."

I knew that was a lie, but I helped Jack get up, and we started walking over to Amos. Then out of the blue, the Eddie guy grabbed my hood as I passed by him, yanking it really hard so I was pulled backward and fell flat on my back. It was a hard fall, and I hurt my elbow pretty bad on a rock. I couldn't really see what happened afterward, except that Amos rammed into the Eddie guy like a monster truck and they both fell down to the ground next to me.

Everything got really crazy after that. Someone pulled me up by my sleeve and yelled, "Run!" and someone else screamed, "Get 'em!" at the same time, and for a few seconds I actually had two people pulling the sleeves of my sweatshirt in opposite directions. I heard them both cursing, until my sweatshirt ripped and the first guy yanked me by my arm and started pulling me behind him as we ran, which I did as fast as I could. I could hear footsteps just behind us, chasing us, and voices shouting and girls screaming, but it was so dark I didn't know whose voices they were, only that everything felt like we were underwater. We were running like crazy, and it was pitch black, and whenever I started to slow down, the guy pulling me by my arm would yell, "Don't stop!"

Voices in the Dark

Finally, after what seemed like a forever of running, someone yelled: "I think we lost them!"

"Amos?"

"I'm right here!" said Amos's voice a few feet behind us.

"We can stop!" Miles yelled from farther up.

"Jack!" I yelled.

"Whoa!" said Jack. "I'm here."

"I can't see a thing!"

"Are you sure we lost them?" Henry asked, letting go of my arm. That's when I realized that he'd been the one who was pulling me as we ran.

"Yeah."

"Shh! Let's listen!"

We all got super quiet, listening for footsteps in the dark. All we could hear were the crickets and frogs and our own crazy panting. We were out of breath, stomachs hurting, bodies bent over our knees.

"We lost them," said Henry.

"Whoa! That was intense!"

"What happened to the flashlight?"

"I dropped it!"

"How did you guys know?" said Jack.

"We saw them before."

"They looked like jerks."

"You just rammed into him!" I said to Amos.

"I know, right?" laughed Amos.

"He didn't even see it coming!" said Miles.

"He was like, 'Are you a freak, too?' and you were like, *bam!*" said Jack.

"Bam!" said Amos, throwing a fake punch in the air. "But after I tackled him, I was like, run, Amos, you schmuck, he's ten times bigger than you! And I got up and started running as fast as I could!"

We all started laughing.

"I grabbed Auggie and I was like, 'Run!'" said Henry.

"I didn't even know it was you pulling me!" I answered.

"That was wild," said Amos, shaking his head.

"Totally wild."

"Your lip is bleeding, dude."

"I got in a couple of good punches," answered Amos, wiping his lip.

"I think they were seventh graders."

"They were huge."

"Losers!" Henry shouted really loudly, but we all shushed him.

We listened for a second to make sure no one had heard him.

"Where the heck are we?" asked Amos. "I can't even see the screen."

"I think we're in the cornfields," answered Henry.

"Duh, we're in the cornfields," said Miles, pushing a cornstalk at Henry.

"Okay, I know exactly where we are," said Amos. "We have to go back in this direction. That'll take us to the other side of the field."

"Yo, dudes," said Jack, hand high in the air. "That was really cool of you guys to come back for us. Really cool. Thanks."

"No problem," answered Amos, high-fiving Jack. And then Miles and Henry high-fived him, too.

"Yeah, dudes, thanks," I said, holding my palm up like Jack just had, though I wasn't sure if they'd high-five me, too.

Amos looked at me and nodded. "It was cool how you stood your ground, little dude," he said, high-fiving me.

"Yeah, Auggie," said Miles, high-fiving me, too. "You were like, 'We're littler than you guys' . . ."

"I didn't know what else to say!" I laughed.

"Very cool," said Henry, and he high-fived me, too. "Sorry I ripped your sweatshirt."

I looked down, and my sweatshirt was completely torn down the middle. One sleeve was ripped off, and the other was so stretched out it was hanging down to my knees.

"Hey, your elbow's bleeding," said Jack.

"Yeah." I shrugged. It was starting to hurt a lot.

"You okay?" said Jack, seeing my face.

I nodded. Suddenly I felt like crying, and I was trying really hard not to do that.

"Wait, your hearing aids are gone!" said Jack.

"What!" I yelled, touching my ears. The hearing aid band was definitely gone. That's why I felt like I was underwater! "Oh no!" I said, and that's when I couldn't hold it in anymore. Everything that had just happened kind of hit me and I couldn't help it: I started to cry. Like big crying, what Mom would call "the waterworks." I was so embarrassed I hid my face in my arm, but I couldn't stop the tears from coming.

The guys were really nice to me, though. They patted me on the back.

"You're okay, dude. It's okay," they said.

"You're one brave little dude, you know that?" said Amos, putting his arm around my shoulders. And when I kept on crying, he put both his arms around me like my dad would have done and let me cry.

The Emperor's Guard

We backtracked through the grass for a good ten minutes to see if we could find my hearing aids, but it was way too dark to see anything. We literally had to hold on to each other's shirts and walk in single file so we wouldn't trip over one another. It was like black ink had been poured all around.

"This is hopeless," said Henry. "They could be anywhere."

"Maybe we can come back with a flashlight," answered Amos.

"No, it's okay," I said. "Let's just go back. Thanks, though."

We walked back toward the cornfields, and then cut through them until the back of the giant screen came into view. Since it was facing away from us, we didn't get any light from the screen at all until we'd walked around to the edge of the woods again. That's where we finally started seeing a little light.

There was no sign of the seventh graders anywhere.

"Where do you think they went?" said Jack.

"Back to the food trucks," said Amos. "They're probably thinking we're going to report them."

"Are we?" asked Henry.

They looked at me. I shook my head.

"Okay," said Amos, "but, little dude, don't walk around here alone again, okay? If you need to go somewhere, tell us and we'll go with you."

"Okay." I nodded.

As we got closer to the screen, I could hear *High on a hill was a lonely goatherd*, and could smell the cotton candy from one of the concession stands near the food trucks. There were lots of kids milling around in this area, so I pulled what was left of my hoodie over my head and kept my face down, hands in pockets, as we made our way through the crowd. It had been a long time since I'd been out without my hearing aids, and it felt like I was miles under the earth. It felt like that song Miranda used to sing to me: *Ground Control to Major Tom, your circuit's dead, there's something wrong . . .*

I did notice as I walked that Amos had stayed right next to me. And Jack was close on the other side of me. And Miles was in front of us and Henry was in back of us. They were surrounding me as we walked through the crowds of kids. Like I had my own emperor's guard.

Sleep

*Then they came out of the narrow valley and at once she saw the
reason. There stood Peter and Edmund and all the rest of Aslan's
army fighting desperately against the crowd of horrible creatures
whom she had seen last night; only now, in the daylight, they
looked even stranger and more evil and more deformed.*

I stopped there. I'd been reading for over an hour and sleep
still didn't come. It was almost two a.m. Everyone else was asleep.
I had my flashlight on under the sleeping bag, and maybe the
light was why I couldn't sleep, but I was too afraid to turn it off. I
was afraid of how dark it was outside the sleeping bag.

When we got back to our section in front of the movie
screen, no one had even noticed we'd been gone. Mr. Tushman
and Ms. Rubin and Summer and all the rest of the kids were just
watching the movie. They had no clue how something bad had
almost happened to me and Jack. It's so weird how that can be,
how you could have a night that's the worst in your life, but to
everybody else it's just an ordinary night. Like, on my calendar at
home, I would mark this as being one of the most horrific days of
my life. This and the day Daisy died. But for the rest of the world,
this was just an ordinary day. Or maybe it was even a good day.
Maybe somebody won the lottery today.

Amos, Miles, and Henry brought me and Jack over to where
we'd been sitting before, with Summer and Maya and Reid, and
then they went and sat where they had been sitting before, with
Ximena and Savanna and their group. In a way, everything was

exactly as we had left it before we went looking for the toilets. The sky was the same. The movie was the same. Everyone's faces were the same. Mine was the same.

But something was different. Something had changed.

I could see Amos and Miles and Henry telling their group what had just happened. I knew they were talking about it because they kept looking over at me while they were talking. Even though the movie was still playing, people were whispering about it in the dark. News like that spreads fast.

It was what everyone was talking about on the bus ride back to the cabins. All the girls, even girls I didn't know very well, were asking me if I was okay. The boys were all talking about getting revenge on the group of seventh-grade jerks, trying to figure out what school they were from.

I wasn't planning on telling the teachers about any of what had happened, but they found out anyway. Maybe it was the torn sweatshirt and the bloody elbow. Or maybe it's just that teachers hear everything.

When we got back to the camp, Mr. Tushman took me to the first-aid office, and while I was getting my elbow cleaned and bandaged up by the camp nurse, Mr. Tushman and the camp director were in the next room talking with Amos and Jack and Henry and Miles, trying to get a description of the troublemakers. When he asked me about them a little later, I said I couldn't remember their faces at all, which wasn't true.

It's their faces I kept seeing every time I closed my eyes to sleep. The look of total horror on the girl's face when she first saw me. The way the kid with the flashlight, Eddie, looked at me as he talked to me, like he hated me.

Like a lamb to the slaughter. I remember Dad saying that ages ago, but tonight I think I finally got what it meant.

276

Aftermath

Mom was waiting for me in front of the school along with all the other parents when the bus arrived. Mr. Tushman told me on the bus ride home that they had called my parents to tell them there had been a "situation" the night before but that everyone was fine. He said the camp director and several of the counselors went looking for the hearing aid in the morning while we all went swimming in the lake, but they couldn't find it anywhere. Broarwood would reimburse us the cost of the hearing aids, he said. They felt bad about what happened.

I wondered if Eddie had taken my hearing aids with him as a kind of souvenir. Something to remember the orc.

Mom gave me a tight hug when I got off the bus, but she didn't slam me with questions like I thought she might. Her hug felt good, and I didn't shake it off like some of the other kids were doing with their parents' hugs.

The bus driver started unloading our duffel bags, and I went to find mine while Mom talked to Mr. Tushman and Ms. Rubin, who had walked over to her. As I rolled my bag toward her, a lot of kids who don't usually say anything to me were nodding hello, or patting my back as I walked by them.

"Ready?" Mom said when she saw me. She took my duffel bag, and I didn't even try to hold on to it: I was fine with her carrying it. If she had wanted to carry me on her shoulders, I would have been fine with that, too, to be truthful.

As we started to walk away, Mr. Tushman gave me a quick, tight hug but didn't say anything.

Home

Mom and I didn't talk much the whole walk home, and when we got to the front stoop, I automatically looked in the front bay window, because I forgot for a second that Daisy wasn't going to be there like always, perched on the sofa with her front paws on the windowsill, waiting for us to come home. It made me kind of sad when we walked inside. As soon as we did, Mom dropped my duffel bag and wrapped her arms around me and kissed me on my head and on my face like she was breathing me in.

"It's okay, Mom, I'm fine," I said, smiling.

She nodded and took my face in her hands. Her eyes were shiny.

"I know you are," she said. "I missed you so much, Auggie."

"I missed you, too."

I could tell she wanted to say a lot of things but she was stopping herself.

"Are you hungry?" she asked.

"Starving. Can I have a grilled cheese?"

"Of course," she answered, and immediately started to make the sandwich while I took my jacket off and sat down at the kitchen counter.

"Where's Via?" I asked.

"She's coming home with Dad today. Boy, did she miss you, Auggie," Mom said.

"Yeah? She would have liked the nature reserve. You know what movie they played? *The Sound of Music*."

"You'll have to tell her that."

"So, do you want to hear about the bad part or the good part first?" I asked after a few minutes, leaning my head on my hand.

"Whatever you want to talk about," she answered.

"Well, except for last night, I had an awesome time," I said. "I mean, it was just awesome. That's why I'm so bummed. I feel like they ruined the whole trip for me."

"No, sweetie, don't let them do that to you. You were there for more than forty-eight hours, and that awful part lasted one hour. Don't let them take that away from you, okay?"

"I know." I nodded. "Did Mr. Tushman tell you about the hearing aids?"

"Yes, he called us this morning."

"Was Dad mad? Because they're so expensive?"

"Oh my gosh, of course not, Auggie. He just wanted to know that you were all right. That's all that matters to us. And that you don't let those . . . thugs . . . ruin your trip."

I kind of laughed at the way she said the word "thugs."

"What?" she asked.

"Thugs," I teased her. "That's kind of an old-fashioned word."

"Okay, jerks. Morons. Imbeciles," she said, flipping over the sandwich in the pan. "Cretinos, as my mother would have said. Whatever you want to call them, if I saw them on the street, I would . . ." She shook her head.

"They were pretty big, Mom." I smiled. "Seventh graders, I think."

She shook her head. "Seventh graders? Mr. Tushman didn't tell us that. Oh my goodness."

"Did he tell you how Jack stood up for me?" I said. "And Amos was like, bam, he rammed right into the leader. They both crashed to the ground, like in a real fight! It was pretty awesome. Amos's lip was bleeding and everything."

"He told us there was a fight, but . . . ," she said, looking at me with her eyebrows raised. "I'm just . . . *phew* . . . I'm just so grateful you and Amos and Jack are fine. When I think about what could have happened . . . ," she trailed off, flipping the grilled cheese again.

"My Montauk hoodie got totally shredded."

"Well, that can be replaced," she answered. She lifted the grilled cheese onto a plate and put the plate in front of me on the counter. "Milk or white grape juice?"

"Chocolate milk, please?" I started devouring the sandwich. "Oh, can you do it that special way you make it, with the froth?"

"How did you and Jack end up at the edge of the woods in the first place?" she said, pouring the milk into a tall glass.

"Jack had to go to the bathroom," I answered, my mouth full. As I was talking, she spooned in the chocolate powder and started rolling a small whisk between her palms really fast. "But there was a huge line and he didn't want to wait. So we went toward the woods to pee." She looked up at me while she was whisking. I know she was thinking we shouldn't have done that. The chocolate milk in the glass now had a two-inch froth on top. "That looks good, Mom. Thanks."

"And then what happened?" she said, putting the glass in front of me.

I took a long drink of the chocolate milk. "Is it okay if we don't talk about it anymore right now?"

"Oh. Okay."

"I promise I'll tell you all about it later, when Dad and Via come home. I'll tell you all every detail. I just don't want to have to tell the whole story over and over, you know?"

"Absolutely."

I finished my sandwich in two more bites and gulped down the chocolate milk.

"Wow, you practically inhaled that sandwich. Do you want another one?" she said.

I shook my head and wiped my mouth with the back of my hand.

"Mom? Am I always going to have to worry about jerks like that?" I asked. "Like when I grow up, is it always going to be like this?"

She didn't answer right away, but took my plate and glass and put them in the sink and rinsed them with water.

"There are always going to be jerks in the world, Auggie," she said, looking at me. "But I really believe, and Daddy really believes, that there are more good people on this earth than bad people, and the good people watch out for each other and take care of each other. Just like Jack was there for you. And Amos. And those other kids."

"Oh yeah, Miles and Henry," I answered. "They were awesome, too. It's weird because Miles and Henry haven't even really been very nice to me at all during the year."

"Sometimes people surprise us," she said, rubbing the top of my head.

"I guess."

"Want another glass of chocolate milk?"

"No, I'm good," I said. "Thanks, Mom. Actually, I'm kind of tired. I didn't sleep too good last night."

"You should take a nap. Thanks for leaving me Baboo, by the way."

"You got my note?"

She smiled. "I slept with him both nights." She was about to say something else when her cell phone rang, and she answered. She started beaming as she listened. "Oh my goodness, really?

What kind?" she said excitedly. "Yep, he's right here. He was about to take a nap. Want to say hi? Oh, okay, see you in two minutes." She clicked it off.

"That was Daddy," she said excitedly. "He and Via are just down the block."

"He's not at work?" I said.

"He left early because he couldn't wait to see you," she said. "So don't take a nap quite yet."

Five seconds later Dad and Via came through the door. I ran into Dad's arms, and he picked me up and spun me around and kissed me. He didn't let me go for a full minute, until I said, "Dad, it's okay." And then it was Via's turn, and she kissed me all over like she used to do when I was little.

It wasn't until she stopped that I noticed the big white cardboard box they had brought in with them.

"What is that?" I said.

"Open it," said Dad, smiling, and he and Mom looked at each other like they knew a secret.

"Come on, Auggie!" said Via.

I opened the box. Inside was the cutest little puppy I've ever seen in my life. It was black and furry, with a pointy little snout and bright black eyes and small ears that flopped down.

Bear

We called the puppy Bear because when Mom first saw him, she said he looked just like a little bear cub. I said: "That's what we should call him!" and everyone agreed that that was the perfect name.

I took the next day off from school—not because my elbow was hurting me, which it was, but so I could play with Bear all day long. Mom let Via stay home from school, too, so the two of us took turns cuddling with Bear and playing tug-of-war with him. We had kept all of Daisy's old toys, and we brought them out now, to see which ones he'd like best.

It was fun hanging out with Via all day, just the two of us. It was like old times, like before I started going to school. Back then, I couldn't wait for her to come home from school so she could play with me before starting her homework. Now that we're older, though, and I'm going to school and have friends of my own that I hang out with, we never do that anymore.

So it was nice hanging out with her, laughing and playing. I think she liked it, too.

The Shift

When I went back to school the next day, the first thing I noticed was that there was a big shift in the way things were. A monumental shift. A seismic shift. Maybe even a cosmic shift. Whatever you want to call it, it was a big shift. Everyone—not just in our grade but every grade—had heard about what had happened to us with the seventh graders, so suddenly I wasn't known for what I'd always been known for, but for this other thing that had happened. And the story of what happened had gotten bigger and bigger each time it was told. Two days later, the way the story went was that Amos had gotten into a major fistfight with the kid, and Miles and Henry and Jack had thrown some punches at the other guys, too. And the escape across the field became this whole long adventure through a cornfield maze and into the deep dark woods. Jack's version of the story was probably the best because he's so funny, but in whatever version of the story, and no matter who was telling it, two things always stayed the same: I got picked on because of my face and Jack defended me, and those guys—Amos, Henry, and Miles—protected me. And now that they'd protected me, I was different to them. It was like I was one of them. They all called me "little dude" now—even the jocks. These big dudes I barely even knew before would knuckle-punch me in the hallways now.

Another thing to come out of it was that Amos became super popular and Julian, because he missed the whole thing, was really out of the loop. Miles and Henry were hanging out with Amos all the time now, like they switched best friends. I'd like to be able to say that Julian started treating me better, too, but that wouldn't be true. He still gave me dirty looks across the room. He still never talked to me or Jack. But he was the only one who was like that now. And me and Jack, we couldn't care less.

Ducks

The day before the last day of school, Mr. Tushman called me into his office to tell me they had found out the names of the seventh graders from the nature retreat. He read off a bunch of names that didn't mean anything to me, and then he said the last name: "Edward Johnson."

I nodded.

"You recognize the name?" he said.

"They called him Eddie."

"Right. Well, they found this in Edward's locker." He handed me what was left of my hearing aid headband. The right piece was completely gone and the left one was mangled. The band that connected the two, the Lobot part, was bent down the middle.

"His school wants to know if you want to press charges," said Mr. Tushman.

I looked at my hearing aid.

"No, I don't think so." I shrugged. "I'm being fitted for new ones anyway."

"Hmm. Why don't you talk about it with your parents tonight? I'll call your mom tomorrow to talk about it with her, too."

"Would they go to jail?" I asked.

"No, not jail. But they'd probably go to juvie court. And maybe they'll learn a lesson that way."

"Trust me: that Eddie kid is not learning any lessons," I joked.

He sat down behind his desk.

"Auggie, why don't you sit down a second?" he said.

I sat down. All the things on his desk were the same as when I first walked into his office last summer: the same mirrored cube, the same little globe floating in the air. That felt like ages ago.

"Hard to believe this year's almost over, huh?" he said, almost like he was reading my mind.

"Yeah."

"Has it been a good year for you, Auggie? Has it been okay?"

"Yeah, it's been good." I nodded.

"I know academically it's been a great year for you. You're one of our top students. Congrats on the High Honor Roll."

"Thanks. Yeah, that's cool."

"But I know it's had its share of ups and downs," he said, raising his eyebrows. "Certainly, that night at the nature reserve was one of the low points."

"Yeah." I nodded. "But it was also kind of good, too."

"In what way?"

"Well, you know, how people stood up for me and stuff?"

"That was pretty wonderful," he said, smiling.

"Yeah."

"I know in school things got a little hairy with Julian at times."

I have to admit: he surprised me with that one.

"You know about that stuff?" I asked him.

"Middle-school directors have a way of knowing about a lot of stuff."

"Do you have, like, secret security cameras in the hallways?" I joked.

"And microphones everywhere," he laughed.

"No, seriously?"

He laughed again. "No, not seriously."

"Oh!"

"But teachers know more than kids think, Auggie. I wish you

and Jack had come to me about the mean notes that were left in your lockers."

"How do you know about that?" I said.

"I'm telling you: middle-school directors know *all*."

"It wasn't that big a deal," I answered. "And we wrote notes, too."

He smiled. "I don't know if it's public yet," he said, "though it will be soon anyway, but Julian Albans is not coming back to Beecher Prep next year."

"What!" I said. I honestly couldn't hide how surprised I was.

"His parents don't think Beecher Prep is a good fit for him," Mr. Tushman continued, raising his shoulders.

"Wow, that's big news," I said.

"Yeah, I thought you should know."

Then suddenly I noticed that the pumpkin portrait that used to be behind his desk was gone and my drawing, my *Self-Portrait as an Animal* that I drew for the New Year Art Show, was now framed and hanging behind his desk.

"Hey, that's mine!" I pointed.

Mr. Tushman turned around like he didn't know what I was talking about. "Oh, that's right!" he said, tapping his forehead. "I've been meaning to show this to you for months now."

"My self-portrait as a duck." I nodded.

"I love this piece, Auggie," he said. "When your art teacher showed it to me, I asked her if I could keep it for my wall. I hope that's okay with you."

"Oh, yeah! Sure. What happened to the pumpkin portrait?"

"Right behind you."

"Oh, yeah. Nice."

"I've been meaning to ask you since I hung this up . . . ," he said, looking at it. "Why did you choose to represent yourself as a duck?"

"What do you mean?" I answered. "That was the assignment."

"Yes, but why a duck?" he said. "Is it safe to assume that it was because of the story of the . . . um, the duckling that turns into a swan?"

"No," I laughed, shaking my head. "It's because I think I look like a duck."

"Oh!" said Mr. Tushman, his eyes opening wide. He started laughing. "Really? Huh. Here I was looking for symbolism and metaphors and, um . . . sometimes a duck is just a duck!"

"Yeah, I guess," I said, not quite getting why he thought that was so funny. He laughed to himself for a good thirty seconds.

"Anyway, Auggie, thanks for chatting with me," he said, finally. "I just want you to know it's truly a pleasure having you here at Beecher Prep, and I'm really looking forward to next year." He reached across the desk and we shook hands. "See you tomorrow at graduation."

"See you tomorrow, Mr. Tushman."

The Last Precept

This was written on Mr. Browne's chalkboard when we walked into English class for the last time:

> MR. BROWNE'S JUNE PRECEPT:
>
> JUST FOLLOW THE DAY AND REACH
> FOR THE SUN!
>
> (The Polyphonic Spree)
>
> Have a great summer vacation, Class 5B!
>
> It's been a great year and you've been a wonderful group of students.
>
> If you remember, please send me a postcard this summer with YOUR personal precept. It can be something you made up for yourself or something you've read somewhere that means something to you. (If so, don't forget the attribution, please!) I really look forward to getting them.
>
> Tom Browne
> 563 Sebastian Place
> Bronx, NY 10053

The Drop-Off

The graduation ceremony was held in the Beecher Prep Upper School auditorium. It was only about a fifteen-minute walk from our house to the other campus building, but Dad drove me because I was all dressed up and had on new shiny black shoes that weren't broken in yet and I didn't want my feet to hurt. Students were supposed to arrive at the auditorium an hour before the ceremony started, but we got there even earlier, so we sat in the car and waited. Dad turned on the CD player, and our favorite song come on. We both smiled and started bobbing our heads to the music.

Dad sang along with the song: "*Andy would bicycle across town in the rain to bring you candy.*"

"Hey, is my tie on straight?" I said.

He looked and straightened it a tiny bit as he kept on singing: "*And John would buy the gown for you to wear to the prom . . .*"

"Does my hair look okay?" I said.

He smiled and nodded. "Perfect," he said. "You look great, Auggie."

"Via put some gel in it this morning," I said, pulling down the sun visor and looking in the little mirror. "It doesn't look too puffy?"

"No, it's very, very cool, Auggie. I don't think you've ever had it this short before, have you?"

"No, I got it cut yesterday. I think it makes me look more grown-up, don't you?"

"Definitely!" He was smiling, looking at me and nodding.

"But I'm the luckiest guy on the Lower East Side, 'cause I got wheels, and you want to go for a ride."

"Look at you, Auggie!" he said, smiling from ear to ear. "Look at you, looking so grown-up and spiffy. I can't believe you're graduating from the fifth grade!"

"I know, it's pretty awesome, right?" I nodded.

"It feels like just yesterday that you started."

"Remember I still had that *Star Wars* braid hanging from the back of my head?"

"Oh my gosh, that's right," he said, rubbing his palm over his forehead.

"You hated that braid, didn't you, Dad?"

"Hate is too strong a word, but I definitely didn't love it."

"You hated it, come on, admit it," I teased.

"No, I didn't hate it." He smiled, shaking his head. "But I will admit to hating that astronaut helmet you used to wear, do you remember?"

"The one Miranda gave me? Of course I remember! I used to wear that thing all the time."

"Good God, I hated that thing," he laughed, almost more to himself.

"I was so bummed when it got lost," I said.

"Oh, it didn't get lost," he answered casually. "I threw it out."

"Wait. What?" I said. I honestly didn't think I heard him right.

"The day is beautiful, and so are you," he was singing.

"Dad!" I said, turning the volume down.

"What?" he said.

"You threw it out?!"

He finally looked at my face and saw how mad I was. I couldn't believe he was being so matter-of-fact about the whole thing. I mean, to me this was a major revelation, and he was acting like it was no big deal.

"Auggie, I couldn't stand seeing that thing cover your face anymore," he said clumsily.

"Dad, I loved that helmet! It meant a lot to me! I was bummed beyond belief when it got lost—don't you remember?"

"Of course I remember, Auggie," he said softly. "Ohh, Auggie, don't be mad. I'm sorry. I just couldn't stand seeing you wear that thing on your head anymore, you know? I didn't think it was good for you." He was trying to look me in the eye, but I wouldn't look at him.

"Come on, Auggie, please try to understand," he continued, putting his hand under my chin and tilting my face toward him. "You were wearing that helmet all the time. And the real, real, real, real truth is: I missed seeing your face, Auggie. I know *you* don't always love it, but you have to understand . . . *I* love it. I *love* this face of yours, Auggie, completely and passionately. And it kind of broke my heart that you were always covering it up."

He was squinting at me like he really wanted me to understand.

"Does Mom know?" I said.

He opened his eyes wide. "No way. Are you kidding? She would have killed me!"

"She tore the place apart looking for that helmet, Dad," I said. "I mean, she spent like a week looking for it in every closet, in the laundry room, everywhere."

"I know!" he said, nodding. "That's why she'd kill me!"

And then he looked at me, and something about his expression made me start laughing, which made him open his mouth wide like he'd just realized something.

"Wait a minute, Auggie," he said, pointing his finger at me. "You have to promise me you will *never* tell Mommy anything about this."

I smiled and rubbed my palms together like I was about to get very greedy.

"Let's see," I said, stroking my chin. "I'll be wanting that new Xbox when it comes out next month. And I'll definitely be wanting my own car in about six years, a red Porsche would be nice, and . . ."

He started laughing. I love it when I'm the one who makes Dad laugh, since he's usually the funnyman that gets everybody else laughing.

"Oh boy, oh boy," he said, shaking his head. "You really have grown up."

The part of the song we love to sing the most started to play, and I turned up the volume. We both started singing.

"I'm the ugliest guy on the Lower East Side, but I've got wheels and you want to go for a ride. Want to go for a ride. Want to go for a ride. Want to go for a riiiiiiiiiiiiiiiiiiide."

We always sang this last part at the top of our lungs, trying to hold that last note as long as the guy who sang the song, which always made us crack up. While we were laughing, we noticed Jack had arrived and was walking over to our car. I started to get out.

"Hold on," said Dad. "I just want to make sure you've forgiven me, okay?"

"Yes, I forgive you."

He looked at me gratefully. "Thank you."

"But don't ever throw anything else of mine out again without telling me!"

"I promise."

I opened the door and got out just as Jack reached the car.

"Hey, Jack," I said.

"Hey, Auggie. Hey, Mr. Pullman," said Jack.

"How you doin', Jack?" said Dad.

"See you later, Dad," I said, closing the door.

"Good luck, guys!" Dad called out, rolling down the front window. "See you on the other side of fifth grade!"

We waved as he turned on the ignition and started to pull away, but then I ran over and he stopped the car. I put my head in the window so Jack wouldn't hear what I was saying.

"Can you guys not kiss me a lot after graduation?" I asked quietly. "It's kind of embarrassing."

"I'll try my best."

"Tell Mom, too?"

"I don't think she'll be able to resist, Auggie, but I'll pass it along."

"Bye, dear ol' Dad."

He smiled. "Bye, my son, my son."

Take Your Seats, Everyone

Jack and I walked right behind a couple of sixth graders into the building, and then followed them to the auditorium.

Mrs. G was at the entrance, handing out the programs and telling kids where to go.

"Fifth graders down the aisle to the left," she said. "Sixth graders go to the right. Everyone come in. Come in. Good morning. Go to your staging areas. Fifth graders to the left, sixth grade to the right . . ."

The auditorium was huge inside. Big sparkly chandeliers. Red velvet walls. Rows and rows and rows of cushioned seats leading up to the giant stage. We walked down the wide aisle and followed the signs to the fifth-grade staging area, which was in a big room to the left of the stage. Inside were four rows of folding chairs facing the front of the room, which is where Ms. Rubin was standing, waving us in as soon as we walked in the room.

"Okay, kids, take your seats. Take your seats," she was saying, pointing to the rows of chairs. "Don't forget, you're sitting alphabetically. Come on, everybody, take your seats." Not too many kids had arrived yet, though, and the ones who had weren't listening to her. Me and Jack were sword-fighting with our rolled-up programs.

"Hey, guys."

It was Summer walking over to us. She was wearing a light pink dress and, I think, a little makeup.

"Wow, Summer, you look awesome," I told her, because she really did.

"Really? Thanks, you do, too, Auggie."

"Yeah, you look okay, Summer," said Jack, kind of matter-of-factly. And for the first time, I realized that Jack had a crush on her.

"This is so exciting, isn't it?" said Summer.

"Yeah, kind of," I answered, nodding.

"Oh man, look at this program," said Jack, scratching his forehead. "We're going to be here all freakin' day."

I looked at my program.

Headmaster's Opening Remarks:
Dr. Harold Jansen

Middle-School Director's Address:
Mr. Lawrence Tushman

"Light and Day":
Middle-School Choir

Fifth-Grade Student Commencement Address:
Ximena Chin

Pachelbel: "Canon in D":
Middle-School Chamber Music Ensemble

Sixth-Grade Student Commencement Address:
Mark Antoniak

"Under Pressure":
Middle-School Choir

Middle-School Dean's Address:
Ms. Jennifer Rubin

Awards Presentation (see back)

Roll Call of Names

"Why do you think that?" I asked.

"Because Mr. Jansen's speeches go on forever," said Jack. "He's even worse than Tushman!"

"My mom said she actually dozed off when he spoke last year," Summer added.

"What's the awards presentation?" I asked.

"That's where they give medals to the biggest brainiacs," Jack answered. "Which would mean Charlotte and Ximena will win everything in the fifth grade, like they won everything in the fourth grade and in the third grade."

"Not in the second grade?" I laughed.

"They didn't give those awards out in the second grade," he answered.

"Maybe *you'll* win this year," I joked.

"Not unless they give awards for the most Cs!" he laughed.

"Everybody, take your seats!" Ms. Rubin started yelling louder now, like she was getting annoyed that nobody was listening. "We have a lot to get through, so take your seats. Don't forget you're sitting in alphabetical order! A through G is the first row! H through N is the second row; O through Q is the third row; R through Z is the last row. Let's go, people."

"We should go sit down," said Summer, walking toward the front section.

"You guys are definitely coming over my house after this, right?" I called out after her.

"Definitely!" she said, taking her seat next to Ximena Chin.

"When did Summer get so hot?" Jack muttered in my ear.

"Shut up, dude," I said, laughing as we headed toward the third row.

"Seriously, when did that happen?" he whispered, taking the seat next to mine.

"Mr. Will!" Ms. Rubin shouted. "Last time I checked, *W* came between *R* and *Z*, yes?"

Jack looked at her blankly.

"Dude, you're in the wrong row!" I said.

"I am?" And the face he made as he got up to leave, which was a mixture of looking completely confused and looking like he's just played a joke on someone, totally cracked me up.

A Simple Thing

About an hour later we were all seated in the giant auditorium waiting for Mr. Tushman to give his "middle-school address." The auditorium was even bigger than I imagined it would be—bigger even than the one at Via's school. I looked around, and there must have been a million people in the audience. Okay, maybe not a million, but definitely a lot.

"Thank you, Headmaster Jansen, for those very kind words of introduction," said Mr. Tushman, standing behind the podium on the stage as he talked into the microphone. "Welcome, my fellow teachers and members of the faculty. . . .

"Welcome, parents and grandparents, friends and honored guests, and most especially, welcome to my fifth- and sixth-grade students. . . .

"Welcome to the Beecher Prep Middle School graduation ceremonies!!!"

Everyone applauded.

"Every year," continued Mr. Tushman, reading from his notes with his reading glasses way down on the tip of his nose, "I am charged with writing two commencement addresses: one for the fifth- and sixth-grade graduation ceremony today, and one for the seventh- and eighth-grade ceremony that will take place tomorrow. And every year I say to myself, Let me cut down on my work and write just one address that I can use for both situations. Seems like it shouldn't be such a hard thing to do, right? And yet each year I still end up with two different speeches, no matter what my intentions, and I finally figured out why this year. It's not, as you might assume, simply because tomorrow I'll be talking to an older crowd with a middle-school experience that is largely behind them—whereas your middle-school experience is largely in front of you. No, I think it has to do more with this particular age that you are right now, this particular moment in your lives that, even after twenty years of my being around students this age, still moves me. Because you're at the cusp, kids. You're at the edge between childhood and everything that comes after. You're in transition.

"We are all gathered here together," Mr. Tushman continued, taking off his glasses and using them to point at all of us in the audience, "all your families, friends, and teachers, to celebrate not only your achievements of this past year, Beecher middle schoolers—but your endless possibilities.

"When you reflect on this past year, I want you all to look at where you are now and where you've been. You've all gotten a little taller, a little stronger, a little smarter . . . I hope."

Here some people in the audience chuckled.

"But the best way to measure how much you've grown isn't by inches or the number of laps you can now run around the track, or even your grade point average—though those things are important, to be sure. It's what you've done with your time, how you've chosen to spend your days, and whom you have touched this year. That, to me, is the greatest measure of success.

"There's a wonderful line in a book by J. M. Barrie—and no, it's not *Peter Pan*, and I'm not going to ask you to clap if you believe in fairies. . . ."

Here everyone laughed again.

"But in another book by J. M. Barrie called *The Little White Bird* . . . he writes . . ." He started flipping through a small book on the podium until he found the page he was looking for, and then he put on his reading glasses. " 'Shall we make a new rule of life . . . always to try to be a little kinder than is necessary?' "

Here Mr. Tushman looked up at the audience. "Kinder than is necessary," he repeated. "What a marvelous line, isn't it? Kinder than is *necessary*. Because it's not enough to be kind. One should be kinder than needed. Why I love that line, that concept, is that it reminds me that we carry with us, as human beings, not just the capacity to be kind, but the very choice of kindness. And what does that mean? How is that measured? You can't use a yardstick. It's like I was saying just before: it's not like measuring how much you've grown in a year. It's not exactly quantifiable, is it? How do we know we've been kind? What *is* being kind, anyway?"

He put on his reading glasses again and started flipping through another small book.

"There's another passage in a different book I'd like to share with you," he said. "If you'll bear with me while I find it. . . . Ah, here we go. In *Under the Eye of the Clock*, by Christopher Nolan, the main character is a young man who is facing some extraordinary challenges. There's this one part where someone helps him: a kid in his class. On the surface, it's a small gesture. But to this young man, whose name is Joseph, it's . . . well, if you'll permit me . . ."

He cleared his throat and read from the book: "'It was at moments such as these that Joseph recognized the face of God in human form. It glimmered in their kindness to him, it glowed in their keenness, it hinted in their caring, indeed it caressed in their gaze.'"

He paused and took off his reading glasses again.

"It glimmered in their kindness to him," he repeated, smiling. "Such a simple thing, kindness. Such a simple thing. A nice word of encouragement given when needed. An act of friendship. A passing smile."

He closed the book, put it down, and leaned forward on the podium.

"Children, what I want to impart to you today is an understanding of the value of that simple thing called kindness. And that's all I want to leave you with today. I know I'm kind of infamous for my . . . um . . . verbosity . . ."

Here everybody laughed again. I guess he knew he was known for his long speeches.

". . . but what I want you, my students, to take away from your middle-school experience," he continued, "is the sure knowledge that, in the future you make for yourselves, anything is possible. If every single person in this room made it a rule that wherever you are, whenever you can, you will try to act a little kinder than is necessary—the world really would be a better place. And if you do this, if you act just a little kinder than is necessary, someone else, somewhere, someday, may recognize in you, in every single one of you, the face of God."

He paused and shrugged.

"Or whatever politically correct spiritual representation of universal goodness you happen to believe in," he added quickly, smiling, which got a lot of laughs and loads of applause, especially from the back of the auditorium, where the parents were sitting.

Awards

I liked Mr. Tushman's speech, but I have to admit: I kind of zoned out a little during some of the other speeches.

I tuned in again as Ms. Rubin started reading off the names of the kids who'd made the High Honor Roll because we were supposed to stand up when our names were called. So I waited and listened for my name as she went down the list alphabetically. Reid Kingsley. Maya Markowitz. August Pullman. I stood up. Then when she finished reading off the names, she asked us all to face the audience and take a bow, and everyone applauded.

I had no idea where in that huge crowd my parents might be sitting. All I could see were the flashes of light from people taking photos and parents waving at their kids. I pictured Mom waving at me from somewhere even though I couldn't see her.

Then Mr. Tushman came back to the podium to present the medals for academic excellence, and Jack was right: Ximena Chin won the gold medal for "overall academic excellence in the fifth grade." Charlotte won the silver. Charlotte also won a gold medal for music. Amos won the medal for overall excellence in sports, which I was really happy about because, ever since the nature retreat, I considered Amos to be like one of my best friends in school. But I was really, really thrilled when Mr. Tushman called out Summer's name for the gold medal in creative writing. I saw Summer put her hand over her mouth when her name was called, and when she walked up onto the stage, I yelled: "Woo-hoo, Summer!" as loudly as I could, though I don't think she heard me.

After the last name was called, all the kids who'd just won awards stood next to each other onstage, and Mr. Tushman said to the audience: "Ladies and gentlemen, I am very honored to present to you this year's Beecher Prep School scholastic achievers. Congratulations to all of you!"

I applauded as the kids onstage bowed. I was so happy for Summer.

"The final award this morning," said Mr. Tushman, after the kids onstage had returned to their seats, "is the Henry Ward Beecher medal to honor students who have been notable or exemplary in certain areas throughout the school year. Typically, this medal has been our way of acknowledging volunteerism or service to the school."

I immediately figured Charlotte would get this medal because she organized the coat drive this year, so I kind of zoned out a bit again. I looked at my watch: 10:56. I was getting hungry for lunch already.

". . . Henry Ward Beecher was, of course, the nineteenth-century abolitionist—and fiery sermonizer for human rights—after whom this school was named," Mr. Tushman was saying when I started paying attention again.

"While reading up on his life in preparation for this award, I came upon a passage that he wrote that seemed particularly consistent with the themes I touched on earlier, themes I've been ruminating upon all year long. Not just the nature of kindness, but the nature of *one's* kindness. The power of *one's* friendship. The test of *one's* character. The strength of *one's* courage—"

And here the weirdest thing happened: Mr. Tushman's voice cracked a bit, like he got all choked up. He actually cleared his throat and took a big sip of water. I started paying attention, for real now, to what he was saying.

"The strength of one's courage," he repeated quietly, nodding and smiling. He held up his right hand like he was counting off. "Courage. Kindness. Friendship. Character. These are the qualities that define us as human beings, and propel us, on occasion, to greatness. And this is what the Henry Ward Beecher medal is about: recognizing greatness.

"But how do we do that? How do we measure something like greatness? Again, there's no yardstick for that kind of thing. How do we even define it? Well, Beecher actually had an answer for that."

He put his reading glasses on again, leafed through a book, and started to read. "'Greatness,' wrote Beecher, 'lies not in being strong, but in the right using of strength. . . . He is the greatest whose strength carries up the most hearts . . .'"

And again, out of the blue, he got all choked up. He put his two index fingers over his mouth for a second before continuing.

"'He is the greatest,'" he finally continued, "'whose strength carries up the most hearts by the attraction of his own.' Without further ado, this year I am very proud to award the Henry Ward Beecher medal to the student whose quiet strength has carried up the most hearts.

"So will August Pullman please come up here to receive this award?"

Floating

People started applauding before Mr. Tushman's words actually registered in my brain. I heard Maya, who was next to me, give a little happy scream when she heard my name, and Miles, who was on the other side of me, patted my back. "Stand up, get up!" said kids all around me, and I felt lots of hands pushing me upward out of my seat, guiding me to the edge of the row, patting my back, high-fiving me. "Way to go, Auggie!" "Nice going, Auggie!" I even started hearing my name being chanted: "Aug-gie! Aug-gie! Aug-gie!" I looked back and saw Jack leading the chant, fist in the air, smiling and signaling for me to keep going, and Amos shouting through his hands: "Woo-hoo, little dude!"

Then I saw Summer smiling as I walked past her row, and when she saw me look at her, she gave me a secret little thumbs-up and mouthed a silent "cool beans" to me. I laughed and shook my head like I couldn't believe it. I really couldn't believe it.

I think I was smiling. Maybe I was beaming, I don't know. As I walked up the aisle toward the stage, all I saw was a blur of happy bright faces looking at me, and hands clapping for me. And I heard people yelling things out at me: "You deserve it, Auggie!" "Good for you, Auggie!" I saw all my teachers in the aisle seats, Mr. Browne and Ms. Petosa and Mr. Roche and Mrs. Atanabi and Nurse Molly and all the others: and they were cheering for me, *woo-hooing* and whistling.

I felt like I was floating. It was so weird. Like the sun was shining full force on my face and the wind was blowing. As I got closer to the stage, I saw Ms. Rubin waving at me in the front row, and then next to her was Mrs. G, who was crying hysterically—a happy crying—smiling and clapping the whole time. And as I walked up the steps to the stage, the most amazing thing happened: everyone started standing up. Not just the front rows, but the whole audience suddenly got up on their feet, whooping, hollering, clapping like crazy. It was a standing ovation. For me.

I walked across the stage to Mr. Tushman, who shook my hand with both his hands and whispered in my ear: "Well done, Auggie." Then he placed the gold medal over my head, just like they do in the Olympics, and had me turn to face the audience. It felt like I was watching myself in a movie, almost, like I was someone else. It was like that last scene in *Star Wars Episode IV: A New Hope* when Luke Skywalker, Han Solo, and Chewbacca are being applauded for destroying the Death Star. I could almost hear the *Star Wars* theme music playing in my head as I stood on the stage.

I wasn't even sure why I was getting this medal, really.

No, that's not true. I knew why.

It's like people you see sometimes, and you can't imagine what it would be like to be that person, whether it's somebody in a wheelchair or somebody who can't talk. Only, I know that I'm that person to other people, maybe to every single person in that whole auditorium.

To me, though, I'm just me. An ordinary kid.

But hey, if they want to give me a medal for being me, that's okay. I'll take it. I didn't destroy a Death Star or anything like that, but I did just get through the fifth grade. And that's not easy, even if you're not me.

Pictures

Afterward there was a reception for the fifth and sixth graders under a huge white tent in the back of the school. All the kids found their parents, and I didn't mind at all when Mom and Dad hugged me like crazy, or when Via wrapped her arms around me and swung me left and right about twenty times. Then Poppa and Tata hugged me, and Aunt Kate and Uncle Po, and Uncle Ben—everyone kind of teary-eyed and wet-cheeked. But Miranda was the funniest: she was crying more than anyone and squeezed me so tight that Via had to practically pry her off of me, which made them both laugh.

Everyone started taking pictures of me and pulling out their Flips, and then Dad got me, Summer, and Jack together for a group shot. We put our arms around each other's shoulders, and for the first time I can remember, I wasn't even thinking about my face. I was just smiling a big fat happy smile for all the different cameras clicking away at me. *Flash, flash, click, click*: smiling away as Jack's parents and Summer's mom started clicking. Then Reid and Maya came over. *Flash, flash, click, click.* And then Charlotte came over and asked if she could take a picture with us, and we were like, "Sure, of course!" And then Charlotte's parents were snapping away at our little group along with everyone else's parents.

And the next thing I knew, the two Maxes had come over, and Henry and Miles, and Savanna. Then Amos came over, and Ximena. And we were all in this big tight huddle as parents clicked away like we were on a red carpet somewhere. Luca.

Isaiah. Nino. Pablo. Tristan. Ellie. I lost track of who else came over. Everybody, practically. All I knew for sure is that we were all laughing and squeezing in tight against each other, and no one seemed to care if it was my face that was next to theirs or not. In fact, and I don't mean to brag here, but it kind of felt like everyone wanted to get close to me.

The Walk Home

We walked to our house for cake and ice cream after the reception. Jack and his parents and his little brother, Jamie. Summer and her mother. Uncle Po and Aunt Kate. Uncle Ben, Tata and Poppa. Justin and Via and Miranda. Mom and Dad.

It was one of those great June days when the sky is completely blue and the sun is shining but it isn't so hot that you wish you were on the beach instead. It was just the perfect day. Everyone was happy. I still felt like I was floating, the *Star Wars* hero music in my head.

I walked with Summer and Jack, and we just couldn't stop cracking up. Everything made us laugh. We were in that giggly kind of mood where all someone has to do is look at you and you start laughing.

I heard Dad's voice up ahead and looked up. He was telling everyone a funny story as they walked down Amesfort Avenue. The grown-ups were all laughing, too. It was like Mom always said: Dad could be a comedian.

I noticed Mom wasn't walking with the group of grown-ups, so I looked behind me. She was hanging back a bit, smiling to herself like she was thinking of something sweet. She seemed happy.

I took a few steps back and surprised her by hugging her as she walked. She put her arm around me and gave me a squeeze.

"Thank you for making me go to school," I said quietly.

She hugged me close and leaned down and kissed the top of my head.

"Thank *you*, Auggie," she answered softly.

"For what?"

"For everything you've given us," she said. "For coming into our lives. For being you."

She bent down and whispered in my ear. "You really are a wonder, Auggie. You are a wonder."

APPENDIX

MR. BROWNE'S PRECEPTS

SEPTEMBER
When given the choice between being right or being kind, choose kind. —Dr. Wayne W. Dyer

OCTOBER
Your deeds are your monuments. —inscription on an Egyptian tomb

NOVEMBER
Have no friends not equal to yourself. —Confucius

DECEMBER
Audentes fortuna iuvat. (Fortune favors the bold.) —Virgil

JANUARY
No man is an island, entire of itself. —John Donne

FEBRUARY
It is better to know some of the questions than all of the answers. —James Thurber

MARCH
Kind words do not cost much. Yet they accomplish much. —Blaise Pascal

APRIL
What is beautiful is good, and who is good will soon be beautiful.
—Sappho

MAY
Do all the good you can,
By all the means you can,
In all the ways you can,
In all the places you can,
At all the times you can,
To all the people you can,
As long as you ever can.
—John Wesley's Rule

JUNE
Just follow the day and reach for the sun! —The Polyphonic
Spree, "Light and Day"

POSTCARD PRECEPTS

CHARLOTTE CODY'S PRECEPT
It's not enough to be friendly. You have to be a friend.

REID KINGSLEY'S PRECEPT
Save the oceans, save the world! —Me!

TRISTAN FIEDLEHOLTZEN'S PRECEPT
Your deeds may be your monuments, but a good joke goes a
long way, too!
—Tristan Fiedleholtzen

SAVANNA WITTENBERG'S PRECEPT
Flowers are great, but love is better. —Justin Bieber

HENRY JOPLIN'S PRECEPT
Don't be friends with jerks. —Henry Joplin

MAYA MARKOWITZ'S PRECEPT
All you need is love. —The Beatles

AMOS CONTI'S PRECEPT
Don't try too hard to be cool. It always shows, and that's uncool.
—Amos Conti

XIMENA CHIN'S PRECEPT
To thine own self be true. —*Hamlet*, Shakespeare

JULIAN ALBANS'S PRECEPT
Sometimes it's good to start over. —Julian Albans

SUMMER DAWSON'S PRECEPT
If you can get through middle school without hurting anyone's
feelings, that's really cool beans. —Summer Dawson

JACK WILL'S PRECEPT
Keep calm and carry on! —some saying from World War II

AUGUST PULLMAN'S PRECEPT
Everyone in the world should get a standing ovation at least once
in their life because we all overcometh the world. —Auggie

Auggie & Me

three wonder stories

The Julian Chapter

Be kind, for everyone you meet is fighting a hard battle.

–Ian Maclaren

Before

Perhaps I have created the stars and the sun

and this enormous house, but I no longer remember.

—Jorge Luis Borges, "The House of Asterion"

•   •   •

Fear can't hurt you any more than a dream.

—William Golding, *Lord of the Flies*

Ordinary

Okay, okay, okay.

I know, I know, I know.

I haven't been nice to August Pullman!

Big deal. It's not the end of the world, people! Let's stop with the drama, okay? There's a whole big world out there, and not everyone is nice to everyone else. That's just the way it is. So, can you please get over it? I think it's time to move on and get on with your life, don't you?

Jeez!

I don't get it. I really don't. One minute, I'm like, the most popular kid in the fifth grade. And the next minute, I'm like, I don't know. Whatever. This bites. This whole year bites! I wish Auggie Pullman had never come to Beecher Prep in the first place! I wish he had kept his creepy little face hidden away like in *The Phantom of the Opera* or something. Put a mask on, Auggie! Get your face out of my face, please. Everything would be a lot easier if you would just disappear.

At least for me. I'm not saying it's a picnic for him, either, by the way. I know it can't be easy for him to look in the mirror every day, or walk down the street. But that's not my problem. My problem is that everything's different since he's been coming to my school. The kids are different. I'm different. And it sucks big-time.

I wish everything was the way it used to be in the fourth grade. We had so, so, so much fun back then. We would play tackle-tag in the yard, and not to brag, but everyone always wanted a piece of me, you know? I'm just sayin'. Everyone always wanted to be my partner when we'd do social studies projects. And everyone always laughed when I said something funny.

At lunchtime, I'd always sit with my peeps, and we were like, it. We were totally *it*. Henry. Miles. Amos. Jack. We were it! It was so cool. We had all these secret jokes. Little hand signals for stuff.

I don't know why that had to change. I don't know why everyone got so stupid about stuff.

Actually, I do know why: it was because of Auggie Pullman. The moment he showed up, that's when things stopped being the way they used to be. Everything was totally ordinary. And now things are messed up. And it's because of him.

And Mr. Tushman. In fact, it's kind of totally Mr. Tushman's fault.

The Call

I remember Mom made a big deal about the call we got from Mr. Tushman. At dinner that night, she went on and on about what a big honor it was. The middle-school director had called us at home to ask if I could be a welcome buddy to some new kid in school. Wow! Big news! Mom acted like I won an Oscar or something. She said it showed her that the school really did recognize who the "special" kids were, which she thought was awesome. Mom had never met Mr. Tushman before, because he was the middle-school director and I was still in the lower school, but she couldn't stop raving about how nice he'd been on the phone.

Mom's always been kind of a bigwig at school. She's on this board of trustees thing, which I don't even know what it is but apparently it's a big deal. She's always volunteering for stuff, too. Like, she's always been the class mom for every grade I've been in at Beecher. Always. She does a lot for the school.

So, the day I was supposed to be a welcome buddy,

she dropped me off in front of the middle school. She wanted to take me inside, but I was like, "Mom, it's middle school!" She took the hint and drove off before I went inside.

Charlotte Cody and Jack Will were already in the front lobby, and we said hello to each other. Jack and I did our peeps' handshake and we said hello to the security guard. Then we went up to Mr. Tushman's office. It was so weird being in the school when there was no one there!

"Dude, we could totally skateboard in here and no one would know!" I said to Jack, running and gliding on the smooth floor of the hallway after the security guard couldn't see us anymore.

"Ha, yeah," said Jack, but I noticed that the closer we got to Mr. Tushman's office, the quieter Jack got. In fact, he kind of looked like he was going to blow chunks.

As we got near the top of the stairs, he stopped.

"I don't want to do this!" he said.

I stopped next to him. Charlotte had already gotten to the top landing.

"Come on!" she said.

"You're not the boss!" I answered.

She shook her head and rolled her eyes at me. I laughed and nudged Jack with my elbow. We loved egging Charlotte Cody on. She was always such a Goody Two-shoes!

"This is so messed up," said Jack, rubbing his hand over his face.

"What is?" I asked.

"Do you know who this new kid is?" he asked. I shook my head.

"You know who he is, right?" Jack said to Charlotte, looking up at her.

Charlotte walked down the stairs toward us. "I think so," she said. She made a face, like she had just tasted something bad.

Jack shook his head and then smacked it three times with his palm.

"I'm such an idiot for saying yes to this!" he said, his teeth clenched.

"Wait, who is it?" I said. I pushed Jack's shoulder so he'd look at me.

"It's that kid called August," he said to me. "You know, the kid with the face?"

I had no idea who he was talking about.

"Are you kidding me?" said Jack. "You never seen that kid before? He lives in this neighborhood! He hangs out in the playground sometimes. You have to have seen him. Everyone has!"

"He doesn't live in this neighborhood," answered Charlotte.

"Yes he does!" Jack answered impatiently.

"No, *Julian* doesn't live in this neighborhood," she answered, just as impatiently.

"What does that have to do with anything?" I said.

"Whatever!" Jack interrupted. "It doesn't matter. Trust me, dude, you've never seen anything like this before."

"Please don't be mean, Jack," Charlotte said. "It's not nice."

"I'm not being mean!" said Jack. "I'm just being truthful."

"What, exactly, does he look like?" I asked.

Jack didn't answer. He just stood there, shaking his head. I looked at Charlotte, who frowned.

"You'll see," she said. "Let's just go already, okay?" She turned around and went up the stairs and disappeared down the hall to Mr. Tushman's office.

"Let's just go already, okay?" I said to Jack, imitating Charlotte perfectly. I thought this would totally make him laugh, but it didn't.

"Jack, dude, come on!" I said.

I pretended to give him a hard slap in the face. This actually did make him laugh a bit, and he threw a slow-motion punch back at me. This led to a quick game of "spleen," which is where we try to jab each other in the rib cage.

"Guys, let's go!" Charlotte commanded from the top of the stairs. She had come back to get us.

"Guys, let's go!" I whispered to Jack, and this time he did kind of laugh.

But as soon as we rounded the corner of the hallway

and got to Mr. Tushman's office, we all got pretty serious.

When we went inside, Mrs. Garcia told us to wait in Nurse Molly's office, which was a small room to the side of Mr. Tushman's office. We didn't say anything to each other while we waited. I resisted the temptation to make a balloon out of the latex gloves that were in a box by the exam table, though I know it would have made everyone laugh.

Mr. Tushman

Mr. Tushman came into the office. He was tall, kind of thin, with messy gray hair.

"Hey, guys," he said, smiling. "I'm Mr. Tushman. You must be Charlotte." He shook Charlotte's hand. "And you are . . . ?" He looked at me.

"Julian," I said.

"Julian," he repeated, smiling. He shook my hand.

"And you're Jack Will," he said to Jack, and shook his hand, too.

He sat down on the chair next to Nurse Molly's desk. "First of all, I just want to thank you guys so much for coming here today. I know it's a hot day and you probably have other stuff you want to do. How's the summer been treating you? Okay?"

We all kind of nodded, looking at each other.

"How's the summer been for you?" I asked him.

"Oh, so nice of you to ask, Julian!" he answered. "It's been a great summer, thank you. Though I am seriously looking forward to the fall. I hate this hot weather."

He pulled his shirt. "I'm so ready for the winter."

All three of us were bobbing our heads up and down like doofballs at this point. I don't know why grown-ups ever bother chitchatting with kids. It just makes us feel weird. I mean, I personally am pretty okay talking to adults—maybe because I travel a lot and I've talked to a lot of adults before—but most kids really don't like talking to grown-ups. That's just the way it is. Like, if I see the parent of some friend of mine and we're not actually in school, I try to avoid eye contact so I don't have to talk to them. It's too weird. It's also really weird when you bump into a teacher outside of school. Like, one time I saw my third-grade teacher at a restaurant with her boyfriend, and I was like, ewww! I don't want to see my teacher hanging out with her boyfriend, you know?

Anyway, so there we were, me, Charlotte, and Jack, nodding away like total bobbleheads as Mr. Tushman went on and on about the summer. But finally—finally!—he got to the point.

"So, guys," he said, kind of slapping his hands against his thighs. "It's really nice of you to give up your afternoon to do this. In a few minutes, I'm going to introduce you to the boy who's coming to my office, and I just wanted to give you a heads-up about him beforehand. I mean, I told your moms a little bit about him—did they talk to you?"

Charlotte and Jack both nodded, but I shook my head.

"My mom just said he'd had a bunch of surgeries," I said.

"Well, yes," answered Mr. Tushman. "But did she explain about his face?"

I have to say, this is the point when I started thinking, *Okay, what the heck am I doing here?*

"I mean, I don't know," I said, scratching my head. I tried to think back to what Mom had told me. I hadn't really paid attention. I think most of the time she was going on and on about what an honor it was that I'd been chosen: she really didn't emphasize that there was something wrong with the kid. "She said that you said the kid had a lot of scars and stuff. Like he'd been in a fire."

"I didn't quite say that," said Mr. Tushman, raising his eyebrows. "What I told your mom is that this boy has a severe craniofacial difference—"

"Oh, right right right!" I interrupted, because now I remembered. "She did use that word. She said it was like a cleft lip or something."

Mr. Tushman scrunched up his face.

"Well," he said, lifting his shoulders and tilting his head left and right, "it's a little more than that." He got up and patted my shoulder. "I'm sorry if I didn't make that clear to your mom. In any case, I don't mean to make this awkward for you. In fact, it's exactly because I don't want it to be awkward that I'm talking to you right now. I just wanted to give you a heads-up that this boy definitely looks very different from other children. And that's not a secret. He knows he looks different. He was born that way. He gets that. He's a great kid. Very smart. Very nice. He's never gone to a regular school before because he was homeschooled, you know, because of all his surgeries. So that's why I just want you guys to show him around a bit, get to know him, be his welcome buddies. You can totally ask him questions, if you want. Talk to him normally. He's really just a normal kid with a face that . . . you know, is not so normal." He looked at us and took a deep breath. "Oh boy, I think I've just made you all more nervous, haven't I?"

We shook our heads. He rubbed his forehead.

"You know," he said, "one of the things you learn when you get old like me is that sometimes, a new situation will come along, and you'll have no idea what to do. There's no rule book that tells you how to act in every given situation in life, you know? So what I always say is that it's always better to err on the side of kindness. That's the secret. If you don't know what to do, just be kind. You can't go wrong. Which is why I asked you three to help me out here, because I'd heard from your lower-school teachers that you're all really nice kids."

We didn't know what to say to this, so we all just kind of smiled like goobers.

"Just treat him like you would treat any kid you've just met," he said. "That's all I'm trying to say. Okay, guys?"

We nodded at the same time now, too. Bobbling heads.

"You guys rock," he said. "So, relax, wait here a bit, and Mrs. Garcia will come and get you in a few minutes." He opened the door. "And, guys, really, thanks again for doing this. It's good karma to do good. It's a mitzvah, you know?"

With that, he smiled, winked at us, and left the room.

All three of us exhaled at the same time. We looked at each other, our eyes kind of wide.

"Okay," Jack said, "I don't know what the heck karma is and I don't know what the heck mitzvah is!"

This made us all laugh a little, though it was kind of a nervous type of laugh.

First Look

I'm not going to go into detail about the rest of what happened that day. I'm just going to point out that, for the first time in his life, Jack had not exaggerated. In fact, he had done the opposite. Is there a word that means the opposite of exaggerated? "Unexaggerated"? I don't know. But Jack had totally not exaggerated about this kid's face.

The first look I got of August, well, it made me want to cover my eyes and run away screaming. Bam. I know that sounds mean, and I'm sorry about that. But it's the truth. And anyone who says that that's not *their* first reaction when seeing Auggie Pullman isn't being honest. Seriously.

I totally would have walked out the door after I saw him, but I knew I would get in trouble if I did. So I just kept looking at Mr. Tushman, and I tried to listen to what he was saying, but all I heard was yak yak yak yak yak because my ears were burning. In my head, I was like, *Dude! Dude! Dude! Dude! Dude! Dude! Dude! Dude! Dude! Dude!*

Dude! Dude! Dude! Dude! Dude!

I think I said that word a thousand times to myself. I don't know why.

At some point, he introduced us to Auggie. Ahh! I think I actually shook his hand. Triple ahh! I wanted to zoom out of there so fast and wash my hand. But before I knew what was happening, we were headed out the door, down the hallway, and up the stairs.

Dude! Dude! Dude! Dude! Dude! Dude! Dude! Dude!

I caught Jack's eye as we were going up the stairs to homeroom. I opened my eyes really wide at him and mouthed the words, "No way!"

Jack mouthed back, "I told you!"

Scared

When I was about five, I remember watching an episode of *SpongeBob* one night, and a commercial came on TV that totally freaked me out. It was a few days before Halloween. A lot of commercials came on during that time of year that were kind of scary, but this one was for a new teen thriller I'd never heard about before. Suddenly, while I was watching the commercial, a close-up of a zombie's face popped up on the screen. Well, it totally and completely terrified me. I mean, terrified me like the kind of terrified where you actually run out of the room screaming with your arms in the air. TERRRRR-IFFF-FIED!

After that, I was so scared of seeing that zombie face again, I stopped watching any TV until Halloween was over and the movie was no longer playing in theaters. Seriously, I stopped watching TV completely—that's how scared I was!

Not too long after that, I was on a playdate with some kid whose name I don't even remember. And this kid was really into Harry Potter, so we started watching one of the Harry Potter movies (I'd never seen any of them before). Well, when I saw Voldemort's face for the first time, the same thing happened that had happened when the Halloween commercial came on. I started screaming hysterically, wailing like a total baby. It was so bad, the kid's mother couldn't calm me down, and she had to call my mother to come pick me up. My mom got really annoyed at the kid's mom for letting me watch the movie, so they ended up getting into an argument and—long story short—I never had another playdate there again. But anyway, between the Halloween zombie commercial and Voldemort's noseless face, I was kind of a mess.

Then, unfortunately, my dad took me to the movies at around that same time. Again, I was only about five. Maybe six by now. It shouldn't have been an issue: the movie we went to see was rated G, totally fine, not scary at all. But one of the trailers that came on was for *Scary Fairy*, a movie about demon fairies. I know—fairies are so lame!—and when I look back I can't believe I was so scared of this stuff, but I freaked out at this trailer. My dad had to take me out of the theater because—yet again!—I couldn't stop crying. It was so embarrassing! I mean, being scared of fairies? What's next? Flying ponies? Cabbage Patch dolls? Snowflakes? It was crazy! But there I was, shaking and screaming as I left the movie theater, hiding my face in my dad's coat. I'm sure there were three-year-olds in the audience who were looking at me like I was the biggest loser!

That's the thing about being scared, though. You can't control it. When you're scared, you're scared. And when you're scared, everything seems scarier than it ordinarily would be—even things that aren't. Everything that scares you kind of mushes together to become this big, terrifying feeling. It's like you're covered in this blanket of fear, and this blanket is made out of broken glass and dog poop and oozy pus and bloody zombie zits.

I started having awful nightmares. Every night, I'd wake up screaming. It got to a point where I was afraid to go to sleep because I didn't want to have another nightmare, so then I started sleeping in my parents' bed. I wish I could say this was just for a couple of nights, but it went like this for six weeks. I wouldn't let them turn off the lights. I had a panic attack every time I started drifting off to sleep. I mean, my palms would literally start to sweat and my heart would start to race, and I'd start to cry and scream before going to bed.

My parents took me to see a "feelings" doctor, which I only later realized was a child psychologist. Dr. Patel helped me a little bit. She said what I was experiencing were "night terrors," and it did help me to talk about them with her. But I think what really got me over the nightmares were the Discovery Channel nature videos my mom brought home for me one day. Woo-hoo for those nature videos! Every night, we'd pop one of them into the DVD player and I'd fall asleep to the sound of some guy with an English accent talking about meerkats or koalas or jellyfish.

Eventually, I did get over the nightmares, though. Everything went back to normal. But every once in a while, I'd have what Mom would call a "minor setback." Like, for instance, although I love *Star Wars* now, the very first time I saw *Star Wars: Episode II*, which was at a birthday sleepover when I was eight, I had to text my mom to come get me at two a.m. because I couldn't fall asleep: every time I'd close my eyes, Darth Sidious's face would pop into my head. It took about three weeks of nature videos to get over that setback (and I stopped going to sleepovers for about a year after that, too). Then, when I was nine, I saw *Lord of the Rings: The Two Towers* for the first time, and the same thing happened to me again, though this time it only took me about a week to get over Gollum.

By the time I turned ten, though, all those nightmares had pretty much gone away. Even the fear of having a nightmare was gone by then, too. Like, if I was at Henry's house and he would say, "Hey, let's watch a scary movie," my first reaction wasn't to think, *No, I might have a nightmare!* (which is what it used to be). My first reaction would be like, *Yeah, cool! Where's the popcorn?* I finally started being able to see all kinds of movies again. I even started getting into zombie apocalypse stuff, and none of it ever bothered me. That nightmare stuff was all behind me.

Or at least I thought it was.

But then, the night after I met Auggie Pullman, I started having nightmares again. I couldn't believe it. Not just passing bad dreams, but the full-blown, heart-pounding, wake-up-screaming kind of nightmares I used to have when I was a little kid. Only, I wasn't a little kid anymore.

I was in the fifth grade! Eleven years old! This wasn't supposed to be happening to me anymore!

But there I was again—watching nature videos to help me fall asleep.

Class Picture

I tried to describe what Auggie looked like to my mom, but she didn't get it until the school pictures arrived in the mail. Up until then, she'd never really seen him. She'd been away on a business trip during the Thanksgiving Sharing Festival, so she didn't see him then. On Egyptian Museum day, Auggie's face had been covered with mummy gauze. And there hadn't been any after-school concerts yet. So, the first time Mom saw Auggie and *finally* started understanding my nightmare situation was when she opened that large envelope with my class picture in it.

It was actually kind of funny. I can tell you exactly how she reacted because I was watching her as she opened it. First, she excitedly slit open the top of the envelope with a letter opener. Then, she pulled out my individual portrait. She put her hand on her chest.

"Awww, Julian, you look so handsome!" she said. "I'm so glad you wore that tie Grandmère sent you."

I was eating some ice cream at the kitchen table, and just smiled and nodded at her.

Then I watched her take the class picture out of the envelope. In lower school, every class would get its own picture taken with its own teacher, but in middle school, it's just one group picture of the entire fifth grade. So sixty kids standing in front of the entrance to the school. Fifteen kids in each row. Four rows. I was in the back row, in between Amos and Henry.

Mom was looking at the photo with a smile on her face.

"Oh, there you are!" she said when she spotted me.

She continued looking at the picture with a smile on her face.

"Oh my, look at how big Miles got!" said Mom. "And is that Henry? He looks like he's getting a mustache! And who is—"

And then she stopped talking. The smile on her face stayed frozen for a second or two, and then her face slowly transformed into a state of shock.

She put the photo down and stared blankly in front of her. Then she looked at the photo again.

Then she looked at me. She wasn't smiling.

"This is the kid you've been talking about?" she asked me. Her voice had completely changed from the way it sounded moments before.

"I told you," I answered.

340

She looked at the picture again. "This isn't just a cleft palate."

"No one ever said it *was* a cleft palate," I said to her. "Mr. Tushman never said that."

"Yes he did. On the phone that time."

"No, Mom," I answered her. "What he said was 'facial issues,' and you just assumed that he meant cleft palate. But he never actually said 'cleft palate.' "

"I could swear he said the boy had a cleft palate," she answered, "but this is so much worse than that." She really looked stunned. She couldn't stop staring at the photo. "What does he have, exactly? Is he developmentally delayed? He looks like he might be."

"I don't think so," I said, shrugging.

"Does he talk okay?"

"He kind of mumbles," I answered. "He's hard to understand sometimes."

Mom put the picture down on the table and sat down. She started tapping her fingers on the table.

"I'm trying to think of who his mother is," she said, shaking her head. "There are so many new parents in the school, I can't think of who it might be. Is she blond?"

"No, she has dark hair," I answered. "I see her at drop-off sometimes."

"Does she look . . . like the son?"

"Oh no, not at all," I said. I sat down next to her and picked up the picture, squinting at it so my eyes wouldn't see it too clearly. Auggie was in the front row, all the way on the left. "I told you, Mom. You didn't believe me, but I told you."

"It's not that I didn't believe you," she answered defensively. "I'm just kind of . . . surprised. I didn't realize it was this severe. Oh, I think I know who she is, his mom. Is she very pretty, kind of exotic, has dark wavy hair?"

"What?" I said, shrugging. "I don't know. She's a mom."

"I think I know who she is," answered Mom, nodding to herself. "I saw her on parents' night. Her husband's handsome, too."

"I have no idea," I said, shaking my head.

"Oh, those poor people!" She put her hand over her heart.

"Now you get why I've been having nightmares again?" I asked her.

She ran her hands through my hair.

"But are you still having nightmares?" she asked.

"Yes. Not every night like I did for the first month of school, but yeah!" I said, throwing the picture down on the tabletop. "Why did he have to come to Beecher Prep, anyway?"

I looked at Mom, who didn't know what to say. She started putting the picture back into the envelope.

"Don't even think of putting that in my school album, by the way," I said loudly. "You should just burn it or something."

"Julian," she said.

Then, out of the blue, I started crying.

"Oh, my darling!" said Mom, kind of surprised. She hugged me.

"I can't help it, Mom," I said through my tears. "I hate that I have to see him every day!"

That night, I had the same nightmare I've been having since the start of school. I'm walking down the main hallway, and all the kids are in front of their lockers, staring at me, whispering about me as I walk past them. I keep walking up the stairwell until I get to the bathroom, and then I look in the mirror. When I see myself, though, it's not me I'm seeing. It's Auggie. And then I scream.

Photoshop

The next morning, I overheard Mom and Dad talking as they were getting ready for work. I was getting dressed for school.

"They should have done more to prepare the kids," Mom said to Dad. "The school should have sent home a letter or something, I don't know."

"Come on," answered Dad. "Saying what? What can they possibly say? There's a homely kid in your class? Come on."

"It's much more than that."

"Let's not make too big a deal about it, Melissa."

"You haven't seen him, Jules," said Mom. "It's quite severe. Parents should have been told. I should have been told! Especially with Julian's anxiety issues."

"Anxiety issues?" I yelled from my room. I ran into their bedroom. "You think I have anxiety issues?"

"No, Julian," said Dad. "No one's saying that."

"Mom just said that!" I answered, pointing at Mom.

344

"I just heard her say 'anxiety issues.' What, so you guys think I have mental problems?"

"No!" they both said.

"Just because I get nightmares?"

"No!" they yelled.

"It's not my fault he goes to my school!" I cried. "It's not my fault his face freaks me out!"

"Of course it's not, darling," said Mom. "No one is saying that. All I meant is that because of your history of nightmares, the school should have alerted me. Then at least I would have known better about the nightmares you're having. I would have known what triggered them."

I sat down on the edge of their bed. Dad had the class picture in his hands and had obviously just been looking at it.

"I hope you're planning on burning that," I said. And I wasn't joking.

"No, darling," said Mom, sitting on the other side of me. "We don't need to burn anything. Look what I've done."

She picked up a different photo from the nightstand and handed it to me to look at. At first, I thought it was just another copy of the class picture, because it was exactly the same size as the class picture Dad had in his hands, and everything in it was exactly the same. I started to look away in disgust, but Mom pointed to a place on the photo—the place where Auggie used to be! He was nowhere in the photo.

I couldn't believe it! There was no trace of him!

I looked up at Mom, who was beaming.

"The magic of Photoshop!" she said happily, clapping her hands. "Now you can look at this picture and not have to have your memory of fifth grade tarnished," she said.

"That's so cool!" I said. "How did you do that?"

"I've gotten pretty good at Photoshop," she answered. "Remember last year, how I made all the skies blue in the Hawaii pictures?"

"You would never have known it rained every day," answered Dad, shaking his head.

"Laugh if you want," said Mom. "But now, when I look at those pictures, I don't have to be reminded of the bad weather that almost ruined our trip. I can remember it for the beautiful vacation that it was! Which is exactly how I want you to remember your fifth-grade year at Beecher Prep. Okay, Julian? Good memories. Not ugly ones."

"Thanks, Mom!" I said, hugging her tightly.

I didn't say it, of course, but even though she changed the skies to light blue on the photos, all I ever really remembered about our Hawaii trip was how cold and wet it was when we were there—despite the magic of Photoshop.

Mean

Look, I didn't start out being mean. I mean, I'm not a mean kid! Sure, sometimes I make jokes, but they're not mean jokes. They're just teasing jokes. People have to lighten up a little! Okay, maybe sometimes my jokes are a little mean, but I only make those jokes behind someone's back. I never say stuff to anyone's face that will actually hurt someone. I'm not a bully like that! I'm not a hater, dudes!

Attention, people! Stop being so sensitive!

Some people totally got the whole Photoshop thing, and some didn't. Henry and Miles thought it was so cool and wanted my mom to email their moms the photo. Amos thought it was "weird." Charlotte completely disapproved. I don't know what Jack thought, because he had gone over to the dark side by now. It's like he totally abandoned his peeps this year and only hangs out with Auggie now. Which bugged me, because that meant I couldn't hang out with him anymore. No way was I going to catch the "plague" from that freak.

That was the name of the game I invented. The Plague. It was simple. If you touched Auggie, and you didn't wash off the contamination, you died. Everyone in the whole grade played. Except Jack.

And Summer.

So here's the strange thing. I've known Summer since we were in third grade, and I never really paid any attention to her, but this year Henry started liking Savanna and they were like, "going out." Now, by "going out" I don't mean like high-school stuff, which would be kind of gross barf disgusting. All it means when you're "going out" is that you hang out together and meet each other at the lockers and sometimes go to the ice-cream shop on Amesfort Avenue after school. So, first Henry started going out with Savanna, and then Miles started going out with Ximena. And I was like, "Yo, what about me?" And then Amos said, "I'm going to ask Summer out," and I was like, "No way, I'm asking her out!" So that's when I started kind of liking Summer.

But it totally bit that Summer, like Jack, was on Team Auggie. It meant I couldn't hang out with her at all. I couldn't even say "Wassup" to her because the freak might think I was talking to him or something. So I told Henry to have Savanna invite Summer to the Halloween party at her house. I figured I could hang out with her and maybe even ask her to go out with me. That didn't work, though, because she ended up leaving the party early. And ever since then, she's been spending all her time with the freak.

Okay, okay. I know it's not nice to call him "the freak," but like I said before, people have to start being a little less sensitive around here! It's only a joke, everyone! Don't take me so seriously! I'm not being mean. I'm just being funny.

And that's all I was doing, being totally funny, the day that Jack Will punched me. I had been totally joking! Fooling around.

I didn't see it coming at *all*!

The way I remember it, we were just goofing together, and all of a sudden, he whacks me in the mouth for no reason! Boom!

And I was like, *Owwwww! You crazy jerkface! You punched me? You actually punched me?*

And the next thing I know, I'm in Nurse Molly's office, holding one of my teeth in my hand, and Mr. Tushman is there, and I hear him on the phone with my mom saying they're taking me to the hospital. I could hear my mom screaming on the other end of the line. Then Ms. Rubin, the dean, is leading me into the back of an ambulance and we're on the way to a hospital! Crazy stuff!

When we were riding in the ambulance, Ms. Rubin asked me if I knew why Jack hit me. I was like, *Duh, because he's totally insane!* Not that I could talk much, because my lips were swollen and there was blood all over my mouth.

Ms. Rubin stayed with me in the hospital until Mom showed up. Mom was more than a little hysterical, as you can imagine. She was crying kind of dramatically every time she saw my face. It was, I have to admit, a little embarrassing.

Then Dad showed up.

"Who did this?" was the first thing he said, shouting at Ms. Rubin.

"Jack Will," answered Ms. Rubin calmly. "He's with Mr. Tushman now."

"Jack Will?" cried Mom in shock. "We know the Wills! How could that happen?"

"There will be a thorough investigation," answered Ms. Rubin. "Right now, what's most important is that Julian's going to be fine . . ."

"Fine?" yelled Mom. "Look at his face! Do you think that's fine? I don't think that's fine. This is outrageous. What kind of school is this? I thought kids didn't punch each other at a school like Beecher Prep. I thought that's why we pay forty thousand dollars a year, so that our kids don't get hurt."

"Mrs. Albans," said Ms. Rubin, "I know you're upset . . ."

"I'm assuming the kid will get expelled, right?" said Dad.

"Dad!" I yelled.

"We will definitely deal with this matter in the appropriate way, I promise," answered Ms. Rubin, trying

350

to keep her voice calm. "And now, if you don't mind, I think I'll leave you guys alone for a bit. The doctor will be back and you can check in with him, but he said that nothing was broken. Julian's fine. He lost a lower first molar, but that was on its way out anyway. He's going to give him some pain medication and you should keep icing it. Let's talk more in the morning."

It was only then that I realized that poor Ms. Rubin's blouse and skirt were completely covered in my blood. Boy, mouths do bleed a lot!

Later that night, when I could finally talk again without it hurting, Mom and Dad wanted to know every detail of what had happened, starting with what Jack and I had been talking about right before he hit me.

"Jack wath upthet becauth he wath paired up with the deformed kid," I answered. "I told him he could thwitch partnerth if he wanted to. And then he punched me!"

Mom shook her head. That was it for her. She was literally madder than I'd ever seen her before (and I've seen my mom pretty mad before, believe me!).

"This is what happens, Jules!" she said to Dad, crossing her arms and nodding quickly. "This is what happens when you make little kids deal with issues they're not equipped to deal with! They're just too young to be exposed to this kind of stuff! That Tushman is an *idiot!*"

And she said a whole bunch of other things, too, but

those are kind of too inapro-pro (if you know what I mean) for me to repeat.

"But, Dad, I don't want Jack to get ecthpelled from thkool," I said later on in the night. He was putting more ice on my mouth because the painkiller they had given me at the hospital was wearing off.

"That's not up to us," he answered. "But I wouldn't trouble myself about it if I were you. Whatever happens, Jack will get what he deserves for this."

I have to admit, I started feeling kind of bad for Jack. I mean, sure, he was a total dipstick for punching me, and I wanted him to get in trouble—but I really didn't want him to get kicked out of school or anything.

But Mom, I could tell, was on one of her missions now (as Dad would say). She gets like that sometimes, when she gets so outraged about something that there's just no stopping her. She was like that a few years ago when a kid got hit by a car a couple of blocks away from Beecher Prep, and she had like a million people sign a petition to have a traffic light installed. That was a super-mom moment. She was also like that last month when our favorite restaurant changed its menu and they no longer made my favorite dish the way I liked it. That was another super-mom moment because after she talked to the new owner, they agreed to special-order the dish—just for me! But Mom also gets like that for not-so-nice stuff, like when a waiter messes up a food order. That's a not-so-super-mom moment because, well, you know, it can get kind of weird when your mom starts talking to a waiter like he's five years old. *Awkward!* Also, like Dad says, you don't want to get a waiter mad at you, you know? They have your food in *their* hands—duh!

So, I wasn't totally clear on how I felt when I realized that my mom was declaring war on Mr. Tushman, Auggie Pullman, and all of Beecher Prep. Was it going to be a super-mom moment or a not-so-super-mom moment? Like, would it end up with Auggie going to a different school—yay!—or with Mr. Tushman blowing his nose in my cafeteria food—ugh!

Party

It took about two weeks for the swelling to go completely down. Because of that, we ended up not going to Paris over winter break. Mom didn't want our relatives to see me looking like I'd been in a "prize fight." She also wouldn't take any pictures of me over the holidays because she said she didn't want to remember me looking like that. For our annual Christmas card, we used one of the rejects from last year's photo shoot.

Even though I wasn't having a lot of nightmares anymore, the fact that I had started having nightmares again really worried Mom. I could tell she was totally stressed out about it. Then, the day before our Christmas party, she found out from one of the other moms that Auggie had not been through the same kind of admissions screening that the rest of us had been. See, every kid who applies to Beecher Prep is supposed to be interviewed and take a test at the school—but some kind of exception had been made for Auggie. He didn't come to the school for the interview and he got to take the admissions test at home. Mom thought that was really unfair!

"This kid should not have gotten into the school," I heard her telling a group of other moms at the party. "Beecher Prep is just not set up to handle situations like this! We're not an inclusion school! We don't have the psychologists needed to deal with how it affects the other kids. Poor Julian had nightmares for a whole month!"

Ugh, Mom! I hate your telling people about my nightmares!

"Henry was upset as well," Henry's mom said, and the other moms nodded.

"They didn't even prepare us beforehand!" Mom went on. "That's what gets me the most. If they're not going to provide additional psychological support, at least warn the parents ahead of time!"

"Absolutely!" said Miles's mom, and the other moms nodded again.

"Obviously, Jack Will could have used some therapy," Mom said, rolling her eyes.

"I was surprised they didn't expel him," said Henry's mom.

"Oh, they would have!" answered Mom, "but we asked them not to. We've known the Will family since kindergarten. They're good people. We don't blame Jack, really. I think he just cracked under the pressure of having to be this kid's caretaker. That's what happens when you put little kids into these kinds of situations. I honestly don't know what Tushman was thinking!"

"I'm sorry, I just have to step in here," said another mom (I think it was Charlotte's mom because she had the same bright blond hair and big blue eyes). "It's not like there's anything wrong with this kid, Melissa. He's a great kid, who just happens to look different, but . . ."

"Oh, I know!" Mom answered, and she put her hand over her heart. "Oh, Brigit, no one's saying he's not a great kid, believe me. I'm sure he is. And I hear the parents are lovely people. That's not the issue. To me, ultimately, the simple fact of the matter is that Tushman didn't follow protocol. He flagrantly disregarded the applications process by not having the boy come to Beecher Prep for the interview—or take the test like every one of our kids did. He broke the rules. And rules are rules. That's it." Mom made a sad face at Brigit. "Oh dear, Brigit. I can see you totally disapprove!"

"No, Melissa, not at all," Charlotte's mom said, shaking her head. "It's a tough situation all around. Look, the fact is, your son got punched in the face. You have every right to feel angry and demand some answers."

"Thank you." Mom nodded and crossed her arms. "I just think the whole thing's been handled terribly, that's all. And I blame Tushman. Completely."

"Absolutely," said Henry's mom.

"He's got to go," agreed Miles's mom.

356

I looked at Mom, surrounded by nodding moms, and I thought, *Okay, so maybe this is going to turn out to be one of those really super-mom moments.* Maybe everything she was doing would make it so that Auggie ended up going to a different school, and then things could go back to the way it used to be at Beecher Prep. That would be so awesome!

But a part of me was thinking, *Maybe this is going to turn into a not-so-super-mom moment.* I mean, some of the stuff she was saying sounded kind of . . . I don't know. Kind of harsh, I guess. It's like when she gets mad at a waiter. You end up feeling sorry for the waiter. The thing is, I know she's on this anti-Tushman mission because of me. If I hadn't started getting nightmares again, and if Jack hadn't punched me, none of this would be happening. She wouldn't be making a big deal about Auggie, or Tushman, and she'd be concentrating all her time and energy on good stuff, like raising money for the school and volunteering at the homeless shelter. Mom does good stuff like that all the time!

So I don't know. On the one hand, I'm happy she's trying to help me. And on the other hand, I would love for her to stop.

Team Julian

The thing that annoyed me the most when we got back from winter break was that Jack had gone back to being friends with Auggie again. They had had some kind of fight after Halloween, which is why Jack and I started being bros again. But after winter break was over, they were best buds again.

It was so lame!

I told everyone we needed to really ice Jack out, for his own good. He had to choose, once and for all, whether he wanted to be on Team Auggie or Team Julian and the Rest of the World. So we started completely ignoring Jack: not talking to him, not answering his questions. It was like he didn't exist.

That'll show him!

And that's when I started leaving my little notes. One day, someone had left some Post-it notes on one of the benches in the yard, which is what gave me the idea. I wrote in this really psycho-killer handwriting:

Nobody likes you anymore!

358

I slipped it into the slits in Jack's locker when no one was looking. I watched him out of the corner of my eye when he found it. He turned around and saw Henry opening his locker nearby.

"Did Julian write this?" he asked.

But Henry was one of my peeps, you know? He just iced Jack out, pretended like no one was even talking to him. Jack crumpled the Post-it and flicked it into his locker and banged the door shut.

After Jack left, I went over to Henry.

"Hollah!" I said, giving him the devil's sign, which made Henry laugh.

Over the next couple of days, I left a few more notes in Jack's locker. And then I started leaving some in Auggie's locker.

They were not—I repeat, not—a big deal. They were mostly stupid stuff. I didn't think anyone would ever take them seriously. I mean, they were actually kind of funny!

Well, kind of. At least, some of them were.

> *You stink, big cheese!*
> *Freak!*
> *Get out of our school, orc!*

No one but Henry and Miles knew that I was writing these notes. And they were sworn to secrecy.

Dr. Jansen's Office

I don't know how the heck Mr. Tushman found out about them. I don't think Jack or Auggie would have been dumb enough to rat on me, because they had started leaving me notes in my locker, too. I mean, how stupid would you have to be to rat someone out about something that you were doing, too?

So, here's what happened. A few days before the Fifth-Grade Nature Retreat, which I was totally looking forward to, Mom got a phone call from Dr. Jansen, the headmaster of Beecher Prep. He said he wanted to discuss something with her and Dad, and asked for a meeting.

Mom assumed it probably had to do with Mr. Tushman, that maybe he was getting fired. So she was actually kind of excited about the meeting!

They showed up for the appointment at ten a.m., and they were waiting in Dr. Jansen's office when, all of a sudden, they see me walking into the office, too. Ms. Rubin had taken me out of class, asked me to follow her,

360

and brought me there: I had no idea what was up. I'd never even been to the headmaster's office before, so when I saw Mom and Dad there, I looked as confused as they looked.

"What's going on?" Mom said to Ms. Rubin. Before Ms. Rubin could say anything, Mr. Tushman and Dr. Jansen came into the office.

Everyone shook hands and they were all smiles as they greeted one another. Ms. Rubin said she had to go back to class but that she would call Mom and Dad later to check in. This surprised Mom. I could tell she started thinking that maybe this wasn't about Mr. Tushman getting fired, after all.

Then Dr. Jansen asked us to sit on the sofa opposite his desk. Mr. Tushman sat down in a chair next to us, and Dr. Jansen sat behind his desk.

"Well, thank you so much for coming, Melissa and Jules," Dr. Jansen said to my parents. It was strange hearing him call them by their first names. I knew they all knew each other from being on the board, but it sounded weird. "I know how busy you are. And I'm sure you're wondering what this is all about."

"Well, yes . . ." said Mom, but her voice drifted off. Dad coughed into his hand.

"The reason we asked you here today is because, unfortunately," Dr. Jansen continued, "we have a serious matter on our hands, and we'd like to figure out the best way to resolve it. Julian, do you have any inkling of what I might be talking about?" He looked at me.

I opened my eyes wide.

"Me?" I snapped my head back and made a face. "No."

Dr. Jansen smiled and sighed at me at the same time. He took off his glasses.

"You understand," he said, looking at me, "we take bullying very seriously at Beecher Prep. There's zero tolerance for any kind of bullying. We feel that every single one of our students deserves the right to learn in a caring and respectful atmosphere—"

"Excuse me, but can someone tell me what's going on here?" Mom interrupted, looking at Dr. Jansen impatiently. "We obviously know the mission statement at Beecher Prep, Hal: we practically wrote it! Let's cut to the chase—what's going on?"

Evidence

Dr. Jansen looked at Mr. Tushman. "Why don't you explain, Larry?" he said.

Mr. Tushman handed an envelope to Mom and Dad. Mom opened it and pulled out the last three Post-it notes I had left in Auggie's locker. I knew immediately that's what they were because these were actually pink Post-its and not yellow ones like all the others had been.

So, I thought: *Ah-ha! So it was Auggie who told Mr. Tushman about the Post-it notes! What a turd!!*

Mom read through the notes quickly, raised her eyebrows, and passed them to Dad. He read them and looked at me.

"You wrote these, Julian?" he said, holding the notes out for me.

I swallowed. I looked at him kind of blankly. He handed me the notes, and I just stared at them.

"Um . . . well," I answered. "Yeah, I guess. But, Dad, they were writing notes, too!"

"Who was writing notes?" asked Dad.

"Jack and Auggie," I answered. "They were writing notes to me, too! It wasn't just me!"

"But you started the note writing, didn't you?" asked Mr. Tushman.

"Excuse me," Mom interjected angrily. "Let's not forget that it was Jack Will who punched Julian in the mouth, not the other way around. Obviously, there's going to be residual anger—"

"How many of these notes did you write, Julian?" Dad interrupted, tapping on the Post-its I was holding.

"I don't know," I said. It was hard for me to get the words out. "Like, six or something. But the other ones weren't this . . . you know, bad. These notes are worse than the other ones I wrote. The other ones weren't so . . ." My voice kind of drifted off as I reread what I'd written on the three notes:

Yo, Darth Hideous. You're so ugly you should wear a mask every day!

And:

I h8 u, Freak!

And the last one:

I bet your mother wishes you'd never been born. You should do everybody a favor—and die.

Of course, looking at them now, they seemed a lot worse than when I wrote them. But I was mad then— super mad. I had just gotten one of their notes and . . .

"Wait!" I said, and I reached into my pocket. I found

the last Post-it that Auggie and Jack had left for me in my locker, just yesterday. It was kind of crumpled up now, but I held it out to Mr. Tushman to read. "Look! They wrote mean stuff to me, too!"

Mr. Tushman took the Post-it, read it quickly, and handed it to my parents. My mom read it and then looked at the floor. My dad read it and shook his head, puzzled.

He handed me the Post-it and I reread it.

Julian, you're so hot! Summer doesn't like you, but I want to have your babies! Smell my armpits! Love, Beulah.

"Who the heck is Beulah?" asked Dad.

"Never mind," I answered. "I can't explain." I handed the Post-it back to Mr. Tushman, who gave it to Dr. Jansen to read. I noticed he actually tried to hide a smile.

"Julian," said Mr. Tushman, "the three notes you wrote don't compare at all to this note in content."

"I don't think it's for anyone else to judge the semantics of a note," said Mom. "It doesn't matter whether you think one note is worse than the other— it's how the person reading the note reads it. The fact is, Julian's had a little crush on this Summer girl all year long, and it probably hurt his feelings—"

"Mom!" I yelled, and I covered my face with my hands. "That's so embarrassing!"

"All I'm saying is that a note can be hurtful to a child—whether *you* see it or not," Mom said to Mr. Tushman.

"Are you kidding me?" answered Mr. Tushman, shaking his head. He sounded angrier than I had ever heard him before. "Are you telling me you don't find the Post-its your son wrote completely horrifying? Because I do!"

"I'm not defending the notes!" answered Mom. "I'm just reminding you that it was a two-way street. You have to realize that Julian was obviously writing those notes as a reaction to something."

"Look," said Dr. Jansen, holding his hand out in front of him like a crossing guard. "There's no doubt there's some history here."

"Those notes hurt my feelings!" I said, and I didn't mind that I sounded like I was going to cry.

"I don't doubt that their notes hurt your feelings, Julian," Dr. Jansen answered. "And you were trying to hurt their feelings. That's the problem with stuff like this—everyone keeps trying to top one another, and then things escalate out of control."

"Exactly!" said Mom, and it almost sounded like she screamed it.

"But the fact is," Dr. Jansen continued, holding up his finger, "there is a line, Julian. There is a line. And your notes crossed that line. They're completely unacceptable. If Auggie had read these notes, how do you think he'd feel?"

He was looking at me so intensely that I felt like disappearing under the sofa.

366

"You mean he hasn't read them?" I asked.

"No," answered Dr. Jansen. "Thank goodness someone reported the notes to Mr. Tushman yesterday, and he opened Auggie's locker and intercepted them before Auggie ever saw them." I nodded and lowered my head. I have to admit—I was glad Auggie hadn't read them. I guess I knew what Dr. Jansen meant about "crossing the line." But then I thought, *So if it wasn't Auggie who ratted me out, who was it?*

We were all quiet for a minute or two. It was awkward beyond belief.

The Verdict

"Okay," said Dad finally, rubbing his palm over his face. "Obviously, we understand the seriousness of the situation now, and we will . . . do something about it."

I don't think I'd ever seen Dad look so uncomfortable. I'm sorry, Dad!

"Well, we have some recommendations," answered Dr. Jansen. "Obviously, we want to help everyone involved . . ."

"Thank you for understanding," said Mom, getting her pocketbook ready as if she were getting up.

"But there are consequences!" said Mr. Tushman, looking at Mom.

"Excuse me?" she shot back at him.

"As I said in the beginning," Dr. Jansen interjected, "the school has a very strict anti-bullying policy."

"Yeah, we saw how strict it was when you *didn't* expel Jack Will for punching Julian in the mouth," Mom answered quickly. Yeah, take that, Mr. Tushman!

"Oh, come on! That was completely different," Mr. Tushman answered dismissively.

"Oh?" answered Mom. "Punching someone in the face isn't bullying to you?"

"Okay, okay," said Dad, raising his hand to keep Mr. Tushman from answering. "Let's just cut to the chase, okay? What exactly are your recommendations, Hal?"

Dr. Jansen looked at him.

"Julian is being suspended for two weeks," he said.

"What?" yelled Mom, looking at Dad. But Dad didn't look back.

"In addition," said Dr. Jansen, "we're recommending counseling. Nurse Molly has the names of several therapists who we think Julian should see—"

"This is outrageous," interrupted Mom, steaming.

"Wait," I said. "You mean, I can't go to school?"

"Not for two weeks," answered Mr. Tushman. "Starting immediately."

"But what about the trip to the nature retreat?" I asked.

"You can't go," he answered coldly.

"No!" I said, and now I really was about to cry. "I want to go to the nature retreat!"

"I'm sorry, Julian," Dr. Jansen said gently.

"This is absolutely ridiculous," said Mom, looking at Dr. Jansen. "Don't you think you're overreacting a little? That kid didn't even read the notes!"

"That's not the point!" answered Mr. Tushman.

"I'll tell you what I think!" said Mom. "This is because you admitted a kid into the school who shouldn't have been admitted into the school in the first place. And you broke the rules to do it. And now you're just taking this out on my kid because I'm the one who had the guts to call you on it!"

"Melissa," said Dr. Jansen, trying to calm her down.

"These children are too young to deal with things like this . . . facial deformities, disfigurement," Mom continued, talking to Dr. Jansen. "You must see that! Julian's had nightmares because of that boy. Did you know that? Julian has anxiety issues."

"Mom!" I said, clenching my teeth.

"The board should have been consulted about whether Beecher Prep was the right place for a child like that," Mom continued. "That's all I'm saying! We're just not set up for it. There are other schools that are, but we're not!"

"You can choose to believe that if you want," answered Mr. Tushman, not looking at her.

Mom rolled her eyes.

"This is a witch hunt," she muttered quietly, looking out the window. She was fuming.

I had no idea what she was talking about. Witches? What witches?

"Okay, Hal, you said you had some recommendations," Dad said to Dr. Jansen. He sounded gruff. "Is that it? Two-week suspension and counseling?"

"We'd also like for Julian to write a letter of apology to August Pullman," said Mr. Tushman.

"Apology for what exactly?" answered Mom. "He wrote some stupid notes. Surely he's not the only kid in the world who's ever written a stupid note."

"It's more than a stupid note!" answered Mr. Tushman. "It's a pattern of behavior." He started counting on his fingers. "It's the making faces behind the kid's back. It's the 'game' he initiated, where if someone touches Auggie he has to wash his hands . . ."

I couldn't believe Mr. Tushman even knew about the Plague game! How do teachers know so much?

"It's social isolation," Mr. Tushman continued. "It's creating a hostile atmosphere."

"And you know for a fact that it's Julian who initiated all this?" asked Dad. "Social isolation? Hostile atmosphere? Are you saying that Julian was the only kid who wasn't nice to this boy? Or are you suspending every kid who stuck his tongue out at this kid?"

Good one, Dad! Score one for the Albanses!

"Doesn't it trouble you at all that Julian doesn't seem to be showing the least bit of remorse?" said Mr. Tushman, squinting at Dad.

"Okay, let's just stop right here," Dad said quietly, pointing his finger in Mr. Tushman's face.

"Please, everyone," said Dr. Jansen. "Let's calm down a bit. Obviously, this is difficult."

"After all we've done for this school," Mom answered,

shaking her head. "After all the money and the time we've put into this school, you would think we'd get just a little bit of consideration." She put her thumb and her index finger together. "Just a little."

Dad nodded. He was still looking angrily at Mr. Tushman, but then he looked at Dr. Jansen. "Melissa's right," he said. "I think we deserved a little better than this, Hal. A friendly warning would have been nice. Instead, you call us in here like children . . ." He stood up. "We deserved better."

"I'm sorry you feel that way," said Dr. Jansen, standing up as well.

"The board of trustees will hear about this," said Mom. She got up, too.

"I'm sure they will," answered Dr. Jansen, crossing his arms and nodding.

Mr. Tushman was the only adult still sitting down.

"The point of the suspension isn't punitive," he said quietly. "We're trying to help Julian, too. He can't fully understand the ramifications of his actions if you keep trying to justify them away. We want him to feel some empathy—"

"You know, I've heard just about enough!" said Mom, holding her palm in front of Mr. Tushman's face. "I don't need parenting advice. Not from someone who doesn't have kids of his own. You don't know what it's like to see your kid having a panic attack every time he shuts his eyes to go to sleep, okay? You don't know what it's like."

372

Her voice cracked a bit, like she was going to cry. She looked at Dr. Jansen. "This affected Julian deeply, Hal. I'm sorry if that's not politically correct to say, but it's the truth, and I'm just trying to do what I think is best for my son! That's all. Do you understand?"

"Yes, Melissa," Dr. Jansen answered softly.

Mom nodded. Her chin quivered. "Are we done here? Can we go now?"

"Sure," he answered.

"Come on, Julian," she said, and she walked out of the office.

I stood up. I admit, I wasn't exactly sure what was going on.

"Wait, is that it?" I asked. "But what about my things? All my stuff 's in my locker."

"Ms. Rubin will get your things ready and she'll get them to you later this week," answered Dr. Jansen. He looked at Dad. "I'm really sorry it came to this, Jules." He held out his hand for a handshake.

Dad looked at his hand but didn't shake it. He looked at Dr. Jansen.

"Here's the only thing I want from you, Hal," he said quietly. "I want that this—all of this—be kept confidential. Is that clear? It doesn't go beyond this room. I don't want Julian turned into some kind of anti-bullying poster boy by the school. No one is to know he's been suspended. We'll make up some excuse about why he's not in school, and that's it. Are we clear, Hal? I don't want him made into an example. I'm not going to stand by while this school drags my family's reputation through the mud."

Oh, by the way, in case I hadn't mentioned it before: Dad's a lawyer.

Dr. Jansen and Mr. Tushman exchanged looks.

"We are not looking to make an example of any of our students," Dr. Jansen answered. "This suspension really is about a reasonable response to unreasonable behavior."

"Give me a break," answered Dad, looking at his watch. "It's a massive overreaction."

Dr. Jansen looked at Dad, and then he looked at me.

"Julian," he said, looking me right in the eye. "Can I ask you something point-blank?"

I looked at Dad, who nodded. I shrugged.

"Do you feel at all remorseful for what you've done?" Dr. Jansen asked me.

I thought about it a second. I could tell all the grown-ups were watching me, waiting for me to answer something magical that would make this whole situation better.

"Yes," I said quietly. "I'm really sorry I wrote those last notes."

Dr. Jansen nodded. "Is there anything else you feel remorse for?" he asked.

I looked at Dad again. I'm not an idiot. I knew what

he was dying for me to say. I just wasn't going to say it. So I looked down and shrugged.

"Can I ask you this, then?" said Dr. Jansen. "Will you consider writing Auggie a letter of apology?"

I shrugged again. "How many words does it have to be?" was all I could think to say.

I knew the moment I said it that I probably shouldn't have. Dr. Jansen looked at my dad, who just looked down.

"Julian," said Dad. "Go find Mom. Wait for me by the reception area. I'll be out in a second."

Just as I closed the door on my way out, Dad started whispering something to Dr. Jansen and Mr. Tushman. It was a hushed, angry whisper.

When I got to the reception area, I found Mom sitting on a a chair with her sunglasses on. I sat down next to her. She rubbed my back but she didn't say anything. I think she had been crying.

I looked at the clock: 10:20 a.m. Right about now, Ms. Rubin was probably going over the results of yesterday's quiz in science class. As I looked around the lobby, I had a blip of a memory— that day before school started, when me, Jack Will, and Charlotte had met up here before meeting our "welcome buddy" for the first time. I remember how nervous Jack had been that day, and how I didn't even know who Auggie was.

So much had happened since then.

Out of School

Dad didn't say anything when he met us in the lobby. We just walked out the doors without saying goodbye— even to the security guard at the reception desk. It was weird leaving the school when everyone was still inside. I wondered what Miles and Henry would think when I didn't come back to class. I hated that I was going to miss PE that afternoon.

My parents were quiet the whole way back to the house. We live on the Upper West Side, which is about a half-hour drive from Beecher Prep, but it felt like it took forever to get home.

"I can't believe I got suspended," I said, just as we pulled into the parking garage in our building.

"It's not your fault, honey," answered Mom. "They have it in for us."

"Melissa!" Dad yelled, which surprised Mom a bit. "Yes, of course it's his fault. This whole situation is his fault! Julian, what the heck were you thinking, writing notes like that?"

"He was goaded into writing them!" answered Mom.

We had pulled to a stop inside the garage. The parking-garage attendant was waiting for us to get out of the car, but we didn't get out.

Dad turned around and looked at me. "I'm not saying I think the school handled this right," he said. "Two weeks' suspension is ridiculous. But, Julian, you should know better!"

"I know!" I said. "It was a mistake, Dad!"

"We all make mistakes," said Mom.

Dad turned back around. He looked at Mom. "Jansen's right, Melissa. If you keep trying to justify his actions—"

"That's not what I'm doing, Jules."

Dad didn't answer right away. Then he said, "I told Jansen that we're pulling Julian out of Beecher Prep next year."

Mom was literally speechless. It took a second for what he said to hit me. "You *what?*" I said.

"Jules," Mom said slowly.

"I told Jansen that we'll finish out this year at Beecher Prep," Dad continued calmly. "But next year, Julian's going to a different school."

"I can't believe this!" I cried. "I love Beecher Prep, Dad! I have friends! Mom!"

"I'm not sending you back to that school, Julian," Dad said firmly. "No way am I spending another dime on that school. There are plenty of other great private schools in New York City."

"Mom!" I said.

Mom wiped her hand across her face. She shook her head. "Don't you think we should have talked about this first?" she said to Dad.

"You don't agree?" he countered.

She rubbed her forehead with her fingers.

"No, I do agree," she said softly, nodding.

"Mom!" I screamed.

She turned around in her seat. "Honey, I think Daddy's right."

"I can't believe this!" I yelled, punching the car seat.

"They have it in for us now," she continued. "Because we complained about the situation with that boy . . ."

"But that was your fault!" I said through clenched teeth. "I didn't tell you to try and get Auggie thrown out of the school. I didn't want you to get Tushman fired. That was you!"

"And I'm sorry about that, sweetheart," she said meekly.

"Julian!" said Dad. "Your mom did everything she did to try and protect you. It's not her fault you wrote those notes, is it?"

"No, but if she hadn't made such a big stink about everything . . ." I started to say.

"Julian, do you hear yourself?" said Dad. "Now you're blaming your mom. Before you were blaming the other boys for writing those notes. I'm starting to wonder if what they were saying is right! Don't you feel any remorse for what you've done?"

"Of course he does!" said Mom.

"Melissa, let him answer for himself!" Dad said loudly.

"No, okay?" I yelled. "I'm not sorry! I know everybody thinks I should be all, *I'm sorry for being mean to Auggie, I'm sorry I talked smack about him, I'm sorry I dissed him.* But I'm not. So sue me."

Before Dad could respond, the garage attendant knocked on the car window. Another car had pulled into the garage and they needed us to get out.

Spring

I didn't tell anyone about the suspension. When Henry texted me a few days later asking why I wasn't in school, I told him I had strep throat. That's what we told everyone.

It turns out, two weeks' suspension isn't so bad, by the way. I spent most of my time at home watching *SpongeBob* reruns and playing *Knights of the Old Republic*. I was still supposed to keep up on my schoolwork, though, so it's not like I totally got to goof off. Ms. Rubin dropped by the apartment one afternoon with all my locker stuff: my textbooks, my loose-leaf book, and all the assignments I would need to make up. And there was a lot!

Everything went really well with social studies and English, but I had so much trouble doing the math homework that Mom got me a math tutor.

Despite all the time off, I really was excited about going back. Or at least I thought I was. The night before my first day back, I had one of my nightmares again.

Only this time, it wasn't me who looked like Auggie—it was everyone else!

I should have taken that as a premonition. When I got back to school, as soon as I arrived, I could tell something was up. Something was different. The first thing I noticed is that no one was really excited about seeing me again. I mean, people said hello and asked me how I was feeling, but no one was like, "Dude, I missed you!"

I would have thought Miles and Henry would be like that, but they weren't. In fact, at lunchtime, they didn't even sit at our usual table. They sat with Amos. So I had to take my tray and find a place to squeeze in at Amos's table, which was kind of humiliating. Then I overheard the three of them talking about hanging out at the playground after school and shooting hoops, but no one asked me to come!

The thing that was weirdest of all, though, was that everyone was being really nice to Auggie. Like, ridiculously nice. It was like I had entered the portal to a different dimension, an alternate universe in which Auggie and I had changed places. Suddenly, he was the popular one, and I was the outsider.

Right after last period, I pulled Henry over to talk to him.

"Yo, dude, why is everyone being so nice to the freak all of a sudden?" I asked.

"Oh, um," said Henry, looking around kind of

nervously. "Yeah, well, people don't really call him that anymore."

And then he told me all about the stuff that had gone down at the nature retreat. Basically, what had happened was that Auggie and Jack got picked on by some seventh-grade bullies from another school. Henry, Miles, and Amos had rescued them, got into a fight with the bullies—like with real punches flying—and then they all escaped through a corn maze. It sounded really exciting, and as he was telling me, I got mad all over again that Mr. Tushman had made me miss it.

"Oh man," I said excitedly. "I wish I'd been there! I totally would have creamed those jerks."

"Wait, which jerks?"

"The seventh graders!"

"Really?" He looked puzzled, though Henry always looked a little puzzled. "Because, I don't know, Julian. I kind of think that if you had been there, we might not have rescued them at all. You probably would have been cheering for the seventh graders!"

I looked at him like he was an idiot. "No I wouldn't," I said.

"Seriously?" he said, giving me a look.

"No!" I said.

"Okay!" he answered, shrugging.

"Yo, Henry, are you coming?" Amos called out from down the hallway.

"Look, I gotta go," said Henry.

382

"Wait," I said.

"Gotta go."

"Want to hang out tomorrow after school?"

"Not sure," he answered, backing away. "Text me tonight and we'll see."

As I watched him jog away, I had this terrible feeling in the pit of my stomach. Did he really think I was that awful that I would have been rooting for some seventh graders while they beat Auggie up? Is that what other people think? That I would have been that much of a dirtwad?

Look, I'm the first one to say I don't like Auggie Pullman, but I would never want to see him get beat up or anything! I mean, come on! I'm not a psycho. It really annoyed me that that's what people thought about me.

I texted Henry later on: "Yo, btw, I would never have just stood by and let those creeps beat Auggie and Jack up!"

But he never texted me back.

Mr. Tushman

That last month in school was awful. It's not like anyone was out-and-out mean to me, but I felt iced out by Amos and Henry and Miles. I just didn't feel popular anymore. No one really ever laughed at my jokes. No one wanted to hang out with me. I felt like I could disappear from the school and nobody would miss me. Meanwhile, Auggie was walking down the hallways like some cool dude, getting high-fived by all the jocks in the upper grades.

Whatever.

Mr. Tushman called me into his office one day.

"How's it going, Julian?" he asked me.

"Fine."

"Did you ever write that apology letter I asked you to write?"

"My dad says I'm leaving the school, so I don't have to write anything," I answered.

"Oh," he said, nodding. "I guess I was hoping you'd want to write it on your own."

"Why?" I said back. "Everyone thinks I'm this big dirtbag now anyway. What the heck is writing a letter going to accomplish?"

"Julian—"

"Look, I know everyone thinks I'm this unfeeling kid who doesn't feel 'remorse'!" I said, using air quotes.

"Julian," said Mr. Tushman. "No one—"

Suddenly, I felt like I was about to cry, so I just interrupted him. "I'm really late for class and I don't want to get in trouble, so can I please go?"

Mr. Tushman looked sad. He nodded. Then I left his office without looking back.

A few days later, we received an official notice from the school telling us that they had withdrawn their invitation to re-enroll in the fall.

I didn't think it mattered, since Dad had told them we weren't going back anyway. But we still hadn't heard from the other schools I had applied to, and if I didn't get into any of them, we had planned on my going back to Beecher Prep. But now that was impossible.

Mom and Dad were furious at the school. Like, *crazy* mad. Mostly because they had already paid the tuition for the next year in advance. And the school wasn't planning on returning the money. See, that's the thing with private schools: they can kick you out for any reason.

Luckily, a few days later, we did find out that I'd gotten into my first-choice private school, not far from where I lived. I'd have to wear a uniform, but that was okay. Better than having to go to Beecher Prep every day!

Needless to say, we skipped the graduation ceremony at the end of the year.

After

"That is only tears such as men use," said Bagheera.

"Now I know thou art a man, and a man's cub no longer.

The jungle is shut indeed to thee henceforward.

Let them fall, Mowgli. They are only tears."

—Rudyard Kipling, *The Jungle Book*

. . .

Oh, the wind, the wind is blowing,

through the graves the wind is blowing,

freedom soon will come;

then we'll come from the shadows.

—Leonard Cohen, "The Partisan"

Summer Vacation

My parents and I went to Paris in June. The original plan was that we would return to New York in July, since I was supposed to go to rock-and-roll camp with Henry and Miles. But after everything that happened, I didn't want to do that anymore. My parents decided to let me stay with my grandmother for the rest of the summer.

Usually, I hated staying with Grandmère, but I was okay about it this time. I knew that after my parents went home, I could spend the entire day in my PJs playing *Halo*, and Grandmère wouldn't care in the least. I could pretty much do whatever I wanted.

Grandmère wasn't exactly the typical "grandma" type. No baking cookies for Grandmère. No knitting sweaters. She was, as Dad always said, something of a "character." Even though she was in her eighties, she dressed like a fashion model. Super glamorous. Lots of makeup and perfume. High heels. She never woke up until two in the afternoon, and then she'd take at least two hours to get dressed. Once she was up, she would take me out shopping or to a museum or a fancy restaurant. She wasn't into doing kid stuff, if you know what I mean. She'd never sit through a PG movie with me, for instance, so I ended up seeing a lot of movies that were totally age-inappropriate. Mom, I knew, would go completely ballistic if she got wind of some of the movies Grandmère took me to see. But Grandmère was French, and was always saying my parents were too "American" anyway.

Grandmère also didn't talk to me like I was a little kid. Even when I was younger, she never used baby words or talked to me the way grown-ups usually talk to little kids. She used regular words to describe everything. Like, if I would say, "*Je veux faire pipi*," meaning "I want to make pee-pee," she would say, "You need to urinate? Go to the lavatory."

And she cursed sometimes, too. Boy, she could curse! And if I didn't know what a curse word meant, all I had to do was ask her and she would explain it to me—in detail. I can't even tell you some of the words she explained to me!

Anyway, I was glad to be away from NYC for the whole summer. I was hoping that I would get all those kids out of my head. Auggie. Jack. Summer. Henry. Miles. All of them. If I never saw any of those kids again, seriously, I would be the happiest kid in Paris.

Mr. Browne

The only thing I was a little bummed about is that I never got to say goodbye to any of my teachers at Beecher Prep. I really liked some of them. Mr. Browne, my English teacher, was probably my favorite teacher of all time. He had always been really nice to me. I loved writing, and he was really complimentary about it. And I never got to tell him I wasn't coming back to Beecher Prep.

At the beginning of the year, Mr. Browne had told all of us that he wanted us to send him one of our own precepts over the summer. So, one afternoon, while Grandmère was sleeping, I started thinking about sending him a precept from Paris. I went to one of the tourist shops down the block and bought a postcard of a gargoyle, one of those at the top of Notre-Dame. The first thing I thought when I saw it was that it reminded me of Auggie. And then I thought, *Ugh! Why am I still thinking about him? Why do I still see his face wherever I go? I can't wait to start over!*

390

And that's when it hit me: my precept. I wrote it down really quickly.

Sometimes it's good to start over.

There. Perfect. I loved it. I got Mr. Browne's address from his teacher page on the Beecher Prep website, and dropped it in the mail that same day.

But then, after I sent it, I realized he wasn't going to understand what it meant. Not really. He didn't have the whole background story about why I was so happy to be leaving Beecher Prep and starting over somewhere new. So, I decided to write him an email to tell him everything that had happened last year. I mean, not *everything*. Dad had specifically told me not to ever tell anyone at the school about the mean stuff I did to Auggie—for legal reasons. But I wanted Mr. Browne to know enough so that he would understand my precept. I also wanted him to know that I thought he was a great teacher. Mom had told everyone that I wasn't going back to Beecher Prep because we were unhappy with the academics—and the teachers. I felt kind of bad about that because I didn't want Mr. Browne to ever think I was unhappy with him.

So, anyway, I decided to send Mr. Browne an email.

To: tbrowne@beecherschool.edu
Fr: julianalbans@ezmail.com
Re: My precept

Hi, Mr. Browne! I just sent you my precept in the mail:

"Sometimes it's good to start over." It's on a postcard of a gargoyle. I wrote this precept because I'm going to a new school in September. I ended up hating Beecher Prep. I didn't like the students. But I DID like the teachers. I thought your class was great. So don't take my not going back personally.

I don't know if you know the whole long story, but basically the reason I'm not going back to Beecher Prep is . . . well, not to name names, but there was one student I really didn't get along with. Actually, it was two students. (You can probably guess who they are because one of them punched me in the mouth.) Anyway, these kids were not my favorite people in the world. We started writing mean notes to each other. I repeat: each other. It was a 2-way street! But I'm the one who got in trouble for it! Just me! It was so unfair! The truth is, Mr. Tushman had it in for me because my mom was trying to get him fired. Anyway, long story short: I got suspended for two weeks for writing the notes! (No one knows this, though. It's a secret so please don't tell anyone.) The school said it had a "zero tolerance" policy against bullying. But I don't think what I did was bullying! My parents got so mad at the school! They decided to enroll me in a different school next year. So, yeah, that's the story.

I really wish that that "student" had never come to Beecher Prep! My whole year would have been so much better! I hated having to be in his classes. He gave me nightmares. I would still be going to Beecher

Prep if he hadn't been there. It's a bummer.

    I really liked your class, though. You were a great teacher. I wanted you to know that.

I thought it was good that I hadn't named "names." But I figured he'd know who I was talking about. I really didn't expect to hear back from him, but the very next day, when I checked my in-box, there was an email from Mr. Browne. I was so excited!

To: julianalbans@ezmail.com
Fr: tbrowne@beecherschool.edu
Re: re: My precept

Hi, Julian. Thanks so much for your email! I'm looking forward to getting the gargoyle postcard. I was sorry to hear you wouldn't be coming back to Beecher Prep. I always thought you were a great student and a gifted writer.

    By the way, I love your precept. I agree, sometimes it's good to start over. A fresh start gives us the chance to reflect on the past, weigh the things we've done, and apply what we've learned from those things to the future. If we don't examine the past, we don't learn from it.

    As for the "kids" you didn't like, I do think I know who you're talking about. I'm sorry the year didn't turn out to be a happy one for you, but I hope you take a little time to ask yourself why. Things that happen to us, even the bad stuff, can often teach us a little bit about ourselves. Do you ever wonder why you had such a hard time with these two students? Was it, perhaps, their friendship that bothered you? Were you troubled by Auggie's physical appearance? You mentioned that you started having nightmares. Did you ever consider that maybe you were just a little afraid of Auggie, Julian? Sometimes fear can make even the nicest kids say and do things they wouldn't ordinarily say or do. Perhaps you should explore these feelings further?

In any case, I wish you the best of luck in your new school, Julian. You're a good kid. A natural leader. Just remember to use your leadership for good, huh? Don't forget: always choose kind!

I don't know why, but I was so, so, *so* happy to get that email from Mr. Browne! I knew he would be understanding! I was so tired of everyone thinking I was this demon-child, you know? It was obvious that Mr. Browne knew I wasn't. I reread his email like, ten times. I was smiling from ear to ear.

"So?" Grandmère asked me. She had just woken up and was having her breakfast: a croissant and *café au lait* delivered from downstairs. "I haven't seen you this happy all summer long. What is it that you are reading, *mon cher?*"

"Oh, I got an email from one of my teachers," I answered. "Mr. Browne."

"From your old school?" she asked. "I thought they

were all bad, those teachers. I thought it was 'good riddance' to all of them!" Grandmère had a thick French accent that was hard to understand sometimes.

"What?"

"Good riddance!" she repeated. "Never mind. I thought the teachers were all stupid." The way she pronounced "stupid" was funny: like stew-peed!

"Not all. Not Mr. Browne," I answered.

"So, what did he write to make you so happy?"

"Oh, nothing much," I said. "It's just . . . I thought everyone hated me, but now I know Mr. Browne doesn't."

Grandmère looked at me.

"Why would everyone hate you, Julian?" she asked. "You are such a good boy."

"I don't know," I answered.

"Read me the email," she said.

"No, Grandmère . . ." I started to say.

"Read," she commanded, pointing her finger at the screen.

So I read Mr. Browne's letter aloud to her. Now, Grandmère knew a little bit about what had happened at Beecher Prep, but I don't think she knew the whole story. I mean, I think Mom and Dad told her the version of the story they told everyone else, with maybe a few more details. Grandmère knew there were a couple of kids who had made my life miserable, for instance, but she didn't know the specifics. She knew I'd gotten punched in the mouth, but she didn't know why. If anything, Grandmère probably assumed I had gotten bullied, and that's why I was leaving the school.

So, there were parts of Mr. Browne's email she really didn't understand.

"What does he mean," she said, squinting as she tried to read off my screen. "Auggie's 'physical appearance'? *Qu'est-ce que c'est?*"

"One of the kids that I didn't like, Auggie, he had like this awful . . . facial deformity," I answered. "It was really bad. He looked like a gargoyle!"

"Julian!" she said. "That is not very nice."

"Sorry."

"And this boy, he was not *sympathique?*" she asked innocently. "He was not nice to you? Was he a bully?"

I thought about that. "No, he wasn't a bully."

"So, why did you not like him?"

I shrugged. "I don't know. He just got on my nerves."

"What do you mean, you don't know?" she answered quickly. "Your parents told me you were leaving school because of some bullies, no? You got punched in the face? No?"

"Well, yeah, I got punched, but not by the deformed kid. By his friend."

"Ah! So his friend was the bully!"

"No, not exactly," I said. "I can't say they were bullies, Grandmère. I mean, it wasn't like that. We just didn't get along, that's all. We hated each other. It's kind of hard to explain, you kind of had to be there. Here, let me show you what he looked like. Then maybe you'll understand a little better. I mean, not to sound mean, but it was really hard having to look at him every day. He gave me nightmares."

I logged on to Facebook and found our class picture, and zoomed in on Auggie's face so she could see. She put her glasses on to look at it and spent a long time studying his face on the computer screen. I thought she would react the way Mom had reacted when she first saw that picture of Auggie, but she didn't. She just nodded to herself. And then she closed the laptop.

"Pretty bad, huh?" I said to her.

She looked at me.

"Julian," she said. "I think maybe your teacher is right. I think you were afraid of this boy."

"What? No way!" I answered. "I'm not afraid of Auggie! I mean, I didn't like him—in fact, I kind of hated him—but not because I was afraid of him."

"Sometimes we hate the things we are afraid of," she said.

I made a face like she was talking crazy.

She took my hand.

"I know what it is like to be afraid, Julian," she said, holding her finger up to my face. "There was a little boy that I was afraid of when I was a little girl."

"Let me guess," I answered, sounding bored. "I bet he looked just like Auggie."

Grandmère shook her head. "No. His face was fine."

"So, why were you afraid of him?" I asked. I tried to make my voice sound as uninterested as possible, but Grandmère ignored my bad attitude.

She just sat back in her chair, her head slightly tilted, and I could tell by looking into her eyes that she had gone somewhere far away.

Grandmère's Story

"I was a very popular girl when I was young, Julian," said Grandmère. "I had many friends. I had pretty clothes. As you can see, I have always liked pretty clothes." She waved her hands down her sides to make sure I noticed her dress. She smiled.

"I was a frivolous girl," she continued. "Spoiled. When the Germans came to France, I hardly took any notice. I knew that some Jewish families in my village were moving away, but my family was so cosmopolitan. My parents were intellectuals. Atheists. We didn't even go to synagogue."

She paused here and asked me to bring her a wine glass, which I did. She served herself a full glass and, as she always did, offered me some, too. And, as I always did, I said, *"Non, merci."* Like I said, Mom would go ballistic if she knew the stuff Grandmère did sometimes!

"There was a boy in my school called . . . well, they called him Tourteau," she continued. "He was . . . how do you say the word . . . a crippled? Is that how you say it?"

"I don't think people use that word anymore, Grandmère," I said. "It's not exactly politically correct, if you know what I mean."

She flicked her hand at me. "Americans are always coming up with new words we can't say anymore!" she said. "*Alors*, well, Tourteau's legs were deformed from the polio. He needed two canes to walk with. And his back was all twisted. I think that's why he was called *tourteau*, crab: he walked sideways like a crab. I know, it sounds very harsh. Children were meaner in those days."

I thought about how I called August "the freak" behind his back. But at least I never called him that to his face!

Grandmère continued talking. I have to admit: at first I wasn't into her telling me one of her long stories, but I was getting into this one.

"Tourteau was a little thing, a skinny thing. None of us ever talked to him because he made us uncomfortable. He was so different! I never even looked at him! I was afraid of him. Afraid to look at him, to talk to him. Afraid he would accidentally touch me. It was easier to pretend he didn't exist."

She took a long sip of her wine.

"One morning, a man came running into our school. I knew him. Everyone did. He was a Maquis, a partisan. Do you know what that is? He was against the Germans.

He rushed into the school and told the teachers that the Germans were coming to take all the Jewish children away. What? What is this? I could not believe what I was hearing! The teachers in the school went around to all the classes and gathered the Jewish children together. We were told to follow the Maquis into the woods. We were going to go hide. Hurry hurry hurry! I think there were maybe ten of us in all! Hurry hurry hurry! Escape!"

Grandmère looked at me, to make sure I was listening—which, of course, I was.

"It was snowing that morning, and very cold. And all I could think was, *If I go into the woods, I will ruin my shoes!* I was wearing these beautiful new red shoes that Papa had brought me, you see. As I said before, I was a frivolous girl—perhaps even a little stupid! But this is what I was thinking. I did not even stop to think, *Well, where is Maman and Papa? If the Germans were coming for the Jewish children, had they come for the parents already?* This did not occur to me. All I could think about were my beautiful shoes. So, instead of following the Maquis into the woods, I snuck away from the group and went to hide inside the bell tower of the school. There was a tiny room up there, full of crates and books, and there I hid. I remember thinking I would go home in the afternoon after the Germans came, and tell Maman and Papa all about it. This is how stupid I was, Julian!"

I nodded. I couldn't believe I had never heard this story before!

"And then the Germans came," she said. "There was a narrow window in the tower, and I could see them perfectly. I watched them run into the woods after the children. It did not take them very long to find them. They all came back together: the Germans, the children, the Maquis soldier."

Grandmère paused and blinked a few times, and then she took a deep breath.

"They shot the Maquis in front of all the children," she said quietly. "He fell so softly, Julian, in the snow. The children cried. They cried as they were led away in a line. One of the teachers, Mademoiselle Petitjean, went with them—even though she was not Jewish! She said she would not leave her children! No one ever saw her again, poor thing. By now, Julian, I had awakened from my stupidity. I was not thinking of my red shoes anymore. I was thinking of my friends who had been taken away. I was thinking of my parents. I was waiting until it was nighttime so I could go home to them!

"But not all the Germans had left. Some had stayed behind, along with the French police. They were searching the school. And then I realized, they were looking for me! Yes, for me, and for the one or two other Jewish children who had not gone into the woods. I realized then that my friend Rachel had not been among the Jewish children who were marched away.

Nor Jakob, a boy from another village who all the girls wanted to marry because he was so handsome. Where were they? They must have been hiding, just like I was!

"Then I heard creaking, Julian. Up the stairs, I heard footsteps up the stairs, coming closer to me. I was so scared! I tried to make myself as small as possible behind the crate, and hid my head beneath a blanket."

Here, Grandmère covered her head with her arms, as if to show me how she was hiding.

"And then I heard someone whisper my name," she said. "It was not a man's voice. It was a child's voice.

"*Sara?* the voice whispered again.

"I peeked out from the blanket.

"*Tourteau!* I answered, astonished. I was so surprised, because in all the years I had known him, I don't think I had ever said a word to him, nor him to me. And yet, there he was, calling my name.

"*They will find you here,* he said. *Follow me.*

"And I did follow him, for by now I was terrified. He led me down a hallway into the chapel of the school, which I had never really been to before. We went to the back of the chapel, where there was a crypt—all this was new to me, Julian! And we crawled through the crypt so the Germans would not see us through the windows, because they were looking for us still. I heard when they found Rachel. I heard her screaming in the courtyard as they took her away. Poor Rachel!

"Tourteau took me down to the basement beneath

the crypt. There must have been one hundred steps at least. These were not easy for Tourteau, as you can imagine, with his terrible limp and his two canes, but he hopped down the steps two at a time, looking behind him to make sure I was following.

"Finally, we arrived at a passage. It was so narrow we had to walk sideways to get through. And then we were in the sewers, Julian! Can you imagine? I knew instantly because of the smell, of course. We were knee-deep in refuse. You can imagine the smell. So much for my red shoes!

"We walked all night. I was so cold, Julian! Tourteau was such a kind boy, though. He gave me his coat to wear. It was, to this day, the most noble act anyone has ever done for me. He was freezing, too—but he gave me his coat. I was so ashamed for the way I had treated him. Oh, Julian, I was so ashamed!"

She covered her mouth with her fingers, and swallowed. Then she finished the glass of wine and poured herself another.

"The sewers lead to Dannevilliers, a small village about fifteen kilometers away from Aubervilliers. Maman and Papa had always avoided this town because of the smell: the sewers from Paris drained onto the farmland there. We wouldn't even eat apples grown in Dannevilliers! But it's where Tourteau lived. He took me to his house, and we cleaned ourselves by the well, and then Tourteau brought me to the barn behind his house. He wrapped me up in a horse blanket and told me to wait. He was going to get his parents.

"No, I pleaded. *Please don't tell them.* I was so frightened. I wondered if, when they saw me, they would call the Germans. You know, I had never met them before!

"But Tourteau left, and a few minutes later, he returned with his parents. They looked at me. I must have seemed quite pathetic there—all wet and shivering. The mother, Vivienne, put her arms around me to comfort me. Oh, Julian, that hug was the warmest hug I have ever felt! I cried so hard in this woman's arms, because I knew then, I knew I would never cry in my own maman's arms again. I just knew it in my heart, Julian. And I was right. They had taken Maman that same day, along with all the other Jews in the city. My father, who had been at work, had been warned that the Germans were coming and managed to escape. He was smuggled to Switzerland. But it was too late for Maman. She was deported that day. To Auschwitz. I never saw her again. My beautiful maman!"

She took a deep breath here, and shook her head.

Tourteau

Grandmère was silent for a few seconds. She was looking into the air like she could see it all happening again right in front of her. Now I understood why she'd never talked about this before: it was too hard for her.

"Tourteau's family hid me for two years in that barn," she continued slowly. "Even though it was so dangerous for them. We were literally surrounded by Germans, and the French police had a large headquarters in Dannevilliers. But every day, I thanked my maker for the barn that was my home, and the food that Tourteau managed to bring me—even when there was hardly any food to go around. People were starving in those days, Julian. And yet they fed me. It was a kindness that I will never forget. It is always brave to be kind, but in those days, such kindnesses could cost you your life."

Grandmère started to get teary-eyed at this point. She took my hand.

"The last time I saw Tourteau was two months before the liberation. He had brought me some soup. It wasn't even soup. It was water with a little bit of bread and onions in it. We had both lost so much weight. I was in rags. So much for my pretty clothes! Even so, we managed to laugh, Tourteau and I. We laughed about things that happened in our school. Even though I could not go there anymore, of course, Tourteau still went every day. At night, he would tell me everything he had learned so that I would stay smart. He would tell me about all my old friends, too, and how they were doing. They all still ignored him, of course. And he never revealed to any of them that I was still alive. No one could know. No one could be trusted! But Tourteau was an excellent narrator, and he made me laugh a lot. He could do wonderful imitations, and he even had funny nicknames for all my friends. Imagine that, Tourteau was making fun of them!

"*I had no idea you were so mischievous! I told him. All those years, you were probably laughing at me behind my back, too!*

"*Laughing at you? he said. Never! I had a crush on you; I never laughed at you. Besides, I only laughed at the kids who made fun of me. You never made fun of me. You simply ignored me.*

"*I called you Tourteau.*

"*And so? Everyone called me that. I really don't mind. I like crabs!*

"*Oh, Tourteau, I am so ashamed!* I answered, and I remember I covered my face with both my hands."

At this point, Grandmère covered her face with her hands. Although her fingers were bent with arthritis now, and I could see her veins, I pictured her young hands covering her young face so many years ago.

"Tourteau took my hands with his own hands," she continued, slowly removing her hands from her face. "And he held my hands for a few seconds. I was fourteen years old then, and I had never kissed a boy, but he kissed me that day, Julian."

Grandmère closed her eyes. She took a deep breath.

"After he kissed me, I said to him, *I don't want to call you Tourteau anymore. What is your name?*"

Grandmère opened her eyes and looked at me. "Can you guess what he said?" she asked.

I raised my eyebrows as if to say, "No, how would I know?" Then she closed her eyes again and smiled.

"He said, *My name is Julian.*"

Julian

"Oh my God!" I cried. "That's why you named Dad Julian?" Even though everyone called him Jules, that was his name.

"Oui," she said, nodding.

"And I'm named after Dad!" I said. "So I'm named after this kid! That is so cool!"

She smiled and ran her fingers through my hair. But she didn't say anything.

Then I remembered her saying, "The last time I saw Tourteau . . ."

"So what happened to him?" I asked. "To Julian?"

Almost instantaneously, tears rolled down Grand-mère's cheeks.

"The Germans took him," she said, "that same day. He was on his way to school. They were making another sweep of the village that morning. By now, Germany was losing the war and they knew it."

"But . . ." I said, "he wasn't even Jewish!"

"They took him because he was crippled," she said

between sobs. "I'm sorry, I know you told me that word is a bad word, but I don't know another word in English. He was an *invalide*. That is the word in French. And that is why they took him. He was not perfect." She practically spat out the word. "They took all the imperfects from the village that day. It was a purge. The Gypsies. The shoemaker's son, who was . . . simple. And Julian. My *tourteau*. They put him in a cart with the others. And then he was put on a train to Drancy. And from there to Auschwitz, like my mother. We heard later from someone who saw him there that they sent him to the gas chambers right away. Just like that, poof, he was gone. My savior. My little Julian."

She stopped to wipe her eyes with a handkerchief, and then drank the rest of the wine.

"His parents were devastated, of course, M. Beaumier and Mme. Beaumier," she continued. "We didn't find out he was dead until after the liberation. But we knew. We knew." She dabbed her eyes. "I lived with them for another year after the war. They treated me like a daughter. They were the ones who helped track down Papa, although it took some time to find him. So much chaos in those days. When Papa finally was able to return to Paris, I went to live with him. But I always visited the Beaumiers—even when they were very old. I never forgot the kindness they showed me."

She sighed. She had finished her story.

"Grandmère," I said, after a few minutes. "That's like,

the saddest thing I've ever heard! I didn't even know you were in the war. I mean, Dad's never talked about any of this."

She shrugged. "I think it's very possible that I never told your father this story," she said. "I don't like to talk about sad things, you know. In some ways, I am still the frivolous girl I used to be. But when I heard you talking about that little boy in your school, I could not help but think of Tourteau, of how afraid I had once been of him, of how badly we had treated him because of his deformity. Those children had been so mean to him, Julian. It breaks my heart to think of it."

When she said that, I don't know, something just really broke inside of me. Completely unexpected. I looked down and, all of a sudden, I started to cry. And when I say I started to cry, I don't mean a few tears rolling down my cheeks—I mean like, full-scale, snot-filled crying.

"Julian," she said softly.

I shook my head and covered my face with my hands.

"I was terrible, Grandmère," I whispered. "I was so mean to Auggie. I'm so sorry, Grandmère!"

"Julian," she said again. "Look at me."

"No!"

"Look at me, *mon cher.*" She took my face in her hands and forced me to look at her. I felt so embarrassed. I really couldn't look her in the eyes. Suddenly, that

411

word that Mr. Tushman had used, that word that everyone kept trying to force on me, came to me like a shout. REMORSE!

Yeah, there it was. That word in all its glory.

REMORSE. I was shaking with remorse. I was crying with remorse.

"Julian," said Grandmère. "We all make mistakes, *mon cher.*"

"No, you don't understand!" I answered. "It wasn't just one mistake. I was those kids who were mean to Tourteau . . . I was the bully, Grandmère. It was me!"

She nodded.

"I called him a freak. I laughed behind his back. *I left mean notes!*" I screamed. "Mom kept making excuses for why I did that stuff . . . but there wasn't any excuse. I just did it! And I don't even know why. I don't even know."

I was crying so hard I couldn't even speak.

Grandmère stroked my head and hugged me.

"Julian," she said softly. "You are so young. The things you did, you know they were not right. But that does not mean you are not capable of doing right. It only means that you chose to do wrong. This is what I mean when I say you made a mistake. It was the same with me. I made a mistake with Tourteau.

"But the good thing about life, Julian," she continued, "is that we can fix our mistakes sometimes. We learn from them. We get better. I never made a mistake like the one I made with Tourteau again, not with anyone in my life. And I have had a very, very long life. You will learn from your mistake, too. You must promise yourself that you will never behave like that with anyone else again. One mistake does not define you, Julian. Do you understand me? You must simply act better next time."

I nodded, but I still cried for a long, long time after that.

My Dream

That night, I dreamt about Auggie. I don't remember the details of the dream, but I think we were being chased by Nazis. Auggie was captured, but I had a key to let him out. And in my dream, I think I saved him. Or maybe that's what I told myself when I woke up. Sometimes, it's hard to know with dreams. I mean, in this dream the Nazis all looked like Darth Vader's Imperial officers anyway, so it's hard to put too much meaning into dreams.

But what was really interesting to me, when I thought about it, is that it had been a dream—not a nightmare. And in the dream, Auggie and I were on the same side.

I woke up super early because of the dream, and didn't go back to sleep. I kept thinking about Auggie, and Tourteau— Julian—the heroic boy I was named for. It's weird: This whole time I had been thinking about Auggie like he was my enemy, but when Grandmère told me that story, I don't know, it all kind of just sank in with me. I kept thinking of how ashamed the original

Julian would be to know that someone who carried his name had been so mean.

I kept thinking about how sad Grandmère was when she told the story. How she could remember all the details, even though it happened like, seventy years ago. Seventy years! Would Auggie remember me in seventy years? Would he still remember the mean things I called him?

I don't want to be remembered for stuff like that. I would want to be remembered the way Grandmère remembers Tourteau!

Mr. Tushman, I get it now! R. E. M. O. R. S. E.

I got up as soon as it was light out, and wrote this note.

> *Dear Auggie,*
> *I want to apologize for the stuff I did last year. I've been thinking about it a lot. You didn't deserve it. I wish I could have a do-over. I would be nicer.*
> *I hope you don't remember how mean I was when you're eighty years old. Have a nice life.*
>
> *Julian*
>
> *PS: If you're the one who told Mr. Tushman about the notes, don't worry. I don't blame you.*

When Grandmère woke up that afternoon, I read her the note.

"I'm proud of you, Julian," she said, squeezing my shoulder.

"Do you think he'll forgive me?"

She thought about it.

"That's up to him," she answered. "In the end, *mon cher*, all that matters is that you forgive yourself. You are learning from your mistake. Like I learned with Tourteau."

"Do you think Tourteau would forgive me?" I asked. "If he knew his namesake had been so mean?"

She kissed my hand.

"Tourteau would forgive you," she answered. And I could tell she meant it.

Going Home

I realized I didn't have Auggie's address, so I wrote another email to Mr. Browne asking him if I could send him my note to Auggie and have him mail it to him for me. Mr. Browne emailed me back immediately. He was happy to do it. He also said he was proud of me.

I felt good about that. I mean like, really good. And it felt good to feel good. Kind of hard to explain, but I guess I was tired of feeling like I was this awful kid. I'm not. Like I keep saying over and over again, I'm just an ordinary kid. A typical, normal, ordinary kid. Who made a mistake.

But now, I was trying to make it right.

My parents arrived a week later. Mom couldn't stop hugging and kissing me. This was the longest I'd ever been away from home.

I was excited to tell them about the email from Mr. Browne, and the note I had written to Auggie. But they told me their news first.

"We're suing the school!" said Mom excitedly.

"What?" I cried.

"Dad is suing them for breach of contract," she said. She was practically chirping.

I looked at Grandmère, who didn't say anything. We were all having dinner.

"They had no right to withdraw the enrollment contract," Dad explained calmly, like a lawyer. "Not before we had been placed in another school. Hal told me—in his office—that they would wait to rescind their enrollment offer until *after* we had gotten accepted into another school. And they would return the money. We had a verbal agreement."

"But I was going to another school anyway!" I said.

"Doesn't matter," he said. "Even if they returned the money, it's the principle of the thing."

"What principle?" said Grandmère. She got up from the table. "This is nonsense, Jules. Stupid. Stew-peed! Complete and utter nonsense!"

"Maman!" said Dad. He looked really surprised. So did Mom.

"You should drop this stupidity!" said Grandmère.

"You don't really know the details, Maman," said Dad.

"I know *all* the details!" she yelled, shaking her fist in the air. She looked fierce. "The boy was wrong, Jules! *Your* boy was in the wrong! He knows it. You know it. He did bad things to that other boy and he is sorry for them, and you should let it be."

Mom and Dad looked at each other.

"With all due respect, Sara," said Mom, "I think we know what's best for—"

"No, you don't know anything!" yelled Grandmère. "You don't know. You two are too busy with lawsuits and stupid things like that."

"Maman," said Dad.

"She's right, Dad," I said. "It was all my fault. All that stuff with Auggie. It was my fault. I was mean to him, for no reason. It was my fault Jack punched me. I had just called Auggie a freak."

"What?" said Mom.

"I wrote those awful notes," I said quickly. "I did mean stuff. It was my fault! I was the bully, Mom! It wasn't anyone else's fault but mine!"

Mom and Dad didn't seem to know what to answer.

"Instead of sitting there like two idiots," said Grandmère, who always said things like they were, "you should be praising Julian for this admission! He is taking responsibility! He is owning up to his mistakes. It takes much courage to do this kind of thing."

"Yes, of course," said Dad, rubbing his chin and looking at me. "But . . . I just don't think you understand all the legal ramifications. The school took our tuition and refused to return it, which—"

"Blah! Blah! Blah!" said Grandmère, waving him away.

"I wrote him an apology," I said. "To Auggie. I wrote

him an apology and I sent it to him in the mail! I apologized for the way I acted."

"You what?" said Dad. He was getting mad now.

"And I told Mr. Browne the truth, too," I added. "I wrote Mr. Browne a long email telling him the whole story."

"Julian . . ." said Dad, frowning angrily. "Why did you do that? I told you I didn't want you to write anything that acknowledged—"

"Jules!" said Grandmère loudly, waving her hand in front of Dad's face. "*Tu as un cerveau comme un sandwich au fromage!*"

I couldn't help but laugh at this. Dad cringed.

"What did she say?" asked Mom, who didn't know French.

"Grandmère just told Dad he has a brain like a cheese sandwich," I said.

"Maman!" Dad said sternly, like someone who was about to begin a long lecture.

But Mom reached out and put her hand on Dad's arm.

"Jules," she said quietly. "I think your mom is right."

Unexpected

Sometimes people surprise you. Never in a million years would I have thought my mom would be the one to back down from anything, so I was completely shocked by what she had just said. I could tell Dad was, too. He looked at Mom like he couldn't believe what she was saying. Grandmère was the only one who didn't seem surprised.

"Are you kidding me?" Dad said to Mom.

Mom shook her head slowly. "Jules, we should end this. We should move on. Your mother's right."

Dad raised his eyebrows. I knew he was mad but trying not to show it. "You're the one who got us on this warpath, Melissa!"

"I know!" she answered, taking her glasses off. Her eyes were really shiny. "I know, I know. And I thought it was the right thing to do at the time. I still don't think Tushman was right, the way he handled everything, but . . . I'm ready to put all this behind us now, Jules. I think we should just . . . let go and move forward." She shrugged. She looked at me. "It was very big of Julian to reach out to that boy, Jules. It takes a lot of guts to do that." She looked back at Dad. "We should be supportive."

"I am supportive, of course," said Dad. "But this is such a complete about-face, Melissa! I mean . . ." He shook his head and rolled his eyes at the same time.

Mom sighed. She didn't know what to say.

"Look here," said Grandmère. "Whatever Melissa did, she did it because she wanted Julian to be happy. And that is all. *C'est tout.* And he's happy now. You can see it in his eyes. For the first time in a long time, your son looks completely happy."

"That's exactly right," said Mom, wiping a tear from her face.

I felt kind of sorry for Mom at that moment. I could tell she felt bad about some of the things she had done.

"Dad," I said, "please don't sue the school. I don't want that. Okay, Dad? Please?"

Dad leaned back in his chair and made a soft whistle sound, like he was blowing out a candle in slow motion. Then he started clicking his tongue against the roof of his mouth. It was a long minute that he stayed like that. We just watched him.

Finally he sat back up in his chair and looked at us. He shrugged.

"Okay," he said, his palms up. "I'll drop the lawsuit.

We'll just walk away from the tuition money. Are you sure that's what you want, Melissa?"

Mom nodded. "I'm sure."

Grandmère sighed. "Victory at last," she mumbled into her wine glass.

Starting Over

We went home a week later, but not before Grandmère took us to a very special place: the village she grew up in. It seemed amazing to me, that she had never told Dad the whole Tourteau story. The only thing he knew was that a family in Dannevilliers had helped her during the war, but she had never told him any of the details. She had never told him that his own grandmother had died in a concentration camp.

"Maman, how come you never told me any of this?" Dad asked her while we were driving in the car to her village.

"Oh, you know me, Jules," she answered. "I do not like to dwell on the past. Life is ahead of us. If we spend too much time looking backward, we can't see where we are going!"

Much of the village had changed. Too many bombs and grenades had been dropped. Most of the original houses had been destroyed in the war. Grandmère's school was gone. There was really nothing much to see. Just Starbucks and shoe stores.

But then we drove to Dannevilliers, which is where Julian had lived: that village was intact. She took us to the barn where she had stayed for two years. The old farmer who lived there now let us walk around and take a look. Grandmère found her initials scrawled in a little nook in one of the horse stalls, which is where she would hide under piles of hay whenever the Nazis were nearby. Grandmère stood in the middle of the barn, with one hand on her face as she looked around. She seemed so tiny there.

"How are you doing, Grandmère?" I asked.

"Me? Ah! Well," she said, smiling. She tilted her head. "I lived. I remember thinking, when I was staying here, that the smell of horse manure would never leave my nostrils. But I lived. And Jules was born because I lived. And you were born. So what is the smell of horse manure against all that? Perfume and time make everything easier to bear. Now, there's one more place I want to visit . . ."

We drove about ten minutes away to a tiny cemetery on the outskirts of the village. Grandmère took us directly to a tombstone at the edge of the graveyard.

There was a small white ceramic plaque on the tombstone. It was in the shape of a heart, and it read:

ICI REPOSENT

Vivienne Beaumier
née le 27 avril 1905
décédée le 21 novembre 1985

Jean-Paul Beaumier
né le 15 mai 1901
décédé le 5 juillet 1985

Mère et père de
Julian Auguste Beaumier
né le 10 octobre 1930
tombé en juin 1944
Puisse-t-il toujours marcher le front haut
dans le jardin de Dieu

I looked at Grandmère as she stood looking at the plaque. She kissed her fingers and then reached down to touch it. She was trembling.

"They treated me like their daughter," she said, tears rolling down her cheeks.

She started sobbing. I took her hand and kissed it.

Mom took Dad's hand. "What does the plaque say?" she asked softly.

Dad cleared his throat.

"Here rests Vivienne Beaumier . . ." he translated softly. "And Jean-Paul Beaumier. Mother and father of

Julian Auguste Beaumier, born October 10, 1930. Killed June 1944. May he walk forever tall in the garden of God."

New York

We got back to NYC a week before my new school was scheduled to start. It was nice, being in my room again. My things were all the same. But I felt, I don't know, a little different. I can't explain it. I felt like I really was starting over.

"I'll help you unpack in a minute," said Mom, running off to the bathroom as soon as we stepped through the door.

"I'm good," I answered. I could hear Dad in the living room listening to our answering-machine messages. I started unpacking my suitcase. Then I heard a familiar voice on the machine.

I stopped what I was doing and walked into the living room. Dad looked up and paused the machine. Then he replayed the message for me to hear.

It was Auggie Pullman.

"Oh, hi, Julian," said the message. "Yeah, so . . . umm . . . I just wanted to tell you I got your note. And, um . . . yeah, thanks for writing it. No need to call me back. I just wanted to say hey. We're good. Oh, and by the way, it wasn't me who told Tushman about the notes, just so you know. Or Jack or Summer. I really don't know how he found out, not that it matters anyway. So, okay. Anyway. I hope you like your new school. Good luck. Bye!"

Click.

Dad looked at me to see how I would react.

"Wow," I said. "I didn't expect that at all."

"Are you going to call him back?" asked Dad.

I shook my head. "Nah," I answered. "I'm too chicken."

Dad walked over to me and put his hand on my shoulder.

"I think you've proven that you're anything *but* chicken," he said. "I'm proud of you, Julian. Very proud of you." He leaned over and hugged me. "*Tu marches toujours le front haut.*"

I smiled. "I hope so, Dad."

I hope so.

Pluto

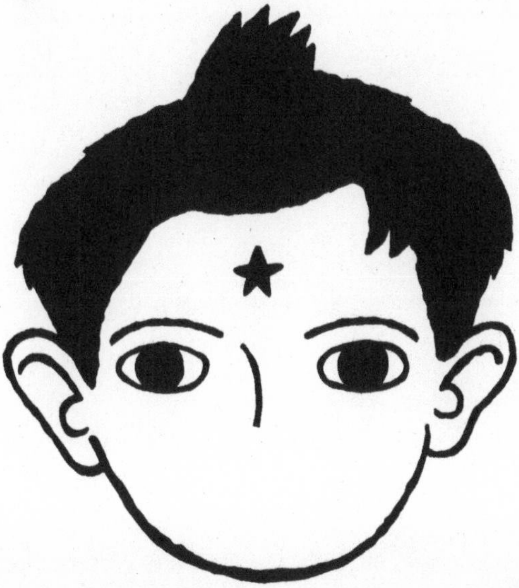

Contemporary observations are changing our understanding of planetary systems, and it is important that our nomenclature for objects reflect our current understanding. This applies, in particular, to the designation "planets." The word "planet" originally described "wanderers" that were known only as moving lights in the sky. Recent discoveries lead us to create a new definition, which we can make using currently available scientific information.
—International Astronomical Union (IAU),
excerpt from Resolution B5

.   .   .

I guess there is no one to blame
We're leaving ground
Will things ever be the same?
—Europe, "The Final Countdown"

.   .   .

It is such a mysterious place, the land of tears.
—Antoine de Saint-Exupéry, *The Little Prince*

Introductions

I was two days old the first time I met Auggie Pullman. I don't remember the occasion myself, obviously, but my mom told me about it. She and Dad had just brought me home from the hospital for the first time, and Auggie's parents had just brought him home from the hospital for the first time, too. But Auggie was already three months old by then. He had to stay in the hospital, because he needed some surgeries that would allow him to breathe and swallow. Breathing and swallowing are things most of us don't ever think about, because we do them automatically. But they weren't automatic for Auggie when he was born.

My parents took me over to Auggie's house so we could meet each other. Auggie was hooked up to a lot of medical equipment in their living room. My mom picked me up and brought me face to face with Auggie.

"August Matthew Pullman," she said, "this is Christopher Angus Blake, your new oldest friend."

And our parents applauded and toasted the happy occasion.

My mom and Auggie's mom, Isabel, became best friends before we were born. They met at the supermarket on Amesfort Avenue right after my parents moved to the neighborhood. Since both of them were having babies soon, and they lived across the street from each other, Mom and Isabel decided to form a mothers' group. A mothers' group is when a bunch of moms hang out together and have playdates with other kids' moms. There were about six or seven other moms in the mothers' group at first. They hung out together a couple of times before any of the babies were born. But after Auggie was born, only two other moms stayed in the mothers' group: Zachary's mom and Alex's mom. I don't know what happened to the other moms in the group.

Those first couple of years, the four moms in the mothers' group—along with us babies—hung out together almost every day. The moms would go jogging through the park with us in our strollers. They would take long walks along the riverfront with us in our baby slings. They would have lunch at the Heights Lounge with us in our baby chairs.

The only times Auggie and his mom didn't hang out with the mothers' group was when Auggie was back in the hospital. He needed a lot of operations, because, just like with breathing and swallowing, there were other things that didn't come automatically to him. For instance, he couldn't eat. He couldn't talk. He couldn't really even close his mouth all the way. These were things that the doctors had to operate on him so that he could do them. But even after the surgeries, Auggie never really ate or talked or closed his mouth all the way like me and Zack and Alex did. Even after the surgeries, Auggie was very different from us.

I don't think I really understood *how* different Auggie was from everyone else until I was four years old. It was wintertime, and Auggie and I were wrapped in our parkas and scarves while we played outside in the playground. At one point, we climbed up the ladder to the ramp at the top of the jungle gym and waited in line to go down the tall slide. When we were almost next, the little girl in front of us got cold feet about going down the tall slide, so she turned around to let us pass. That's when she saw Auggie. Her eyes opened really wide and her jaw dropped down, and she started screaming and crying hysterically. She was so upset, she couldn't even climb down the ladder. Her mom had to climb up the ramp to get her. Then Auggie started to cry, because he knew the girl was crying because of him. He covered his face with his scarf so nobody could see him, and then his mom had to climb up the ramp to get him, too. I don't remember all the details, but I remember there was a big commotion. A little crowd had formed around the slide. People were whispering. I remember us leaving the playground very quickly. I remember seeing tears in Isabel's eyes as she carried Auggie home.

That was the first time I realized how different Auggie was from the rest of us. It wasn't the last time, though. Like breathing and swallowing, crying comes automatically to most kids, too.

7:08 a.m.

I don't know why I was thinking about Auggie this morning. It's been three years since we moved away, and I haven't even seen him since his bowling party in October. Maybe I'd had a dream about him. I don't know. But I was thinking about him when Mom came into my room a few minutes after I turned off my alarm clock.

"You awake, sweetie?" she said softly.

I pulled my pillow over my head as an answer.

"Time to wake up, Chris," she said cheerfully, opening the curtains of my window. Even under my pillow with my eyes closed, I could tell my room was way too bright now.

"Close the curtains!" I mumbled.

"Looks like it's going to rain all day today," she sighed, not closing the curtains. "Come on, you don't want to be late again today. And you have to take a shower this morning."

"I took a shower, like, two days ago."

438

"Exactly!"

"Ugh!" I groaned.

"Let's go, honeyboy," she said, patting the top of my pillow.

I pulled the pillow off my face. "Okay!" I yelled. "I'm up! Are you happy?"

"You're such a grump in the morning," she said, shaking her head. "What happened to my sweet fourth grader from last year?"

"Lisa!" I answered.

She hated when I called her by her first name. I thought she'd leave my room then, but she started picking some clothes off my floor and putting them in my hamper.

"Did something happen last night, by the way?" I said, my eyes still closed. "I heard you on the phone with Isabel when I was going to sleep last night. It sounded like something bad . . ."

She sat down on the edge of my bed. I rubbed my eyes awake.

"What?" I said. "Is it really bad? I think I had a dream about Auggie last night."

"No, Auggie's fine," she answered, scrunching up her face a bit. She pushed some hair out of my eyes. "I was going to wait till later to—"

"What!" I interrupted.

"I'm afraid Daisy died last night, sweetie."

"What?"

"I'm sorry, honey."

"Daisy!" I covered my face with my hands.

"I'm sorry, sweetie. I know how much you loved Daisy."

Darth Daisy

I remember the day Auggie's dad brought Daisy home for the first time. Auggie and I were playing Trouble in his room when, all of a sudden, we heard high-pitched squealing coming from the front door. It was Via, Auggie's big sister. We could also hear Isabel and Lourdes, my babysitter, talking excitedly. So we ran downstairs to see what the commotion was about.

Nate, Auggie's dad, was sitting on one of the kitchen chairs, holding a squirming, crazy yellow dog in his lap. Via was kneeling down in front of the dog, trying to pet it, but the dog was kind of hyper and kept trying to lick her hand, which Via kept pulling away.

"A dog!" Auggie screamed excitedly, running over to his dad.

I ran over, too, but Lourdes grabbed me by the arm.

"Oh no, *papi*," she said to me. She had just started babysitting me in those days, so I didn't know her very well. I remember she used to put baby powder in my sneakers, which I still do now because it reminds me of her.

Isabel's hands were on the sides of her face. It was obvious that Nate had just come through the door. "I can't believe you did this, Nate," she was saying over and over again. She was standing on the other side of the room next to Lourdes.

"Why can't I pet him?" I asked Lourdes.

"Because Nate says three hours ago this dog lived on the street with a homeless man," she answered quickly. "Is disgusting."

"She's not disgusting—she's beautiful!" said Via, kissing the dog on her forehead.

"In my country, dogs stay outside," said Lourdes.

"He's so cute!" Auggie said.

"It's a *she*!" Via said quickly, nudging Auggie.

"Be careful, Auggie!" said Isabel. "Don't let her lick you in the face."

But the dog was already licking Auggie all over his face.

"The vet said she's perfectly healthy, guys," Nate said to both Isabel and Lourdes.

"Nate, she was living on the street!" Isabel answered quickly. "Who knows what she's carrying."

"The vet gave her all her shots, a tick bath, checked for worms," answered Nate. "This puppy's got a clean bill of health."

"That is *not* a puppy, Nate!" Isabel pointed out.

442

That was true: The dog was definitely not a puppy. She wasn't little, or soft and round, like puppies usually are. She was skinny and pointy and wild-eyed, and she had this crazy, long black tongue kind of pouring out of the side of her mouth. And she wasn't a small dog, either. She was the same size as my grandmother's labradoodle.

"Okay," said Nate. "Well, she's puppy*like*."

"What kind of dog is she?" asked Auggie.

"The vet thinks a yellow lab mix," answered Nate. "Maybe some chow?"

"More like pit bull," said Isabel. "Did he at least tell you how old she is?"

Nate shrugged. "He couldn't tell for sure," he answered. "Two or three? Usually they judge from the teeth, but hers are in bad shape because, you know, she's probably been eating junk food all her life."

"Garbage and dead rats," Lourdes said, like it was for sure.

"Oh God!" Isabel muttered, rubbing her hand over her face.

"Her breath does smell pretty bad," said Via, waving her hand in front of her nose.

"Isabel," said Nate, looking up at her. "She was destined for us."

"Wait, you mean we're *keeping* her?" Via said excitedly, her eyes opening up really wide. "I thought we were just babysitting her until we could find her a home!"

"I think *we* should be her home," said Nate.

"Really, Daddy?" cried Auggie.

Nate smiled and pointed his chin at Isabel. "But it's up to Mommy, guys," he said.

"Are you kidding me, Nate?" cried Isabel as Via and Auggie ran over to her and started pleading with her, putting their hands together, like they were praying in church.

"Please please please please please please please please please?" they kept saying over and over again. "Please pretty please please please please?"

"I can't believe you're doing this to me, Nate!" said Isabel, shaking her head. "Like our lives aren't complicated enough?"

Nate smiled and looked down at the dog, who was looking at him. "Look at her, honey! She was starving and cold. The homeless guy offered to sell her to me for ten bucks. What was I going to do, say no?"

"Yes!" said Lourdes. "Very easy to do."

"It's good karma to save a dog's life!" answered Nate.

"Don't do it, Isabel!" said Lourdes. "Dogs are dirty, and smelly. And they have germs. And you know who will end up walking her all the time, picking up all the poo-poo?" She pointed at Isabel.

"That's not true, Mommy!" said Via. "I promise I'll walk her. Every day."

"Me too, Mommy!" said Auggie.

444

"We'll take care of her completely," continued Via. "We'll feed her. We'll do everything."

"Everything!" added Auggie. "Please please please, Mommy?"

"Please please please, Mommy?" Via said at the same time.

Isabel was rubbing her forehead with her fingers, like she had a headache. Finally she looked at Nate and shrugged. "I think this is crazy, but . . . Okay. Fine."

"Really?" shrieked Via, hugging Isabel tightly. "Thank you, Mommy! Thank you so much! I promise we'll take care of her."

"Thank you, Mommy!" repeated Auggie, hugging Isabel.

"Yay! Thank you, Isabel!" said Nate, clapping the dog's two front paws together.

"Can I please pet her now?" I said to Lourdes, pulling away from her grip before she could stop me again. I slid over between Auggie and Via.

Nate put the dog down on the rug then, and she literally turned over onto her back so that we would all scratch her tummy. She closed her eyes like she was smiling, her long black tongue hanging from the side of her mouth onto the rug.

"That's exactly how I found her today," Nate pointed out.

"I've never seen a longer tongue in my life," said Isabel, crouching down next to us. She still hadn't pet the dog yet, though. "She looks like the Tasmanian Devil."

"I think she's beautiful," said Via. "What's her name?"

"What do you want to name her?" asked Nate.

"I think we should name her Daisy!" answered Via without any hesitation at all. "She's yellow, like a daisy."

"That's a nice name," said Isabel, who started petting the dog. "Then again, she looks a little like a lion. We could call her Elsa."

"I know what you should name her," I said, nudging Auggie. "You should call her Darth Maul!"

"That is the stupidest name in the world for a dog!" Via answered, disgusted.

I ignored her. "Do you get it, Auggie? Darth . . . *maul?* Get it? Because dogs maul . . ."

"Ha ha!" Auggie said. "That's so funny! Darth *Maul!*"

"We're not calling her that!" Via said snottily to the two of us.

"Hi, Darth Maul!" Auggie said to the dog, kissing her on her pink nose. "We can call her Darth for short."

Via looked at Nate. "Daddy, we're not calling her that!"

"I think it's kind of a fun name," Nate answered, shrugging.

"Mommy!" Via said angrily, turning to Isabel.

446

"I agree with Via," said Isabel. "I don't think we should use the word 'maul' for a dog . . . especially one that looks like this one."

"Then we'll just name her Darth," Auggie insisted.

"That's idiotic," said Via.

"I think, since Mommy's letting us keep the dog," answered Nate, "she should be the one who decides what to name her."

"Can we call her Daisy, Mommy?" asked Via.

"Can we call her Darth Maul?" asked Auggie.

Isabel gave Nate a look. "You really are killing me, Nate."

Nate laughed.

And that was how they ended up calling her Darth Daisy.

7:11 a.m.

"How did she die?" I asked Mom. "Was she hit by a car?"

"No." She stroked my arm. "She was old, sweetie. It was her time."

"She wasn't that old."

"She was sick."

"What, so they put her to sleep?" I asked, incensed. "How could they do that?"

"Sweetie, she was in pain," she answered. "They didn't want her to suffer. Isabel said that she died very peacefully in Nate's arms."

I tried to picture what that would look like, Daisy dying in Nate's arms. I wondered if Auggie had been there, too.

"As if that family hasn't been through enough already," Mom added.

I didn't say anything. I just blinked and looked up at the glow-in-the-dark stars on my ceiling. Some of them were coming unstuck, hanging on by just one or two points. A few had fallen down on me, like little pointy raindrops.

"You never fixed the stars, by the way," I said without thinking.

She had no idea what I was talking about. "What?"

"You said you were going to glue them back on," I said, pointing to the ceiling. "They keep falling down on me."

She looked up. "Oh, right," she said, nodding. I think she hadn't expected the conversation about Daisy to be over so quickly. But I didn't want to talk about it anymore.

She got up on top of my bed, took one of the lightsabers leaning on my bookcase, and tried to jam one of the larger stars back into place with the end of the lightsaber.

"They need to be glued, Lisa," I said just as the plastic star fell down on her head.

"Right," she answered, picking the star out of her hair. She jumped down off my bed. "Can you not call me Lisa, please?"

"Okay, Lisa," I answered.

She rolled her eyes and pointed the lightsaber at me, like she was going to jab me.

"Thanks for waking me up with really bad news, by the way," I said sarcastically.

"Hey, you're the one who asked me about it," she

answered, putting the lightsaber back. "I was going to wait until this afternoon to tell you."

"Why? I'm not a baby, Lisa," I answered. "I mean, sure, I love Daisy, but it's not like she was my dog. It's not like I see her anymore."

"I thought you'd be really upset," she answered.

"I am!" I said. "I'm just not, like, going to start crying or anything."

"Okay," she answered, nodding and looking at me.

"What?" I said impatiently.

"Nothing," she answered. "You're right, you're not a baby." She looked at the plastic star that was still stuck on her thumb and then, without saying anything else, leaned down and stuck it on my forehead. "You should call Auggie this afternoon, by the way."

"Why?" I asked.

"Why?" She raised her eyebrows. "To tell him how sorry you are about Daisy. To pay your condolences. Because he's your best friend."

"Oh, right," I mumbled, nodding.

"Oh, right," she repeated.

"Okay, Lisa. I get it!" I said.

"Grumpity grump grump," she said on her way out. "You have three minutes, Chris. Then you've got to get up. I'll turn on the shower for you."

"Close the door behind you!" I called out after her.

"Please!" she yelled from the hallway.

"Close the door behind you, PLEASE!" I groaned.

She slammed the door shut.

She could be so annoying sometimes!

I picked the star off my forehead and looked at it. Mom had put those stars on the ceiling when we first moved in. That was back when she was trying to do everything she could to get me to like our new house in Bridgeport. She had even promised that we would get a dog after we got settled in. But we never got a dog. We got a hamster. But that's hardly a dog. That's not even one quarter of a dog. A hamster is basically just a warm potato with fur. I mean, it moves and it's cute and all, but don't let anyone try to fool you that it's the same as a dog. I called my hamster Luke. But he's no Daisy.

Poor Daisy! It was hard to believe she was gone.

But I didn't want to think about her now.

I started thinking of all the things I had to do this afternoon. Band practice right after school. Study for the math test tomorrow. Start my book report for Friday. Play some *Halo*. Maybe catch up on *The Amazing Race* tonight.

I flicked the plastic star in the air and watched it spin across the room. It landed on the edge of my rug by the door.

Lots of stuff to do. It was going to be a long day.

But even as I was ticking off all the things I had to do today, I knew calling Auggie wasn't going to be one of them.

Friendships

I don't remember exactly when Zack and Alex stopped hanging out with me and Auggie. I think it was about the time we started kindergarten.

Before that, we all used to see each other almost every day. Our moms would usually bring us over to Auggie's house, since there were a lot of times when he couldn't go out because he was sick. Not a contagious kind of sick or anything, but the kind where he couldn't go outside. But we liked going to his house. His parents had turned their basement into a giant playroom. So, basically, it was like a toy store down there. Board games, train sets, air hockey and foosball tables, even a mini trampoline in the back. Zack and Alex and Auggie and I would literally spend hours running around down there, having all-day lightsaber duels and hop ball races. We would have balloon wars. We would pile cardboard bricks into giant mountains and play avalanche. Our moms called us the Four Musketeers, since we did everything together. And even after all the moms—except

Isabel—went back to work, our babysitters got us together every day. They would take us on day trips to the Bronx Zoo, or to see the pirate ships at the South Street Seaport. We'd have picnics in the park. We even went all the way down to Coney Island a few times.

But once we started kindergarten, Zack and Alex started having playdates with other kids. They went to a different school than I did, since they lived on the other side of the park, so we didn't see them as much anymore. Auggie and I would bump into them in the park some-times—Zack and Alex, hanging out with their new buddies—and we tried hanging out with them a couple of times. But their new friends didn't seem to like us. Okay, that's not exactly true. Their new friends didn't like *Auggie*. I know that for a fact, because Zack told me this. I remember telling this to my mom, and she explained that some kids might feel "uncomfortable" around Auggie because of the way he looks. That's how she put it. Uncomfortable. That's not how Zack and Alex had put it, though. They used the word "scared."

But I knew that Zack and Alex weren't uncomfort-able or scared of Auggie, so I didn't understand why *they* stopped hanging out with us. I mean, I had new friends from my school, too, but I didn't stop hanging out with Auggie. Then again, I never hung out with Auggie and my new friends together, because, well, mixing friends can be a weird thing even under the best circumstances.

I guess the truth is, I didn't want anyone to feel uncomfortable or scared, either.

Auggie had his own group of friends, too, by the way. These were kids who belonged to an organization for kids with "craniofacial differences," which is what Auggie has. Every year, all the kids and their families hang out together at Disneyland or some other fun place like that. Auggie loved going on these trips. He'd made friends all over the country. But these friends didn't live near us, so he hardly ever got to hang out with them.

I did meet one of his friends once, though. A kid named Hudson. He had a different syndrome than Auggie has. His eyes were spaced very far apart, and they kind of bulged out a bit. He and his parents were staying with Auggie's family for a couple of days while they were in the city meeting with doctors at Auggie's hospital. Hudson was the same age as me and Auggie. He was really into Pokémon, I remember.

Anyway, I had an okay time playing with him and Auggie that day, though Pokémon has never really been my thing. But then we all went out to dinner together—and that's when things got bad for me. I can't believe how much we got stared at! Like, usually when it was just me and Auggie, people would look at him and not even notice me. I was used to that. But with Hudson there, for some reason, it was just so much worse. People would look at Auggie first, and then they'd look at Hudson, and then they'd automatically look at me like they were wondering what was wrong with me, too. I saw one teenager staring at me like he was trying to figure out what was out of place on my face. It was so annoying! It made me want to scream. I couldn't wait to go home.

The next day, since I knew Hudson was still going to be there, I asked Lourdes if I could have a playdate over at Zack's house after school instead of going to Auggie's house. It's not that I didn't like Hudson, because I did. But I wasn't into Pokémon, and I definitely didn't want to get stared at again if we all went out somewhere.

I ended up having lots of fun at Zack's house. Alex came over, and the three of us played Four Square in front of his stoop. It really felt like old times again—except for the fact that Auggie wasn't there with us. But it was nice. No one stared at us. No one felt uncomfortable. No one got scared. Hanging out with Zack and Alex was just easy. That's when I realized why they didn't hang out with us anymore. Being friends with Auggie could be hard sometimes.

Luckily, Auggie never asked me why I didn't come over to his house that day. I was glad about that. I didn't know how to tell him that being friends with him could be hard for me sometimes, too.

8:26 a.m.

I don't know why, but it's almost impossible for me to get to school on time. Honestly, I don't know why. Every day, it's the same thing. I sleep through my alarm. Mom or Dad wakes me up. Whether I take a shower or not, whether I have a big breakfast or a Pop-Tart, we end up scrambling before we leave, Mom or Dad yelling at me to hurry up and get my coat, hurry up and tie my shoelaces. And even in those rare moments when we do get out the door on time, I'll forget something, so we end up having to turn back anyway. Sometimes it's my homework folder I forget. Sometimes it's my trombone. I don't know why, I really don't. It's just the way it is. Whether I'm sleeping at my mom's house or my dad's house, I'm always running late.

Today, I took a quick shower, got dressed super fast, popped my Pop-Tart, and managed to get out the door on time. It wasn't until we had driven the fifteen minutes it takes to get to school and had pulled into the school parking lot that I realized I had forgotten my science paper, my gym shorts, *and* my trombone. A new record for forgetting things.

"You're kidding, right?" said Mom when I told her. She was looking at me in the rearview mirror.

"No!" I said, biting my nails nervously. "Can we go back?"

"Chris, you're already running late! In this rain, it'll take forty minutes by the time we get home and back. No. You go to class, and I'll write you a note or something."

"I can't show up without my science paper!" I argued. "I have science first period!"

"You should have thought of that before you left the house this morning!" she answered. "Now come on, get out or you'll be late on top of everything. Look, even the school buses are leaving!" She pointed to where the school buses had started driving out of the parking lot.

"Lisa!" I said, panicked.

"What, Chris?" she shot back. "What do you want me to do? I can't teleport."

"Can't you go home and get them for me?"

She passed her fingers through her hair, which had gotten wet from the rain. "How many times have I told you to pack up your stuff the night before so you don't forget anything, huh?"

"Lisa!"

"Fine," she said. "Just go to class, and I'll bring you your stuff. Now go, Chris."

"But you have to hurry!"

"Go!" She turned around and gave me that look she gives me sometimes, when her eyeballs get super big and she kind of looks like an angry bird. "Get out of the car and go to school already!"

"Fine!" I said. I stomped out of the car. It had started raining harder, and of course I didn't have an umbrella.

She lowered the driver's side window. "Be careful walking to the sidewalk!"

"Trombone, science paper, gym shorts," I said to her, counting on my fingers.

"Careful where you're walking," she said, nodding. "This is a parking lot, Chris!"

"Mrs. Kastor will deduct five points off my grade if I don't hand my paper in by the end of first period!" I answered. "You have to be back before first period ends!"

"I know, Chris," she answered quickly. "Now walk to the sidewalk, sweetie."

"Trombone, science paper, gym shorts!" I said, walking backward toward the sidewalk.

"Watch where you're walking, Chris!" she shrieked just as a bike swerved around to avoid hitting me.

"Sorry!" I said to the bicyclist, who had a baby bundled up in the front bike carrier. The guy shook his head and pedaled away.

"Chris! You have to watch where you're going!" Mom screamed.

"Will you stop yelling?" I yelled.

She took a deep breath and rubbed her forehead. "Walk. To. The. Sidewalk. PLEASE." This she said through gritted teeth.

I turned around, looked both ways in an exaggerated way, and crossed the parking lot to the path leading to the school entrance. By now, the last of the school buses was pulling out of the parking lot.

"Happy now?" I said when I reached the sidewalk.

I could hear her sighing from twenty feet away. "I'll leave your stuff at the front desk in the main office," she answered, turning on the ignition and looking behind her as she started slowly backing out of the parking space. "Bye, honey. Have a nice—"

"Wait!" I ran over to the car while it was still moving.

The car screeched to a stop. "Chris!"

"I forgot my backpack," I said, opening the car door to get the backpack that I had left on the backseat. I could see her shaking her head out of the corner of my eye.

I closed the door, looked both ways in a super-obvious way again, and sprinted back toward the sidewalk. By now, the rain was coming down really hard. I pulled my hood over my head.

"Trombone! Science paper! Gym shorts!" I shouted, not looking back at her. I started jogging up the side-walk to the school entrance.

"Love you!" I heard her call out.

"Bye, Lisa!"

I made it inside just before first bell rang.

9:14 a.m.

I kept looking at the clock all through science class. Then, about ten minutes before the bell, I asked for the bathroom pass. I ran over to the main office as fast as I could and asked Ms. Denis, the nice old lady behind the main desk, for the stuff my mother had dropped off.

"Sorry, Christopher," she said. "Your mother hasn't dropped anything off."

"What?" I said.

"Was she supposed to come at a certain time?" she asked, looking at her watch. "I've been here all morning. I'm sure I haven't missed her."

She must have seen the expression on my face, because she waved me to come to the other side of her desk. She pointed to the phone. "Why don't you give her a call, honey?"

I called Mom's cell phone and got her voice mail.

"Hi, Mom. It's me and . . . um, you're not here and it's . . ." I looked at the big clock on the wall. "It's

461

nine-fourteen. I'm totally screwed if you don't show up in the next ten minutes, so, yeah. Thanks a lot, Lisa."

I hung up.

"I'm sure she'll be here any minute now," said Ms. Denis. "There's a lot of traffic on the highway because of all the construction. And it's really pouring outside now . . ."

"Yeah." I nodded and headed back to class.

At first, I thought maybe I'd gotten lucky. Mrs. Kastor didn't mention anything about the paper for the rest of the class. Then, just as the bell rang, she reminded us to drop off our science papers at her desk on the way out.

I waited until everyone else had left and walked over to her at the whiteboard.

"Um, Mrs. Kastor?" I said.

"Yes, Christopher?"

"Yeah, um, sorry, but I left my science paper at home this morning?"

She continued erasing the whiteboard.

"My mom's bringing it to school, but she got caught in the rain?" I said.

I don't know why, but when I talk to teachers and get a little nervous, my voice goes up at the end of every sentence.

"That's the fourth time this semester you've forgotten an assignment, Christopher," she said.

"I know," I answered. Then I raised my shoulders and smiled. "But I didn't know *you* knew! Ha."

462

She didn't even crack a smile at my attempt at humor.

"I just meant I didn't know you were keeping track . . ." I started to say.

"It's five points off, Chris," she said.

"Even if I get it to you next period?" I know I sounded whiny at this point.

"Rules are rules."

"So unfair," I muttered under my breath, shaking my head.

The second bell rang, and I ran to my next class before she could respond.

10:05 a.m.

Mr. Wren, my music teacher, was just as annoyed at me for forgetting my trombone as Mrs. Kastor had been about my science paper. For one thing, I had told Mr. Wren that Katie McAnn, the first trombonist, could take my trombone home today to practice her solo for the spring concert on Wednesday night. Katie's trombone was getting repaired, and the only other spare trombone was so banged up, you couldn't even push the slide past fourth position. So not only was Mr. Wren angry, but Katie was, too. And Katie is the kind of girl you don't want getting mad at you. She's a head taller than everyone else, and she gives really scary dirty looks to people she's mad at.

Anyway, I told Katie that my mom was on her way back to school with my trombone, so she didn't give me the dirty look right away. Mr. Wren gave her the dented trombone to use during class, so she didn't even have to sit out of music. When people forget their instruments, Mr. Wren usually makes them sit quietly off to the side and watch the orchestra rehearse. You're not allowed to read anything, or do homework. You just have to sit and listen to the orchestra rehearse. Not exactly the most thrilling experience in the world. I, of course, did have to sit music out today, since there was no trombone left for me to play.

During break, I ran over to the main office to pick up the stuff Mom should have dropped off by now. But she still hadn't shown up.

"I'm sure she just got stuck in traffic," offered Ms. Denis.

I shook my head. "No, I think I know what happened," I answered grumpily.

It had occurred to me while I was watching the band rehearse.

Isabel.

Duh, of course! Daisy just died. Something else must have happened. Maybe something to do with Auggie. And Isabel called Mom. And Mom, like she always does, dropped whatever she was doing to go help the Pullmans.

For all I knew, she was probably at the Pullman house right now! I bet she'd been on her way back to school with my trombone, science paper, and gym shorts on the backseat of the car when Isabel called, and bam, Mom completely forgot about me. Duh, of course that's what happened! It wouldn't be the first time, either.

"You want to call her again?" said Ms. Denis sweetly, handing me the phone.

"No thanks," I mumbled.

Katie came over to me when I got back to music class.

"Where's the trombone?" she said. Her eyebrows were practically touching in the middle of her forehead. "You said your mom was bringing it!"

"She's stuck in traffic?" I said apologetically. "She'll have it when she picks me up from school today, though?" I guess Katie made me as nervous as teachers did. "Can you meet me after school at five-thirty?"

"Why would I want to wait around till five-thirty?" she answered, making a clucking sound with her tongue. She gave me the same look she gave me when I accidentally emptied my spit valve in her Dixie cup a few weeks ago. "Gee, thanks, Chris! Now I'm going to totally mess up my solo at the spring concert. And it's totally going to be your fault!"

"It's not my fault?" I said. "My mother was supposed to bring me my stuff?"

"You're such a . . . moron," she mumbled.

"No, you are" was my brilliant comeback.

"Your ears stick out." She made both her hands into little fists and walked away with her arms straight at her sides.

"Ugh!" I answered her, rolling my eyes.

And for the rest of the class, she shot me the dirtiest looks you can imagine over her music stand. If looks really could kill, Katie McAnn would be a serial murderer.

All of this could have been avoided if Mom hadn't abandoned me today! I was so mad at her for that. Boy, was she going to be sorry tonight. I could picture it already, how she would pick me up after school and be all, "I'm so sorry, honey! I had to drive over to the Pullmans', because they needed help with yadda yadda yadda."

And I would be like, "Yadda yadda yadda."

And she would be like, "Come on, honey. You know they need our help sometimes."

"Yadda! Yadda! Yadda!"

Space

When Auggie turned five, someone gave him an astronaut helmet as a birthday present. I don't remember who. But Auggie started wearing that helmet all the time. Everywhere. Every day. I know people thought it was because he wanted to cover his face—and maybe part of it *was* that. But I think it was more because Auggie really loved outer space. Stars and planets. Black holes. Anything to do with the *Apollo* missions. He started telling everyone he was going to be an astronaut when he grew up. In the beginning, I didn't get why he was so obsessed with this stuff. But then one weekend, our moms took us to the planetarium at the natural history museum—and that's when I got sucked into it, too. That was the beginning of what we called our space phase.

Auggie and I had gone through a lot of phases by then. ZoobiePlushies. PopBopBots. Dinosaurs. Ninjas. Power Rangers (I'm embarrassed to say). But, until then, nothing had been as intense as our space phase. We watched every DVD we could find about the universe. Space videos. Picture books about the Milky Way. Making 3-D solar systems. Building model rocket ships. We would spend hours playing pretend games about missions to deep space, or landing on Pluto. That became our favorite planet to travel to. Pluto was our Tatooine.

We were still deep into our space phase when my sixth birthday rolled around, so my parents decided to have my party at the planetarium. Auggie and I were so excited! The new space show had just come out, and we hadn't seen it yet. I invited my entire first-grade class. And Zack and Alex, of course. I even invited Via, but she couldn't come because she had a different birthday party to go to that same day.

But then, the morning of my birthday, Isabel called Mom and told her that she and Nate had to take Auggie to the hospital. He had woken up with a high fever, and his eyelids were swollen shut. A few days before, he had had a "minor" surgery to correct a previous surgery to make his lower eyelids less droopy, and now it had become infected. So Auggie had to go to the hospital instead of going to my sixth birthday party.

I was so bummed! But I got even more bummed when Mom told me that Isabel had asked her if she would be able to drop Via off at the other birthday party before going to my party.

Before even checking with me first, Mom had said,

"Yes, of course, whatever we can do to help!" Even though that meant that she might end up being a little late to *my* birthday party!

"But why can't Nate drop Via off at the other party?" I asked Mom.

"Because he's driving Auggie to the hospital, along with Isabel," Mom answered. "It's not a big deal, Chris. I'll take Via in a taxi and then hop on a train."

"But can't someone else take Via? Why does it have to be you?"

"Isabel doesn't have the time to start calling other moms, Chris! So if we don't take Via, she'll have to just go with them to the hospital. Poor Via is always missing out—"

"Mommy!" I interrupted. "I don't care about Via! I don't want you to be late to my birthday party!"

"Chris, what do you want me to say?" Mom answered. "They're our friends. Isabel is my good friend, just like Auggie is your good friend. And when good friends need us, we do what we can to help them, right? We can't just be friends when it's convenient. Good friendships are worth a little extra effort!"

When I didn't say anything, she kissed my hand.

"I promise I'll only be a few minutes late," she said.

But she wasn't just a few minutes late. She ended up being more than an hour late.

"I'm so sorry, honey . . . The A train was out of service . . . No taxis anywhere . . . So sorry . . ."

470

I knew she felt terrible. But I was so angry. I remember even Dad was annoyed.

She was so late, she even missed the space show.

3:50 p.m.

The rest of the day ended up being pretty much as bad as the beginning of the day. I had to sit out of gym, because I didn't have my gym shorts and I didn't have a spare set in my locker. Katie McAnn's entire table kept shooting me dirty looks at lunch. I don't even remember my other classes. Then math was the last class of the day. I knew we were having a big math test tomorrow, which I hadn't studied for over the weekend like I was supposed to. But it wasn't until Ms. Medina started going over the material for tomorrow's test that I realized I was in deep trouble. I didn't understand what the heck we were doing. I mean, seriously, it was like Ms. Medina was suddenly talking in a made-up language that everyone else in class seemed to understand but me. *Gadda badda quotient. Patta beeboo divisor.* At the end of class, she offered to meet with any kids who needed a little extra help studying right after school. *Um, that would be me, thank you!* But I had band practice then, so I couldn't go.

I raced down to the auditorium right after dismissal. The after-school rock band meets every Monday and Tuesday afternoon. I had only joined a few months ago, at the beginning of the spring semester, but I was really into it. I'd been taking guitar lessons since last summer, and my dad, who's a really good guitar player, had been teaching me all these great guitar licks. So when *Santa* gave me an electric guitar for Christmas, I figured I was ready to join the after-school rock band. I was a little nervous in the beginning. I knew the three guys who were already in the band were really good musicians. But then I found out there was a fourth grader named John who was also joining the band in the spring semester, so I knew I wouldn't be the only new kid. John played guitar, too. He wore John Lennon glasses.

The other three guys in the band were Ennio, who plays the drums and is considered to be this prodigy drummer, Harry on lead guitar, and Elijah on bass guitar. Elijah's also the lead singer, and he's kind of the leader of the band. The three of them are all in the sixth grade. They've been in the after-school rock band since they were in the fourth grade, so they're a pretty tight group.

I can't say they were thrilled when John and I first joined the band. Not that they weren't *nice*, but they weren't *nice* nice. They didn't treat us like we were equal members of the band. It was pretty obvious that they didn't think we played as well as they did—and, to be truthful, we really didn't. But still, we were trying really hard to get better.

"So, Mr. B," Elijah said after we had all jammed on our own a bit. "We're thinking we want to play 'Seven Nation Army' for the spring concert on Wednesday."

Mr. Bowles was the after-school rock band adviser. He had gray hair that he kept in a ponytail, and had been a member of a famous folk-rock band in the '80s that my dad, for one, had never heard of. But Mr. Bowles was super nice, and he was always trying to get the other guys to include me and John. This, of course, just got the other guys even more annoyed at us. And it also made them really dislike Mr. Bowles. They made fun of the way he sometimes talked with his eyes closed. They made fun of his ponytail and his taste in music.

"'Seven Nation Army'?" answered Mr. Bowles, like he was impressed by the song choice. "That's an awesome song, Elijah."

"Is that by Europe, too?" John asked, since we'd all agreed a few weeks ago—after much arguing—to play "The Final Countdown" by Europe at the spring concert.

Elijah snickered and made a face. "Dude," he answered, not looking at John or me. "It's the White Stripes."

Elijah had long blond hair that he was really good at talking through.

"Never heard of them!" John said cheerfully, which I

474

wished he hadn't said. Truth is, I hadn't heard of them, either, but I knew enough to pretend I knew them—at least until I could download the song tonight. John wasn't so great at the social stuff that goes on inside a rock band. Lots of group dynamic stuff to sort out. You have to kind of just nod and go along if you want to fit in. Then again, John wasn't very good at fitting in that way.

Elijah laughed and turned around to tune his guitar.

John looked at me over his little round glasses and made an "Is it me, or are they crazy?" face.

I shrugged in response.

John and I had become our own little group inside this rock band. We hung out together during breaks and made jokes, especially since the other three guys hung out together and made their own jokes. Every Thursday after school, I'd go over to John's house and we'd practice together, or we'd listen to some classic rock songs so we could sound like we knew as much about rock music as the other guys. And then we'd make suggestions about what songs we could play. So far, we had suggested "Yellow Submarine" and "Eye of the Tiger." But Elijah, Harry, and Ennio had nixed them both.

That was fine, though, because I was really into "The Final Countdown," which had been Mr. Bowles's suggestion. *It's the final countdown!*

"I don't know, guys," Mr. Bowles said. "I'm not sure there's going to be enough time between today and

Wednesday to learn a brand-new song. Maybe we should stick to 'The Final Countdown' for now?" He played the opening notes of that song on the keyboard, and John started bopping his head.

Then Elijah started playing a great riff on his bass, which turned out to be the opening of "Seven Nation Army." As if on cue, Harry and Ennio started playing, too. It was pretty obvious that they had practiced the song a lot of times before today. I have to say, they sounded amazing.

Somewhere in the second chorus, Mr. Bowles put his hand up for them to stop jamming.

"Okay, dudes," he said, nodding. "You're sounding absolutely awesome. Killer bass, Elijah. But everyone's got to be able to play the song for the spring concert, right? These two dudes need a chance to learn the song, too." He pointed at me and John.

"But it's just basic chords!" said Elijah. "Like C and G! B. D. You do know D, right?" He looked at us like we were an alien species. "You seriously can't do that?"

"I can do that," I answered quickly, forming the chords with my fingers.

"I hate the B chord!" said John.

"It's so easy!" said Elijah.

"But what about 'The Final Countdown'?" John whined. "I've been practicing that for weeks!"

He started playing the same opening part that Mr. B had just played, but he honestly didn't sound that good.

476

"Dude, that was awesome!" said Mr. B, high-fiving John.

I noticed Elijah smiled at Harry, who looked down like he was trying not to laugh.

"Guys, we have to be fair here," said Mr. B to Elijah.

"Here's the thing," answered Elijah. "We can only play one song at the spring concert, and we want it to be 'Seven Nation Army.' Majority rules."

"But it's not what we *said* we were going to play!" yelled John. "It's not fair that you guys agreed to play 'The Final Countdown,' and me and Chris have spent a lot of time learning it . . ."

I have to admit, John had guts talking back to a sixth grader like that.

"Sorry, dude," said Elijah, fiddling with his amp. But he didn't seem sorry.

"Okay, let's settle down, guys," said Mr. B with his eyes closed.

"Mr. B?" said Ennio, holding up his hand like he was in class. "The thing is, this is going to be our last spring concert before the three of us graduate." He pointed his drumstick at Harry and Elijah and himself.

"Yeah, we're going to middle school next year!" agreed Elijah.

"We want to play a song that we feel really good about," Ennio finished. "'The Final Countdown' doesn't represent us musically."

"But that's not fair!" said John. "This is an after-*school* rock band. Not just *your* band! You can't just do that!"

"Dude, you can play whatever you want next year," Elijah answered. He looked like he wanted to flick John's glasses off his face. "You can play 'Puff the Magic Dragon' for all I care."

This made the other guys laugh.

Mr. Bowles finally opened his eyes. "Okay, guys, enough," he said, holding up his hands. "Here's what we're going to do. Let's see how well you two pick up 'Seven Nation Army' today and tomorrow." He said this while pointing at me and John. "We'll practice it a little today. We'll also tighten up 'The Final Countdown.' Then, tomorrow, we'll see which song sounds better. But I'm going to be the one to make the final decision which song we play, okay? Sound good?"

John nodded yes eagerly, but Elijah rolled his eyes.

"So, let's start with 'The Final Countdown,'" said Mr. Bowles. He clapped his hands twice. "From the beginning. Let's go, guys. 'The Final Countdown'! From the top. Ennio, wake up! Harry! Elijah, get us going, man! On four. A one. Two. Three . . ."

We played the song. Even though Elijah and the other guys weren't into it, they totally rocked it. In fact, we sounded pretty amazing together, I thought.

"That sounded awesome!" said John when it was over. He held his hand in the air to high-five me, which I did a little reluctantly.

"Whatever," said Elijah, shaking his hair off his face.

478

We spent the rest of the class running through "Seven Nation Army." But John kept making mistakes and asking us to start over. It didn't sound good at all.

"You guys sound terrific!" said John's mother, who had just come in the band room. She tried to clap while holding her wet umbrella.

Mr. B looked at his watch. "Whoa, it's five-thirty? Oh man! Dudes, I've got a gig tonight. We have to wrap this up. Let's go. Everything in the lock room."

I started putting my guitar in the case.

"Step on it, guys!" said Mr. B, putting the mics away.

We all hurried up and put our instruments in the lock room.

"See you tomorrow, Mr. B!" said John, who was the first to be ready to leave. "Bye, Elijah, bye, Ennio, bye, Harry!" He waved at them. "See you tomorrow!"

I saw the three of them shoot each other looks, but they nodded goodbye to John.

"Bye, Chris!" John said loudly from the door.

"Bye," I mumbled. I liked the guy, I really did. One on one he was awesome. But he could be so clueless, too. It was like being friends with SpongeBob.

After John and his mother had left, Elijah went up to Mr. Bowles, who was wrapping up the mic cords.

"Mr. B," he said, ultra politely. "Can we please play 'Seven Nation Army' on Wednesday night?"

At that moment, Ennio's mom arrived to pick up the three of them.

"We'll see tomorrow, dude," Mr. Bowles answered distractedly, throwing the last of the equipment into the lock room.

"Yeah, you're just gonna choose 'The Final Countdown,'" said Elijah, and then he walked out the door.

"Bye, guys," I said to Harry and Ennio as they followed Elijah out.

"Bye, dude," they both said to me.

Mr. B turned the key in the lock room. Then he looked at me, like he was surprised I was still there.

"Where's your mom?"

"I guess she's running late."

"Don't you have a cell phone?"

I nodded, fished my phone out of my backpack, and turned it on. There were no texts or missed calls from Mom.

"Just call her!" he said after a few minutes. "I've got to get out of here, dude."

5:48 p.m.

Just as I was about to call, my dad knocked on the band-room door. I was totally surprised. He's never picked me up from school on a Monday before.

"Dad!" I said.

He smiled and walked in. "Sorry I'm late," he said, shaking out his umbrella.

"This is Mr. Bowles," I said to him.

"Nice to meet you!" said Mr. B quickly, but he'd already started out the door. "Sorry, I can't stay and chat. You've got a nice kid there!" Then he left.

"Don't forget to lock the door behind you, Chris!" he yelled out a second later from down the hallway.

"I will!" I said, loud enough for him to hear me.

I turned to Dad. "What are you doing here?"

"Mom asked me to get you," he answered, picking up my backpack.

"Let me guess," I said sarcastically, putting on my jacket. "She went to Auggie's house today, right?"

Dad looked surprised. "No," he said. "Everything is

fine, Chris. Pull your hood up—it's raining hard." We started walking out the door.

"Then where is she? Why didn't she bring me my stuff?" I said angrily.

He put his hand on my shoulder as we kept walking. "I don't want you to worry at all, but . . . Mommy got in a little car accident today."

I stopped walking. "What?"

"She's totally fine," he said, squeezing my shoulder. "Nothing to worry about. Promise." He motioned for me to keep walking.

"So, where is she?" I asked.

"She's still in the hospital."

"Hospital?" I yelled. Once again, I stopped walking.

"Chris, she's fine, I promise," he answered, pulling me by the elbow. "She broke her leg, though. She has a huge cast."

"Seriously?"

"Yes." He held the exit door open for me while opening his umbrella. "Pull your hood up, Chris."

I pulled my hood over my head as we hurried across the parking lot. It was really pouring. "Was she hit by a car?"

"No, she was driving," he answered. "Apparently, the rain caused some flooding on the parkway, and a construction truck hit a ditch, and Mom swerved to avoid hitting it but then got sideswiped by the car in the left lane. The woman in the other car was fine, too. Mommy's fine. Her leg will be fine. Everyone is fine, thank God."

He stopped at a red hatchback I had never seen before.

"Is this new?" I said, confused.

"It's a rental," he answered quickly. "Mom's car got totaled. Come on, get in."

I got into the backseat. By now my sneakers were soaking wet. "Where's your car?"

"I went to the hospital straight from the train station," he answered.

"We should sue whoever was driving that construction truck," I said, putting my seat belt on.

"It was a freak accident," he muttered. He started driving out of the parking lot.

"When did it happen?" I asked.

"This morning."

"What time this morning?"

"I don't know. About nine? I had just gotten to work when they called me from the hospital."

"Wait, did the person who called you know that you and Mom are getting a divorce?"

He looked at me in the rearview mirror. "Chris," he said. "Your mom and I will always be there for one another. You know that."

"Right," I said, shrugging.

I looked out the window. It was that time of day when the sun's gone down but the streetlights haven't come on yet. The streets were black and shiny because of the rain. You could see the reflections of all the red and white lights of the cars in the puddles along the highway.

I pictured Mom driving in the rain this morning. Did it happen right after she dropped me off, or when she was driving back to school with my stuff?

"Why did you think she was on her way to Auggie's house?" Dad asked.

"I don't know," I answered, still looking out the window. "Because Daisy died. I thought maybe—"

"Daisy died?" he said. "Oh no, I didn't know that. When did that happen?"

"They put her to sleep last night."

"Had she been sick?"

"Dad, I don't know any details!"

"Okay, don't bite my head off."

"It's just . . . I wish you had told me about the accident earlier in the day! Someone should have told me."

Dad looked at me in the rearview mirror again. "There was no need to alarm you, Chris. Everything was under control. There was nothing you could have done anyway."

"I was waiting for Mom to come back with my stuff all morning!" I said, crossing my arms.

"It was a crazy day for all of us, Chris," he answered. "I spent the day dealing with accident reports and insurance forms, rental cars, going back and forth to the hospital . . ."

"I could have gone to the hospital with you," I said.

"Well, you're in luck," he said, drumming the steering wheel. "Because that's where we're going right now."

"Wait, we're going to the hospital?" I said.

"Mom just got discharged, so we're picking her up." He looked at me in the mirror again, but I looked away. "Isn't that great?"

"Yeah."

We drove quietly for a few seconds. The rain was coming down in sheets. Dad made the windshield wipers go faster. I leaned my head against the window.

"This day sucked," I said quietly. I blew some hot air on the window and drew a sad face with my finger.

"You okay, Chris?"

"Yes," I mumbled. "I hate hospitals, that's all."

The Hospital Visit

The first and only time I'd ever been to a hospital before was to visit Auggie. This was when we were about six years old. Auggie had had like a million surgeries before then, but this was the first time my mom thought I was old enough to go and visit him.

The surgery had been to remove the "buttonhole" on his neck. This is what he used to call his trach tube, a little plastic thingy that was literally inserted into his neck below his Adam's apple. The "buttonhole" is what the doctors put inside Auggie when he was born to allow him to breathe. The doctors were removing it now, because they were pretty sure Auggie could breathe on his own.

Auggie was really excited about this surgery. He hated his buttonhole. And when I say he hated it, I mean he *haaaated* it. He hated that it was so noticeable, since he wasn't allowed to cover it up. He hated that he couldn't go swimming in a pool because of it. Most of all, he hated how sometimes it would get blocked up, for no reason, and he would start to cough like he was choking, like he couldn't breathe. Then Isabel or Nate would have to jab a tube into the hole, to suction it, so that he could breathe again. I watched this happen a couple of times, and it was pretty scary.

I remember I was really happy about visiting Auggie after his surgery. The hospital was downtown, and Mom surprised me by stopping off at FAO Schwarz so I could pick out a nice big present to bring to Auggie (a *Star Wars* Lego set) and a small present for me (an Ewok plushie). After we bought the toys, Mom and I got lunch at my favorite restaurant, which makes the best foot-long hot dogs and iced hot chocolate milk shakes on the planet.

And then, after lunch, we went to the hospital.

"Chris, there are going to be other kids who are having facial surgeries," Mom told me quietly as we walked through the hospital doors. "Like Auggie's friend Hudson, okay? Remember not to stare."

"I would never stare!" I answered. "I hate when kids stare at Auggie, Mommy."

As we walked down the hall to Auggie's room, I remember seeing lots of balloons everywhere, and posters of Disney princesses and superheroes taped to the hallway walls. I thought it was cool. It felt like a giant birthday party.

I peeked into some of the hospital rooms as we passed, and that's when I realized what my mom meant. These were kids like Auggie. Not that they looked like him, though a couple of them did, but they had other facial differences. Some of them had bandages on their faces. One girl, I saw quickly, had a huge lump on her cheek that was the size of a lemon.

I squeezed my mom's hand and remembered not to stare, so I looked down at my feet as we walked and held on tight to my Ewok plushie.

When we reached Auggie's room, I was glad to see that Isabel and Via were already there. They both came over to the door when they saw us and kissed us hello happily.

They walked us over to Auggie, who was in the bed by the window. As we passed the bed closest to the door, I got the impression that Isabel was trying to block me from looking at the kid lying in that bed. So I took a quick peek behind me after we had passed. The boy in the bed, who was probably only about four, was watching me. Under his nose, where the top of his mouth was supposed to be, was an enormous red hole, and inside the hole was what looked like a piece of raw meat. There seemed to be teeth stuck into the meat, and pieces of jagged skin hanging over the hole. I looked away as quickly as I could.

Auggie was asleep. He seemed so tiny in the big hospital bed! His neck was wrapped up in white gauze, and there was blood on the gauze. He had some tubes sticking out of his arm, and one sticking into his nose.

His mouth was wide open, and his tongue was kind of hanging out of his mouth onto his chin. It looked a little yellow and was all dried up. I've seen Auggie asleep before, but I'd never seen him sleep like that.

I heard my mom and Isabel talking about the surgery in their quiet voices, which they used when they didn't want me or Auggie to hear what they were saying. Something about "complications" and how it had been "touch and go" for a while. My mom hugged Isabel. I stopped listening.

I stared at Auggie, wishing he would close his mouth in his sleep.

Via came over and stood next to me. She was about ten years old then. "It was nice of you to come visit Auggie," she said.

I nodded. "Is he going to die?" I whispered.

"No," she whispered back.

"Why is he bleeding?" I asked.

"It's where they operated on him," she answered. "It'll heal."

I nodded. "Why is his mouth open?"

"He can't help it."

"What's wrong with the little boy in the other bed?"

"He's from Bangladesh. He has a cleft lip and palate. His parents sent him here to have surgery. He doesn't speak any English."

I thought of the big empty red hole in the boy's face. The jagged flap of skin.

"Are you okay, Chris?" Via asked gently, nudging me. "Lisa? Lisa, I don't think Chris is looking so good . . ."

That's when the foot-long hot dog and iced hot chocolate milk shake kind of just exploded out of me. I threw up all over myself, the giant Lego box I'd gotten for Auggie, and most of the floor in front of his bed.

"Oh my goodness!" cried Mom as she looked around for paper towels. "Oh, sweetie!"

Isabel found a towel and started cleaning me with it. My mom, meanwhile, was frantically wiping the floor with a newspaper.

"No, Lisa! Don't worry about that," said Isabel. "Via, sweetie, go find a nurse and tell her we need a cleanup here." She said this as she was picking hot-dog chunks off my chin.

Via, who looked like she might throw up herself, turned around calmly and headed out the door. Within a few minutes, some nurses had come into the room with mops and buckets.

"Can we go home, Mommy?" I remember saying, the vomit taste still fresh in my mouth.

"Yes, honey," said Mom, taking over from Isabel and cleaning me off.

"I'm so sorry, Lisa," said Isabel, wetting another towel at the sink. She dabbed my face with it.

By now, I was sweating profusely. I turned to leave even before Mom and Isabel had finished cleaning me off. But then I accidentally caught a glimpse of the little boy in the bed, who was still looking at me. I started to cry when I looked into the big empty red hole above his mouth.

At that point, Mom kind of hugged me and glided me out the door at the same time. When we got outside the room, she half carried me to the lobby by the elevators. My face was buried in her coat, and I was crying hysterically.

Isabel and Via followed us out.

"I'm so sorry," Isabel said to us.

"I'm so sorry," said Mom. They were both kind of mumbling sorries to each other at the same time. "Please tell Auggie we're sorry we couldn't stay."

"Of course," said Isabel. She knelt down in front of me and started wiping my tears. "Are you okay, honey? I'm so sorry. I know it's a lot to process."

I shook my head. "It's not Auggie," I tried to say.

Her eyes got very wet suddenly. "I know," she whispered. Then she put both her hands on my face, like she was cradling it. "Auggie's lucky to have a friend like you."

The elevator came, Isabel hugged me and Mom, and then we got inside the elevator.

I saw Via waving at me as the elevator doors closed. Even though I was only six at the time, I remember thinking I felt sorry for her that she couldn't leave with us.

As soon as we were outside, Mom sat me down on a

bench and hugged me for a long time. She didn't say anything. She just kissed the top of my head over and over again.

When I finally calmed down, I handed her the Ewok.

"Can you go back and give it to him?" I said.

"Oh, honey," she answered. "That's so sweet of you. But Isabel can clean the Lego set. It'll be good as new for Auggie, don't worry."

"No, for the other kid," I answered.

She looked at me for a second, like she didn't know what to say.

"Via said he doesn't speak any English," I said. "It must be really scary for him, being in the hospital."

She nodded slowly. "Yeah," she whispered. "It must be."

She closed her eyes and hugged me again. And then she took me over to the security desk, where I waited until she went back up the elevator and, after about five minutes, came back down again.

"Did he like it?" I asked.

"Honeyboy," she said softly, brushing the hair out of my eyes. "You made his day."

7:04 p.m.

When we got to Mom's hospital room, we found her sitting up in a wheelchair watching TV. She had a huge cast that started from her thigh and went all the way down to her ankle.

"There's my guy!" she said happily as soon as she saw me. She held her arms out to me, and I went over and hugged her. I was relieved to see that Daddy had told the truth: except for the cast and a couple of scratches on her face, Mom looked totally fine. She was dressed and ready to go.

"How are you feeling, Lisa?" said Dad, leaning over and kissing her cheek.

"Much better," she answered, clicking off the TV set. She smiled at us. "Totally ready to go home."

"We got you these," I said, giving her the vase of flowers we had bought downstairs in the gift store.

"Thank you, sweetie!" she said, kissing me. "They're so pretty!"

I looked down at her cast. "Does it hurt?" I asked her.

"Not too much," she answered quickly.

"Mommy's very brave," said Dad.

"What I am is very lucky," Mom said, knocking the side of her head.

"We're all very lucky," added Dad quietly. He reached over and squeezed Mom's hand.

For a few seconds, no one said anything.

"So, do you need to sign any discharge papers or anything?" asked Dad.

"All done," she answered. "I'm ready to go home."

Dad got behind the wheelchair.

"Wait, can I push her?" I said to Dad, grabbing one of the handles.

"Let me just get her out the door here," answered Dad. "It's a little hard to maneuver with her leg."

"How was your day, Chris?" asked Mom as we wheeled her into the hallway.

I thought about what an awful day it had been. All of it, from beginning to end. Science, music, math, rock band. Worst day ever.

"Fine," I answered.

"How was band practice? Is Elijah being any nicer these days?" she asked.

"It was good. He's fine." I shrugged.

"I'm sorry I didn't bring your stuff," she said, stroking my arm. "You must have been wondering what happened to me!"

"I figured you were running errands," I answered.

494

"He thought you went to Isabel's house," laughed Dad.

"I did not!" I said to him.

We had reached the nurses' station and Mom was saying goodbye to the nurses, who were waving back, so she didn't really hear what Dad had said.

"Didn't you ask me if Mom had gone to—" Dad said to me, confused.

"Anyway!" I interrupted, turning to Mom. "Band was fine. We're playing 'Seven Nation Army' for the spring concert on Wednesday. Can you still come?"

"Of course I can!" she answered. "I thought you were playing 'The Final Countdown.'"

"'Seven Nation Army' is a great song," said Dad. He started humming the bass line and playing air guitar as we waited for the elevator.

Mom smiled at him. "I remember you playing that at the Parlor."

"What's the Parlor?" I asked.

"The pub down the road from our dorm," answered Mom.

"Before you were born, buddy," said Dad.

The elevator doors opened, and we got in.

"I'm starving," I said.

"You guys haven't eaten dinner yet?" Mom asked, looking at Dad.

"We came straight here from school," he answered. "When were we going to stop for dinner?"

"Can we stop for some McDonald's on the way home?" I asked.

"Sounds good to me," answered Dad.

We reached the lobby, and the elevator doors opened.

"Now can I push the wheelchair?" I said.

"Yep," he answered. "You guys wait for me over there, okay?" He pointed to the farthest exit on the left. "I'll pull the car around."

He jogged out the front entrance toward the parking lot. I pushed Mom's wheelchair to where he'd pointed.

"I can't believe it's still raining," said Mom, looking out the lobby windows.

"I bet you could pop a wheelie on this thing!" I said.

"Hey, hey! No!" Mom screamed, squeezed the sides of the wheelchair as I tilted it backward. "Chris! I've had enough excitement for the day."

I put the wheelchair down. "Sorry, Mom." I patted her head.

She rubbed her eyes with the palms of her hand. "Sorry, it's just been a really long day."

"Did you know that a day on Pluto is 153.3 hours long?" I asked.

"No, I didn't know that."

We didn't say anything for a few minutes.

"Hey, did you give Auggie a call, by the way?" she said out of the blue.

"Mom," I groaned, shaking my head.

"What?" she said. She tried to turn around in her

496

wheelchair to look at me. "I don't get it, Chris. Did you and Auggie have a fight or something?"

"No! There's just so much going on right now."

"Chris . . ." She sighed, but she sounded too tired to say anything else about it.

I started humming the bass line of "Seven Nation Army."

After a few minutes, the red hatchback pulled up in front of the exit, and Dad came jogging out of the car, holding an open umbrella. I pushed Mom outside the front doors. Dad gave her the umbrella to hold, and then he pushed her down the wheelchair ramp and around to the passenger side of the car. The wind was picking up now, and the umbrella Mom was holding went inside out after a strong gust.

"Chris, get inside!" said Dad. He started picking Mom up under her arms to transfer her to the front seat of the car.

"Kind of nice being waited on," Mom joked. But I could tell she was in pain.

"Worth a broken femur?" Dad joked back, out of breath.

"What's a femur?" I asked, scooching into the backseat.

"The thighbone," answered Dad. He was soaking wet by now as he tried to help Mom find her seat belt.

"Sounds like an animal," I answered. "Lions and tigers and femurs."

Mom tried to laugh at my joke, but she was sweating.

Dad hurried around to the back of the car and spent a few minutes trying to figure out how to fold the wheelchair to get it inside. Then he came around to the driver's seat, sat down, and closed the door. We all kind of sat there quietly for a second, the wind and rain howling outside the windows. Then Dad started the car. We were all soaking wet.

"Mommy," I said after we'd been driving a few minutes, "when you got in the accident this morning, were you on your way home after dropping me off? Or were you driving back to school with my stuff?"

Mom took a second to answer. "It's actually kind of a blur, honey," she answered, reaching her arm behind her so that I would take her hand. I squeezed her hand.

"Chris," said Dad, "Mommy's kind of tired. I don't think she wants to think about it right now."

"I just want to know."

"Chris, now's not the time," said Dad, giving me a stern look in the rearview mirror. "The only thing that's important is that everything worked out okay and that Mommy's safe and sound, right? We have a lot to be thankful for. Today could have been so much worse."

It took me a second to realize what he meant. And then when I did, I felt a shiver go up my spine.

FaceChat

The first year after we moved to Bridgeport, our parents tried really hard to get Auggie and me together at least a couple of times a month—either at our place or at Auggie's. I had a couple of sleepovers at Auggie's house, and Auggie tried a sleepover at my place once, though that didn't work out. But it's a long car ride between Bridgeport and North River Heights, and eventually we only got together every couple of months or so. We started FaceChatting each other a lot around that time. Like, practically every day in third grade, Auggie and I would hang out together on FaceChat. We had decided to grow our Padawan braids before I moved away, so it was a great way to check how long they had gotten. Sometimes we wouldn't even talk: we'd just keep the screens on while we both watched a TV show together or built the same Lego set at the same time. Sometimes we would trade riddles. Like, what has a foot but no leg? Or, what does a poor man have, a rich man need, and you would die if you ate it? Stuff like that could keep us going for hours.

Then, in the fourth grade, we started FaceChatting less. It wasn't a thing we did on purpose. I just started having more things to do in school. Not only did I get more homework now, but I was doing a lot of after-school stuff. Soccer a couple of times a week. Tennis lessons. Robotics in the spring. It felt like I was always missing Auggie's Face-Chat requests, so finally we decided to schedule our chats for right before dinner on Wednesdays and Saturdays.

And that worked out fine, though it ended up being only Wednesday nights because Saturdays I had too much going on. It was somewhere toward the end of the fourth grade that I told Auggie I had cut off my Padawan braid. He didn't say it, but I think that hurt his feelings.

Then this year, Auggie started going to school, too.

I almost couldn't imagine Auggie at school, or how it would be for him. I mean, being a new kid is hard enough. But being a new kid that looks like Auggie? That would be insane. And not only was he starting school, he was starting *middle* school! That's how they do it in his school—fifth graders walking down the same hallways as ninth graders! Crazy! You have to give Auggie his props—that takes guts.

The only time I FaceChatted with Auggie in September was a few days after school had started, but he didn't seem to want to talk. I did notice he had cut off his Padawan braid, but I didn't ask him about it. I figured it was for the same reason I had cut mine off. I mean, you know, nerd alert.

I was curious to go to Auggie's bowling party a few weeks before Halloween. I got to meet his new friends, who seemed nice enough. There was this one kid named Jack Will who was pretty funny. But then I think something happened with Jack and Auggie, because when I FaceChatted with Auggie after Halloween, he told me they weren't friends anymore.

The last time I FaceChatted with Auggie was right after winter break had ended. My friends Jake and Tyler were over my place and we were playing *Age of War II* on my laptop when Auggie's FaceChat request came up on my screen.

"Guys," I said, turning the laptop toward me. "I need to take this."

"Can we play on your Xbox?" asked Jake.

"Sure," I said, pointing to where they could find the extra controllers. And then I kind of turned my back to them, because I didn't want them to see Auggie's face. I tapped "accept" on the laptop, and a few seconds later, Auggie's face came on the screen.

"Hey, Chris," he said.

"Sup, Aug," I answered.

"Long time no see."

"Yeah," I answered.

Then he started talking about something else. Something about a war at his school? Jack Will? I didn't really follow what he was saying, because I was completely distracted by Jake and Tyler, who had started nudging one another, mouths open, half laughing, the moment Auggie had come on-screen. I knew they had seen Auggie's face. I walked to the other side of the room with the laptop.

"Mm-hmm," I said to Auggie, trying to tune out the things Jake and Tyler were whispering to each other. But I heard this much:

"Did you see that?"

"Was that a mask?"

". . . a fire?"

"Is there someone there with you?" asked Auggie.

I guess he must have noticed that I wasn't really listening to him.

I turned to my friends and said, "Guys, shh!"

That made them crack up. They were very obviously trying to get a closer look at my screen.

"Yeah, I'm just with some friends," I mumbled quickly, walking to yet another side of my room.

"Hi, Chris's friend!" said Jake, following me.

"Can we meet your friend?" asked Tyler loudly so Auggie would hear.

I shook my head at them. "No!"

"Okay!" said Auggie from the other side of the screen.

Jake and Tyler immediately came on either side of me so the three of us were facing the screen and seeing Auggie's face.

502

"Hey!" Auggie said. I knew he was smiling, but sometimes, to people who didn't know, his smile didn't look like a smile.

"Hey," both Jake and Tyler said quietly, nodding politely. I noticed that they were no longer laughing.

"So, these guys are my friends Jake and Tyler," I said to Auggie, pointing my thumb back and forth at them. "And that's Auggie. From my old neighborhood."

"Hey," said Auggie, waving.

"Hey," said Jake and Tyler, not looking at him directly.

"So," said Auggie, nodding awkwardly. "So, yeah, what are you guys doing?"

"We were just turning on the Xbox," I answered.

"Oh, nice!" answered Auggie. "What game?"

"*House of Asterion.*"

"Cool. What level are you on?"

"Um, I don't know exactly," I said, scratching my head. "Second maze, I think."

"Oh, that's a hard one," Auggie answered. "I've almost unlocked Tartarus."

"Cool."

I noticed out of the corner of my eye that Jake was poking Tyler behind my back.

"Yeah, well," I said, "I think we're going to start playing now."

"Oh!" said Auggie. "Sure. Good luck with the second maze!"

"Okay. Bye," I said. "Hope the war thing works out."

"Thanks. Nice meeting you guys," Auggie added politely.

"Bye, Auggie!" Jake said, smirking.

Tyler started laughing, so I elbowed him out of screen view.

"Bye," Auggie said, but I could tell he noticed them laughing. Auggie always noticed stuff like that, even though he pretended not to.

I clicked off. As soon as I did, both Jake and Tyler started cracking up.

"What the heck?" I said to them, annoyed.

"Oh, dude!" said Jake. "What was up with that kid?"

"I've never seen anything that ugly in my life," said Tyler.

"Hey!" I answered defensively. "Come on."

"Was he in a fire?" asked Jake.

"No. He was born like that," I explained. "He can't help the way he looks. It's a disease."

"Wait, is it contagious?" asked Tyler, pretending to be afraid.

"Come on," I answered, shaking my head.

"And you're friends with him?" asked Tyler, looking at me like I was a Martian. "Whoa, dude!" He was snickering.

"What?" I looked at him seriously.

He opened his eyes wide and shrugged. "Nothing, dude. I'm just saying."

I saw him look at Jake, who squeezed his lips together like a fish. There was an awkward silence.

"Are we playing or not?" I asked after a few seconds. I grabbed one of the controllers.

We started playing, but it wasn't a great game. I was in a bad mood, and they just continued being goofballs. It was irritating.

After they left, I started thinking about Zack and Alex, how they had ditched Auggie all those years ago.

Even after all this time, it can still be hard being friends with Auggie.

8:22 p.m.

As soon as Dad wheeled Mom into our house, I plopped down on the sofa in front of the TV with my half-finished McDonald's Happy Meal. I clicked the TV on with the remote.

"Wait," said Dad, shaking out the umbrella. "I thought you had homework to do."

"I just want to watch the rest of *Amazing Race* while I eat," I answered. "I'll do my homework when it's over."

"Is it okay for him to do that?" Dad said to Mom.

"It's almost over anyway, Mommy!" I said to Mom. "Please?"

"So long as you start right after the show's over," she answered, but I knew she wasn't really paying attention. She was looking up at the staircase, shaking her head slowly. "How am I going to do this, Angus?" she said to Dad. She looked really tired.

"That's what I'm here for," Dad answered. He turned her wheelchair around toward him, reached under her, wrapped his other arm around her back, and lifted her out of the wheelchair. This made Mom scream in a giggly sort of way.

"Wow, Dad, you're strong!" I said, popping a french fry in my mouth as I watched them. "You guys should be on *The Amazing Race*. They're always having divorced couples."

Dad started climbing the staircase with Mom in his arms. They were both laughing as they bumped into the railing and the walls on the way up. It was nice seeing them like this. Last time we were all together, they were screaming at each other.

I turned around and watched the rest of the show. Just as Phil the host was telling the last couple to arrive at the pit stop that they have been eliminated, my phone buzzed.

It was a text from Elijah.

Yo chris. so me and the guys decided we're dropping out of after school rock band. we're starting our own band. we're playing 7NationArmy on Wednesday.

I reread the text. My mouth was literally hanging open. Dropping out of the band? Could they do that? John would go ballistic when none of them showed up at band practice tomorrow. And what did that mean for the after-school rock band? Would it be just me and John playing "The Final Countdown"? That would be awful!

Then another text came through.

do you want to join our band? we want YOU to join. but

ABSOLUTLY NOT john. He sucks. We're practicing at my place tomorrow after school. Bring your guitar.

Dad came downstairs. "Time for homework, Chris," he said quietly. Then he saw my face. "What's the matter?"

"Nothing," I said, clicking off the phone. I was kind of in a state of shock. They want me in their band? "I just remembered, I need to practice for the spring concert."

"Okay, but it needs to be quiet," answered Dad. "Mom is out like a light, and we have to let her rest, okay? Don't make a lot of noise going up the stairs. I'm in the guest room if you need anything."

"Wait, you're staying here tonight?" I asked.

"For a few days," he answered. "Until your mom can get around herself."

He started walking back upstairs with the crutches they had given Mom in the hospital.

"Can you print out the chords for 'Seven Nation Army' for me?" I asked. "I have to learn them by tomorrow."

"Sure," he said at the top of the stairs. "But remember, keep it down!"

North River Heights

Our new house is much bigger than our old house in North River Heights. Our old house was actually a brownstone, and we lived on the first floor. We only had one bathroom, and a tiny yard. But I loved our apartment. I loved our block. I missed being able to walk everywhere. I even missed the ginkgo trees. If you don't know what ginkgo trees are, they're the trees that drop these little squishy nuts that smell like dog poop mixed with cat pee mixed with some toxic waste when you step on them. Auggie used to say they smelled like orc vomit, which I always thought was funny. Anyway, I missed everything about our old neighborhood, even the ginkgo trees.

When we lived in North River Heights, Mom owned a little floral shop on Amesfort Avenue called Earth Laughs in Flowers. She worked really long hours, which is why they hired Lourdes to babysit me. That was another thing I missed: Lourdes. I missed her empanadas. I missed how she used to call me *papi*. But we didn't need Lourdes after we moved to Bridgeport, because Mom had sold her floral shop and no longer worked full-time. Now Mom picks me up from school on Mondays through Wednesdays. On Thursday nights, she picks me up from John's house and drops me off at Dad's place, which is where I stay until Sunday.

When we lived in North River Heights, Dad was usually home by seven p.m. But now he can't get home before nine p.m. because of the long commute from the city. Originally the plan was that that was only going to be a temporary thing, because he was going to be transferred to a Connecticut office, but it's been three years and he still has his old job in Manhattan. Mom and Dad used to argue about that a lot.

On Fridays, Dad leaves work early so that he can pick me up from school. We usually order Chinese food for dinner, jam a little on our guitars, and watch a movie. Mom gets annoyed with Dad that he doesn't make me do my homework over the weekend when I'm with him, so by the time I go back home on Sunday night, I'm always kind of grumpy as I scramble to finish my homework with her. This weekend, for instance, I should have been studying for my math test, but Dad and I went bowling and I just never got around to doing that. My bad.

I got used to the new house in Bridgeport, though. My new friends. Luke the hamster that's not a dog. But what I miss the most about North River Heights is that my parents seemed together then.

Dad moved out of our house last summer. My parents had been fighting a lot before that, but I don't know why he moved out over the summer. Just that one day, out of nowhere, they told me that they were separating. They "needed some time apart" to figure out if they wanted to continue living together. They told me that this had nothing to do with me, and they would "both go on loving me" and seeing me as much as before. They said they still loved each other, but that sometimes marriages are like friendships that get tested, and people have to work through things.

"Good friendships are worth a little extra effort," I remember saying to them.

I don't think Mom even remembered that she's the one who told me that once.

I listened to "Seven Nation Army" while I did my homework. And I tried not to think too much about how
John would react tomorrow when I told him I was
joining the other band. I mean, I didn't think I really
had a choice. If I stayed in the after-school rock band,
it'd just be me and John playing "The Final Countdown"
at the spring concert, with Mr. B playing drums, and
we'd look like the world's biggest dweebs. We were just
not good enough to play by ourselves. I remembered how
Harry was trying not to laugh when John played the
guitar solo today. If it was just the two of us up there, *all*
the kids in the audience would be trying not to laugh.

What I couldn't figure out was what John would do
when he found out. Any sane person would just forget
about playing in the spring concert on Wednesday at
all. But knowing John, I could pretty much bet that he
would go ahead and play "The Final Countdown."
He didn't care about making a fool of himself that way.
I could picture him singing his heart out, strumming

the guitar, with Mr. Bowles rocking out behind him on the keyboards. *Ladies and gentlemen, the after-school rock band!* Just the thought of it made me cringe for him. He would never live that down.

It was hard to concentrate on my homework, so it took me a lot longer than I thought it would. I didn't even start studying for the math test until almost ten p.m. That's when I remembered that I was totally screwed in math. I waited to the last minute to study, and I didn't understand any of it.

Dad was in bed working on his laptop when I opened the door of the guest bedroom. I was holding my ridiculously heavy fifth-grade math textbook in my hands.

"Hey, Dad."

"You're not in bed yet?" he asked, looking at me over his reading glasses.

"I need some help studying for my math test tomorrow."

He glanced over at the clock on the bedside table. "Kind of late to be discovering this, no?"

"I had so much homework," I answered. "And I had to learn the new song for the spring concert, which is the day after tomorrow. There's so much going on, Dad."

He nodded. Then he put his laptop down and patted the bed for me to sit next to him, which I did. I turned to page 151.

"So," I said, "I'm having trouble with word problems."

"Oh, well, I'm great at word problems!" he answered, smiling. "Lay it on me."

I started reading from the textbook. "Jill wants to buy honey at an outdoor market. One vendor is selling a twenty-six-ounce jar for $3.12. Another vendor is selling a sixteen-ounce jar for $2.40. Which is the better deal, and how much money per ounce will Jill save by choosing it?"

I put the textbook down and looked at Dad, who looked at me blankly.

"Okay, um . . ." he said, scratching his ear. "So, that was twenty-six ounces for . . . what again? I'm going to need a piece of paper. Pass me my notebook over there?"

I reached over to the other end of the bed and passed him his notebook. He started scribbling in it, asked me to repeat the question again, and then kept scribbling.

"Okay, okay, so . . ." he said, turning his notebook around for me to look at his scribbled numbers. "So, first you want to divide the numbers to figure out what the cost per ounce is, then you want . . ."

"Wait, wait," I said, shaking my head. "That's the part I don't get. When do you know you have to divide? What do you need to do? How do you know?"

He looked down at the scribbles on his notebook again, as if the answer were there.

"Let me see the question?" he said, pushing his

reading glasses back up on his nose and looking at where I pointed in the textbook. "Okay, well, you know you have to divide, because, um, well, you want to figure out the price per ounce . . . because it says so right here." He pointed to the problem.

I looked quickly at where he pointed but shook my head. "I don't get it."

"Well, look, Chris. Right there. It asks how much the cost per ounce is."

I shook my head again. "I don't get it!" I said loudly. "I hate this. I suck at this."

"No, you don't, Chris," he answered calmly. "You just have to take a deep breath and—"

"No! You don't understand," I said. "I don't get this at all!"

"Which is why I'm trying to explain it to you."

"Can I ask Mom?"

He took his eyeglasses off and rubbed his eyes with his wrist. "Chris, she's asleep. We should just let her rest tonight," he answered slowly. "I'm sure we can figure this out ourselves."

I started poking my knuckles into my eyes, so he pulled my hands down off my face gently. "Why don't you call one of your friends at school? How about John?"

"He's in the fourth grade!" I said impatiently.

"Okay, well, someone else," he said.

"No!" I shook my head. "There's no one I can call.

I'm not friends with anyone like that this year. I mean, my *friend* friends aren't in the same math class I'm in. And I don't know the kids in this math class that well."

"Then call your other friends, Chris," he said, reaching over for his cell phone. "What about Elijah and those guys in the band? I'm sure they've all taken that class."

"No! Dad! Ugh!" I covered my face with my hands. "I'm totally going to fail this test. I don't get it. I just don't get it."

"Okay, calm down," he said. "What about Auggie? He's kind of a math whiz, isn't he?"

"Never mind!" I said, shaking my head. I took the textbook from him. "I'll figure it out myself!"

"Christopher," he said.

"It's fine, Dad," I said, getting up. "I'll just figure it out. Or I'll text someone. It's fine."

"Just like that?"

"It's fine. Thanks, Dad." I closed the textbook and got up.

"I'm sorry I couldn't help you," he answered, and for a second, I felt sorry for him. He sounded a little defeated. "I mean, I think we can figure it out together if you give me another chance."

"No, it's okay!" I answered, walking toward the door.

"Good night, Chris."

"Night, Dad."

I went to my room, sat at my desk, and opened the

textbook to page 151 again. I tried rereading the word problem, but all I could hear in my head were the words to "Seven Nation Army." And those made no sense to me, either.

No matter how hard I stared at the problem, I just couldn't think of what to do.

Pluto

A few weeks before we moved to Bridgeport, Auggie's parents were over at our house helping my parents pack for the big move. Our entire apartment was filled with boxes.

Auggie and I were having a Nerf war in the living room, turning the boxes into hostile aliens on Pluto. Occasionally, one of our Nerf darts would hit Via, who was trying to read her book on the sofa. Okay, maybe we were doing it a little bit on purpose, *tee-hee*.

"Stop it!" she finally screamed when one of my darts zinged her book. "Mom!" she yelled.

But Isabel and Nate were all the way on the other side of the apartment with my parents, taking a coffee break in the kitchen.

"Can you guys please stop?" Via said to us seriously.

I nodded, but Auggie shot another Nerf dart at her book.

"That's a fart dart," said Auggie. This made us both crack up.

518

Via was furious. "You guys are such geeks," she said, shaking her head. "*Star Wars.*"

"Not *Star Wars.* Pluto!" answered Auggie, pointing his Nerf blaster at her.

"That's not even a real planet," she said, opening her book to read.

Auggie shot another Nerf dart at her book. "What are you talking about? Yes, it is."

"Stop it, Auggie, or I swear I'll . . ."

Auggie lowered his Nerf blaster. "Yes, it is," he repeated.

"No, it's not," answered Via. "It *used* to be a planet. I can't believe you two geniuses don't know that after all the space videos you've watched!"

Auggie didn't answer right away, like he was processing what she just said. "But my very educated mother just showed us nine planets! That's how Mommy said people remember the planets in our solar system."

"My very educated mother just served us nachos!" answered Via. "Look it up. I'm right." She started looking it up on her phone.

It may be that in all our reading science books and watching videos, this information had made its way to us before. But I guess we never really understood what it meant. We were still little kids when we were in our space phase. We barely knew how to read.

Via started reading aloud from her phone: "From Wikipedia: 'The understanding that Pluto is only one of several large icy bodies in the outer solar system prompted the International Astronomical Union (IAU) to formally define "planet" in 2006. This definition excluded Pluto and reclassified it as a member of the new "dwarf planet" category (and specifically as a plutoid).' Do I need to go on? Basically what that means is that Pluto was considered too puny to be a real planet, so there. I'm right."

Auggie looked really upset.

"Mommy!" he yelled out.

"It's not a big deal, Auggie," said Via, seeing how upset he was getting.

"Yes, it is!" he said, running down the hallway.

Via and I followed him to the kitchen, where our parents were sitting around the table over a bagel and cream cheese spread.

"You said it was 'my very educated mother just showed us nine planets'!" said Auggie, charging over to Isabel.

Isabel almost spilled her coffee. "What—" she said.

"Why are you making such a big deal about this, Auggie?" Via interrupted.

"What's going on, guys?" asked Isabel, looking from Auggie to Via.

"It *is* a big deal!" Auggie screamed at the top of his lungs. It was so loud and unexpected, that scream, that everyone in the room just looked at one another.

"Whoa, Auggie," said Nate, putting his hand on Auggie's shoulder. But Auggie shrugged it off.

"You told me Pluto was one of the nine planets!" Auggie yelled at Isabel. "You said it was the littlest planet in the solar system!"

"It is, sweetness," Isabel answered, trying to get him to calm down.

"No, it's not, Mom," Via said. "They changed Pluto's planetary status in 2006. It's no longer considered one of the nine planets in our solar system."

Isabel blinked at Via, and then she looked at Nate. "Really?"

"I knew that," Nate answered seriously. "They did the same thing to Goofy a few years ago."

This made all the adults laugh.

"Daddy, this isn't funny!" Auggie shrieked. And then, out of the blue, he started to cry. Big tears. Sobbing crying.

No one understood what was happening. Isabel wrapped her arms around Auggie, and he sobbed into her neck.

"Auggie Doggie," Nate said, gently rubbing Auggie on the back. "What's going on here, buddy?"

"Via, what happened?" Isabel asked sharply.

"I have no idea!" said Via, opening her eyes wide. "I didn't do anything!"

"Something must have happened!" said Isabel.

"Chris, do you know why Auggie's so upset?" asked Mom.

"Because of Pluto," I answered.

"But what does that mean?" asked Mom.

I shrugged. I understood why he was so upset, but I couldn't explain it to them exactly.

"You said . . . it was . . . a planet . . ." Auggie finally said in between gulps. Even under ordinary circumstances, Auggie could be hard to understand sometimes. In the middle of a crying fit, it was even harder.

"What, sweetness?" whispered Isabel.

"You said . . . it was . . . a planet," Auggie repeated, looking up at her.

"I thought it was, Auggie," she answered, wiping his tears with her fingertips. "I don't know, sweetness. I'm not a real science teacher. When I was growing up, there were nine planets. It never even occurred to me that that could change."

Nate knelt down beside him. "But even if it's not considered a planet anymore, Auggie, I don't understand why that should upset you so much."

Auggie looked down. But I knew he couldn't explain his Plutonian tears.

10:28 p.m.

By about ten-thirty, I was getting desperate about the math test tomorrow. I had texted Jake, who's in my math class, and messaged a few other kids on Facebook. When my phone buzzed, I assumed it was one of these kids, but it wasn't. It was Auggie.

Hey, Chris. Just heard about your mom being in hospital. Sorry, hope she's ok.

I couldn't believe he was texting me, just when I'd been thinking about him. Kind of psychic.

Hey, Aug, I texted back. *Thx. She's ok. She broke her femur. She has this huge cast.*

He texted me a sad-face emoticon.

I texted: *My dad had to carry her up the stairs! They kept bumping into the wall.*

Ha ha. He texted me a laughing-face icon.

I texted: *I was going to call u today. To tell u sorry about Daisy.* :(((((

Oh yeah. Thx. He texted a string of crying-face emoticons.

Hey, remember the Galactic Adventures of Darth Daisy?
I texted.

This was a comic strip we used to draw together about two astronauts named Gleebo and Tom who lived on Pluto and had a dog named Darth Daisy.

Ha ha. Yeah, Major Gleebo.

Major Tom.

Good times good times, he texted back.

Daisy was the GR8EST DOG IN UNIVERSE! I thumbed loudly. I was smiling.

He texted me a picture of Daisy. It had been such a long time since I had seen her. In the picture, her face had gotten completely white, and her eyes were kind of foggy. But her nose was still pink and her tongue was still super long as it hung out of her mouth.

So cute! Daisy!!!!!!! I texted.

DARTH Daisy!!!!!!!!!!!!!!!

Ha ha. Take that, Via! I wrote.

Remember those fart darts?

Hahahahahaha. I was smiling a lot at this point. It was the happiest part of my day, to be truthful. *That was when we were still into Pluto.*

Were we into Star Wars yet?

Getting into it. Do you still have all your miniatures?

Yeah but I put some away too. So anyway, Gleebo, my mom's telling me I gots to go to bed now. Glad your mom is okay.

I nodded. There was no way I could ask him for help

in math at this point. It would just be too lame. I sat down on the edge of my bed and started responding to his text.

Before I could finish, he texted: *my mom actually wants to talk to you. she wants to FaceChat. R U free?*

I stood up. *Sure.*

Two seconds later, I got a request to FaceChat. I saw Isabel on the phone.

"Oh, hey, Isabel," I said.

"Hi, Chris!" she answered. I could tell she was in her kitchen. "How are you? I talked to your mom earlier. I wanted to make sure you guys got home okay."

"Yeah, we did."

"And she's doing okay? I didn't want to wake her if she's sleeping."

"Yeah, she's sleeping," I answered.

"Oh good. She needs her rest. That was a big cast!"

"Dad's staying here tonight."

"Oh, that's so great!" she answered happily. "I'm so glad. And how are you doing, Chris?"

"I'm good."

"How's school?"

"Good."

Isabel smiled. "Lisa told me you got her beautiful flowers today."

"Yeah," I answered, smiling and nodding.

"Okay. Well, I just wanted to check in on you and say

hello, Chris. I want you to know we're thinking about you guys, and if there's anything we can do—"

"I'm sorry about Daisy," I blurted out.

Isabel nodded. "Oh. Thank you, Chris."

"You guys must be so sad."

"Yeah, it's sad. She was such a presence in our house. Well, you know. You were there when we first got her, remember?"

"She was so skinny!" I said. I was smiling, but suddenly, out of the blue, my voice got a little shaky.

"With that long tongue of hers!" She laughed.

I nodded. I felt a lump in my throat, like I was going to cry.

She looked at me carefully. "Oh, sweetie, it's okay," she said quietly.

Auggie's mom had always been like a second mom to me. I mean, aside from my parents, and maybe my grandmother, Isabel Pullman knew me better than anyone.

"I know," I whispered. I was still smiling, but my chin was trembling.

"Sweetie, where's your dad?" she asked. "Can you put him on the phone?"

I shrugged. "I think . . . he might be asleep by now."

"I'm sure he won't care if you wake him up," she answered softly. "Go get him. I'll wait on the phone."

Auggie nudged his way into view on the screen.

"What's the matter, Chris?" he asked.

I shook my head, fighting back tears. I couldn't talk. I knew if I did, I'd start to cry.

"Christopher," Isabel said, coming close to the screen. "Your mom is going to be fine, sweetie."

"I know," I said, my voice cracking, but then it just came out of me. "But she was in the car because of me! Because I forgot my trombone! If I hadn't forgotten my stuff, she wouldn't have gotten into an accident! It's my fault, Isabel! She could have died!"

This all came pouring out of me in a string of messy crying bursts.

10:52 p.m.

Isabel put Auggie on the phone while she called Dad's
cell phone to let him know I was crying hysterically in
my room. A minute later, Dad came into my room and
I hung up on Auggie. Dad put his arms around me
and hugged me tightly.

"Chris," said Dad.

"It was my fault, Daddy! It was my fault she was
driving."

He untangled himself from my hug and put his face
in front of my face.

"Look at me, Chris," he said. "It's not your fault."

"She was on her way back to school with my stuff."
I sniffled. "I told her to hurry. She was probably
speeding."

"No, she wasn't, Chris," he answered. "I promise you.
What happened today was just an accident. It wasn't
anyone's fault. It was a fluke. Okay?"

I looked away.

"Okay?" he repeated.

I nodded.

"And the most important thing is that no one got seriously hurt. Mom is fine. Okay, Chris?"

He was wiping my tears away as I nodded.

"I kept calling her Lisa," I said. "She hates when I do that. The last thing she said to me was 'Love you!' and all I answered was 'Bye, Lisa.' And I didn't even turn around!"

Dad cleared his throat. "Chris, please don't beat yourself up," he said slowly. "Mom knows you love her so much. Listen, this was a scary thing that happened today. It's natural for you to be upset. When something scary like this happens, it acts like a wake-up call, you know? It makes us reassess what's important in life. Our family. Our friends. The people we love." He was looking at me while he was talking, but I almost felt like he was talking to himself. His eyes were very moist. "Let's just be grateful she's fine, okay, Chris? And we'll take really good care of her together, okay?"

I nodded. I didn't try to say anything, though. I knew it would just come out as more tears.

Dad pulled me close to him, but he didn't say anything, either. Maybe for the same reason.

10:59 p.m.

After Dad had gotten me to calm down a bit, he called Isabel back to let her know everything was fine. They chatted, and then Dad handed the phone to me.

It was Auggie on the line.

"Hey, your dad told my mom you need some help with math," he said.

"Oh yeah," I answered shyly, blowing my nose. "But it's so late. Don't you need to go to bed?"

"Mom's totally fine with my helping you. Let's Face Chat."

Two seconds later, he was on-screen.

"So, I'm having trouble with word problems," I said, opening my textbook. "I just . . . I'm not getting how you know what operation to use. When do you multiply and when do you divide? It's so confusing."

"Oh, that." He nodded. "Yeah, I definitely had trouble with that, too. Have you memorized the clue words, though? That helped me a lot."

I had no idea what he was talking about.

"Let me send you a PDF," he said.

Two seconds later, I printed out the PDF he sent me, which listed a whole bunch of different math words.

"If you know what clue words to look for in the word problem," Auggie explained, "you know what operation to use. Like 'per' or 'each' or 'equally' means you have to divide. And 'at this rate' or 'doubled' means multiplication. See?"

He went over the whole list of words with me, one by one, until it finally began to make some sense. Then we went over all the math problems in the textbook. We started with the sample problems first, and it turned out he was right: once I found the clue word in each problem, I knew what to do. I was able to do most of the worksheet problems on my own, though we went over each and every one of them after I was done, just to be sure I had really gotten it.

11:46 p.m.

My favorite types of books have always been mysteries. Like, you don't know something at the beginning of the book. And then at the end of the book, you know it. And the clues were there all along, you just didn't know how to read them. That's what I felt like after talking to Auggie. Like this colossal mystery I couldn't understand before was now completely, suddenly solved.

"I can't believe I'm finally getting this now," I said to him after we had gone over the last problem. "Thank you so much, Aug. Seriously, thank you."

He smiled and got in close to the screen. "It's cool beans," he said.

"I totally owe you one."

Auggie shrugged. "No problem. That's what friends are for, right?"

I nodded. "Right."

"G'night, Chris. Talk soon!"

"Night, Aug! Thanks again! Bye!"

He hung up. I closed my textbook.

I went to the guest room to tell Dad that Auggie had helped me figure out all the math stuff, but he wasn't in the room. I knocked on the bathroom door, but he wasn't in there, either. Then I noticed Mom's bedroom door was open. I could see Dad's legs stretched out on the chair next to the dresser. I couldn't see his face from the hallway, so I walked in quietly to let him know that I was finished talking with Auggie.

That's when I saw that he had fallen asleep in the chair. His head was drooping to one side. His glasses were on the edge of his nose, and his computer was on his lap.

I tiptoed to the closet, got a blanket, and placed it over his legs. I did it really softly so he wouldn't wake up. I took the computer from his lap and put it on the dresser.

Then I walked over to the side of the bed where Mom was sleeping. When I was little, Mom used to fall asleep reading to me at bedtime. I would nudge her awake if she fell asleep before finishing the book, but sometimes, she just couldn't help it. She'd fall asleep next to me, and I would listen to her soft breathing until I fell asleep, too.

It had been a long time since I'd seen her sleeping, though. As I looked at her now, she seemed kind of little to me. I didn't remember the freckle on her cheek. I'd never noticed the tiny lines on her forehead.

I watched her breathing for a few seconds.

"I love you, Mommy."

I didn't say this out loud, though, because I didn't want to wake her up.

11:59 p.m.

It was almost midnight by the time I went back to my room. Everything was exactly the way I had left it this morning. My bed was still unmade. My pajamas were jumbled up on the floor. My closet door was wide open. Usually, Mom would make my room look nice after she dropped me off at school in the morning, but today, of course, she never got the chance to do that.

It felt like days had passed since Mom woke me up this morning.

I closed the closet door, and that's when I noticed the trombone resting against the wall. So the accident didn't happen as she was bringing me my stuff this morning! I don't know why exactly, but this made me feel so much better.

I put the trombone right next to the bedroom door so I wouldn't forget it again on my way to school tomorrow, and I packed my science paper and gym shorts inside my backpack.

Then I sat down at my desk.

Without thinking anything more about it, I replied to Elijah's text.

Hey, Elijah. Thanks for the offer to join your band. But I'm going to stick with John at the spring concert. Good luck with Seven Nation Army.

Even if I looked like a total dweeb at the spring concert, I couldn't let John down like that. That's what friends are for, right? *It's the final countdown!*

Sometimes friendships are hard.

I put my pajamas on, brushed my teeth, and got into bed. Then I turned off the lamp on my night-stand. The stars on my ceiling were glowing bright neon green now, as they always did right after I turned the lights off.

I turned over on my side, and my eyes fell on a small star-shaped green light on my floor. It was the star Mom had placed on my forehead this morning, which I had flicked across the room.

I got out of bed, picked it up, and stuck it on my forehead. Then I got back in my bed and closed my eyes.

We're leaving together
But still it's farewell
And maybe we'll come back
To Earth, who can tell

I guess there is no one to blame
We're leaving ground
Will things ever be the same again?

It's the final countdown . . .

Shingaling

But every Spring
It groweth young again,
And fairies sing.
—Cicely Mary Barker, "Flower
Fairies of the Spring", 1923

• • •

Nobody can do the shingaling like I do.
—The Isley Brothers, "Nobody But Me"

How I Walked to School

There was a blind old man who played the accordion on Main Street, who I used to see every day on my way to school. He sat on a stool under the awning of the A&P supermarket on the corner of Moore Avenue, his seeing-eye dog lying down in front of him on a blanket. The dog wore a red bandanna around its neck. It was a black Labrador. I know because my sister Beatrix asked him one day.

"Excuse me, sir. What kind of dog is that?"

"Joni is a black Labrador, missy," he answered.

"She's really cute. Can I pet her?"

"Best not. She's working right now."

"Okay, thank you. Have a good day now."

"Bye, missy."

My sister waved at him. He had no way of knowing this, of course, so he didn't wave back.

Beatrix was eight then. I know because it was my first year at Beecher Prep, which means I was in kindergarten.

I never talked to the accordion-man myself. I hate to admit it, but I was kind of afraid of him back then. His eyes, which were always open, were kind of glazed and cloudy. They were cream-colored, and looked like white-and-tan marbles. It spooked me. I was even a little afraid of his dog, which really made no sense because I usually love dogs. I mean, I *have* a dog! But I was afraid of his dog, who had a gray muzzle and whose eyes were kind of gloopy, too. But—and here's a big but—even though I was afraid of both of them, the accordion-man *and* his dog, I always dropped a dollar bill into the open accordion case in front of them. And somehow, even though he was playing the accordion, and no matter how quietly I crept over, the accordion-man would always hear the *swoosh* of the dollar bill as it fell into the accordion case.

"God bless America," he would say to the air, nodding in my direction.

That always made me wonder. How could he hear that? How did he know what direction to nod at?

My mom explained that blind people develop their other senses to make up for the sense they've lost. So, because he was blind, he had super hearing.

That, of course, got me wondering if he had other superpowers, too. Like, in the winter when it was freezing cold, did his fingers have a magical way of keeping warm while they pressed the keys? And how did the rest of him stay warm? On those really frigid days when my teeth would start to chatter after walking just a few blocks against the icy wind, how did he stay warm enough to play his accordion? Sometimes, I'd even see little rivers of ice forming in parts of his mustache and beard, or I'd see him reach down to make sure his dog was covered by the blanket. So I knew he *felt* the cold, but how did he keep playing? If that's not a superpower, I don't know what is!

In the wintertime, I always asked my mom for *two* dollars to drop into his accordion case instead of just one.

Swoosh. Swoosh.

"God bless America."

He played the same eight or ten songs all the time. Except at Christmastime, when he'd play "Rudolph the Red-Nosed Reindeer" and "Hark! The Herald Angels Sing." But otherwise, it was the same songs. My mom knew the names of some of them. "Delilah." "Lara's Theme." "Those Were the Days." I downloaded all the titles she named, and she was right, those *were* the songs. But why just those songs? Were they the only songs he ever learned to play, or were they the only songs he remembered? Or did he know a whole bunch of other songs, but chose to play just those songs?

And all that wondering got me wondering even more! When did he learn to play the accordion? When he was a little boy? Could he see back then? If he couldn't see, how could he read music? Where did he grow up?

544

Where did he live when he wasn't on the corner of Main Street and Moore Avenue? I saw him and his dog walking together sometimes, his right hand holding the dog's harness and his left hand holding the accordion case. They moved so slowly! It didn't seem like they could get very far. So where *did* they go?

There were a lot of questions I would have asked him if I hadn't been afraid of him. But I never asked. I just gave him one-dollar bills.

Swoosh.

"God bless America."

It was always the same.

Then, when I got older and wasn't *that* afraid of him anymore, the questions I used to have about him didn't seem to matter as much to me. I guess I got so accustomed to seeing him, I didn't really think about his foggy eyes or if he had superpowers. It's not like I stopped giving him a dollar when I passed by him or anything. But it was more like a habit now, like swiping a MetroCard through a subway turnstile.

Swoosh.

"God bless America."

By the time I started fifth grade, I stopped seeing him completely because I no longer walked past him on my way to school. The Beecher Prep middle school is a few blocks closer to my house than the lower school was, so now I walk *to* school with Beatrix and my oldest sister, Aimee, and I walk home *from* school with my best friend, Ellie, as well as Maya and Lina, who live near me. Once in a while, at the beginning of the school year, we would go get snacks at the A&P after school before heading home, and I'd see the accordion-man and give him a dollar and hear him bless America. But as the weather got colder, we didn't do that as much. Which is why it wasn't until a few days into winter break, when I went to the A&P with my mom one afternoon, that I realized that the blind old man who played the accordion on Main Street wasn't there anymore.

He was gone.

How I Spent My Winter Vacation

People who know me always say I'm so dramatic. I have no idea why they say that, because I'm really, really, really *not* dramatic. But when I found out the accordion-man was gone, I kind of lost it! I really don't know why, but I just couldn't stop obsessing about what had happened to him. It was like a mystery that I had to solve! What in the world happened to the blind old man who played the accordion on Main Street?

Nobody seemed to know. My mom and I asked the cashiers in the supermarket, the lady in the dry cleaner's, and the man in the eye shop across the street if they knew anything about him. We even asked the policeman who gave out parking tickets on that block. Everyone knew who he was, but no one knew what had happened to him, just that one day—*poof!*—he wasn't there anymore. The policeman told me that on really cold days, homeless people are actually taken to the city shelters so they won't freeze to death. He thought that's probably what happened to the accordion-man.

547

But the dry-cleaning lady said that she knew for a fact that the accordion-man wasn't homeless. She thought he lived somewhere up in Riverdale because she'd see him getting off the Bx3 bus early in the mornings with his dog. And the eye-shop man said that he was certain that the accordion-man had been a famous jazz musician once and was actually loaded, so I shouldn't worry about him.

You would think these answers would have helped me, right? But they didn't! They just raised a whole bunch of other questions that made me even *more* curious about him. Like, was he in a homeless shelter for the winter? Was he living in his own beautiful house in Riverdale? Had he really been a famous jazz musician? Was he rich? If he was rich, why was he playing for money?

My whole family got sick and tired of my talking about this, by the way.

Beatrix was like: "Charlotte, if you talk about this one more time, I'm going to throw up all over you!"

And Aimee said, "Charlotte, will you just *drop* it already?"

My mom's the one who suggested that a good way to "channel" my energy would be to start a coat drive in our neighborhood to benefit homeless people. We put up flyers asking people to donate their "gently worn" coats by dropping them off in plastic bags in a giant bin we left in front of our brownstone. Then, after we'd collected about ten huge garbage bags full of coats, my mom and dad and I drove all the way downtown to the Bowery Mission to donate the coats. I have to say, it felt really good to give all those coats to people who really needed them! I looked around when I was inside the mission with my parents to see if maybe the accordion-man was there, but he wasn't. Anyway, I knew he had a nice coat already: a bright orange Canada Goose parka that made my mom hopeful that the rumors about his being rich might actually be true.

"You don't see many homeless people wearing Canada Goose," observed Mom.

When I got back to school after winter break, Mr. Tushman, the middle school director, congratulated me on having started a coat drive. I'm not sure how he knew, but he knew. It was generally agreed upon that Mr. Tushman had some kind of secret surveillance drone keeping tabs on everything going on at Beecher Prep: there was no other way he could know all the stuff he seemed to know.

"That's a beautiful way to spend your winter vacation, Charlotte," he said.

"Aw, thank you, Mr. Tushman!"

I loved Mr. Tushman. He was always really nice. What I liked was that he was one of those teachers that never talks to you like you're some little kid. He always uses big words, assuming you know and understand them, and he never looks away when you're talking to him. I also loved that he wore suspenders and a bow tie and bright red sneakers.

"Do you think you could help me organize a coat drive here at Beecher Prep?" he asked. "Now that you're an expert at it, I would love your input."

"Sure!" I answered.

Which is how I ended up being part of the first annual Beecher Prep Coat Drive.

In any case, between the coat drive and all the other drama going on at school when I got back from winter vacation (more on that soon!), I didn't really get a chance to solve the mystery of what happened to the blind old man who played the accordion on Main Street. Ellie didn't seem the least bit interested in helping me solve the mystery, though it was the kind of thing that she might have been into just a few months before. And neither Maya nor Lina seemed to remember him at all. In fact, no one seemed to care about what happened to him in the least, so finally, I just dropped the subject.

I still thought about the accordion-man sometimes, though. Every once in a while, one of the songs he used to play on his accordion would come back to me. And then I'd hum it all day long.

How the Boy War Started

The only thing everybody *could* talk about when we got back from winter break was "the war," also referred to as "the boy war." The whole thing started right before winter break. A few days before recess, Jack Will had gotten suspended for punching Julian Albans in the mouth. *Talk about drama!* Everyone was gossiping about it. But no one knew exactly why Jack did it. Most people thought it had something to do with Auggie Pullman. To explain that a bit, you have to know that Auggie Pullman is this kid at our school who was born with very severe facial issues. And by severe, I mean *severe*. Like, *really* severe. None of his features are where they're supposed to be. And it's kind of shocking when you see him at first because it's like he's wearing a mask or something. So when he started at Beecher Prep, *everybody* noticed him. He was impossible not to notice.

A few people—like Jack and Summer and *me*—were nice to him from the beginning. Like, when I would pass him in the hall, I'd always say, "Hey, Auggie, how're you doing?" and stuff like that. Now, sure, part of that was because Mr. Tushman had asked me to be a welcome buddy to Auggie before school had started, but I would have been nice to him even if he hadn't asked me to do that.

Most people, though—like Julian and his group—were not at *all* nice to Auggie, especially in the beginning. I don't think people were even trying to be mean necessarily. I think they were just a little weirded out by his face, is all. They said stupid things behind his back. Called him *Freak*. Played this game called The Plague, which I did *not* participate in, by the way! (If I've never touched Auggie Pullman, it's only because I've never had a reason to—that's all!) Nobody ever wanted to hang out with him or get partnered up with him on a class project. At least in the beginning of the year. But after a couple of months, people did start getting used to him. Not that they were really nice or anything, but at least they stopped being mean. Everyone, that is, *except* for Julian, who continued to make such a big deal about him! It's like he couldn't get over the fact that Auggie looks the way he looks! As if the poor guy could help it, right?

Anyway, so what everyone thinks happened is that Julian said something horrible about Auggie to Jack. And Jack—being a good friend—punched Julian. *Boom.*

And then Jack got suspended. *Boom.*

And now he's back from suspension! *Boom!*
And that's the *drama!*
But that's not all there is to it!

Because then what happened is this: over winter break, Julian had this huge party and, basically, turned everyone in the fifth grade against Jack. He spread this rumor that the school psychologist had told his mom that Jack was emotionally unstable. And that the pressure of being friends with Auggie had made him snap and turn into an angry maniac. Crazy stuff! Of course, none of it was true, and most people knew that, but it didn't stop Julian from spreading that lie.

And now the boys are all in this war. And that's how it started. And it's so *stupid!*

How I Stayed Neutral

I know one thing people say about me is that I'm a goody two-shoes. I have no idea why they say that. Because I'm really *not* that much of a goody two-shoes. But I'm also not someone who's going to be mean to *someone* just because *someone* else says I should be mean to them. I hate when people do stuff like that.

So, when all the boys started giving Jack the cold shoulder, and Jack didn't know why, I thought the least I could do was tell him what was going on. I mean, I've known Jack since we were in kindergarten. He's a good kid!

The thing is, I didn't want anyone to *see* me talking to him. Some of the girls, like Savanna's group, had started taking sides with the Julian boys, and I really wanted to stay neutral because I didn't want any of them to get mad at *me*. I was still hoping that maybe, one of these days, I'd work my way into that group myself. The last thing I wanted was to do anything to mess up my chances with them.

So, one day right before last period, I slipped Jack a note to meet me in room 301 after school. Which he did. And then I told him everything that was going on. You should have seen Jack's face! It was bright red! Seriously! The poor kid! We pretty much agreed that this whole thing was *so* messed up! I really felt sorry for him.

Then, after we were done talking, I sneaked out of the room without anyone seeing me.

How I Wanted to Tell Ellie About My Talk with Jack Will

At lunch the next day, I was going to tell Ellie that I'd talked to Jack. Ellie and I both had had a tiny *secret* crush on Jack Will going back to the fourth grade, when he played the Artful Dodger in *Oliver!* and we thought he looked adorable in a top hat.

I went over to her when she was emptying her lunch tray. We don't sit at the same lunch table anymore, ever since she switched to Savanna's lunch table around Halloween. But I still trusted Ellie. We've been BFFs since first grade! That counts for a lot!

"Hey," I said, nudging into her with my shoulder.

"Hey!" she said, nudging me back.

"Why weren't you in chorus yesterday?"

"Oh, didn't I tell you?" she said. "I switched electives when I came back from winter break. I'm in band now."

"*Band?* Seriously?" I said.

"I'm playing the clarinet!" she answered.

"Wow," I said, nodding. "Sweet."

This bit of news was really surprising to me, for a lot of reasons.

"Anyhow, what's up with you, Charly?" she said. "I feel like I've hardly seen you since we got back from winter break!" She picked up my wrist to inspect my new bangle.

"I know, right?" I answered, though I didn't point out that that was because she had canceled on me every single time we'd made plans to hang out after school.

"How's Maya's dots tournament going?"

She was referring to Maya's obsession with making the world's largest dot game to play at lunchtime. We kind of made fun of it behind her back.

"Good," I answered, smiling. "I keep meaning to ask you about this whole boy-war thing. It's so lame, isn't it?"

She rolled her eyes. "It's totally out of control!"

"Right?" I said. "I feel kind of sorry for Jack. Don't you think Julian should just call it quits already?"

Ellie started twisting a strand of hair around her finger. She took a fresh juice box off the counter and popped the straw into the hole. "I don't know, Charly," she answered. "Jack's the one who punched *him* in the mouth. Julian has every right to be mad." She took a long sip. "I'm actually starting to think that Jack has serious anger-management issues."

Hold up. What? I've known Ellie since forever, and the Ellie I know would never use a phrase like "anger-management issues." Not that Ellie isn't smart, but she's not *that* smart. *Anger-management issues?* That sounded more like something Ximena Chin would say in that sarcastic way of hers. Ever since Ellie started hanging out with Ximena and Savanna, she's been acting weirder and weirder!

Wait a minute! I just remembered something: Ximena plays clarinet! *That* explains why Ellie switched electives! Now it's all making sense!

"Either way," said Ellie, "I don't think we should get involved. It's a boy thing."

"Yeah, whatever," I answered, deciding it was better if I didn't tell Ellie I had spoken with Jack.

"So are you ready for the dance tryouts today?" she asked cheerfully.

"Yeah," I answered, pretending to get excited. "I think Mrs. Atanabi is—"

"Ready, Ellie?" said Ximena Chin, who had just appeared out of nowhere. She nodded a quick hello my way without really looking at me, and then turned around and headed to the lunchroom exit.

Ellie dropped her unfinished juice box into the trash can, clumsily heaved her backpack onto her right shoulder, and trotted after Ximena. "See you later, Charly!" she mumbled halfway across the lunchroom.

"Later," I answered, watching her catch up to Ximena. Together, they joined Savanna and Gretchen, a sixth grader, who were waiting for them by the exit.

The four of them were all about the same height, and they all had super-long hair, with wavy curls at the ends. Their hair colors were different, though. Savanna's was golden blond. Ximena's was black. Gretchen's was red. And Ellie's was brown. I actually wondered sometimes if Ellie hadn't gotten into that popular group because of her hair, which was just the right color and length to fit in.

My hair is white-blond, and so straight and flat, there's no way it would ever end in a curl without massive doses of hair spray. And it's short. Like me.

How to Use Venn Diagrams
(Part 1)

In Ms. Rubin's science class, we learned about Venn diagrams. You draw Venn diagrams to see the relationships between different groups of things. Like, if you want to see the common characteristics between mammals, reptiles, and fish, for instance, you draw a Venn diagram and list all the attributes of each one inside a circle. Where the circles intersect is what they have in common. In the case of mammals, reptiles, and fish, it would be that they all have backbones.

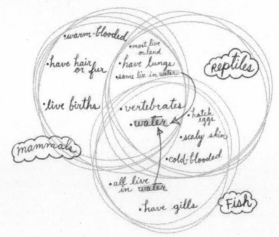

Anyway, I love Venn diagrams. They're so useful for explaining so many things. I sometimes draw them to explain friendships.

Ellie and me in first grade.

As you can see, Ellie and I had a lot in common. We've been friends since the first day of first grade, when Ms. Diamond put us both at the same table. I remember that day very clearly. I kept trying to talk to Ellie, but she was shy and didn't want to talk. Then, at snack time, I started ice-skating with my fingers on the top of the desk we shared. If you don't know what that is, it's when you make an upside-down peace sign and let your fingers glide over the glossy desk, like they were figure skaters. Anyway, Ellie watched me do that for a little while, and then she started ice-skating with her fingers, too. Pretty soon, we were both making figure eights all over the desk. After that, we were inseparable.

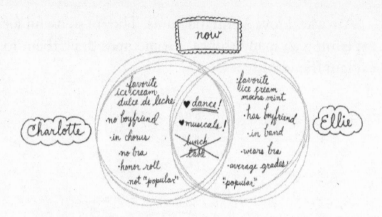

Ellie and me now.

How I Continued to Stay Neutral

Ellie, Savanna, and Ximena were hanging out in front of the lockers outside the performance space when I showed up for the dance tryouts after school. I knew the moment they looked at me that they'd just been talking about me.

"You're not really taking *Jack's* side in the boy war, are you?" said Savanna, making an *eww* expression with her lips.

I glanced at Ellie, who had obviously shared some of my lunch conversation with Savanna and Ximena. She chewed a strand of hair and looked away.

"I'm not on Jack's side," I said calmly. I popped open my locker and shoved my backpack inside. "All I said is that I think this whole boy-war thing is dumb. *All* the boys are just being so jerky."

"Yeah, but Jack started it," said Savanna. "Or are you saying it's okay that he punched Julian?"

"No, it's definitely not okay that he did that," I answered, pulling out my dance gear.

"So how could you be on Jack's side?" Savanna asked quickly, still making that *eww* face with her mouth.

"Is it because you *like* him?" asked Ximena, smiling mischievously.

Ximena, who probably hasn't said more than thirty words to me all year long, is asking me if I *like* Jack?

"No," I answered, but I could feel my ears turning red. I glanced up at Ellie as I sat down to put on my jazz sneakers. She was twirling yet another part of her hair in preparation for putting it into her mouth. I can't believe she told them about Jack! What a traitor!

At that moment, Mrs. Atanabi came into the room, clapping to get everyone's attention in her usual, theatrical way. "Okay, girls, if you haven't signed your name on the tryout sheet, please do so now," she said, pointing to the clipboard on the table next to her. There were about eight other girls standing in line to sign in. "And if you've already signed in, please take a spot on the dance floor and start doing your stretches."

"I'll sign in for you," Ximena said to Savanna, walking over to the table.

"Do you want me to sign in for you, Charly?" Ellie asked me. I knew that was her way of checking to see if I was mad at her. *Which I was!*

"I already signed in," I answered quietly, not looking at her.

"Of course she signed in," Savanna said quickly, rolling her eyes. "Charlotte's *always* the first to sign in."

How (and Why) I Love to Dance

I've been taking dance lessons since I was four. Ballet. Tap. Jazz. Not because I want to be a prima ballerina when I grow up, but because I intend on becoming a Broadway star someday. To do that, you really have to learn how to sing and dance and perform. Which is why I work so hard on my dance lessons. And my singing lessons. I take them very seriously, because I know that someday, when I get my big break, I'll be ready for it. And why will I be ready for it? Because I've worked hard for it—my whole life! People seem to think that Broadway stars just come out of nowhere—but that's not true! They practice until their feet hurt! They rehearse like maniacs! If you want to be a star, you have to be willing to work harder than everyone else to achieve your goals and dreams! The way I see it, a dream is like a drawing in your head that comes to life. You have to imagine it first. Then you have to work extremely hard to make it come true.

So, when Savanna says, "Charlotte's *always* the first

to sign in," on the one hand it's kind of a compliment because she's saying, "Charlotte's always on top of things, which is why her hard work pays off for her." But when she says, "Charlotte's *always* the first to sign in," with that *eww* expression on her face, it's more like she's saying, "Charlotte only gets what she wants because she's first in line." Or at least that's what I hear. A put-down.

Savanna's really good at those kinds of put-downs, where it's all in the eyes and the corners of the mouth. It's too bad, because she didn't used to be like that. In lower school, Savanna and Ellie and me and Maya and Summer: we were all friends. We played together after school. We had tea parties. It's only been since we started middle school—ever since she got popular—that Savanna's become less nice than she used to be.

How Mrs. Atanabi
Introduced Her Dance

"Okay, ladies," said Mrs. Atanabi, clapping her hands and motioning for us to walk toward her, "everybody on the dance floor, please! Take your positions. Everybody spread out. So what we're going to do today is, I'm going to show you a couple of different dances from the sixties that I'd like you to try. The twist. The Hully Gully. And the mambo. Just those three. Sound good?"

I had taken up a position behind Summer, who smiled and waved one of her cute happy hellos at me. When I was little and still into Flower Fairies, I used to think that Summer Dawson looked exactly like the Lavender Fairy. Like she should have been born with violet wings.

"Since when have you been into dance?" I asked her, because she had never been one of the girls I'd see at dance recitals.

Summer shrugged shyly. "I started taking classes this summer."

"Sweet!" I answered, smiling encouragingly.

"Mrs. Atanabi?" said Ximena, raising her hand. "What is this audition even for?"

"Oh my goodness!" answered Mrs. Atanabi, tapping her forehead with her fingers. "Of course. I completely forgot to tell you guys what we're doing here."

I, personally, have always loved Mrs. Atanabi—with her long flowy dresses and scarves and the messy bun. I love that she always has the breathless appearance of someone who's just come back from a great journey. I like that. But a lot of people think she's flaky and weird. The way she throws her head back when she laughs. The way she mumbles to herself sometimes. People have said she looks exactly like Mrs. Puff in *SpongeBob SquarePants*. They call her Mrs. Fatanabi behind her back, which I think is incredibly mean.

"I've been asked to put together a dance piece to perform at the Beecher Prep Benefit Gala," she started explaining. "Which is in mid-March. It's not a performance that other students will ever see. It's for the parents, faculty, and alumni. But it's kind of a big deal. They're having it at Carnegie Hall this year!"

Everyone made little excited chirpy sounds.

Mrs. Atanabi laughed. "I thought you'd all like that!" she said. "I'm adapting a piece I choreographed years ago, which had gotten considerable attention at the time, I don't mind saying. And it should be a lot of fun. But it will take plenty of work! Which reminds me: if you're chosen for this dance, it will require a *big* time commitment! I want to be clear about that right from the start, ladies. Ninety minutes of rehearsal, after school, three times a week. From now, through March. So if you can't commit to that, don't even try out. Okay?"

"But what if we have soccer practice?" asked Ruby, in the middle of a *plié*.

"Ladies, sometimes in life you have to choose," Mrs. Atanabi answered. "You can't have soccer practice *and* be in this dance. It's as simple as that. I don't want to hear any excuses about homework assignments or tests or anything else. Even one missed rehearsal is too much! Remember, this is *not* something you're required to do for school! You don't *have* to be here, girls. You won't be getting extra credit. If the appeal of dancing on one of the world's most famous stages isn't enough for you, then please *don't* try out." She extended her arm all the way and pointed to the exit. "I won't take it personally."

We all looked at each other. Ruby and Jacqueline both smiled apologetically at Mrs. Atanabi, waved goodbye, and left. I couldn't believe anyone would do that! To give up the chance to dance at Carnegie Hall? That's as famous as Broadway!

Mrs. Atanabi blinked but didn't say anything. Then she rubbed her head, like she was warding off a headache. "One last thing," she said. "If you're not selected for this particular routine, please remember there's still the big dance number in the spring variety show—and

569

everyone can dance in that one. So if you don't make this performance, *please don't* have your mom email me. There are only spots for three girls."

"Only *three?*" cried Ellie, covering her mouth with her hand.

"Yes, *only* three," Mrs. Atanabi responded, sounding exactly like Mrs. Puff sounds when she says, *Oh, SpongeBob.*

I knew what Ellie was thinking: *Please let it be me, Ximena, and Savanna.*

But even as she wished that, she probably knew it wasn't going to work out that way. The thing is, everybody knows that Ximena is the best dancer in the whole school. She got selected for the summer intensives at the School of American Ballet. She's at *that* level. So it was a pretty safe bet that Ximena would make it in.

And everybody knows that Savanna made the finals in two different regionals last year, and had come close to placing at a national—so there was a good chance that she would make it in.

And everybody knows that— Well, not to brag, but dance is kind of my thing, and I have a bunch of huge trophies on my shelf that prove it.

Ellie, though? Sorry, but she's just not in the same league as either Ximena or Savanna. Or me. Sure, she's been into dance all these years, but she's always been kind of lazy about it. I don't know, maybe if there were room for four girls. But not if there can only be *three.*

Nope, it seemed pretty clear as I looked around the room at the competition: the final three would be Ximena, Savanna. And me! *Sorry, Ellie!*

And maybe, just *maybe*, this would be my chance to finally work my way into the Savanna group, once and for all. I could go back to having Ellie as my best friend. Savanna could have Ximena. It could all work out.

The twist. The Hully Gully. And the mambo.

Got it.

How to Use Venn Diagrams (Part 2)

In middle school, your lunch-table group isn't always the same as your friend group. Like, it's very possible—in fact, it's *probable!*—that you may end up sitting at a lunch table with a bunch of girls that you're friends with—but who aren't necessarily your *friend* friends. How you ended up at that table is completely random: Maybe there wasn't enough room at the table with the girls you really wanted to sit with. Or maybe you just happened to end up with a group of girls because of the class you had right before lunch. That's actually what happened to me. On the first day of school, Maya, Megan, Lina, Rand, Summer, Ellie, and I were all in Ms. Petosa's advanced math class together. When the lunch bell rang, we flew down the stairs in a big huddle, not knowing exactly how to get to the cafeteria. When we finally did find it, we all just sat down at a table in a pack. It was like we were playing musical chairs, with everyone scrambling to get a seat. There were actually only supposed to be six kids to a table, but the seven of us squeezed in and made it work.

Lina Summer Megan Rand

Ellie Charlotte Maya

At first, I thought it was the greatest table in the whole lunchroom! I was sitting right between Ellie, my best friend from first grade, and Maya, my other best friend from lower school. I was sitting directly across from Summer and Megan, both of whom I knew from lower school, too, even if we weren't necessarily good friends. *And* I knew Lina from the Beecher Prep Summer Camp program. The only person I didn't know at all was Rand, but she seemed nice enough. So, all in all, it looked like a totally awesome lunch table!

But then, that very first day, Summer switched tables to go sit with Auggie Pullman. It was so shocking! One second we were all sitting there, talking about him, watching him eat his lunch. Lina said something really mean that I won't repeat. And the next second, Summer,

573

without saying anything to *anyone*, just picked up her lunch tray and walked over to him. It was so unexpected! Lina, I remember, looked like she was watching a car accident.

"Stop staring!" I said to her.

"I can't believe she's *eating* with him," she whispered, horrified.

"It's not *that* big a deal," I said, rolling my eyes.

"Then why aren't *you* having lunch with him?" she answered. "Aren't you supposed to be his welcome buddy?"

"That doesn't mean I have to sit with him at lunch," I answered quickly, regretting that I'd told anyone that Mr. Tushman had chosen me to be Auggie's welcome buddy. Yes, it was an honor that he had asked me, along with Julian and Jack—but I didn't want anyone throwing it in my face!

All around the cafeteria, people were doing the exact same thing we were doing at our lunch table: staring at Auggie and Summer eating together. We were literally only a few hours into middle school, but people had already started calling him the *Zombie Kid* and *Freak*.

Beauty and the Freak. That's what people were whispering about Summer and Auggie.

No way was I going to have people whisper stuff behind my back, too!

"Besides," I said to Lina, taking a bite of my Caesar salad. "I like *this* table. I don't want to switch."

And that was true! I *did* like this table!

At least, at first I did.

But then, as I got to know everyone a little better, I realized that maybe I didn't have as much in common with them as I would have liked. It turned out that Lina, Megan, and Rand were *all* super into sports (Maya played soccer, but that was all). So there was this whole world of soccer games and swim meets and "away games" that Ellie and I couldn't really talk to them about. Another thing is that they had all chosen to be in orchestra, while Ellie and I had chosen chorus. And the last thing, very simply, was that they weren't into a lot of the stuff *we* were into! They never watched *The Voice* or *American Idol*. They weren't into movie stars or old movies. They had never even seen *Les Misérables*, for crying out loud! I mean, how could I have a serious friendship with someone who had no interest in seeing *Les Mis*?

But as long as I had Ellie to talk to, with Maya there to round us out, everything was totally fine by me. The three of us would chat about the stuff *we* wanted to talk about on our side of the table, and Megan, Lina, and Rand would chat about the stuff *they* wanted to talk about on their side of the table. And then we'd all catch up about the stuff we had in common—schoolwork, homework, teachers, tests, bad cafeteria food—in the middle of the table.

Which is why everything was good. Until Ellie switched tables!

And now it's just me. And Maya.

Maya, who was only really fun to talk to when Ellie was there. Or if you wanted to play a rousing game of dots.

Look, I'm not mad at Ellie for switching tables. I honestly *don't* blame her. Ever since we heard that Amos had a crush on her, it was like she'd gotten a free pass into the popular group. Savanna had asked her to sit with them at lunch, and then arranged it so Amos and Ellie sat next to each other. That's how all the "couples" in the grade got together. Ximena and Miles. Savanna and Henry. And now, Amos and Ellie. In arranged group huddles. The popular boys and the popular girls. It was natural that they'd all want to stick together. Nobody else in our grade is dating or even *close* to dating! I know for a fact that the girls at *my* lunch table still act like boys have cooties! And, from what I can tell, most of the boys act like girls don't exist.

So, yeah, I totally get why Ellie switched lunch tables. I really do. And I'm not about to be super-mad at her, like Maya is. It's hard when you've been invited to a better lunch table. There's kind of no looking back.

All I can do is sit and wait, talk to Maya, and hope that Savanna will ask me to join them at the popular table someday.

In the meanwhile, I draw Venn diagrams. And play lots and lots of dots.

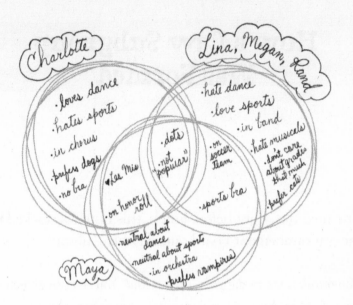

Charlotte
- loves dance
- hates sports
- in chorus
- prefers dogs
- no bra

Lina, Megan, Band
- hate dance
- love sports
- in band
- hate musicals
- don't care about grades that much
- prefer cats
- on soccer team
- sports bra

♥Les Mis

- dots
- "not popular"
- on honor roll

Maya
- neutral about dance
- neutral about sports
- in orchestra
- prefers vampires

How a New Subgroup Was Formed

The next day, right before lunch, this note was tacked to the announcement board outside of the library:

Congratulations to the girls listed below! You've been chosen to participate in Mrs. Atanabi's 1960s dance performance. I've posted a rehearsal schedule on the website. Mark your calendars! No absences. No excuses. Our first rehearsal is tomorrow at 4:00 p.m. in the performance space. DO NOT DARE TO BE LATE!—Mrs. Atanabi

Ximena Chin
Charlotte Cody
Summer Dawson

OMG, I got in! Yay!!!!!! I was so happy when I read my name on the list! Overjoyed! Ecstatic! Woo-hoo!

So it was me, Ximena—and *Summer*?

Whaaat! *Summer*? That was such a surprise! I was so positively sure it was going to be Savanna! I mean,

Summer had just started taking dance! Did she really beat out Savanna?

Oh boy: I could only imagine how mad Savanna was at that. I bet her *eww* frown stretched clear across her face when she saw the list! And Ellie? Actually, I bet Ellie was somewhat relieved. She would have had a hard time keeping up with Ximena and Savanna, and Ellie never *really* loved dancing that much. I always kind of thought she was only into it because *I'd* always been into it. I was happy it worked out for her this way. I mean, she might not act like it, but she's still *my* BFF.

And I was happy for me, too! Because even though I was hoping to get a bit closer to the Savanna group, I had also been a little stressed wondering if the Savanna and Ximena pairing would have iced me out.

But having Summer in the group along with Ximena? That was going to be awesome! Maybe the combined power of Summer's niceness and my niceness would turn Ximena into one of us. At the very least, it might keep her from being the mean girl everyone seems to think she is. Not that I think she's a mean girl. In fact, I barely know her! Either way, having Summer be the third girl in the dance made me so happy. I almost couldn't stop smiling all day.

How I Saw Savanna

At lunch, I squeezed in next to Maya and Rand, who were hunched over yet another one of Maya's giant dot games, which were getting more and more elaborate.

"So!" I said happily. "Good news, guys! I got picked to be in Mrs. Atanabi's sixties dance show for the benefit in March! Yay!"

"Yay!" Maya answered, not looking up from the dot game. "That's great, Charlotte."

"Yay," echoed Rand. "Congrats."

"Summer got in, too."

"Oh yay, good for her," said Maya. "I like Summer. She's always so nice."

Rand, who was marking a row of boxes she had just closed off with her initial, looked up at Maya and smiled. "Fifteen!" she said.

"Argh!" said Maya, grinding her teeth. She had just gotten braces, and was making a lot of funny movements with her mouth these days.

I flicked my eraser at them. "That sure is one intense

game of dots you're playing there," I said sarcastically.

"Ha-ha!" said Maya, leaning into me with her shoulder. "That's so funny I forgot to laugh."

"The mean-girl table is looking at you," said Rand.

"What?" I said. Both Maya and I turned around in the direction she was staring.

But Savanna, Ximena, Gretchen, and Ellie turned away the moment I glanced in their direction.

"They were *so* just talking about you!" said Maya, giving them her dirtiest look through her black-framed glasses.

"Stop that, Maya," I said to her.

"Why? I don't care," she answered. "Let them see me."

She bared her teeth at them like some kind of crazy ferret.

"Stop looking at them, Maya!" I whispered through my own gritted teeth.

"Fine," she said.

She went back to playing her colossal game of dots with Rand, and I concentrated on eating my ravioli. At one point, I could feel someone's eyes burning into my back, so I turned around to sneak a peek at the Savanna table again. This time around, Ximena, Gretchen, and Ellie were talking together, completely oblivious to me. But Savanna was glaring right at me! And she didn't look away when our eyes met. She just continued staring me down. Then, right before she finally stopped, she poked her tongue out at me. It happened so fast, no one else would have seen it. And it seemed so childish, I almost couldn't believe it!

That's when I realized that I got it wrong before, about Summer taking the third spot in Mrs. Atanabi's dance piece. I had thought that spot should have gone to Savanna, *not* Summer. But in Savanna's view, it wasn't Summer who had taken that spot from her. It was *me*! "Charlotte's *always* the first to sign in," she had said.

Savanna blamed *me* for taking her rightful spot in the dance!

How We Got Off to an Awkward Start

All the next day, the threat of a snowstorm made everyone kind of giddy and uncertain, since there was talk that the school would close early if it came down as bad as the forecast predicted. Luckily—because the last thing in the world I wanted was for our first rehearsal to be canceled!—the snow only started falling in the late afternoon. Not hard at all. So I made my way up to the performance space as quickly as I could after the last bell. Given that Mrs. Atanabi had issued such a threatening warning about being late, I wasn't surprised that both Summer and Ximena were already there, too.

We said hello to one another before changing into our dance clothes. It was a little awkward at first, I guess. The three of us had never really hung out together before. We were from different groups, our own version of mammals, reptiles, and fish. Summer and I only had one class together. And, like I said before, I *barely* knew Ximena. The longest conversation we'd ever had was back in December, in Ms. Rubin's class, when she asked me—without a shred of remorse—if I would mind switching partners with her so she could be paired up with Savanna. Which is how I ended up with Remo as my science fair project partner, but that's a whole other story not worth telling.

We started doing warm-ups and stretches to pass the time. Mrs. Atanabi was now almost half an hour late!

"Do you think this is how it's always going to be?" said Ximena, mid-*battement*. "Mrs. Atanabi being late?"

"She's *never* on time to theater class," I said, shaking my head.

"Right?" Ximena said. "That's what I'm afraid of."

"Maybe she just got stuck in the snow?" Summer said, somewhat hopefully. "It's starting to come down pretty hard now, I think."

Ximena made a face. "Yeah, maybe she needs a dog-sled," she answered quickly.

"Ha-ha-ha!" I laughed.

But I could tell I sounded dorky.

Please, God, please don't let me seem dorky in front of Ximena Chin.

The truth is: Ximena Chin made me a little nervous. I don't know why exactly. It was just that she was *so* cool, and *so* pretty, and everything about her was always *so* perfect. The way she wrapped her scarf. The way her jeans fit her. The way she fastened her hair into the neatest twist. Everything was so flawless with her!

I remember from the moment Ximena started at

584

Beecher Prep this year, *everybody* had wanted to be her friend. Including me! I'm sure she didn't even remember this, but I was the one who helped her find her locker on the first day of school. I was the one who let her borrow a pencil in third period (which she never returned to me, come to think of it). But Savanna was the one who became her best friend. Savanna managed to zoom in on her within the first nanosecond of school. And then, forget it. It was like the Big Bang of friendships. It just exploded into an instantaneous universe of knowing looks and giggles and clothes and secrets.

There was really no chance of getting to know Ximena better after that. The truth is, she didn't make much of an effort to expand beyond the Savanna group anyway. Maybe she felt like she didn't actually have to. People said she was kind of a snob.

All I really knew about her was that she had the most amazing leg extension I'd ever seen, the highest scores in our grade, and she was snarky. Meaning, she made a lot of "clever observations" about people behind their backs. There were a bunch of people—like Maya, for instance—who couldn't stand her. But I couldn't wait to get to know her better. To be friends with her, maybe! To laugh at her sarcastic gibes. More than anything, though, I just really really *really* wanted her to like me!

"I hope this is all going to be worth the time-suck," Ximena was saying. "I mean, we've got so many other things going on this month! That science fair project?"

"I haven't even started mine," said Summer.

"Me, neither!" I said, though that actually wasn't true at all. Remo and I had finished our diorama of a cell the first week back from winter break.

"I just want to make sure we get enough rehearsal time for this dance," Ximena said, looking at her phone. "I don't want to be onstage at *Carnegie* Hall looking like a *total* idiot because we didn't rehearse enough—all because Mrs. Atanabi was too flaky to show up on time."

"You know," I said, trying to sound casual, "if we ever need a place to rehearse away from school, you guys could come over to my house. I have a mirrored wall in my basement and a barre. My mom used to teach ballet out of our house."

"I remember your basement!" said Summer cheerfully. "You had that Flower Fairy birthday party there once!"

"Back in the second grade," I answered, a little embarrassed she would mention Flower Fairies in front of Ximena.

"Do you live far from here?" Ximena asked me, scrolling through her texts.

"Just ten blocks away."

"Okay, text me your address," she said.

"Sure!" I said, whipping out my phone, thinking *I'm texting Ximena Chin my address* like the big dork that I am. "Umm, sorry, what's your number?"

She didn't look up from her phone but held her hand up to my face, like a crossing guard. There, running vertically down the side of her palm, was her phone number written in neat block letters in dark blue pen. I keyed her number into my contacts and texted her my address.

"Hey, you know," I said as I was texting, "you guys could come over tomorrow after school, if you want. We can start rehearsing then."

"Okay," Ximena mumbled casually, which made me want to gasp. *Ximena Chin is coming over to my house tomorrow!*

"Oh, I actually *can't*," said Summer, squinting her eyes apologetically. "I'm hanging out with Auggie tomorrow."

"What about Friday, then?" I asked.

"Can't," said Ximena. She had obviously finished texting now and looked up.

"Then maybe next week?" I said.

"We'll figure out some other time," Ximena answered indifferently. She started running her fingers through her hair. "I forget you're friends with the freak," she said to Summer, smiling. "What's that like?"

I don't think she was even trying to be mean when she said this. That's really just how a lot of people automatically referred to Auggie Pullman.

I looked at Summer. *Don't say anything*, I thought.

But I knew she would.

How Nobody Gets Mad at the Lavender Fairy

Summer sighed. "Could you please not call him that?" she asked, almost shyly.

Ximena acted like she didn't get it. "Why? He's not here," she said, pulling her hair into a ponytail. "It's just a nickname."

"It's an awful nickname," Summer answered. "It makes me feel bad."

Here's the thing with Summer Dawson: she has this way of talking where she can say stuff like this, and people don't seem to mind. If I had said something like this? Forget it, people would be all over me about being a goody two-shoes! But when the Lavender Fairy does it, with her cute little eyebrows raised like smiles on her forehead, she doesn't come off as preachy. She just seems sweet.

"Oh, okay, I'm sorry," answered Ximena apologetically, her eyes open wide. "I honestly wasn't trying to be mean, Summer. But I won't call him that again, I promise."

She sounded like she was genuinely sorry, but there was something about her expression that always made you wonder if she was being completely sincere. I think it had something to do with the dimple in her left cheek. She almost couldn't help looking mischievous.

Summer looked at her doubtfully. "It's fine."

"I really am sorry," said Ximena, almost like she was trying to smooth out her dimple.

Now Summer smiled. "Totally cool beans," she said.

"I've said it before and I'll say it again," answered Ximena, giving Summer a little squeeze. "You really are a saint, Summer."

For a second, I felt a quick pang of jealousy that Ximena seemed to like Summer so much.

"I don't think anyone should call him a freak, *either*," I said absently.

Now, here I have to stop and say something in my defense—I HAVE NO IDEA WHY I SAID THAT! It literally just came out of me, this stupid string of words hurling from my mouth like vomit! I knew immediately how obnoxious it made me sound.

"So *you've* never called him that," Ximena said, raising one eyebrow high. The way she was looking at me, it was like she was daring me to blink.

"I, um—" I said. I could feel my ears turning red.

No, I'm sorry I said it. Don't hate me, Ximena Chin!

"Let me ask you something," she said quickly. "Would you go out with him?"

It was so out of the blue, I almost didn't know what to say.

"What? No!" I answered immediately.

"Exactly," she said, like she had just proved a point.

"But not because of how he looks," I said, flustered. "Just because we don't have anything in common!"

"Oh, come on!" laughed Ximena. "That's *so* not true."

I didn't know what she was getting at.

"Would *you* go out with him?" I asked.

"Of course not," she answered calmly. "But I'm not about to be hypocritical about it."

I glanced at Summer, who gave me an *ouch, that hurts* look.

"Hey, I don't want to be mean," continued Ximena matter-of-factly. "But when you say, *Oh, I would never call him a freak*, it totally makes me look like a jerk because I had obviously just called him that, and it's kind of annoying because everyone knows that Mr. Tushman *asked* you to be his welcome buddy and *that's* why you don't call him a freak like everybody else does. Summer became friends with him without anyone forcing her to be his welcome buddy, which is why she's a saint."

"I'm not a saint," Summer answered quickly. "And I don't think Charlotte would have called him that, even if Mr. Tushman hadn't asked her to be a welcome buddy."

"See? You're being a saint even now," said Ximena.

"I don't think I would have called him a freak," I said quietly.

Ximena crossed her arms. She was looking at me with a knowing smile.

"You know, you're nicer to him when you're in front of teachers," she said very seriously. "It's been noticed."

Before I could answer—not that I even knew what I *would* have answered—Mrs. Atanabi burst into the performance space through the double doors in the back of the auditorium.

"So sorry I'm late, so sorry I'm late!" she announced breathlessly, covered in snow. She looked like a little snowman as she walked down the stairs carrying four ridiculously full tote bags.

Ximena and Summer ran up the stairs to help her, but I turned around and walked out to the hallway. I pretended to drink at the water fountain, but what I really needed to gulp down was air. Ice-cold air. Because I could feel my cheeks burning, like they were on fire. It felt like I'd just gotten slapped in the face. I could see out the hallway window that the snow really was coming down hard now, and a part of me just wanted to run outside and ice-skate away.

Is that how *other* people saw me? Like I was this hypocritical fake or something? Or was that just Ximena being her typical snarky self?

591

You're nicer to him when you're in front of teachers. It's been noticed.

Is that true? Has it been noticed? I mean, have there been a couple of times when I was being especially nice to Auggie Pullman because I knew it would get back to Mr. Tushman that I was being a good welcome buddy? Maybe. I don't know!

But even if that were the case, at least I can say I've *been* nice to him! That's more than most people can say! That's more than Ximena can say! I still remember that time she was partnered with Auggie in dance class and looked like she was about to throw up. I've never done anything like that to Auggie!

Okay, so maybe I *am* a little nicer to Auggie when teachers are around. Is that *so* horrible?

It's been noticed? What does that even mean? Noticed by *who*? Savanna? Ellie? Is that what they say about me? Is that what they were talking about in the lunchroom yesterday, when they were so obviously talking about me that even Maya—who can be so clueless about social stuff—felt sorry for me?

Here this whole time I had assumed that Ximena Chin didn't even know who I was! And now, it turns out, *I've been noticed*. More than I ever wanted to be.

How I Received My First Surprise of the Day

I walked back inside the performance space as Mrs. Atanabi finished unwrapping herself from all her wintry layers. Her coat, her scarf, and her sweater were all scattered around her on the floor, which was wet from the snow she had brought inside with her.

"Oh my gosh, oh my gosh!" she kept saying over and over again, fanning herself with both hands. "It's really starting to come down now."

She plopped onto the piano bench in front of the stage and caught her breath. "Oh my gosh, I do hate being late!"

I saw Ximena and Summer exchange knowing looks.

"When I was little," Mrs. Atanabi continued, talking in that chatterbox way of hers that some people loved and some people thought made her seem crazy, "my mother actually used to charge my sister and me one dollar every time we were late for something. Literally, *every* time I was late—even if it was just for dinner—I had to pay my mom a dollar!" She laughed and started redoing her bun, holding a couple of bobby pins in her teeth while she talked. "When your entire allowance for the week is only three bucks, you learn to budget your time! That's why I'm conditioned to *hate* being late!"

"And yet," Ximena pointed out, smiling in that sly way of hers, "you were still late today. Maybe we should charge you a dollar from now on?"

"Ha-ha-ha!" laughed Mrs. Atanabi good-naturedly, flicking off her boots. "Yes, I was late, Ximena! And that's actually not a bad idea. Maybe I *should* give all three of you a dollar!"

Ximena kind of laughed, assuming she was joking.

"In fact," Mrs. Atanabi said, reaching for her pocket-book, "I think I'm going to give *each* one of you girls a dollar bill *every* time I'm late to a rehearsal. From now on! That'll force me to be on time!"

Summer shot me a quizzical look. We started to realize that Mrs. Atanabi, who had pulled out her wallet, was serious.

"Oh no, Mrs. Atanabi," said Summer, shaking her head. "You don't have to do that."

"I know! But I'm going to!" answered Mrs. Atanabi, smiling. "Now, here's the rub. I'll agree to give each of you a dollar every time *I'm* late to a rehearsal if you agree to give me a dollar every time *you're* late for a rehearsal."

"Are you allowed to do that?" Ximena asked incredulously. "Take money from a student?"

I was thinking the same thing.

"Why not?" answered Mrs. Atanabi. "You're in private school. You can afford it! *Probably more than I can.*" This last part she muttered. And then she started cracking up.

Mrs. Atanabi was kind of famous for laughing at her own jokes. You pretty much had to get used to it.

She pulled three crisp dollar bills out of her wallet and held them up in the air for us to see.

"So, what do you girls say?" she said. "Is it a deal?"

Ximena looked at both of us. "I know *I'm* never going to be late," she said to us.

"I'm not going to be late, either!" said Summer.

I shrugged, still unable to look Ximena in the eyes. "Me, neither," I said.

"Then it's a deal!" said Mrs. Atanabi, walking over to us.

"For you, *mademoiselle*," she said to Ximena, handing her a spanking-new dollar bill.

"*Merci!*" said Ximena, shooting us a quick smile, which I pretended not to see.

Then Mrs. Atanabi walked over to me and Summer.

"For you, and for you," she said, handing us each a dollar bill.

"God bless America," we both answered at the same time.

Wait. What?

We looked at each other, our mouths and eyes open wide. Suddenly everything that occurred in the last half-hour seemed to lose any importance—if what I *think* just happened *did* just happen.

"The accordion-man?" I whispered excitedly.

Summer gasped and nodded happily. "The accordion-man!"

How We Went to Narnia

It's funny how you can know someone your whole life, but not *really* know them at all. Here, this whole time, I've been living in a parallel world to Summer Dawson, a nice girl I've known since kindergarten who I've always thought looked like the Lavender Fairy. But we'd never actually become *friend* friends! Not for any particular reason. It just worked out that way. The same way that Ellie and I were *destined* to be friends because Ms. Diamond had sat us next to each other on the first day of school, Summer and I were *destined* not to get to know each other because we were never in the same classes. Except for PE and swim, and assembly and concerts and stuff like that, our paths never crossed in lower school. Our moms weren't really friends, so we never had playdates. Sure, I invited her to my Flower Fairy birthday party once. But it really was because Ellie and I thought she looked like the Lavender Fairy! And sure, we'd hang out a bit at other people's bowling parties and at sleepovers and stuff. We were Facebook friends. We had lots of people in common. We were totally *friendly*.

But we were never actually *friends*.

So, when she said "God bless America," it almost felt like I was meeting her for the first time in my life. Imagine finding out that there was someone else in the world who knew a secret that only you knew! It was like an invisible bridge had instantly been built connecting us. Or, like we had stumbled onto a tiny door in the back of a wardrobe and an accordion-playing faun had welcomed us to Narnia.

How I Received My Second
Surprise of the Day

Before Summer and I could say anything else on the subject of the accordion-man, Mrs. Atanabi brushed her hands together and said it was time to "get to work." We spent the rest of the rehearsal time, since there was only half an hour left, listening to Mrs. Atanabi give us a quick overview of the dance while also periodically checking the weather app on her phone. We didn't really do any actual dancing: just some basic steps and a little rough blocking.

"We'll start getting into it next time!" Mrs. Atanabi assured us. "I promise I won't be late! See you Friday! Stay warm! Be careful going home!"

"Bye, Mrs. Atanabi!"

"Bye!"

As soon as she was gone, Summer and I came together like magnets, talking excitedly at the same time.

"I can't believe you know who I'm talking about," I said.

"God bless America!" she answered.

"Do you have any idea what happened to him?"

"No! I asked around and everything."

"I did, too! No one knows what happened to him."

"It's like he just vanished off the face of the earth!"

"It's like *who* vanished off the face of the earth?" asked Ximena, looking at us curiously. I guess the way we were squealing and carrying on, it did seem like something major had *just* happened.

I was still kind of keeping my distance from her because of before, so I let Summer answer.

"This guy who used to play the accordion on Main Street," said Summer. "In front of the A&P on Moore? He was always there with his guide dog? I'm sure you must have noticed him. Whenever you'd drop money into his accordion case, he'd say, 'God bless America.'"

"God bless America," I chimed in at the exact same time.

"Anyway," she continued, "he's been there for *forever*, but a couple of months ago, he just wasn't there anymore."

"And no one knows what happened to him!" I added. "It's like this *mystery*."

"Wait, so this is a *homeless* person you're talking about?" asked Ximena, kind of making the same *eww* face Savanna makes sometimes.

"I don't know if Gordy's homeless, actually," Summer answered.

"You know his name?" I asked, completely surprised.

"Yeah," she answered matter-of-factly. "Gordy Johnson."

"How do you know that?"

"I don't know. My dad used to talk to him," she answered, shrugging. "He was a veteran, and my dad was a marine, and was always like, *That gentleman's a hero, Summer. He served his country.* We used to bring him coffee and a bagel on the way to school sometimes. My mom gave him my dad's old parka."

"Wait, was it an orange Canada Goose parka?" I said, pointing at her.

"Yes!" Summer answered happily.

"I remember that parka!" I screamed, grabbing her hands.

"OMG, you guys are totally geeking out," Ximena laughed. "All this over a homeless guy in an orange parka?"

Summer and I looked at each other.

"It's hard to explain," said Summer. But I could tell she felt it, too: our connection over this. Our bond. It was our version of the Big Bang.

"Oh my God, Summer!" I said, grabbing her arm. "Maybe we could track him down! We could find out where he is and make sure he's okay! If you know his name, we should be able to do that!"

"You think we could?" asked Summer, her eyes doing that little dancing thing they did when she was super-happy. "I would *love* that!"

"Wait, wait, wait," said Ximena, shaking her head. "Are you guys serious? You want to track down some homeless dude you barely know?" She acted like she couldn't believe what she was hearing.

"Yes," we both said, looking at each other happily.

"Who barely knows *you?*"

"He'll know me!" Summer said confidently. "Especially if I tell him I'm Sergeant Dawson's daughter."

"Will he know you, Charlotte?" Ximena asked me, her eyes narrowing doubtfully.

"Of course not!" I answered her quickly, just wanting her to stop talking. "He's blind, *stupid!*"

The moment I said it, everything got quiet. Even the radiator, which had been making all these loud banging noises in the performance space until then, suddenly fell silent. As if the performance space wanted to hear my words echo in the air.

He's blind, stupid. He's blind, stupid. He's blind, stupid.

Another vomit of words. It's almost like I was *trying* to get Ximena Chin to hate me!

I waited for her to hit me with a sarcastic comeback, something that would slap me like an invisible hand across the face.

But, instead, to my utter and complete amazement, she started to laugh.

Summer started to laugh, too. "He's blind, *stupid!*" she said, imitating the way I had said it exactly.

"He's blind, *stupid!*" Ximena repeated.

They both started cracking up. I think the horrified look on my face made it even funnier for them. Every time they looked at me, they laughed harder.

"I'm so sorry I said that, Ximena," I whispered quickly.

Ximena shook her head, wiping her eyes with the palm of her hand.

"It's fine," she answered, catching her breath. "I kind of had that coming."

There wasn't a trace of snarkiness to her right now. She was smiling.

"Look, I didn't mean to insult you earlier," she said. "What I said about Auggie. I know you're not *only* nice to him in front of teachers. I'm sorry I said that."

I couldn't believe she was apologizing.

"No, it's fine," I answered, fumbling.

"Really?" she asked. "I don't want you to be mad at me."

"I'm not!"

"I can be a total jerk sometimes," she said regretfully. "But I really want us to be friends."

"Okay."

"Awww," said Summer, stretching her arms out to us. "Come on, guys. Group hug."

She wrapped her fairy wings around us, and for a few seconds, we came together in an awkward embrace that lasted a second too long and ended in more giggles. This time, I was laughing, too.

That turned out to be the biggest surprise of the day. Not finding out that people have *noticed* me. Not finding out that Summer knew the accordion-man's name.

But realizing that Ximena Chin, under her layers and layers and layers of snarkiness and mischief, could actually be kind of sweet. When she wasn't being kind of mean.

How We Got to Know
Each Other Better

The next few weeks flew by! A crazy blur of snowstorms, and dance rehearsals, and science fair projects, and studying for tests, *and* trying to solve the mystery of what had happened to Gordy Johnson (more on that later).

Mrs. Atanabi turned out to be quite the little drill sergeant! Lovable, in her own cute, waddly way, but *really* pushy. Like, we could *never* practice enough for her. Drills, drills, drills. *En pointe!* Shimmy! Hip roll! Classical ballet! Modern dance! A little bit of jazz! No tap! Downbeat! Half toe! Everything done her way, because she had a lot of very specific dance quirks. Things she obsessed about. The dances themselves weren't hard. The twist. The monkey. The Watusi. The pony. The hitchhike. The swim. The hucklebuck. The shingaling. But it was doing them exactly the way she wanted us to do them that was hard. Doing them as part of a larger choreographed piece. And doing them in sync. That's what we spent most of our time working on. The way we carried our arms. The way we snapped our fingers. Our turnouts. Our jumps. We had to work hard on learning how to dance *alike*—not just together!

The dance we spent the most time working on was the shingaling. It was the centerpiece of Mrs. Atanabi's whole dance number, what she used to transition from one dance style to the next. But there were so many variations to it—the Latin one, the R&B one, the funk shingaling—it was hard not to mix them up. And Mrs. Atanabi was *so* particular about the way each one was danced! Funny how she could be so loosey-goosey about some things—like never *once* getting to a rehearsal on time!—and yet be so strict about other things—like, God forbid you do a diagonal *chassé* instead of a sideways *chassé*! *Uh-oh, careful, the world as you know it might end!*

I'm not saying that Mrs. Atanabi wasn't nice, by the way. I want to be fair. She *was* super-nice. Reassuring us if we were having trouble with a new routine: "Small steps, girls! Everything starts with small steps!" Surprising us with brownies after a particularly intense workout. Driving us home when she kept us rehearsing too late. Telling us funny stories about other teachers. Personal stories about her own life. How she'd grown up in the Barrio. How some of her friends had gone down a "wrong" path. How watching *American Bandstand* had saved her life. How she'd met her husband, who was also a dancer, while performing with Cirque du Soleil in

Quebec. "We fell in love doing arabesques on a tightrope thirty feet in the air."

But it was intense. When I would go to sleep at night, I had so much information bouncing around my head! Bits of music. Things to memorize. Math equations. To-do lists. Mrs. Atanabi saying in her smooth East Harlem accent: *"It's the shingaling, baby!"* There were times when I would just put my headset on to drown out the chatter in my brain.

I was having so much fun, though, I wouldn't have changed a thing. Because the best part about all the crazy rehearsing and Mrs. Atanabi's drills and every-thing else—*and I don't want to sound corny*—was that Ximena, Summer, and I were really starting to get to know each other. Okay, that *does* sound corny. But it's true! Look, I'm not saying we became best friends or anything. Summer still hung out with Auggie. Ximena still hung out with Savanna. I still played dots with Maya. But we were becoming friends. Like, *friend* friends.

Ximena's snarkiness, by the way, was completely put on. Something she could take off whenever she wanted to. Like a scarf you wear as an accessory until it starts feeling itchy around your neck. When she was with Savanna, she wore the scarf. With us, she took it off. That's not to say I didn't still get nervous around her sometimes! OMG. The first time she came over to my house? I was a complete wreck! I was nervous that my mom would embarrass me. I was nervous that the stuffed animals on my bed were too pink. I was nervous about the *Big Time Rush* poster on my bedroom door. I was nervous that my dog, Suki, would pee on her.

But, of course, everything turned out fine! Ximena was totally nice. Said I had a cool room. Offered to do the dishes after dinner. Made fun of a particularly hilarious photo of me when I was three, which was fair because I look like a sock puppet in it! At some point during that afternoon, I don't even know when it was, I actually stopped thinking *Ximena Chin is in my house! Ximena Chin is in my house!* and just started having fun. That was huge for me because it was a turning point, the moment I stopped acting like an idiot around Ximena. No more word vomits. I guess that was when I took my "scarf" off, too.

Anyway, February was intense, but awesome. And by the end of February, we were pretty much hanging out at my place every day after school, dancing in front of the mirrored walls, self-correcting, matching our moves. Whenever we'd get tired, or discouraged, one of us would say in Mrs. Atanabi's accent, "It's the shingaling, baby!" And that would keep us going.

And sometimes we didn't rehearse. Sometimes we just chilled in my living room by the fire doing home-work together. Or hanging out. Or, occasionally, searching for Gordy Johnson.

How I Prefer Happy Endings

One of the things I miss the most about being a little kid is that when you're little, all the movies you watch have happy endings. Dorothy goes back to Kansas. Charlie gets the chocolate factory. Edmund redeems himself. I like that. I like happy endings.

But, as you get older, you start seeing that sometimes stories *don't* have happy endings. Sometimes they even have sad endings. Of course, that makes for more interesting storytelling, because you don't know *what's* going to happen. But it's also kind of scary.

Anyway, the reason I'm bringing this up is because the more we looked for Gordy Johnson, the more I started realizing that this story might *not* have a happy ending.

We had started our search by simply Googling his name. But, it turns out, there are hundreds of Gordy Johnsons. Gordon Johnsons. Gordie Johnsons. There's a famous jazz musician named Gordy Johnson (which we theorized could explain the rumor the eye-shop man had heard about *our* Gordy Johnson). There are politician Gordon Johnsons. Construction worker Gordon Johnsons. Veterans. Lots of obituaries. The Internet doesn't distinguish between names of the living and names of the dead. And every time we clicked on one of those names, we would be relieved that it wasn't *our* Gordy Johnson. But sad that it was someone else's Gordy Johnson.

At first, Ximena didn't really join in the search. She would be doing her homework or texting Miles on one side of the bedroom while Summer and I huddled around my laptop, scrolling through page after page of dead ends. But one day, Ximena pulled her chair next to ours and started looking over our shoulders.

"Maybe you should try searching by image," she suggested.

Which we did. It was still a dead end. But after that, Ximena became as interested in finding out what happened to Gordy Johnson as we were.

How I Discovered
Something About Maya

Meanwhile, at school, everything was business as usual.
We had our science fair. Remo and I got a B+ for our
cell-anatomy diorama, which was more than I thought
we would get considering I spent as little time on that
project as possible. Ximena and Savanna built a sundial.
The most interesting one was probably Auggie and
Jack's, though. It was a working lamp that was powered
by a potato. I figured Auggie probably did most of the
work, since, let's face it, Jack's never been what one
would call a "gifted student," but he was so happy to
have gotten an A on it. He looked so cute!!! Like a little
happy but somewhat clueless emoticon. ☺

And this was my emoticon when I saw him: ☺

By the end of February, the boy war had really
escalated, though. Summer filled me in about what was
going on, since she had the inside scoop on everything
from Auggie and Jack's point of view. Apparently—and
I was sworn to secrecy—Julian had started leaving

really nasty yellow Post-it notes for Jack and Auggie in their lockers.

I felt so bad for them!

Maya felt bad for them, too. She had become obsessed with the boy war herself, though I wasn't sure why at first. It's not like she had ever made any attempts to be friends with Auggie! And she always treated Jack like a goofball. Like, back in the days when Ellie and I would point out how cute he looked in his Artful Dodger top hat, Maya would stick her fingers in her ears and cross her eyes, as if even the thought of him repulsed her. So I figured her interest in the war had to do with the fact that, quirky as she was, Maya had a good heart.

It was only one day at lunch, when I saw her hard at work on some kind of list, that I understood why she cared so much. In her notebook, where she designs her dot games, she had three rows of tiny Post-its with the names of all the boys in the grade. She was sorting them into columns: Jack's side; Julian's side; neutrals.

"I think it'll help Jack to know he's not alone in this war," she explained.

That's when I realized: *Maya has a little crush on Jack Will! Awww, that's so cute!*

"Sweet," I answered, not wanting to make her self-conscious. So I helped her organize the list. We disagreed about some of the neutrals. She ultimately gave in to me. Then she copied the list onto a piece of loose-leaf paper and folded it in half, then in quarters, then in

612

eighths, then in sixteenths. "What are you going to do with it?"

"I don't know," she answered, pushing her glasses back up her nose. "I don't want it to get in the wrong hands."

"You want me to give it to Summer?"

"Yes."

So I gave the list to Summer to give to Jack and Auggie. I think Summer might have assumed that I had made the list myself, which I didn't correct because I *had* helped Maya work on the list, so I thought it was fine.

"How's the dance stuff going?" Maya asked me in her flat-voiced way that same day. I knew she was just trying to be polite, since she couldn't care less. But she was good that way. At least she made an effort to act interested.

"Crazy!!!" I answered, biting into my sandwich. "Mrs. Atanabi is absolutely insane!"

"Ha. Mrs. Mad-anabi," said Maya.

"Yeah," I said. "Good one."

"It's like you've been hibernating the whole month of February, though!" said Maya. "I've barely seen you. You never walk home with us after school."

I nodded. "I know. We've been practicing at lunch-time lately. But we'll be done soon enough. Just a few more weeks. The gala is on March fifteenth."

"Beware the ides of March," she said.

"Oh yeah! Right," I said, though I had absolutely no idea what she was talking about.

"So, want to see the sketches for my newest colossal dot game?"

"Sure," I answered, taking a deep breath.

She pulled out her notebook and launched into a detailed explanation of how she had stopped using grid patterns for her dots and was now using chalk art-style graphics to create murals, so that when the dots got filled in, they would "have a dynamic flow pattern." Or something like that. The truth is, I had trouble following what she was saying. The only part I heard for sure was when she said: "I haven't brought my new dot game to school yet because I want to make sure you're around to play it."

"Oh, sweet," I answered, scratching my head. I couldn't believe how bored I was at the moment.

She started saying something else about the dots, and I glanced over at Summer's table to distract myself. She, Jack, and Auggie were laughing. I could guarantee you one thing: they weren't talking about dots! There were times when I really wished I had the guts to just go and sit with them.

Then I looked over at the Savanna table. They were all laughing and having a good time, too. Savanna. Ellie. Gretchen. *Ximena.* All talking to the boys at the table across from them: Julian, Miles, Henry, Amos.

"Isn't she awful?" said Maya, following my gaze.

"Ellie?" I asked, because that's who I was looking at that exact moment.

"No. Ximena Chin."

I turned around and gave Maya a look. I knew she hated Ximena, but for some reason, the way she had said it, in this seething tone, just surprised me. "So, what is this thing you have against Ximena Chin?" I asked. "It's *Ellie* who ditched us, remember? It's *Savanna* who hasn't been nice to us."

"That's not true," Maya argued. "Savanna's always been nice to me. We used to have playdates all the time when we were in lower school."

I shook my head. "Yeah, but, Maya," I said, "playdates don't count. Half the time, our moms set those up. Now *we* get to choose who *we* want to hang out with. And Savanna is *choosing* not to hang out with us. Ellie is *choosing* not to hang out with us. Just like we're *choosing* not to hang out with some people. It's not that big a deal. But it's certainly not Ximena Chin's fault."

Maya peered over her glasses at the Savanna table. As I watched her, I realized she still looked exactly the way she did in kindergarten, when we would have tetherball games in the playground or go on fairy quests in the park at sunset.

In some ways, Maya hadn't grown up that much since then. Her face, her glasses, and her hair—they were almost identical to what they used to be. She was taller now, of course. But almost everything else remained unchanged. Especially her expressions. They were exactly the same.

"No, Ellie used to be nice to me," she answered very surely. "Just like Savanna was. I blame it all on Ximena Chin."

How February Made Us
Money, Too!

By the end of February, we'd made thirty-six dollars!

Mrs. Atanabi had been late to every single rehearsal.

Every.

Single.

One.

It got so that she would actually come to rehearsal with crisp dollar bills all ready in her hands to give us. She would literally show up, begin talking, hand us the money without even acknowledging it, and start the dance class! It was almost like it was the price of admission. What she paid to get through the door. So funny!

Then at one point halfway through the month, she herself suggested upping the amount of the penalty she would give us for being late from one dollar to five dollars. This, she assured us, would definitely keep her from being late in the future.

But of course that didn't work, either. And now,

instead of coming to rehearsal prepared with crisp one-dollar bills in her hand, she would come in with crisp five-dollar bills. Which she simply dropped on top of our backpacks by the door without saying a word. The price of admission.

Swoosh. Swoosh. Swoosh.

"God bless America."

Even Ximena said that now.

How Ximena Made a Discovery

Ascension **Transcends**
By Melissa Crotts, NYT *MuseTech*, February 1978

Ascension, in its world premiere at the Nelly Regina Theater, is the stunning debut by choreographer Petra Echevarri, recent graduate of Juilliard and winner of the Princess Grace Award. A mesmerizing reinterpretation of the dance fads of the '60s—as seen through the Kodachromic lens of the author's childhood in NYC's Barrio—this piece is a riveting and joyful homage to the scratchy, catchy, and soon-to-be-lost tracks of the decade. Chock-full of breathtaking leaps and innovative steps that belie Ms. Echevarri's own training in the classical style, the work takes one particular dance, the shingaling, and creates a visual narrative through which the rest of the work weaves.

"The reason I chose the shingaling as the centerpiece of this dance," explains Echevarri, "is because it's the only one of the dance fads of the time that actually evolved over the years to reflect the musical styles and genres of the musicians and dancers interpreting it. There are so many types of shingaling: Latin, soul,

619

R&B, funk, psychedelic, and rock and roll. It's the one dance that intersects every genre. The common thread.

"Growing up in the '60s, music was everything to me and my friends. I didn't have money for dance lessons. *American Bandstand* was my dance teacher. Those dance fads of the era were my training."

Echevarri didn't begin formal dance training until the age of twelve, but once she did, there was no looking back. "Once I got into Performing Arts, and then Juilliard," recalls Echevarri, "I knew I could do it. I could defy the odds. None of my neighborhood friends did. The 'hood is a tough place to leave."

When asked why she chose the shingaling as the main theme of her dance, Echevarri grows wistful. "A couple of years ago, about a month before graduating from Juilliard, I attended the funeral of a childhood friend—one of those girls who used to come to my house for *Bandstand*. I hadn't seen her for years, but I'd heard she was in a bad way, had gotten in with the wrong crowd. Anyway, her mother saw me at the funeral, and said her daughter had made a gift for me, a graduation present. I couldn't imagine what it was!"

Echevarri holds up a cassette tape. "This girl had made me a tape of every shingaling song from our childhood. Every single one. 'Chinatown' by Justi Barreto. 'Shingaling Shingaling' by Kako and His Orchestra. 'Sugar, Let's Shing-A-Ling' by Shirley Ellis. 'I've Got Just the Thing' by Lou Courtney. 'Shing-A-Ling Time, Baby!'

by the Liberty Belles. 'El Shingaling' by the Lat-Teens. 'Shing-A-Ling!' by Arthur Conley. 'Shing-A-Ling!' by Audrey Winters. 'Nobody but Me' by the Human Beinz. An incredible song list. I don't even know how she recorded some of them. But when I heard these songs, I knew I was going to create a dance woven around them."

The three dancers in the piece, all recent graduates of Juilliard themselves, bring a distinctive vocabulary to the montage, drawing viewers into an experience that is at once life-affirming and joyful, without any bubble-gum sentimentality. This lack of artifice owes as much to the rousing arrangement of songs, which blend seamlessly together, as it does to Echevarri's poignant narrative. Modern dance at its best.

How We Texted

Thursday 9:18 pm

Ximena Chin

Did you guys see the article I emailed you?

Charlotte Cody

O!M!G!!!! Is THAT really Mrs. Atanabi?

Ximena Chin

:) ;-O Crazy, right?

Charlotte Cody

R U sure? Who is Petra Echevarrrrarara?

Ximena Chin

It's her maiden name. That's her! Trust me. I was googling Gordy Johnson tonight and got bored and started googling Petra Atanabi.

Summer Dawson

I just read the article. Unbelievable! That's the dance WE'RE DOING!!!! Ascension!

Ximena Chin

I know! Amyaazzzinng!

Charlotte Cody

She looks so young and pretty in that photo.

622

Summer Dawson
Aww, that's so sweet, Ximena!
Ximena Chin
W@?????
Summer Dawson
That you were googling Gordy Johnson.
Ximena Chin
Yeah, well, now im curios too. I want to know what happened to him already.
Charlotte Cody
I shuldnt say this but My mom thinks that maybe he's—
Summer Dawson
Oh no!!! I think my mom thinkx so too.
Ximena Chin
Sorry guys. I sorta think maybe I agree . . . ?????
Charlotte Cody
RIP Gordy Johnson?????? 🙁
Summer Dawson
Nooooooo!!!!!
Charlotte Cody
I dont blieve it.
Summer Dawson
Me neither
Ximena Chin
K. 4get I said NEthing.
Summer Dawson
Said whaaaat?

Charlotte Cody

Ximena Chin

On completely unrelated note do yu guys want to sleep over my house 2moro night?

Charlotte Cody

Yea! Let me ask my mom. BRB

Summer Dawson

Sounds fun. Just us?

Ximena Chin

Ya. COme @ 6?

Summer Dawson

OK

Charlotte Cody

My mom says fine so long as your parents home?

Ximena Chin

Natch.

Charlotte Cody

My parental unit who is at this moment violating my personal space and reading my text over my shoulder wants me to finish homework so I GTG. CU2moro! Gnight.

Summer Dawson

Nighty night!

Ximena Chin

Til 2moro! Cant wait! xo

624

How We Went to Ximena Chin's House

It was the first time we went to Ximena's house. Up until then, we'd always hung out at my house or Summer's apartment.

Ximena lived in one of those luxury high-rises on the other side of the park. It was a doorman building, very different from the apartments I was used to in North River Heights. Most of those are brownstones or small apartment buildings that are over a hundred years old. Ximena's apartment was ultra-modern. The elevator opened directly into the apartment.

"Hey!" said Ximena, waiting for us in the foyer.

"Hey!" we said.

"Wow, this is beautiful," said Summer, looking around as she dropped her sleeping bag in the hallway. "Should we take our shoes off?"

"Sure, thanks," said Ximena, taking our coats. "I can't believe it's snowing again."

I dropped my sleeping bag next to Summer's and pulled off my UGGs. A woman I'd never seen before came in from the living room.

"This is Luisa," said Ximena. "This is Summer, and that's Charlotte. Luisa's my babysitter."

"Hi," we both said.

Luisa smiled at us. "So nice meet you!" she said in halting English. And then said something in rapid-fire Spanish to Ximena, who answered by nodding and saying *gracias*.

"You speak *Spanish?*" I said, astonished. We were following Ximena over to the kitchen counter.

Ximena laughed. "You didn't know? *Ximena*'s such a Spanish name. You want something to drink?"

"I thought it was Chinese!" I answered truthfully. "Water's great."

"Me, too," said Summer.

"My dad's Chinese," she explained, filling two glasses full of water from the refrigerator door. "My mom's Spanish. From Madrid. That's where I was born."

"Really?" I said. "That's so cool."

She set the cups of water in front of us while Luisa brought over a tray full of snacks.

"¡*Muchas gracias!*" Summer said to Luisa.

"*Muchas gracias,*" I repeated, in my terrible American accent.

"You guys are so cute," said Ximena, dipping a carrot stick into a little tub of hummus.

"So, did you grow up in Madrid?" I asked. Besides dancing, and horses, and *Les Mis*, the thing I love most in the world is traveling. Not that I had ever done any

626

traveling—yet. So far we'd only gone to the Bahamas once, Florida, and Montreal—but my parents are always talking about taking us to Europe someday. And I plan on becoming a professional traveler after I'm done being a Broadway star.

"No, I didn't grow up there," answered Ximena. "I mean, I spend summers there—except for last summer, when I did the ballet intensive here in the city. But I didn't grow up there. My parents both work for the UN, so I kind of grew up all over the place." She took a bite of the carrot stick. *Crunch.* "Rome for two years. Then before that we lived in Brussels. We lived in Dubai for a year when I was about four, but I don't remember that at all."

"Wow," said Summer.

"That's so cool," I said.

Ximena tapped on the glass she was drinking from with her carrot stick. "It's okay," she said. "But it can be kind of hard, too. Moving around. I'm always the new kid in school."

"Oh yeah," Summer said sympathetically.

"I survived," Ximena answered sarcastically. "I'm not about to complain." She took another bite of her carrot stick.

"So, do you know other languages?" I asked.

She held up three and a half fingers as an answer, since her mouth was full. And then, after she swallowed, she elaborated: "English, because I always went to

American schools. Spanish. Italian. And a little bit of Mandarin from my grandmother."

"That's so cool!" I answered.

"You keep saying *that's so cool*," Ximena pointed out.

"That's so uncool," I answered, which made her laugh.

Luisa came over to Ximena and asked her something.

"Luisa wants to know what you guys would like for dinner," Ximena translated.

Summer and I looked at each other.

"Oh, anything is fine," Summer said very politely to Luisa. "Please don't go to any trouble."

Luisa raised her eyebrows and smiled as Ximena translated. Then she reached over and pinched Summer's cheek affectionately.

"¡Qué muchachita hermosa!" she said. And then she looked at me. "Y ésta se parece a una muñequita."

Ximena laughed. "She says you're very pretty, Summer. And, Charlotte, you look like a little doll."

I looked at Luisa, who was smiling and nodding.

"Aww!" I said. "That's so nice!"

Then she walked away to start dinner for us.

"My parents will be home about 8 p.m.," Ximena said, waving for us to follow her.

She showed us the rest of the apartment, which looked like something out of a magazine. Everything was white. The sofa. The rug. There was even a white ping-pong table in the living room! It made me a little nervous about being klutzy—which I have been known to be—and accidentally spilling something.

We made our way down the hall to Ximena's room, which was probably the biggest bedroom I've ever seen (that wasn't a master bedroom). My bedroom, which I shared with Beatrix, was probably one quarter the size of Ximena's bedroom.

Summer walked into the middle of the room and made a slow spin as she took it all in. "Okay, this room is actually as big as my entire living room and kitchen combined," she said.

"Oh wow," I said, walking over to the floor-to-ceiling windows. "You can see the Empire State Building from here!"

"This is, like, the most beautiful apartment I've ever seen!" said Summer, sitting down in Ximena's desk chair.

"Thanks," Ximena said, nodding and looking around. She seemed a little embarrassed. "Yeah, I mean, we've only been here since this summer so it doesn't quite feel like home to me yet, but—" She plopped down on the bed.

Summer pulled the rolling chair up to the giant bulletin board in back of Ximena's desk, which was completely covered with tiny photos and pictures and quotes and sayings.

"Oh look, a Mr. Browne precept!" she said, pointing to a cutout of Mr. Browne's September precept.

"He's, like, my favorite teacher ever," answered Ximena.

"Mine, too!" I said.

"What a cute picture of you and Savanna," Summer said.

I went over to see what she was pointing at. In between the dozens of little pictures of people from Ximena's life, most of whom we didn't recognize, were camera-booth-type photos of Ximena and Savanna— plus Ximena and Miles, Savanna and Henry, and Ellie and Amos. When I saw Ellie's picture up there, I have to admit, it was kind of strange for me. Like I saw her in a different light. She really did have this whole new life.

"I have to get a picture of *you* two for my wall," Ximena said.

"Oh, come on," said Summer, in her cute, disapproving fairy way as she pointed to a picture on the board. "Ximena!"

It took me a second to realize she hadn't said "Oh, come on" in response to what Ximena had just said.

"Oh, sorry," said Ximena, making a guilty face.

At first I didn't know what the problem was, since it was just our homeroom class picture. Then I realized that over Auggie's face was a tiny yellow Post-it with a drawing of a sad face.

Ximena pulled the Post-it off the picture. "It was just Savanna and those guys fooling around," she said apologetically.

"That's almost as bad as Julian's mom Photoshopping the picture," Summer said.

"It was from a long time ago. I forgot it was even there," said Ximena. I was so used to the dimple in her left cheek by now that I never confused when she was serious with when she was joking anymore. I would say her expression right now was definitely remorseful. "Look, the truth is, I think Auggie's amazing."

"But you never talk to him," said Summer.

"Just because I'm not comfortable around him doesn't mean I'm not amazed by him," explained Ximena.

At that moment, we heard a knock on the open door. Luisa was holding a little boy in her arms, who had obviously just woken up from a nap. He was probably about three or four years old and looked exactly like Ximena, except for the fact that it was very obvious he had Down's syndrome.

"¡Hola, Eduardito!" said Ximena, beaming. She held her arms out to her little brother, who Luisa deposited into her arms. "These are my friends. Mis amigas. This is Charlotte, and that's Summer. Say hi. Di hola." She took Eduardito's hand and waved it at us, and we waved back. Eduardito, who had still not completely woken up, looked at us sleepily while Ximena planted kisses all over his face.

How We Played Truth or Dare

"The day I found out my dad died," Summer said.

The three of us were lying in our sleeping bags on the floor in Ximena's bedroom. The ceiling lights had been turned off, but the red chili Christmas lights that were strung all around the room gave the walls a pink glow in the dark. Our pajamas glowed pink. Our faces glowed pink. It was the perfect lighting for telling secrets and talking about things you would never talk about in the daylight. We were playing a Truth or Dare game, and the Truth card that Summer had drawn read: *What was the worst day of your life?*

My first instinct had been to put the card back and tell her to draw another one. But she didn't seem to mind answering it.

"I was in Mrs. Bob's class when my mom and grandma came to get me," she continued quietly. "I thought they were taking me to the dentist, since I'd lost a tooth that morning. But the second we got inside our car, my grandma started to cry. And then Mom told me that they'd just found out that Dad had been killed in action. *Daddy's in heaven now,* she said. And then we just all cried and cried in the car. Like, these huge, unstoppable tears." She was fidgeting with the zipper of her sleeping bag as she talked, not looking at us. "Anyway, that was the worst day."

Ximena shook her head. "I can't even imagine what that must be like," she said quietly.

"Me, neither," I said.

"It's kind of a blur now, actually," answered Summer, still pulling at the zipper. "Like, I honestly don't remember his funeral. At *all*. The only thing I remember about that day is this picture book about dinosaurs that I was reading. There was this one illustration of a meteor streaking across the sky over the heads of the triceratops. And I remember thinking my dad's death was like that. It's like the extinction of the dinosaurs. A meteor hits your heart and changes everything forever. But you're still here. You go on."

She finally got the zipper to unstick and pulled it up all the way to close her sleeping bag.

"But, anyway . . ." she said.

"I remember your dad," I said.

"Yeah?" she said, smiling.

"He was tall," I answered. "And he had a really deep voice."

Summer nodded happily.

"My mom told me all the moms thought he was *so* handsome," I said.

Summer opened her eyes wide. "Aww," she said.

We were quiet again for a few seconds. Summer started straightening up the card decks.

"Okay, so whose turn is it now?" she asked.

"I think it's mine," I answered, flicking the spinner.

It landed on Truth, so I pulled a card from the Truth deck.

"Oh, this one's so lame," I said, reading aloud. "*What superpower would you like to have and why?*"

"That's fun," said Summer.

"I'd want to fly, of course," I answered. "I could go anywhere I want. Zoom around the world. Go to all those places Ximena's lived in."

"Oh, I think I'd want to be invisible," said Ximena.

"I wouldn't," I answered. "Why? So I could hear what everyone says about me behind my back? And know that everyone thinks I'm such a phony?"

"Oh no!" laughed Ximena. "Not this again."

"I'm teasing, you know."

"I know!" she said. "But for the record, no one thinks you're a phony."

"Thank you."

"Just a faker."

"Ha!"

"But you *do* care too much about what people think of you," she said, somewhat seriously.

"I know," I answered, just as seriously.

"Okay, it's your turn, Ximena," said Summer.

Ximena flicked the spinner. It pointed to Truth. She picked up a card, read it to herself, then groaned.

"*If you could go out with any boy in your school, who would it be?*'" she read aloud. She covered her face with her hand.

"What?" I said. "Wouldn't it be Miles?"

Ximena started laughing and shook her head, embarrassed.

"Whoa!!!" Summer and I both said, pointing at her. "Who? Who? Who?"

Ximena was laughing. It was hard to see in the dim light, but I'm pretty sure she was blushing.

"If I tell you, you have to tell me *your* secret crushes!" she said.

"Not fair, not fair," I answered.

"Yes, fair!" she said.

"Fine!"

"Amos," she said, sighing.

"No way!" said Summer, her mouth open wide. "Does Ellie know?"

"Of course not," said Ximena. "It's just a crush. I wouldn't do anything about it. Besides, he's not into me at all. He really likes Ellie."

I thought about that. How just a few months ago, Ellie and I would talk about Jack. Having a "boyfriend" seemed like such a far-off thing back then.

Ximena looked at me. "I think I know who Charlotte's crush is," she said in a singsongy way.

I covered my face. "*Everybody* knows, thanks to Ellie," I said.

"What about you, Summer?" said Ximena, poking Summer's hand.

"Yeah, Summer, what about you?" I asked.

Summer was smiling, but she shook her head *no*.

"Come on!" said Ximena, pulling Summer's pinky. "There's got to be someone."

"Fine," she said. She hesitated. "Reid."

"Reid?" said Ximena. "Who's Reid?"

"He's in Mr. Browne's class with us!" I answered. "Very quiet? Draws sharks."

"He's not exactly popular," Summer said. "But he's really nice. And I think he's very cute."

"Ohhh!" said Ximena. "Of course I know who Reid is, duh. He's *totally* cute!"

"He *is*, right?" said Summer.

"You'd make a great couple," said Ximena.

"Maybe someday," answered Summer. "I don't want to be a couple *yet*."

"Is that why you didn't want to go out with Julian?" asked Ximena.

"I didn't want to go out with Julian because Julian's a jerk," Summer answered quickly.

"But you weren't really sick on Halloween, right?" said Ximena. "At Savanna's party?"

Summer shook her head. "I wasn't sick."

Ximena nodded. "I thought so."

"Okay, I have a question," I said to Ximena. "But it's not from the cards."

"Oh!" said Ximena, raising her eyebrows and smiling. "Okay."

I hesitated. "Okay. When you say you're 'going out' with Miles, what does that really mean? Like, what do you do?"

"Charlotte!" said Summer, smacking my arm with the back of her hand.

Ximena started laughing.

"No, I just mean—" I said.

"I know what you mean!" said Ximena, grabbing my fingers. "All it means is that Miles meets me at my locker after school every day. And he walks me to the bus stop sometimes. We hold hands."

"Have you ever kissed him?" I asked.

Ximena made a face, like she was sucking on a lemon. She wasn't wearing her contacts now. Just big tortoise-framed glasses, as well as a retainer she was supposed to wear at night. She didn't look at all like the Ximena Chin we were used to seeing in school. "Just once. At the Halloween party."

"Did you like it?" I asked.

"I don't know!" she answered, smiling. "It was a little like kissing your arm. Have you done that? Kiss your arms."

Summer and I obediently kissed our arms. And then we all started giggling.

"Oh, Jack!" I said, making slurpy noises while I kissed myself up and down my wrist.

"Oh, Reid!" said Summer, doing the same thing.

"Oh, Miles!" said Ximena, kissing her wrist. "I mean, Amos!"

We were cracking up.

"*Mija*," Ximena's mom said, knocking on the door. She poked her head in. "I don't want the baby to wake up. Can you keep it down a little?"

"Sorry, *mami*," said Ximena.

"Good night, girls," she said sweetly.

"Good night!" we whispered. "Sorry!"

"Should we go to sleep now?" I said softly.

"No, let's just be much quieter," said Ximena. "Come on, I think it's your turn now, Summer. Truth or Dare."

"I have another question that's not on the card, too," said Summer, pointing to Ximena. "For you."

"Uh-oh, you guys are ganging up on me!" laughed Ximena.

"We haven't done any Dares yet," I pointed out.

"Okay, this is the Dare," said Summer. "You have to sit at my lunch table on Monday, and you can't tell anyone why."

"Oh, come on!" said Ximena. "I can't just ditch my table without saying why."

"Exactly!" answered Summer. "So choose Truth."

"Fine," said Ximena. "So what's the Truth?"

Summer looked at her. "Okay, Truth. If Savanna, Ellie, and Gretchen hadn't gone skiing this weekend, would you still have asked Charlotte and me to a sleepover tonight?"

Ximena rolled her eyes. "Ohhh!" She puffed her cheeks out like a fish.

"You look like Mrs. Atanabi now," I pointed out.

"Come on, Truth or Dare," Summer pressured her.

"Okay, fine," Ximena said finally, hiding her face behind her hands. "It's true! I probably wouldn't have. Sorry." She peeked out at us from between her fingers. "I was *supposed* to go skiing with them this weekend, but then I didn't think it was worth my possibly twisting an ankle or something right before the dance, so I canceled at the last minute, and then I invited you guys over."

"Aha!" said Summer, poking Ximena in the shoulder. "I knew it. We were your plan B for this weekend."

I started poking her, too.

"I'm sorry!" said Ximena, laughing because we had started tickling her. "But it doesn't mean I don't want to hang out with you guys, too!"

"Have you had any other sleepovers in the last month?" Summer asked.

We were tickling her a lot at this point.

"Yes!" she giggled. "I'm sorry! I didn't invite you to those, either. I'm not good at mixing my friend groups! But I'll get better next year, I promise."

"Do you even *like* Savanna?" I said, giving her one last poke.

Ximena made a face that I realized was a perfect imitation of Savanna's *eww* expression.

Now Summer and I started laughing.

"Shh!" said Ximena, patting the air to remind us to keep quiet.

"Shh!" said Summer.

"Shh!" I said.

We all settled down.

"Okay, I have to admit," Ximena said quietly, "she's been *really* annoying ever since I started spending time with you guys rehearsing. She was so mad when she wasn't picked for the dance!"

"Probably mad that I got picked instead of her," said Summer.

"Actually, no, she was mad at Charlotte," Ximena answered, pointing her thumb at me.

"I knew it!" I said.

Ximena leaned her head on one shoulder. "She said—and this is *her* talking, not *me*—that you always get the good parts in shows at Beecher Prep because the teachers know you were in TV commercials when you were little. And that you try really hard to always be a teacher's pet."

"What. The. Heck?" I said, stupefied. "That is the craziest thing I've ever heard."

Ximena shrugged. "I'm just telling you what she told me and Ellie."

"But Ellie knows that's not true," I said.

"Trust me," answered Ximena. "Ellie never says anything to contradict Savanna."

"I don't get why she's always *hated* me," I said, shaking my head.

"Savanna doesn't hate you," Summer answered, reaching over to take Ximena's glasses off her face. "I think, if anything, she's probably always been a little jealous of you and Ellie being best friends."

"Really?" I said. "Why?"

Summer shrugged. She tried on Ximena's glasses. "Well, you know, you and Ellie tended to be kind of cliquey. I think Savanna probably felt a little left out."

This had never, *ever* occurred to me.

"I had no idea anyone felt that way," I said. "I mean, *seriously*, no idea. Are you sure? Did other people feel this way? Did *you?*"

Summer let the glasses fall to the tip of her nose. "Kind of. But I wasn't in any of your classes, so I didn't care. Savanna was in *all* your classes."

"Wow," I said, biting the inside of my cheek, which is a nervous habit I have.

"I wouldn't worry about it, though," said Summer, putting Ximena's glasses on my face now. "It doesn't matter anymore. You look really good in those."

"I don't want Savanna to hate me, though!" I said.

"Why do you care so much about what Savanna thinks?" asked Ximena.

"Don't *you* care what she thinks?" I asked. "Let's face it, you're different when you're around her, too."

"That's true," said Summer, taking the glasses off my face. She started cleaning them with her pajama top.

"You're much nicer when you're not with her," I said.

Ximena was twisting her hair with her finger. "Everyone's a little mean in middle school, don't you think?"

"No!" said Summer, putting the glasses back on Ximena's face.

"Not even a little?" Ximena answered, raising her right eyebrow.

"No," Summer repeated, adjusting the glasses so they were straight. "No one has to be mean. Ever." She leaned back to inspect the glasses.

"Well, that's what you think because you're a saint," teased Ximena.

"Oh my gosh, if you call me that one more time!" laughed Summer, tossing her pillow at Ximena.

"Summer Dawson, you did not just hit me with my favorite 800-fill-power European white goose-down pillow, did you?" said Ximena, standing up slowly. She picked up her own super-fluffy pillow and raised it in the air.

"Is that a challenge?" Summer asked, standing and holding her pillow up like a shield.

I stood up excitedly, holding my pillow in the air.

"Pillow fight!" I said, a little too loudly because I was excited.

"Shh!" Ximena said, holding her finger over her mouth to remind me to keep it down.

"Silent pillow fight!" I whispered loudly.

We spent one long second looking at one another, to see who would strike first, and then we just started going at it. Ximena brought her pillow down on Summer, Summer struck her from below, I made a long sideswipe at Ximena. Then Ximena came up and swung at me from the left, but Summer spun around and struck us both from above. Soon we were smacking each other with more than just pillows: the stuffed animals on Ximena's bed, towels, our rolled-up clothes. And despite our trying to be completely silent, or maybe *because* of it—since there's nothing funnier than trying not to laugh when you want to laugh—it was the single best pillow fight I've ever had in my entire life!

The thing that stopped it, or else it might have gone on too long, was the mysterious trumpet blast of a fart that came from one of us. It stopped the three of us in our tracks as we looked at each other, eyes open wide, and started laughing hysterically when no one took credit for it.

Anyway, two seconds later, Ximena's mom knocked

on the door again, still sounding patient but also obviously a little irritated. It was way past midnight.

We promised her we would go to sleep now and we wouldn't make any more noise.

We were out of breath from laughing so hard. My stomach actually hurt a little.

It took us a while to straighten out our sleeping bags and put the stuffed animals back where they belonged. We folded our clothes and returned the towels to the closet.

We smoothed out our pillows and lay down in our sleeping bags and zipped them up, and then we said good night to one another. I think I probably would have fallen asleep right away, but I got a case of the giggles, and then Summer and Ximena started giggling. We kept trying to shush one another by cupping our hands over each other's mouths.

Finally, once the giggles had passed and it got quiet again, Ximena started singing really softly in the dark. At first, I didn't even realize what she was singing, she was singing so quietly.

No-no, no, no-no, no-no-no-no.

Then Summer took up the song:

No, no-no, no, no, no-no, no-no, no-no.

Finally, I realized what they were singing, and sang:

No-no-no-no, no-no, no, no-no, no!

Then we all started whisper-singing together.

Nobody can do the shingaling

644

Like I do—
Nobody can do the skate
Like I do—
Nobody can do boogaloo
Like I do—
We were lying on our backs side by side as we sang, and made our arms and hands dance in sync above our heads. And we sang the whole song, from beginning to end, as quietly as if we were praying in church.

How Our Venn Diagrams Look

I know. I spend too much time thinking about this stuff. 😊

How We Never Talked About It

On Monday, there was no mention of the sleepover. It's like the three of us knew, instinctively, without having to say it out loud, that when we got back to school, everything would return to being business as usual. Ximena hanging out with the Savanna group. Summer hanging out with her tiny group. Me playing dots with Maya at my lunch table.

No one would have ever guessed that Summer, Ximena, and I had become good friends. Or that just a few days before, we were having silent pillow fights and sharing secrets under the pink glow of the red chili lights in Ximena's bedroom.

How I Failed to Prevent a Social Catastrophe

The night before the gala, Mrs. Atanabi told us to take the day off and get some rest. She wanted us to make sure we had a nice healthy dinner and a good night's sleep. Then she gave us our costumes, which she had somehow managed to sew herself. We had already tried them on the week before, but I was so excited to come home and try mine on again, now that it had been fitted. The costume was inspired by this photo of the Liberty Belles:

THE LIBERTY BELLES
SHOUT RECORDING ARTISTS

MANAGEMENT
HORIZON PROMOTIONS, INC.

So that afternoon, I went home from school with Maya and Lina, the way I used to in the old days before I started hanging out with Summer and Ximena all the time.

It was one of the first nice days in March, when you finally get a hint of spring after the long, crazy cold winter. Lina had the brainstorm to stop at Carvel on our way home, which felt like a very "springtime" thing to do, so we walked in the opposite direction up Amesfort toward the park. As we were walking, I told them how I had heard that Savanna was telling people that the only reason I got a part in Mrs. Atanabi's dance show was because I had been in a TV commercial when I was little.

"No one believes that," Lina said sympathetically, kicking her soccer ball in front of her.

"That's awful!" said Maya, and it kind of made me happy that she got so mad about it. "I can't believe Savanna! She used to be so nice in lower school."

"Savanna was never really that nice to me," I answered.

"She *was* nice to me," Maya insisted, pushing her glasses up her nose. "Now she's evil. That whole group is evil."

I nodded. Then I shook my head. "Well, I don't know about *that*."

"And now they've turned Ellie against us," Maya said. "You know, Ellie barely even says hello to me anymore. Now she's evil, too."

I scratched my nose. Maya had a way of being very black-and-white about things. "I guess."

"I'm telling you, it's Ximena Chin's fault," Maya continued. "It's only because of her. If she hadn't started this year, everything would be the same as it was. She's the bad influence."

I knew that that was how Maya saw things. It was one of the reasons I never went into too much detail about the dance show I was in. She never really got that it was just me, Summer, and the dreaded *Ximena Chin*. And that was fine by me! I didn't want to have to defend my friendship with Ximena to Maya! I honestly don't think she would have understood.

"You know what I hate the most?" Maya said. "I hate that she's probably going to end up giving the fifth-grade commencement speech at graduation this year."

"Well, she does have the best grades of anyone," I answered, trying to sound as impartial as possible.

"I thought you had the best grades, Charlotte," Lina said to me.

"No, Ximena does," Maya interjected. She started counting off on her fingers. "Ximena. Charlotte. Simon. Me. And then either Auggie or Remo. Auggie's actually got better grades than Remo in math, but he didn't do that well in Spanish on his last few quizzes, and that's bringing his whole grade point average down."

Maya always knew what everyone else got on their tests. She kept tabs on homework assignments, essay scores. You name it, if it had a grade attached to it, Maya would ask you about it. And she had an amazing way of remembering all those details, too.

"It's crazy how you can remember everybody's grades," said Lina.

"It's a gift," answered Maya, not even meaning to be funny.

"Hey, did you tell Charlotte about the note?" Lina asked her.

"What note?" I said. Like I mentioned, I was a little out of the loop with these guys because I hadn't hung around them that much these last few weeks.

"Oh, nothing," said Maya.

"She wrote Ellie a note," said Lina.

Maya looked up at me and frowned. "Telling her how I feel," she added, peering at me over the rims of her glasses.

I immediately had a sinking feeling about this note.

"What did you write?" I asked.

She shrugged. "Just a note."

Lina nudged her. "Let her read it!"

"She's going to tell me not to give it to her!" Maya answered, biting the end of her long, curly hair.

"At least *show* it to me?" I said, now really curious. "Come on, Maya!"

We had stopped at the intersection of Amesfort and 222nd Street to wait for the light to change.

"Fine," Maya answered. "I'll show you." She started

digging into her coat pocket and pulled out a well-worn Uglydoll envelope with the word "Ellie" written on the outside in silver marker. "Okay. So, basically, I just wanted to let Ellie know how I feel about the way she's changed this year."

She passed the envelope to me, and then nodded for me to open it and read the note inside.

> *Dear Ellie,*
> *I'm writing as one of your oldest friends to tell you that you've really been acting different lately, and I hope you snap out of it. I don't blame you. I blame it on the evil Ximena Chin, who is negatively influencing you! First she twisted Savanna's brain, and now she's turning you into a pretty zombie just like she is. I hope you stop being friends with her and remember all the good times we used to have. Remember Mr. Browne's November precept: "Have no friends not equal to yourself!" Can we please be friends again?*
>
> > *Your former*
> > *really good friend,*
> > *Maya*

I folded the note up and put it back inside the envelope. She was looking at me expectantly.

"Is it stupid?" she asked me.

I handed the envelope back to her.

"No, it's not stupid," I answered. "But as your friend, I'm telling you that I don't think you should give it to her."

"I knew you would try to talk me out of it!" she said, annoyed and disappointed by my reaction.

"No, I'm not trying to talk you out of it!" I said. "You should give it to her if you *really* want to. I know you *mean* well, Maya."

"I'm not trying to *mean* well," she said angrily. "I'm just trying to be truthful!"

"I know," I said.

By now we had crossed the street and arrived at Carvel, only to see how super-busy it was inside. The line at the counter went all the way to the door, and every single table was full—mostly with Beecher Prep kids.

"Everyone had the same idea as we did," said Lina regretfully.

"It's too crowded," I said. "Let's forget it."

Maya gripped my arm. "Look, there's Ellie," she said.

I followed her gaze and saw Ellie sitting with Ximena, Savanna, and Gretchen—plus Miles, Henry, and Amos—at a table in front of the birthday-cake counter, which was all the way on the other side of the shop.

"Let's just go," I said, pulling Maya by the arm. Lina had already started kicking the ball down the block. But Maya stayed where she was.

"I'm going to give her my note," she said slowly, her expression very serious. She held the note I had just returned to her in her left hand, and now she waved it like a tiny flag.

"Oh no, you're not," I said quickly, pushing her hand down. "Not now at least."

"Why not?"

Lina came back toward us. "Wait, you want to give her the note *now?*" she said incredulously. "In front of *everybody?*"

"Yes!" Maya answered stubbornly.

"No," I said, closing my hand over the note. All I could think of is what a big fool she would make of herself if she did that. Ellie would open the note in front of everyone at her table, and they would get so mad at her for the things she said about Ximena and Savanna. Unforgivable things, really! But even worse, they would totally start laughing at her about this. "This is the kind of thing you would never live down, Maya," I cautioned. "You will absolutely regret it. Don't do this."

I could tell she was reconsidering. Her forehead was all scrunched up.

"You could give it to her some other time," I continued, tugging on her coat sleeve the way Summer sometimes tugged on mine when she was talking. "When she's alone. You could even send it to her in the mail, if you want. But do *not* do it now in front of everyone. I'm begging you. Believe me, Maya. That would be a social catastrophe."

654

I saw her rubbing her face. The thing with Maya is, she's never cared about popularity or social catastrophes. She's so good at keeping tabs on people's test scores and grades, but she doesn't have a clue how to read the social stuff. She gets the basics, of course—but in her black-and-white world, kids are either nice or evil. There's no in-between.

In some ways, that's always been one of the nicest things about her. She'll go up to anyone and just assume they're friends. Or she'll do something really nice for someone out of the blue, like giving Auggie Pullman an Uglydoll keychain, which she did just last week.

But in some ways, it's really bad because she has no defenses ready for when people *aren't* nice to her. She has no good comebacks. She just takes it all seriously. What's worse, though, is that she doesn't always get when people don't feel like talking to her. So she'll just keep chattering on or asking questions until the person walks away. It was Ellie who actually put it kind of perfectly a few months ago when we were griping about how annoying Maya could be sometimes:

"Maya makes it easy for people to be mean to her."

And now Maya was about to make it *really* easy for Ellie to be mean to her—in front of a whole bunch of ice-cream-eating kids! Because, despite my words, despite my basically begging her not to do this, Maya Markowitz walked into the store, wove her way in and out of the crowd of people waiting in line, and marched to the back table where Ellie and that whole group of mighty girls was sitting.

Lina and I watched from the sidewalk outside the Carvel. There was a floor-to-ceiling window in the storefront, which was the perfect place to see events unfold. For a second, it felt like I was looking at one of those nature videos on PBS. I could almost hear a man with a British accent narrating the action.

Observe what happens as the young gazelle, which has just strayed from its herd . . .

I watched Maya say something to Ellie, and how everyone at that table stopped talking and looked up at Maya.

. . . comes to the attention of the lions, who haven't eaten in several days.

I saw her hand the envelope to Ellie, who seemed a bit confused.

"I can't watch," said Lina, closing her eyes.

And now the lions, hungry for fresh meat, begin the hunt.

How I Stayed Neutral
—Again

Pretty much everything I predicted would happen happened as I predicted. After giving Ellie the note in front of everyone at the table, Maya turned around and started walking away. Ellie and the Savanna group exchanged laughing looks, and before Maya had even reached the next table, Savanna, Ximena, and Gretchen got out of their chairs to huddle around Ellie as she opened the envelope. I could see their faces clearly as they read the note. Ximena gasped at one point, while Savanna obviously thought it was hilarious.

Maya kept walking across the room toward the exit, looking at me and Lina as she walked. Believe it or not, she was smiling at us. I could tell she was actually very happy. From her point of view, she was getting something off her chest that had really been bothering her, and, since she didn't give a hoot what the popular group thought about her, she didn't see herself as having anything to lose. The truth is, Maya was beyond their being able to hurt her. It was only Ellie she was mad at because

Ellie had been her friend. But Maya really didn't care what those other girls thought about her, or that they might be laughing at her this very moment.

In a way, I have to admit: I admired Maya's bravery.

Having said that, I knew the last thing in the world I wanted right now was to be seen with her, so I started walking away from the window before she got back outside. I especially didn't want Ximena to see me there, waiting for Maya outside. I didn't want anyone to think I had anything to do with this kind of craziness.

Just like I had managed to stay neutral in a war among the boys, I wanted to stay neutral in what might have turned into a war among the girls.

How Ximena Reacted

Summer texted me later that afternoon. *Did u hear about what Maya did?*

Yes, I texted.

I'm with Ximena right now. We're at my place. She's really upset. Can you come over?

"Mom," I said, just as we were getting ready for dinner. "Can I go to Summer's house?"

Mom shook her head. "No."

"Please? It's kind of an emergency."

She looked at me. "What happened?"

"I can't explain now," I answered quickly, getting my coat. "Please, Mom? I'll be back soon, promise."

"Does it have to do with the dance number?" she asked.

"Kind of," I fibbed.

"Okay, text me when you get there. But I want you home by six-thirty."

Summer only lived four blocks away from me, so I was there within ten minutes. Summer's mom buzzed me in.

"Hi, Charlotte, they're in the back," she said when she opened the front door. She took my coat.

I made my way back to Summer's bedroom, where Ximena, just as Summer had texted, was crying on Summer's bed. Summer had a box of tissues in her hands and was consoling her.

They told me the whole story, which I pretended not to know too much about. Maya had handed Ellie a note in front of everybody, and the note was full of really "venomous" things about Ximena. That's how they described it to me.

"She called me *evil!*" said Ximena, wiping tears from her face. "I mean, what did I ever do to Maya? I don't even *know* her!"

"I was telling Ximena that Maya can be kind of socially awkward sometimes," said Summer, patting Ximena's back like a mom would.

"Socially awkward?" said Ximena. "That's not social awkwardness, that's just mean! Do you know what it's like to have everyone reading something *that* awful about you? They passed her note around the table, and everyone took turns reading it—even the boys. And everybody thought it was *hysterical*. Savanna practically peed her pants, she thought it was so funny. I pretended *I* thought it was funny, too! Ha-ha. Isn't it hilarious that somebody I barely know blames me for turning people into *zombies?*" She put air quotes on the word "zombies." Then she started crying again.

660

"It's awful, Ximena," I said, biting the inside of my cheek. "I'm so sorry she did that."

"I told her we would talk to Maya," Summer said to me.

I gave her a long look. "To do what?" I asked.

"To tell her how upsetting what she wrote was," Summer answered. "Since we're friends with Maya, I figured we could explain how it hurt Ximena's feelings."

"Maya's not going to care," I said quickly. "She won't get it, Ximena, believe me." How to explain to her? "Honestly, Ximena, I've known Maya for years, and in her mind, this wasn't about *you*. It's about Ellie. She's just mad that Ellie doesn't hang out with her anymore."

"Obviously. But that's not *my* fault!" said Ximena.

"I know that," I said, "but Maya *doesn't* know that, and she just wants to blame someone. She wants everything to go back to the way it was in lower school. And she figures it's your fault that things have changed."

"That's just idiotic!" Ximena said.

"I know!" I said. "It's like Savanna being mad at me for having been in a TV commercial once. It makes no sense."

"How do you know all this?" asked Ximena. "Did she tell you?"

"No!" I said.

"Did you know about the note beforehand?"

"No!" I said.

Summer rescued me. "So what did *Ellie* say when she read Maya's note?" she asked Ximena.

"Oh, she was so mad," answered Ximena. "She and Savanna want to go all out on Maya, post something super-mean about her on Facebook or whatever. Then Miles drew this cartoon. They want to post it on Instagram."

She nodded for Summer to hand me a folded-up piece of loose-leaf paper, which I opened. On it was a crude drawing of a girl (who was obviously Maya) kissing a boy (who was obviously Auggie Pullman). Underneath it was written: "Freaks in love."

"Wait, why are they bringing Auggie into it?" Summer asked, incensed.

"I don't know," she said. "Miles was just trying to make me laugh. Everyone was laughing like it's all some kind of giant joke. But I don't think it's funny."

"I'm really sorry, Ximena," I said.

"Why does Maya hate me?" she asked sadly.

"You just have to put it out of your mind," I advised her. "And not take it personally. Remember you told me I have to stop caring so much what people think about me? You have to do the same thing. Forget what Maya thinks about you."

"I didn't ask to be part of Savanna's group when I started at Beecher Prep," said Ximena. "I didn't know who anyone was, or who was friends with who, or who was mad at who. Savanna was the first person who was nice to me, that's all."

662

"Well?" I answered, raising my chin and my shoulders. "That's not exactly true. I was nice to you."

Ximena looked surprised.

"I was nice to you," Summer added.

"What, now you guys are ganging up on me, too?" said Ximena.

"No, no way," said Summer. "Just trying to make you see it from Maya's point of view, that's all. She's not a mean girl, Ximena. Maya doesn't even really have a mean bone in her body. She's mad at Ellie, and Ellie has been kind of mean to *her* lately. That's it."

"Ellie hasn't really even been mean," I said. "She just ditched us for you guys. Which is fine. I don't care. I'm not Maya."

Ximena covered her face with her hands.

"Does everybody hate me?" she said, looking at us between her fingers.

"No!" we both answered.

"*We* certainly don't," said Summer, handing Ximena a box of Kleenex.

Ximena blew her nose. "I guess I haven't been *that* nice to her in general," she said quietly.

"Drawings like this don't help," said Summer, handing the sketch Miles had made back to Ximena.

Ximena took it and ripped it up into lots of little pieces.

"Just so you know," she said, "I would never have posted that. And I told Savanna and Ellie not to dare make any mean comments about Maya on Facebook or anything. I would never be a cyber-bully."

"I know," said Summer. She was about to say something else when there was a knock on the door.

Summer's mom popped her head in.

"Hey, guys," she said cautiously. "Is everything okay?"

"We're fine, Mom," said Summer. "Just some girl drama."

"Charlotte, your mom just called," Summer's mom said. "She says you promised you'd be home in ten minutes."

I looked at my phone. It was already 6:20 p.m.!

"Thanks," I said to Summer's mom. And then to Summer and Ximena: "I better go. Are you going to be okay, Ximena?"

She nodded. "Thanks for coming. Both of you, thanks for being so nice," she said. "I just really wanted to talk to someone about it, but I couldn't actually talk to Savanna and Ellie, you know?"

We nodded.

"I better go home, too," she said, standing up.

The three of us walked down the hallway to the front door, where Summer's mom looked like she was trying to organize the coats.

"Why the long faces, girls?" she asked cheerfully. "I would think you'd be jumping up and down for joy about the big day tomorrow! After all those rehearsals and all the hard work you've put into it. I can't wait to see you guys dancing!"

"Oh yeah," I answered, nodding. I looked at Summer and Ximena. "It *is* pretty exciting."

Summer and Ximena started smiling.

"Yeah," said Ximena.

"I'm actually kind of nervous," said Summer. "I've never danced in front of an audience before!"

"You just have to pretend they're not there," answered Ximena. You would never know that two minutes ago she'd been crying.

"That's awesome advice," said Summer's mom.

"That's what I said, too!" I chimed in.

"Are your parents going to be there, Ximena?" Summer's mom asked. "I look forward to meeting them at the banquet."

"Yeah," she answered politely, smiling with her dimple on full power now.

"All the parents are sitting at the same table," I said. "And Mrs. Atanabi and her husband."

"Oh good," said Summer's mom. "I'm looking forward to hanging out with everyone."

"Bye, Summer. Bye, Mrs. Dawson," said Ximena.

"Bye!" I said.

We walked down the stairs to the lobby together, Ximena and me, and then headed down the block toward Main Street, where she would make a left turn and I would make a right turn.

"You feeling better now?" I said as we stopped on the corner.

"Yeah," she answered, smiling. "Thanks, Charlotte. You've been a really good friend."

"Thanks. You, too."

"Nah." She shook her head, playing with the fringes of my scarf. She gave me a long look. "I know I could've been nicer to you sometimes, Charlotte." Then she hugged me. "Sorry."

I have to say, it felt really awesome hearing that from her.

"Cool beans," I said.

"See you tomorrow."

"Bye."

I walked past the restaurants along Amesfort Avenue, which were finally starting to get busy again now that the weather was becoming warmer. I couldn't stop thinking about what Ximena had just said. Yeah, she could've been nicer to me sometimes. Could I have been nicer to some people, too?

I stopped at the big intersection for the light. That's when I noticed the back of a man in an orange parka boarding a bus. With a black dog next to him. The dog was wearing a red bandanna.

"Gordy Johnson!" I called out, running after him as soon as the light changed.

He turned when he heard his name, but the doors of the bus closed behind him.

How Mrs. Atanabi
Wished Us Well

In the upper-floor studios of Carnegie Hall, which is
where Mrs. Atanabi had us get ready for the show, there's
a hallway with framed pictures and programs of some of
the great dancers who've performed there over the years.
As we walked down that hall on the way to change
into our costumes, Mrs. Atanabi pointed to one of the
photographs. It was a picture of the Duncan Dancers,
Isadora Duncan's daughters, posing very theatrically in
long white tunics. It was dated November 3, 1923.

"Look, they're just like the three of you!" she chirped happily. "Let me take a picture of you girls in front of it," she said, pulling out her phone and aiming it toward us.

The three of us instantly posed next to the picture, standing the same way the dancers were: me on the left, hands in the air facing right; Summer on the right, hands in the air facing left; and Ximena in the middle, arms spread out in front of her facing the camera.

Mrs. Atanabi snapped several shots, until she was content with one, and then the four of us—because Mrs. Atanabi was every bit as excited as we were tonight—giddily trotted to the back room to get into our costumes.

We weren't the only ones performing tonight. The Upper School Jazz Ensemble and the Upper School Chamber Choir were already there. We could hear the sounds of trumpets and saxophones and other instruments echoing through the hallways, and the choir doing warm-ups in a large room next to our dressing room.

Mrs. Atanabi helped us with our hair and makeup. It was so awesome how she transformed each of our hairstyles into big, round bouffants with curled, flicked-up ends, topped by a cloud of hair spray. Although we all had such different types of hair, Mrs. Atanabi somehow made us match perfectly!

We were going on last. It felt like such a long wait!

We held hands the whole time and tried to talk ourselves out of being completely panicked.

When it was finally time for us to go on, Mrs. Atanabi brought us downstairs to the back stage of the Stern Auditorium. We peeked through the curtains at the audience as the Upper School Chamber Choir finished its last song. There were so many people! You couldn't make out anyone's face, because it was so dark, but it was the biggest auditorium I had ever seen—with balconies and gilded arches and velvet walls!

Mrs. Atanabi had us take our positions behind the curtains: Ximena in the middle, me on the left, Summer on the right. Then she faced us.

"Girls, you've worked so hard," she whispered, her voice shaking with emotion. "I can't thank you enough for all the time you've put into making my piece come to life. Your energy, your enthusiasm—"

Her voice cracked. She wiped a tear away excitedly. If we hadn't read that article about her, we might not have understood why this was all so important to her. But we knew. We never told her we had found that article about her. That we knew about her childhood friend. We figured if she had wanted us to know, she would have told us. But knowing that little piece of her story somehow made the dance and everything leading up to it that much more special. Funny how all our stories kind of intertwine. Every person's story weaves in and out of someone else's story.

"I'm just so proud of you, girls!" she whispered, kissing us each on our forehead.

The audience was applauding the choir, which had just finished. As the singers streamed backstage through the wings, Mrs. Atanabi made her way around the front of the stage to wait for Mr. Tushman to introduce her, and we took our positions. We could hear Mrs. Atanabi introducing the number we were about to dance, and us.

"This is it, guys!" Ximena whispered to us as the curtain started to rise.

We waited for the music to start. Five. Six.

Five-six-seven-eight!

It's the shingaling, baby!

How We Danced

I wish I could describe every second of those eleven minutes on stage, every move, every jump. Every shimmy and twist. But of course I can't. All I can say is that the whole thing went ABSOLUTELY PERFECTLY. Not one missed cue or fumble. Basically, for eleven solid minutes, it felt like we were dancing ten feet above the rest of the world. It was the most thrilling, exciting, tiring, emotional, fun, awesome experience of my life, and as we ramped up to the big finish, stoplighting to *Well let me tell you nobody, nobody* before busting into Mrs. Atanabi's signature shingaling, which was a variation she invented, I could feel the energy of the entire audience as they clapped along to the song.

Nobody, nobody
Nobody, nobody
Nobody, nobody . . .

And then we were done. It was over. Out of breath, beaming from ear to ear. Thunderous applause.

The three of us bowed in sync, and then we took our

individual bows. The audience hooted and hollered.

Our parents were ready with flowers for us. And my mom handed me an extra bouquet, which we gave to Mrs. Atanabi when she came onstage with us to take a bow. I wished, for a second, that all the fifth graders who'd ever laughed behind Mrs. Atanabi's back could see her now, right this minute, as I was seeing her. In her beautiful gown, her bun perfectly made—she looked like a queen.

How We Spent the Rest of the Night

A little later, after changing out of our costumes, we joined our parents for dinner in the banquet hall downstairs. As we wound our way through the round tables full of teachers, other parents, and a lot of grown-ups we didn't know, people congratulated us and complimented our dancing. I thought to myself, *This is what it feels like to be famous.* And I loved it.

Our parents were all sitting together at a table by the time we got there, along with Mrs. Atanabi and her husband. There was a little round of applause from them as we sat down, and then, basically, we spent the rest of the evening talking to each other non-stop, breaking down every second of the dance, where we'd been nervous about not making a particular kick, where we'd gotten a little dizzy coming out of a spin.

Before dinner was served, Dr. Jansen, the headmaster of the school, gave a short speech thanking everyone for coming to the benefit, and then asked Mrs. Atanabi, as well as the choir teacher and the jazz teacher, to stand up for another round of applause. Ximena, Summer, and I cheered as loud as we could. Then he talked about other things, like financial goals and fund-raising, and stuff that was so boring I couldn't wait for him to stop. Later, after we'd finished our salads, Mr. Tushman made a speech about the importance of supporting the arts at Beecher Prep so the school could continue to nurture the kind of "talent" they'd watched tonight. And this time he asked all the students who had performed tonight to stand up again for another round of applause. Around the room, the kids from the jazz ensemble and choir stood up with varying degrees of willingness and shyness. The three of us, though, weren't the least bit shy about standing up for another round of applause. What can I say?

Bring it on!

By the time coffee was being served, all the speeches were over, and people had started walking around and mingling. I saw one couple come over to our table, but I couldn't remember who they were until Summer jumped out of her seat to hug them. Then I knew. Auggie's parents. They kissed Summer's mom and then circled around to me and Ximena.

"You guys were so amazing," Auggie's mom said sweetly.

"Thank you so much," I answered, smiling.

"You must be so proud of them," Auggie's dad said to Mrs. Atanabi, who was next to Summer.

"I am!" Mrs. Atanabi said, beaming. "They worked so hard."

"Congrats again, girls," said Auggie's mom, giving my shoulder a little squeeze before making her way back to Summer's mom.

"Say hi to Auggie for me," I called out.

"We will."

"Wait, those were *Auggie's* parents?" said Ximena. "They look like movie stars."

"I know," I whispered back.

"What are you guys whispering about?" said Summer, coming between us.

"She didn't know they were Auggie's parents," I explained.

"Oh," said Summer. "His parents are *so* nice."

"It's really ironic," said Ximena. "They're so good-looking."

"Have you ever seen Auggie's big sister?" I said. "She's *super*-pretty. Like she could be a model. It's crazy."

"Wow," said Ximena. "I guess I thought, I don't know, that they'd all kind of look like Auggie."

"No," Summer said gently. "It's like with your brother. It's just how he was born."

Ximena nodded slowly.

I could tell, smart as she was, she'd never thought of it like that before.

How I Fell Asleep—Finally!

We didn't get home until pretty late that night. I was super-tired as I washed all the makeup off my face and got ready for bed. But then, I don't know why, I couldn't fall asleep. All the night's events kept crashing over me like soft waves. I felt the way you feel like when you're on a boat, rocking back and forth. My bed was floating in an ocean.

After about half an hour of tossing and turning, I picked my phone up from where it was charging on my nightstand.

Anyone up, I texted Summer and Ximena.

It was after midnight. I was sure they were asleep.

Just wanted u guys to know that I thnk ur the two most amazing people in the world and Im glad we got to b such good friends for a while. Ill always remembr this night. Its the shingaling, baby!

I put the phone back on the nightstand and karate-chopped my pillow to make it comfy. I closed my eyes, hoping sleep would come. Just as I felt myself finally drifting off, my phone buzzed.

It wasn't Ximena or Summer. Weirdly enough, it was Ellie.

Hey, Charly, Im sure ur sleeping but my parents just came home from the gala and said you guys were absolutely unbelievably incredible. Proud of you. Wish I coulda been there to see you dance. You deserve it. Lets try to hang out after school next week. Miss u.

It sounds stupid, but her text made me so happy, tears instantly welled up in my eyes.

Thnx so much, Ellie! I texted back. *Wish u could've been there too. Would love to hang next week. Miss U2. G'night.*

How Maya Was Surprised
and Surprised Us All

I woke up feeling so exhausted the next morning, Mom let me go to school late. I saw that both Ximena and Summer had texted me first thing in the morning.
Ximena Chin
I feel the same way, Charlotte. What a night!
Summer Dawson
I <3 U 2!
I didn't text them back because I knew they were in class. I missed the first three periods, and didn't see either of them until lunch. Summer, as usual, was sitting with Auggie and Jack. And Ximena, as usual, was at the Savanna table. For a fraction of a second, I was going to go over and say hello to Ximena, but the image of Maya standing in front of that same group of kids yesterday was still fresh in my head—and I didn't want to give Ximena even the sliver of a chance of disappointing me with anything but a really friendly hello.

So I waved to her and Summer as I walked over to my usual table, and sat down next to Maya. The girls at my table asked me how last night had gone—some of them had heard about it from their parents—but I spared them too many details because I knew they'd lose interest after thirty seconds. Which is exactly what happened.

Not that I could blame them, really.

The main thing on their minds—in fact, the *only* thing they wanted to talk about—was the note that Maya had given to Ellie yesterday in Carvel. That note, it turned out—which by now had been quoted or read aloud by half the grade—was Maya's first ticket to a kind of popularity she'd never experienced before. People were talking about her. Kids were pointing her out to curious sixth graders who had also heard about the note.

"I'm the queen of the underdogs today!" Maya herself said.

I could tell she felt triumphant. She liked the attention she was getting.

I had intended to tell her how hurt Ximena had been by her note, how it had made her cry. But, in a strange way, I also didn't want to rain on Maya's parade.

"Hey, you!" said Summer, nudging me so I could scoot over.

"Hey!" I said, surprised to see her there. I looked over at her table, but Auggie and Jack had already left.

"Hi, Summer," said Maya eagerly. "Did you hear about my note?"

Summer smiled. "Yes, I did!" she answered.

"Did you like it?" Maya asked.

I could tell Summer didn't want to hurt Maya's feelings, either, so she hesitated in answering.

"Where are Auggie and Jack?" I interjected.

"Working on some top-secret notes to leave in Julian's locker," she answered.

"A note like mine?" said Maya.

Summer shook her head. "I don't think so. Love notes from someone named Beulah."

"Who's Beulah?" I said.

Summer laughed. "It's too hard to explain."

I noticed that Ximena was looking at us from all the way across the cafeteria. I smiled at her. She smiled back. Then, to my surprise, she got up and walked over to our table.

Everybody at the table stopped talking as soon as they saw her standing there. Without even being asked, Megan and Rand scooted apart and Ximena sat down between them, directly opposite Maya, me, and Summer.

Maya was completely shocked. Her eyes were open wide, and she almost looked a little scared. I had no idea what would happen next.

Ximena clasped her hands in front of her, leaned forward, and looked straight at Maya.

"Maya," she said, "I just want to apologize if I've ever said or done anything to insult you. I never meant to, if that's the case. I actually think you're a really nice person and super-smart and interesting, and I really hope that we can be friends from now on."

Maya blinked, but she didn't say anything. Her mouth was literally hanging open.

"Anyway," said Ximena, now seeming a little shy, "I just wanted to tell you that."

"That's so nice of you, Ximena," said Summer, smiling.

Ximena looked at us with that winking expression of hers.

"It's the shingaling, baby!" she said, which made us both smile.

Then, as quickly as she'd sat down with us, she got up and walked back to her table. I looked out of the corner of my eye and saw Ellie and Savanna watching her. As soon as she sat down at her table, they came in close to hear what she had to say.

"That was so nice of her, wasn't it?" Summer said to Maya.

"I'm shocked," answered Maya, taking her glasses off to wipe them. "Totally shocked."

Summer gave me a little knowing look.

"Maya, whatever happened to that giant game of dots you were working on?" I said.

"Oh, I have it here!" she answered eagerly. "I told you I was waiting until you're around to play it. Why? You want to play it now?"

"Yeah!" I answered. "I do."

"Me, too," said Summer.

Maya gasped, grabbed her backpack, and pulled out a tube of paper that was folded in thirds and slightly bent at the top. We watched her unfold it and carefully unwind the sheet of paper, which took up the entire width and length of the lunch table. When it was completely stretched out, we all looked at it. Stunned.

There wasn't one square inch of the gigantic paper that wasn't covered in dots. Perfectly drawn, evenly spaced lines of dots. But not *just* dots. Beautiful grid patterns connected by swirls. Waves of lines that ended in spirals, or flowers, or sunbursts. It almost looked like tattoo art, the way blue ink can cover someone's arm so completely, you don't know where one tattoo starts and another ends.

It was the most unbelievably beautiful game of dots I've ever seen.

"Maya, this is incredible," I said slowly.

"Yeah!" she said happily. "I know!"

How Some Things Changed, and Some Things Didn't

That was the only time, and the last time, that Summer, Ximena, and I sat at a lunch table together. Or at any table, for that matter. We went back to our different groups. Ximena with Savanna. Summer and Auggie. Me and Maya.

And that, honestly, was fine with me.

Sure. Maybe there was part of me, the part that loves happy endings, that wished things had changed. Ximena and Ellie would suddenly switch tables and start sitting at my table, along with Summer. Maybe we'd start a new lunch table together, with Jack and Auggie, and Reid—and Amos!—at the table next to ours.

But the truth is, I knew things wouldn't change much. I knew it would be the way it had been after the sleepover. Like we had taken a secret trip together. A voyage that no one else knew about. And when we returned from our journey, we each went back to our own homes. Some friendships are like that. Maybe even the best friendships are like that. The connections are always there. They're just invisible to the eye.

Which is why Savanna would have no idea that Summer and I got to know her friend Ximena as well as we did. And why Maya wouldn't understand the effect her note had on me and Summer. Or why Auggie didn't know the first thing about *any* of this stuff that was going on. "He has his own stuff to worry about," Summer had told me once, when she explained why she had never even told Auggie she'd gotten picked to be in Mrs. Atanabi's dance. "He doesn't need to know about all this girl drama."

That's not to say there haven't been some changes that *have* happened.

As we entered our last few months of fifth grade, I definitely noticed that Ximena made more of an effort to branch out to other girls in our grade. And when she sees me in the hallway now, she always gives me a warm hello—regardless of whether she's with Savanna. Also, even though Ellie and Maya never patched things up, Ellie and I have hung out after school a couple of times. Not that it's like it used to be, of course. But it's something, and I'll take it.

Small steps, as Mrs. Atanabi would say. It starts with small steps.

And the truth is, even if Ximena, Savanna, and Ellie *did* suddenly invite me to sit at their table, I wouldn't go now. It just wouldn't seem right. First of all, I wouldn't want to get an angry note from Maya or have her bare her teeth at me across a room But mostly, it's because I realized something the day she unrolled her magnificent dot game across the lunch table: Maya's been my friend through thick and thin. My *friend* friend. All these years. In her clumsy, loyal, slightly annoying way. She's never judged me. She's always accepted me. And that group of girls at my lunch table, the ones I have nothing in common with? Well, guess what? We have a lunch table in common! And a ridiculously beautiful game of dots that we play over lunch, with the different-colored markers Maya's assigned to each and every one of us. Which we have to use or she gets really mad at us.

But that's just Maya. And that will never change.

How I Talked to
Mr. Tushman

The last day of school, Mr. Tushman's assistant, Mrs. Garcia, found me in seventh period and asked if I would come talk to Mr. Tushman right after school. Maya overheard her and started giggling.

"Ooh, ooh, Charlotte's in trouble," she sang.

We both knew that wasn't the case, though, and that it probably had to do with the awards they were giving out tomorrow. Everyone assumed that I would win the Beecher medal because I had organized the coat drive, and the medal usually went to the student who did the most community service.

I knocked on Mr. Tushman's door right after the last-period bell.

"Come in, Charlotte," he said enthusiastically, signaling for me to sit at the chair in front of his desk.

I always loved Mr. Tushman's office. He had all these fun puzzles on the edge of his desk, and artwork from kids over the years framed and hanging on the walls. I noticed immediately that he had Auggie's self-portrait as a duck displayed behind his desk.

And then suddenly I knew what this meeting was about.

"So, are you excited about tomorrow's graduation ceremony?" he asked, crossing his hands in front of him on the desk.

I nodded. "I can't believe fifth grade is almost over!" I answered, unable to restrain my happiness.

"It's hard to believe, isn't it?" he said. "Do you have plans for summer?"

"I'm going to dance camp."

"Oh, how fun!" he answered. "You three were so amazing at the benefit in March. Like professional dancers. Mrs. Atanabi was so impressed with how hard you worked, and how well you worked together."

"Yeah, it was so much fun," I said excitedly.

"That's great," he said, smiling. "I'm glad you've had a good year, Charlotte. You deserve it. You've been a joyful presence in these hallways, and I appreciate how you've always been nice to everyone. Don't think things like that go unnoticed."

"Thank you, Mr. Tushman."

"The reason I wanted to have a little word with you before tomorrow," he said, "and I'm hoping you can keep it between us, is that I know *you* know that among the many honors I give out tomorrow, one of them is the Beecher medal."

"You're giving it to Auggie," I blurted out. "Right?"

He looked surprised. "Why do you say that?" he asked.

"Everybody's assuming I'm getting it."

He looked at me carefully. Then he smiled.

"You are a very smart girl, Charlotte," he said gently.

"I'm fine with that, Mr. Tushman," I said.

"But I wanted to explain," he insisted. "Because, the truth of the matter is, had this been like any other ordinary year, *you* would probably be getting that medal, Charlotte. You deserve it—not only because of all the hard work you did on the coat drive, but because, like I just said before, you've been a really nice person to everyone. I still remember how, right from the start when I asked you to be Auggie's welcome buddy, you embraced that wholeheartedly and without equivocation."

Have I mentioned how much I love the fact that he uses big words and assumes we understand them?

"But, as you know," he said, "this year has been anything *except* ordinary. And when I was thinking about this award, thinking about what it represents, I realized that it can be about more than community service—not to devalue that at *all*."

"No, I know totally what you mean," I agreed.

"When I look at Auggie and all the challenges he has to face on a daily basis," he said, patting his heart, "I'm in awe of how he manages to simply show up every day. With a smile on his face. And I want him to have validation that this year was a triumph for him. That he's made an impact. I mean, the way the kids rallied around him after the horrible incident at the nature reserve? It was because of *him*. He inspired that kindness in them."

"I completely get what you mean," I said.

"And I want this award to *be* about kindness," he continued. "The kindness we put out in the world."

"Totally," I agreed.

He seemed genuinely delighted by my attitude. And a little relieved, I think.

"I'm so glad you understand, Charlotte!" he said. "I wanted to tell you beforehand, so you wouldn't be disappointed during the ceremony tomorrow, since, as you say, everyone's assuming you're getting it. But you won't tell anyone, right? I wouldn't want to ruin the surprise for Auggie or his family."

"Can I tell *my* parents?"

"Of course! Though I'm planning on giving them a call myself tonight to tell them just how proud I am of you at this very moment."

He got up and reached across the table to shake my hand, so I shook his hand.

"Thank you, Charlotte," he said.

"Thank you, Mr. Tushman."

"See you tomorrow."

"Bye." I started walking toward the door, but then this one thought popped into my head, like a fully formed idea. I had no clue where it came from.

"But the award *can* go to two people, right?" I asked.

He looked up. For a second, I thought I saw the tiniest bit of disappointment in his eyes. "It has, on a *few* occasions, gone to a couple of students who've done a community service project *together*," he answered, scratching his forehead. "But in the case of Auggie and you, I think, the reasons he would be getting it are so different from the reasons you would be—"

"No, I'm not talking about Auggie and me," I interrupted. "I think *Summer* should get that award."

"Summer?"

"She's been such an *amazing* friend to Auggie all year long," I explained. "And not because you *asked* her to be his welcome buddy, like with me and Jack. She just did it! It's like what you just said about kindness."

Mr. Tushman nodded, like he was really listening to what I was saying.

"I mean, I've been *nice* to Auggie," I said, "but Summer was *kind*. That's like nice to the tenth power or something. Do you know what I mean?"

"I know exactly what you mean," he answered, smiling.

I nodded. "Good."

"I really appreciate your telling me all this, Charlotte," he said. "You've given me much to think about."

"Awesome."

He was looking at me and nodding slowly, like he was debating something in his head. "Let me ask you something, though," he said, pausing as if he were trying to find the right words. "Do you think *Summer* would want a medal just for being friends with Auggie?"

The moment he said it, I knew exactly what he meant.

"Oh!" I said. "Wait a minute. You're right. She wouldn't."

For some reason, the image of Maya baring her teeth at the Savanna table across the room popped into my head.

Friends definitely aren't about the medals.

"But let me think about it tonight," he said, getting up.

"No, you're right," I answered. "It's good the way you had it."

"You sure?"

I nodded. "Thanks again, Mr. Tushman. See you tomorrow."

"See you tomorrow, Charlotte."

We shook hands again, but this time he took my hand in both of his own.

"Just so you know," he said. "Being nice is the first step toward being kind. It's a pretty awesome start. I'm supremely proud of you, Charlotte."

Maybe he knew it and maybe he didn't, but for someone like me, words like that are worth all the medals in the world.

How Ximena Rocked
Her Speech

Good morning, Dr. Jansen, Mr. Tushman, Dean Rubin, fellow students, faculty, teachers, and parents.

I'm honored to have been asked to give the commencement speech on behalf of the fifth grade this year. As I look around at all the happy faces, I feel so lucky to be here. As some of you know, this was my first year at Beecher Prep. I won't lie: I was a little nervous about coming here at first! I knew that some kids have been here since kindergarten, and I was afraid I wouldn't make friends. But it turns out that a lot of my classmates were also new to the school, like me. And even the kids who have been here a while, well, middle school is a brand-new ball game for everyone. It's definitely been a learning experience for all of us. With some bumps along the way. Some hits and misses. But it's been a wonderful ride.

Earlier this year, I was asked to perform in a dance choreographed by Mrs. Atanabi for the Beecher Prep Benefit. It was amazing for me. My fellow dancers and

I worked really hard to learn how to dance together as one. That takes a lot of time. And trust. Now, you may not know this about me, but as someone who's gone to a lot of different new schools over the years, trust hasn't always been easy for me to give people. But I really learned to trust these girls. I realized I could be myself with them. And I'll always be grateful for that.

I think what I'm most looking forward to next year, my fellow fifth graders, is building that trust with all of you. My hope is, as we start sixth grade, as we get older and wiser, that we all learn to trust each other enough so that we can truly be ourselves, and accept each other for who we *really* are.

Thank you.

How I Finally Introduced Myself

I had texted Summer and Ximena the day I saw Gordy Johnson getting on an uptown bus, and we were all thrilled to know he was alive and well. There was so much else going on at the time, though, that we really hadn't had the chance to talk about it too much. We got excited, kept our eyes peeled to see if we'd spot him again somewhere else in the neighborhood, but we never did. He was gone. Again.

The next time I saw him wasn't until the beginning of July. Suddenly he was there again, sitting in front of the A&P supermarket awning, playing the same songs on his accordion that he had always played, his black Labrador lying down in front of him.

I watched him for a few minutes. I studied his open eyes, remembering how they used to scare me. I watched his fingers tapping the buttons on the accordion. It's such a mysterious instrument to me. He was playing "Those Were the Days." My favorite song.

I went up to him when he was finished.

694

"Hi," I said.

He smiled in my direction. "Hello."

"I'm glad you're back!" I said.

"Thank you, missy!" he said.

"Where did you go?"

"Oh well," he said, "I went to stay with my daughter down south for a spell. These New York City winters are getting tough on these old bones of mine."

"It was a cold winter, that's for sure," I said.

"That's for sure!"

"Your dog's name is Joni, right?"

"That's right."

"And your name is Gordy Johnson?"

He tilted his head. "Am I so famous that you know my name?" he asked, cackling.

"My friend Summer Dawson knows you," I answered.

He looked up, trying to think of who I might have been talking about.

"Her father was in the marines?" I explained. "He died a few years ago. Sergeant Dawson?"

"Sergeant Dawson!" he said. "Of course I remember him. Glorious man. Sad news. I remember that family well. You tell that little girl I say hello, okay? She was a sweet child."

"I will," I answered. "We actually tried to find you. Summer and I were worried about you when you weren't here anymore."

"Oh, honey," he said. "You don't needs to worry about me. I make my way around all right. I'm not homeless or anything. I got a place of my own uptown. I just like to have something to do with myself, to get out with Joni. I take the express bus in the morning right outside my building. Get out at the last stop. It's a nice ride. I come here out of habit, you know? Nice people here, like Sergeant Dawson was. I like to play for them. You like my music?"

"Yes!" I said.

"Well, that's why I'm out here playing, girl!" he said excitedly. "To brighten up people's days."

I nodded happily.

"Okay," I said. "Thank you, Mr. Johnson."

"You can call me Gordy."

"I'm Charlotte, by the way."

"Nice to meet you, Charlotte," he said.

He extended his hand. I shook it.

"I better go now," I said. "It was nice talking to you."

"Bye-bye, Charlotte."

"Bye-bye, Mr. Johnson."

I reached into my pocket, pulled out a dollar bill, and dropped it into his accordion case.

Swoosh.

"God bless America!" said Gordy Johnson.

ACKNOWLEDGMENTS

I am grateful beyond measure to my amazing agent, Alyssa Eisner Henkin, for loving this manuscript even in its earliest drafts and being such a strong champion for Jill Aramor, R. J. Palacio, or whatever name I decided to call myself. Thanks to Joan Slattery, whose joyful enthusiasm brought me to Knopf. And most especially, thank you to Erin Clarke, editor extraordinaire, who made this book as good as it could be and for taking such good care of Auggie & Company: I knew we were all in good hands.

Thank you to the wonderful team who worked on *Wonder*. Iris Broudy, I am privileged to call you my copy editor. Kate Gartner and Tad Carpenter, thank you for the brilliant jacket. Nancy Hinkel, Judith Haut, John Adamo, Adrienne Weintraub, Tracy Lerner, Chip Gibson, Lisa McClatchy, and most especially Lauren Donovan, my partner-in-crime publicist: "You've been so kind and generous . . . I'm bound to thank you for it" (to quote another Natalie Merchant song). Thank you, too, to Team *Wonder* on the other side of the Atlantic. Starting with Natalie Doherty, who got the *Wonder* ball rolling, to Annie Eaton, Larry Finlay, Larry's son, Jane Lawson, Lauren Bennett, Mads Toy, Philippa Dickinson, and all of you in the UK: it's been absolutely "brilliant" working with you. Long before I wrote this book, I was lucky to work side by side with copy editors, proofreaders, designers, production managers, marketing assistants, publicists, and all the men and women quietly toiling behind the curtain to make books happen—and I know it ain't for the money! It's for love. Thank you to all the sales reps and the booksellers and the librarians who are in this impossible but truly beautiful industry.

Thank you to my amazing sons, Caleb and Joseph, for all the joy you bring me, for understanding all those times when Mom needed to write, and for always choosing "kind." You are my wonders.

And most of all, thank you to my incredible husband, Russell, for your inspiring insights, instincts, and unwavering support—not just for this project but for all of them over the years—and for being my first reader, my first love, my everything. Like Maria said, "Somewhere in my youth or childhood, I must have done something good." How else to explain this life we've built together? I am grateful every day.

Lastly, but not least, I would like to thank the little girl in front of the ice cream shop and all the other "Auggies," whose stories have inspired me to write this book.

—R.J.